WHERE THE SUN SETS

D.M. Litt

This is a work of fiction. Names, characters, organizations, places, events, and incidents are either products of the author's imagination or are used fictitiously.

Copyright © 2018 D.M. Litt
All rights reserved.

No part of this book may be reproduced, or stored in a retrieval system, or transmitted in any form or by any means, electronic, mechanical, photocopying, recording, or otherwise, without express written permission of the publisher.

Published by Inkshares, Inc., Oakland, California
www.inkshares.com

Edited by Nicole Ayers
Cover design by Maria Laguna
Interior design by Kevin G. Summers

Ebook: 9781947848580
Paperback: 9781947848610
LCCN: 2018942674

First edition

Printed in the United States of America

For Michael. It's about time.

*In the universe suddenly restored to its silence,
the myriad wondering little voices of the earth rise up.*
Albert Camus, "The Myth of Sisyphus"

ONE

Sunday, June 21, 2015
Dorset, Ontario, Canada
8:43 p.m. eastern time
8,996 sleeps since

I AM A CHANGED MAN. I knew it before I walked through our weather-worn oak door, its original storm cover rusted and removed years ago. (It doesn't rain enough here to warrant buying another, I remember telling Bay as I struggled to remove it from its hinges. The screws were stripped, and it took me much longer than I anticipated.) I knew I was changed, in the permanent sense, the moment my bare bicycle tire kissed the end of our driveway, and I was unsure whether I'd come home to the right house. I know it now, beyond any shadow of a doubt, as I sit here in the rocking chair that has been sitting in the same corner of our matchbox bedroom since before William was born.

The golden rays of the setting sun have always glimmered this way from the rocking chair, coming into our bedroom. High windows—a surprising feature for a squat bungalow—top the western and southern walls. On sweltering nights, the humid kind we sometimes get here, we would leave all the windows open. The evening breeze would blow through, cooling the sweat on our bodies, transporting us somewhere far away and far more exotic as we lay together, trembling in bed.

Yes, the windows must have kept us here. That, and there was never enough time or money back then to consider going anywhere else.

Recalling how the day's dying light would illuminate Bay's face, calm and smooth as though she hadn't a care in all the world, perplexes me more than anything else I've encountered. I saw this same sun yesterday. This seems impossible because I haven't set foot inside the walls of our home in a quarter century. I've been gone almost twenty-five years. How can it be I'm the only thing that's changed?

If I've learned anything, it's that the word *impossible* is as real as a sun that never sets, waves that never crash, a dreaming soul who never sleeps.

I would say I'm a stranger in my own home, except I'm not. Everything is exactly as I left it, one day ago. Not even the most thirst-quenched blades of grass on our postage-stamp lawn have grown since I saw them last. I'm coming home not as a stranger, but as a lost soul who has found absolution—

I'll stop myself there.

So much time spent alone, living in a silence only stars and planets should come to know, has left its mark. I don't know when I'm rambling, or saying something no one wants to hear.

I close my eyes and empty my mind, make myself steady and clear for the thing I must do next. I've done this many times before, each time more unnerving than the last. This time, this final time, is most unnerving of all. What if I've lost the skill? What if her closed lids never crack light for me again? What if my life has been the cheap trick of a bored bully, and all our suffering and bliss has come down to this precise moment, and I'm about to be the punchline? These echoes, they haunt. Questions are my plague, though I know none of it matters in the end. I've seen all there is to see in this world, and more. If this is how man, this man, discovers he has a destiny, so be it. I have lived enough to be grateful to have been let in on the joke at all.

Ah. There I go again. An old man beneath a gaze that won't bend.

"This is it, Jocko," I mutter to the gray-bearded schnauzer who lays guard next to Bay on the bed. Jock hasn't drawn a single breath in ten years, but he's never looked more alive.

A fit of coughing overtakes me. I wait for it to pass. Water hasn't soothed my throat for many months now, so I don't bother reaching for my bottle.

I can't get over the feeling I've forgotten something important. Maybe the most important thing. A familiar, lingering fear. I feel it every time. My mind isn't as sharp as it used to be. I tell myself it's up to its old tricks again.

I shake my body all over, blow my cheeks and flap my tongue to make noises that would embarrass my mother, and her mother before her, but not Bay. Never Bay.

Thoughts of her help me to relax. I'm as ready as one can be for the cacophony of the universe.

I clear my mind.

A dandelion appears in the empty expanse between my ears where rambling thoughts recently echoed. It's the kind of dandelion that's covered in fluffy seeds, like tiny feather parasols, waiting to be carried off on a hazy day's warm breeze. I don't need to remember the dandelion, or anything at all for that matter, but I do because I like the ritual of it. It's like tipping my hat to the universe before it swings wide the door for me to step through. *Besides,* my darkest corners whisper, *if I stop giving thanks, maybe next time I'll be refused passage.* I'll be locked somewhere I don't want to be, and Bay will never know if we made it. So, I pick a memory (rather, one picks me, since all I do is invite any to pop into my mind), and I give thanks.

I recall the dandelion moment and whisper, "Go," in the same instant. *Tapered kernels carrying the promise of new life, each with its own feather cap, scatter like a trail of breadcrumbs up across the sky. Pluck them from their cloud beds and plant them in the earth, one by one, a thousand at a time.* Go.

The sudden lack of quiet is overwhelming, but I've been waiting a long time to hear her speak. I'm attuned to her gentle notes. I can't miss it in the din.

"Vole." A feather's sigh. Her voice is like that now, feathery and light, as though every pump of her lungs is shallow and barely there.

I feel a warm tongue on the back of my hand and a cold nose pushing into my palm. My fingers move, automatically locating the spot behind Jock's salt-and-pepper moustache. The dog leans into my touch. I revel in the pulsing weight of his head. We're great friends now, he and I. Before I used to rub him down and give him treats no more than once a day, but for the past twenty-four hours of his life, I've barely stopped; though, in all that time, he never once leaned into my hand like he is now.

"How long this time?"

It takes me a moment to understand her words. Gathering meaning from sound is a skill, like riding a bike. The first few times you try after years of negligence, you're wobbly and slow and wont to do something stupid.

I shake my head, still my trembling arms, take a swallow of water.

"Vole?"

"I'm sorry, honeybee," I apologize, squeeze her hand.

I'd forgotten she can no longer see.

"It hasn't been long," I tell her. She smiles in my direction, a blaze of sunshine and hope cast broadly (she could do that—lighten up a dark room with her bright smile), but she says nothing back. Hours ago, she would've fought me and insisted on hearing every detail of every day that passed between us while she took a blink, but she's too tired now. Instead, her sightless eyes turn inward, and I listen to her think.

"Did we make it?" she asks after some time.

"We did, my flower."

"I thought so. Will you tell me how it went? From the beginning. Please. I want to hear everything, one more time, before . . ." She trails off before asking, "Will you do that for me?"

I'm grateful, for once, she can't see, because she'd be disturbed by the tears cascading down my cracked cheeks and dribbling off my chin. Bay hated seeing anyone cry. It made her cry a thousand times harder. She has a special kind of beauty of the soul. The rare kind that absorbs pain from others and grants them freedom and relief in turn, but she suffers for it.

As though she can sense my distress, she brings my skeleton hand to her lips and trails kisses, pollen-sweet, across my knuckle. "*Shhh.*" She shushes me like she once shushed our baby boy in his pinewood crib. "Don't be sad. Not for me. I'm the luckiest girl in the world because of you."

My throat eases barely enough to release a chuckle. It's our own private joke, this thing called *luck*—a concept I would've disregarded for most of our marriage. Where once I would've scoffed, said luck has nothing to do with anything, that hard work and patience is king, today I give credit where credit is due.

"You were born lucky, honeybee. I had nothing to do with it. Are you comfortable?"

"I am."

She taps the soft mattress next to her, and Jock abandons my roving fingers to sit by his mistress. The dog and I seek to share a lot in common.

"Good," I say. "Your medicine's right next to you." I guide her hand to the cup that holds her pills. I help her swallow them down with small sips of water. One at a time. A pause between each. Sip, sip. Another. She's so tired.

"From the beginning?"

"From the very beginning," I confirm, and I lie down next to her.

A gentle wind pushes and pulls; shadows, dappled, tickle my peripheries. I take pleasure in pretending to ignore these barest of movements while letting them wash over me in silence. I'm reminded of how busy life is supposed to be.

I place her head on my chest as gently as I would a newborn babe and wrap her in my arms, as drafty and thin as they are. These days my creaky body is most at ease sitting, but now I'm home, and twisted sinew gives way. The downy softness of our bed cradles me in comfort, and relief cascades through my bones. We've slept this way, in this bed, for decades. Barely missing more than a day. The mattress knows the curves and dips of our bodies well. When the disease began to eat away at Bay's frame, the spaces in our bed that formed over years seemed to envelop her. Now, we are both so frail we must look like little James tucked inside his giant peach as we curl up close to one another.

"I love you," I whisper and wait to hear what comes next. It's the longest moment of them all.

"I love you too, you old sap."

Her head rises and falls with my quiet laugh. I'm foolish to doubt her love, she reminds me. She doesn't know what doubt feels like the way I do. How it can grow so large it blots out everything familiar and good. Then again, maybe she does.

Who am I to know what nightmares come alive inside her? I've spent an eternity alone, and I've barely come to know those that haunt me.

Jock presses against Bay closer than ever before. The three of us lie there, fitted together like the nested measuring spoons William gave us years ago. They were one of the first gifts he ever bought, paid for with money he earned himself by sweeping floors at the pharmacy down the street. No matter how dented and scratched those spoons got, Bay refused to trade them in for a newer set.

The touch of Bay's skin and the scent of her hair distracts me. Little things, like the way she smells, and the way the tips of her once-long brown hair (now graying and shoulder-length, silky and soft) brush across her shoulders, are my greatest comforts. I've become used to a world unchanging and these constants have come to anchor me.

I digress, and I'm ashamed for wasting the most precious minutes of all. I must go back to the beginning as Bay has asked me to do. Back to when I was her husband, and she was

my wife, and we'd finished celebrating thirty-five years of marriage together. To when the fruit of this world we'd been waiting our entire lives to pluck folded in on itself, and everything came crashing down.

TWO

Saturday, June 20, 2015
Rosabella Memorial Hospital, Dorset, Ontario
7:32 p.m. eastern time

ON THE GRAY wall, behind Dr. Sheppard's head and in Vole's direct line of sight, was a bulletin board. Tacked to it was a faded, paper sign. WELCOME, CATHARINE! it read, typed in a large Times New Roman font. It was vibrant, once. Now, the paper was dull and the ink was gray, and the words blended into the memos tacked around it. A spreading numbness, rooted in Vole's bottom and traveling quickly up his spine, reminded him no one within hospital walls was actually welcome, and it took all his restraint not to jump to his feet and send his chair crashing into the stupid sign.

"Acute onset multiple organ dysfunction," Vole demanded, sitting tall and motionless in his uncomfortable seat. "What the hell does that *mean*?!" He'd already heard the doctor's explanation many times before, but each time it was lacking. Not once did Dr. Sheppard follow up with what he wanted to hear most: "But she'll get through it." He knew in his heart the words would come.

The doctor leaned forward and set clasped hands down between them. To Vole, who'd never sat with a psychotherapist before, Dr. Sheppard behaved like a psychotherapist. The doctor spoke in deliberate staccato and enunciated every single word with care. He seemed an experienced and removed practitioner. One who was accustomed to reading from a well-rehearsed script.

"It is impossible to say what will happen exactly, but we do know Baylotta's body will not be able to sustain multiple organ systems failing all at once. Her organs are under exorbitant amounts of strain. We can help ease her discomfort with medication. But . . ." The doctor opened his palms and spread his fingers. *See? There's no blame to lay here.* "My only suggestion, at this point, is to speak with your family and confirm your affairs are in order. She does not have long."

"H-how long are you talking?"

"It is impossible to—"

"How long?"

The doctor shook his head. He seemed to know better than to write the expiry sticker himself. In normal circumstances, he probably wouldn't have. Once again, Vole was reminded theirs weren't normal circumstances.

"I would say she has twenty-four, maybe forty-eight hours. I understand this comes as a terrible shock. I am . . . so sorry."

Vole didn't know what to say. Sense vanished into the gaping black pit inside of him, long ago. Nothing was right. Everything was wrong. He and Bay walked side by side, together. Not apart. The years turned slowly. Time was a constant. Why was everything spinning and unspooling so fast?

When Bay collapsed the first time, a few short months ago, Vole rushed her to Rosabella Memorial Hospital. Staff poked her with needles and filled her with fluids. They sent her to Toronto to see a specialist. By the time she returned home, the

Gibbons knew what the coming weeks held for them. The disease was deep inside Bay's body, where it had lurked unbridled and unseen for longer than either of them knew.

She'd been getting thinner. Complaining of aches and pains. She was a strong woman who had learned, long ago, to carry pain as though it were a striking piece of jewelry—hidden to everyone from most angles, but when she allowed it to be seen, it became impossible to miss.

If they caught it sooner, they may have stood a chance. At this late stage, at this rapid rate, all they had left was a narrow sliver of time.

"I . . . she . . ." *Why?* he wondered, over and over, though he couldn't possibly know the *why* of anything anymore. Everything was impossible enough when he thought they had weeks.

What will we say to William?

"Do you want to be there when I tell her?" Dr. Sheppard asked.

"*Yes.*"

"I will give you a moment on your own. You will hear a knock on the door before I come in. If you need more time, knock twice back, and I will leave you for another fifteen minutes."

Vole blinked.

"It is hard for her, Vole, but remember it is hard for you also. Read this." He placed a pamphlet titled *Life After Death* on the table in front of him. "There is more literature at the nurse's station. The nurses will tell you more if you ask. You should know there is help available for you too."

Vole blinked again and the doctor got to his feet. He didn't say anything more. On his way out of the room, he gripped Vole's shoulder. Then his warmth was gone, and Vole's head sagged.

Alone in the small doctor's office that had no windows and smelled like plastic and bleach, Vole let his head drop into his hands, and he began to weep.

Telling Bay was the easy part. She closed her eyes when the words were said, and opened them again before too much time passed, and nodded when she was supposed to, before closing her eyes once more. Uncharacteristically long blinks and long-held silences were two of many small habits they kept in common. Everything about them, the weird and the wonderful, had grown entwined. *We're like two peas in a pod*, Vole thought, before he imagined how lonely a single pea in a pod meant for two would be.

Stop feeling sorry for yourself, Vole berated. *She's the one going through hell right now. But what's the point of living for anything, much less tomorrow, if Bay's not going to be there with me?*

Vole supposed feeling this way was inevitable, and he hadn't the slightest clue what to do about it.

The doctor described what would happen as Bay's body began to reject normal function and the tumor continued to grow, as though he were talking to a tenth-grade biology class. *You turn the specimen over, make a straight vertical incision along its stomach with the tip of your scalpel, and begin to cut into any organ that looks like rubber and is dyed blue. Any questions? No? Very well then. You're free to eviscerate the specimen.*

The silence between them when Dr. Sheppard left was so vast, Vole vanished into it like a drop in the sea.

"Will you call Will and tell him for me?" Bay asked, shattering the miserable silence with a voice that came out thin and raw. "I-I don't think I can do it."

Vole blinked.

"And will you bring me my diary?"

He nodded.

"Please . . . I need you here with me."

Vole blinked, nodded, cleared his throat, and swallowed three times.

"I'm here, honeybee. Forever and always. Whatever you need, you tell me."

Bay looked so frail. A thin, disease-worn husk trying to cling to life in a bed that was built for a person five times her size.

"I want to write . . ." her bottom lip trembled ". . . goodbye."

"Bay . . ." Vole said, sounding small, like a child. "I don't want to leave you."

"I'll be here when you get back."

"Do you promise?"

"I do."

What else could she have said?

Vole didn't know when he posed the question to himself, and he didn't know as he turned the key in the ignition of their silver, spot-covered sedan. The parking lot was sparse, but he barely made note of it. He was too preoccupied with the task at hand. Vole was to fetch the things Bay had requested from home. Her diary, her pajama bottoms—the worn flannel ones with a small hole in the left knee—the photograph on her nightstand of William and Jock, her reading glasses, and her bedside paperback.

When Vole stepped inside their home, he shivered. If it hadn't been for Jock, their thirteen-year-old miniature schnauzer, who welcomed him home with a wriggling dance, Vole would have said their house already felt like a tomb.

All the items Bay asked him to bring were kept inside their bedroom. Vole moved about like a ghost, gathering everything, saving the most personal, her diary, for last. As he retrieved the well-used notebook from their shared chest of drawers, a piece of folded paper fell out. It was light pink. The same shade hospitals used to identify baby girls from baby boys, and the page was silken to the touch. The quality of it reminded him of back when perfumed love letters were made to contain secrets. He supposed it must have been tucked inside the book. He wondered what it was.

Vole turned the folded piece of paper in his fingers. Round and round it went, pinned between his long thumb and longer forefinger.

Peering closer, he was surprised to discover it had been opened and folded so many times that it appeared moth-eaten where creases split to holes. The edges were fuzzy and soft where once they were fresh and sharp.

He unfolded it, slowly, and a strange feeling overtook him. In all the years they'd been married, he never once ventured past the unspoken bounds of privacy. Now, with Bay on the brink of the abyss, it seemed insane to care about something so trivial as personal space.

When the paper lay open on their bed next to him, Vole's heart skipped a beat. A title stood out, passion against pale. *Bay's List of Wonders*, it read. Only the title withstood the years whole. Her list of wonders, a secret account of her aspirations and all the places she dreamed of seeing, had faded. So few of her hopes remained on what was once a vibrant page.

THREE

October 1979

HALLOWEEN WAS AROUND the corner, and it was the first ice-slicked day of the cold season. The same day drivers across southern Ontario thought about snow tires for the first time in months. A bit early in the year, perhaps, but late fall cold snaps weren't uncommon in those parts.

Vole was pulling up to the intersection when the light flicked to red and he recalled something important: he needed to place a phone call to a high-value commercial banking client first thing in the morning. The red light proved the perfect opportunity to jot down a reminder before he forgot again. After having come to a careful stop, Vole slipped his right hand into his worn leather brief bag—it sat upright on the passenger seat next to him—and went searching for a pen.

At the exact moment his outstretched fingers found a pen, his upper body snapped backward. His whole body lurched forward. An orchestral crash filled the car. A loud crunch, a sickening crack, an agonized yelp. *Bop, bang, boom.* Heavy quiet.

Startled and stinging from the impact of being rear-ended at full stop, Vole reached across the wheel with his left hand to shut the car engine off and rested his forehead against the Montcalm's steering wheel.

"Damned black ice," he cursed, trying to ignore the ache taking over his right arm, which was still stuck inside his bag. *A bit of flippin' frost is all it takes to turn the roads into a bloody nightmare circus*, he thought.

A voice came from outside his car. He ignored it. A sharp, persistent knock sounded on his window. He turned to glare at the unwelcome percussionist.

A young woman with long brown hair covered by a bright blue winter hat was saying something to him from the other side of the glass.

"What did you say?" he called back.

She gestured for him to lower the window.

Vole lowered the window.

"Are you all right?" she demanded, followed by, "What is *wrong* with you? Why the hell would you stop on a yellow? You're in Canada, for Christ's sake! Learn how to drive in the winter. I swear, all it takes is *one* night below zero to bring out all the worst drivers!"

Vole opened his mouth to dispute who was the worse driver when a stabbing pain in his right forearm stopped him short.

"Shit," the woman swore. "You don't look all right. What's wrong? There's a dent in your back bumper. It's not bad. Your car will still drive. My front will need some work, but at least we're both still alive. That's something!"

Perhaps it was the effortless swing of her disposition, or perhaps it was the cocktail of chemicals swirling inside his body from having survived a crash—whatever the reason, in that moment, something happened. Something Vole had never experienced before and certainly not something he'd planned on happening.

"Winter, eh?" he tittered, pretending to be entirely unaffected. *Don't be an idiot,* he thought. *Love at first sight isn't real.* "Awful season. The worst. It's not November yet!

"Since you asked, I think my right arm might be broken, but it doesn't hurt," he lied, trying to save face. "And I like your thinking. You're right, we're alive! That's what's important. Tell you what, how about we don't worry about putting this through insurance? We can settle it between us. Keep it off the record. What do you think?"

Concern colored her face.

"Come on," she said. "Let me take a look at your arm. Not here. We should get off the road."

Vole agreed, never one to like being in someone else's way. When the woman returned to her car, he extracted his right arm from the bag, gingerly. Panting with exertion, he cradled it in his lap.

One after the other (she went ahead), they pulled their damaged vehicles into the parking lot next to the intersection and found two remote side-by-side spots. They parked their cars and stood outside their vehicles. She peeled back the sleeve of his shirt.

"Are you a doctor?" he said through gritted teeth, trying to sound light.

"No."

Wincing, "A nurse?"

"*No.*"

"An animal doctor?"

"Hmm. We should sit." They sat down together on the cold concrete curb. She still had hold of his arm, and still he pretended it didn't ache. "You mean a veterinarian. Would you please stop talking? You're moving around too much. I need you to relax."

Vole tried to relax.

"My father coached a hockey team," she clarified. His arm jerked in immediate response and his vision went dark before becoming a flurry of small explosions. "I said don't move!" The woman's hot breath drew a cloud in the air between them.

Vole wheezed, "I fail to see how having a hockey coach father certifies you to poke at my broken—*Arghm!*" Then, "*Ah . . .*" in significant relief.

"You have a minor distal fracture of the radius," she explained, returning his limb to him. "The bone was out of place, so I set it. You'll be okay. Bones crack and get bent out of shape all the time. My old man had to set broken arms and wrists for players. He did it his whole life. One day it became what I did for him. You'll need a cast, though, and something to make sure it doesn't get infected. Oh, and don't bump into anything."

Vole had never met anyone so fascinating.

"I see. Thanks. So. About—"

"Hey," she said. "You already said we could avoid going through insurance."

"—your name," he finished, ignoring the interruption. "I'm Vole Gibbons. I'd shake your hand, but you've already broken it."

Her face flushed.

"What kind of first name is *Vole?*"

"A shrewd one."

She smiled.

"Prairie voles are monogamous and capable of deep love," Vole continued. Piddly rodents be damned—he never had forgiven his father for his chosen name—all he wanted was to discuss her soft fingers and curving mouth. After that, painkillers, and maybe the hospital too. "It's not my fault," he continued. "Blame my father. He thought it was romantic."

Her smile broadened and another brilliant moment flashed by. Hers was a smile that put sunsets to shame.

"I'm Bay. Here's my number," she said, jotting it down in a notebook she'd pulled from her purse. She ripped the page out and handed it to him. "Can you call me when you hear back from the garage? I've got to be going."

"Already?"

"I don't want to be late," she explained. "For reasons I know you can appreciate, I'm already running behind."

He fiddled with the paper that had her number scrawled across it in his left hand.

"Late for what?"

"An interview."

"What job?"

"It's with a new airline."

"Oh." What did it mean that she was destined for a life packed with far more adventure than his own? "Are you prepared?"

"Yes," she replied and shook of her head. "I don't know why I said that. I don't feel prepared. They're hiring thirty stewardesses, and I'm going into the second round of interviews, but I didn't get any sleep last night thinking about it. I've been feeling sick all morning. I hate interviews. They're worse than exams."

"I'm no good at exams either."

Vole barely made it through his own interview at the bank, and he knew there was no way he would've gotten the job as a teller if it hadn't been for Mr. McKinsey, the bank manager, whose mother was a friend of the family.

"I didn't say I was bad. I said I hate them."

Vole felt his face get hot. "Let me help you get into the mindset," he pressed on, unsure why he was willing to make such a fool of himself. "I know this question will come up. It's an important one, so pay close attention. When they ask you, 'If you could go anywhere, where in the world would you go on your honeymoon?' what will you say?"

She crossed her arms.

"I happen to know they won't ask that question," she said.

"Oh?"

"They already asked it in the first interview."

"Well, what did you say? Do you want to get married one day, and go on a honeymoon?"

"I have to be going."

He became desperate.

"Can I see you again? Please. I'd like to."

She paused, then smiled her sunset smile. "I can't believe I'm doing this," she said. "You're a complete stranger. I broke your arm, for Christ's sake. . . I'd like to see you again too. However," she paused, and his breath caught, "I have one condition. You have to guess my answer correctly.

"Where do you think someone like me wants to go on her honeymoon? Assuming I'm someone who thinks marriage is a good idea, that is."

It was a difficult, thrilling question.

"Well?" she insisted after several seconds had passed.

"I don't want to rush this. This is a big deal, guessing the first place a pretty girl wants to go as a married woman."

"You're not seriou—"

"Got it!" he interrupted. "You're far too smart for cliché, which rules out London and Las Vegas. Certainly not Paris. You deserve to go somewhere grand and exotic. You'd likely fly to . . . to Belarus! No, to Egypt! Yes, my guess is Egypt. To gaze upon the Nile and contemplate the pyramids."

Bay's flush deepened to crimson.

"How did I do?" Vole asked. "Did I get it right? Is it Egypt?"

"No."

"Belgium? Dammit. I knew I should have said Belgium."

"It's Paris," she blurted. "I want to honeymoon in Paris. Don't laugh. It's supposed to be beautiful. France has been on my list since I was in grade school. So has Egypt, and Belgium too, for that matter."

Vole was enchanted.

"Your list?" he asked.

"Of wondrous places I'll one day visit. That's why I want this job. I'll get paid to fly around the world and *live* its wonders, not just read about them in books!"

"Oh! Oh. You should go. I don't want you to be late."

He didn't want her to leave.

"Neither do I. Goodbye, Vole. It was nice to meet you."

"Goodbye, Bay."

Still, Vole didn't turn away, and neither did Bay.

Saturday, June 20, 2015
Gibbons' residence, Dorset, Ontario
8:25 p.m. eastern time

In the following decades, it never once occurred to Vole that Bay's list of wondrous places was a real thing. He hadn't thought of it once since the serendipitous day they met, when Bay rescheduled her interview (due to a traffic collision, no fault of her own), and went to the hospital with him instead. They sat together in the emergency waiting room and laughed over the impossibility of love at first sight. They shared a box of honey-coated doughnut holes—a new and exciting novelty at the time.

Vole presumed Bay kept her list of wonders inside her head, next to all the other fantasies a young romantic, who believes in love and seeks adventure, kept; and when she took a job answering phones at her dentist's office, citing their love carried her to higher places than a pair of metal wings ever could, Vole grew further enthralled.

He never once considered what else keeping her grounded could have meant.

Now, holding the list in his hand, Vole counted the places that weren't scribbled over; Bay's list had only twelve places left on it. A dozen left from eighty-four. Four of the remaining locations were underlined numerous times. One of them, which Vole could see was originally written in pencil and drawn over later in blue ink, had a star next to it. *The Graveyard*, it read. *Great-grandma's and grandpa's resting place.*

Among her list of shining cities were other places like the graveyard. Special spots on Bay's list, locations that marked some gauzy moment in time. She was the type to turn a memory into an occasion, paying tribute to it with a physical visit; and he shouldn't have been surprised, but he was.

It was easy for him to forget that Bay was a dreamer, because she was also as pragmatic as he. Unlike him, who sometimes underwhelmed, she made sure to give holiday celebrations their due whimsy and celebration—birthdays, graduations, religious holidays. The remaining days of the year she spent the same as he, getting from one minute to the next, as smooth and trouble free as the world they could afford would allow—and he thought they were happy.

Wasn't she happy?

Drops, salty and plump, splashed sorrow down onto the pink page. Dramatic bursts of fuchsia speckled its surface and tired ink swirled. Vole refolded and tucked the dampened piece of paper into his breast pocket—he hoped Bay wouldn't miss it in her book.

Vole sat down on the edge of their bed and became lost in thought. They never bought a king-sized mattress. It would have meant buying a new box spring and frame. Vole made their bed frame years ago. He got angry when Bay asked why he didn't make it larger. He remembered how his back ached from bending over, and his fingers were bruised from misplaced hammer strikes. *Soon two will become three*, she reasoned with him at the time, *and we could use the extra space.*

Shortly thereafter, Bay sanded the frame and coated it in ivory-colored paint. He was shocked she could maneuver in such tight spaces with her round and heavy belly. "Please be careful," he begged, thinking of their last two pregnancies, which never took long enough for Bay to show. She smiled and told him he was being foolish. "I am careful. You needn't worry so much. This one's different."

Looking back, Vole was happy he hadn't made their bed any bigger. When William was a toddler, he would often snuggle in with them at night. Vole was happiest when the three of them were together, safe and held tight. If they had more space between them as a family to share, his memories may not be as secure. Soon, memories would be all he had left of her.

Vole stilled his bouncing and stared down at his hands.

Why were we so careful? Why did we put off so much? Was it for this, to learn what it is to regret?

No matter how many times he turned the questions over in his mind, a turning bed post on a lathe, an answer never took shape. They never lied, cheated, or stole. They never hurt anyone. They never put on airs, and they saved their pennies. They gave their son a good education neither of them had. Vole never once blamed anyone else for his problems. After the housing market crashed and everything took a turn for the worse, he never pointed fingers. "Know your numbers and know your heart," he would say at the dinner table. "Control what you can and the rest will be." Dinnertime was family time. The words gave him courage. Saying them out loud in front of William and Bay kept him grounded. Reminded him he was in control of his own destiny. They worked hard to be good people.

Why is this happening to us?

"I wish . . ." He stopped, unfamiliar with how the words felt on his lips. "I wish," he tried again. "I wish . . . Dammit, why is this so hard? Why can't there be more time! I wish we had more time!"

His voice dropped, and with it, his demeanor turned inward and grave.

"Please," he said. "Please let us have more time together. *Please.*"

It was the sort of first wish a man with a broken heart would make. Maybe it was the first wish the universe had ever answered. Maybe strange things happened so near the summer equinox all the time. Vole didn't know. In truth, he never gave it much thought. He knew he could never be sure. All he could be sure of was that the unthinkable happened.

Everything went still.

Saturday, June 20, 2015
Gibbons' residence, Dorset, Ontario
8:29 p.m. eastern time

He felt it in his stomach first. Like he stepped off a gravity-defying carnival ride—the kind young William squealed about because it let him turn upside down and crawl across walls—into a gelatin-filled swimming pool. Vole could sense something monumental had occurred, but had no idea what. Everything looked the same. Everything smelled the same. Everything was quiet. Everything . . . didn't feel the same. That was it. The air felt different around him. It had become heavy. Viscous, almost.

Behind him, Vole noticed their curtains, stuck in a blowing position, as though caught in a breeze. They remained motionless, and no sensation of wind moved across his skin, there was no tingle inside his ears. In fact, there was no sound whatsoever. The quiet was too quiet.

Vole got to his feet, grateful for his clothing's rustle.

"Jock!" he called out. A look from his old friend would help ease his mind, he was sure of it. He called out once more when he didn't hear the usual scrambling of claws. A few seconds passed, and Vole's concern grew to alarm when Jock still didn't appear.

He strode into the living room. Jock was sprawled out on top of their loveseat, not moving, as though he were ill.

"Jock?" Vole cried, rushing to his companion's side.

Oh no, not you too!

When he got close, he could see Jock looked well. Perky. His eyes were open, his body warm, and his nose was moist and cold to the touch.

"Treats?" Vole asked, using the magic word. "Would you like a *treat?*"

Nothing.

"TREAT?!" he burst, unable to contain his alarm.

The dog made no reaction. He wouldn't budge. No amount of shaking, petting, or cajoling could get Jock to move.

Disturbed, Vole glanced down at his watch. It was twenty-nine minutes past eight. He needed to get back. The hospital was a few minutes away. The notion of spending any more seconds away from Bay was appalling, and the thick quiet was suffocating, but he couldn't leave Jock in such a queer state. The dog needed to see a vet.

Vole tried to massage Jock into wakefulness once more. It didn't work. Giving up, he retrieved the vet's phone number from Bay's family contact list and jogged back to their bedroom to pick up her things.

He glanced down at his watch a second time. It was 8:29 p.m. Still.

"That's not right."

Slowly, ever so slowly, the pieces began to move. A murky picture formed inside his mind.

First, he made his wish. Then, a subtle yet dramatic change occurred in his surroundings. It was like the magnetic fields that held the world together shifted. Maybe that's what made the wind stop blowing. Then there was his watch. It displayed the same time after he knew many minutes had gone by. He changed its battery the other day. And there was Jocko, who seemed perfectly normal but looked as though he was frozen in time—

No! Vole thought. *Not possible!*

With what seemed to Vole to be at the urging of a single thought, everything went back to normal.

The intense quiet was suddenly gone. It was replaced by a steady vibration brought on by an incessant and pervasive noise. The noise was all around. Everything seemed to be contributing to it. It was coming from him too. How could that be?

There it was. A light hum he never noticed before emanated out from his body and blended with an invisible stream of sound that flowed all around him.

"Why does everything get more confusing with time?" Vole grumbled to himself, fussing with his shirt, rubbing his hands up and down his thighs. It was the first of many instances the question would occur to him in the coming years, though he didn't know it yet.

A sharp bark rang out. Jock was standing in the doorway of their bedroom, watching Vole.

"Well. Well, well, well. I suppose you got lucky this time, Jocko."

Jock hated going on car rides. At his age, a car ride rarely meant anything good. Vole was sure if his furry companion knew how close he'd come to being bundled up and placed inside the Sebring, he wouldn't look so happy.

What Vole wasn't sure about, however, was what to think about what just happened.

FOUR

Saturday, June 20, 2015
Rosabella Memorial Hospital, Dorset, Ontario
8:43 p.m. eastern time

BAY WAS DOZING when Vole peered into room 1221 of the hospital's west wing. Her eyes flitted open as he crossed the threshold and entered. She was a light sleeper, sensitive on every level. One of the many reasons she took such good care of them. Of him. What would come of him when she was gone? Would all her care disappear with her? It certainly felt as though he'd vanish into thin air when she did. That's what was supposed to happen, because that's how important decisions were made. Together. How could she leave him all alone in the dark?

Quelling a sharp pang, Vole said, "You never change, my sleeping beauty." None of this was her fault.

Bay shuffled over to make space for him to sit on the bed. "Strange question," he said, "but did anything odd happen a few minutes ago?"

"Odd?"

"Odd. Unlike anything you've ever felt before. A sudden quiet. A twitch, or abnormal niggling inside your stomach, perhaps?" The words felt stiff and awkward inside his mouth.

"Oh dear. I don't want to think about my stomach, much less an abnormal niggling inside of it.

"How's Jocko doing?" she asked, shifting focus.

"He misses you. He hadn't touched his food by the time I left."

"He'll eat if you stay and keep him company."

Vole knew but didn't say so.

"I brought over everything you asked for," he said and held up the bag to show her proof. "Is there anything else I can get you?"

Her lips twisted.

"A new body?"

"Honeybee . . ."

How could he do this? How could he sit there, knowing every second might be her last, her second last, her third last . . . ?

A new idea struck him. What if—and he knew it was insane to consider—but what if, for a moment back at the house, time *had* stopped? What if it happened because he *made* it happen?

Vole had never tried to stop time before. He didn't know how these things worked. William might have a theory—their son seemed to know a lot about many things that didn't make sense to Vole—but William wasn't around, and the thought of explaining the inexplicable to their son, now, as adult as he'd become, seemed an insurmountable challenge. Stopping time shouldn't be possible, which is exactly what William would say.

"I want you to do something for me," Vole appealed on a desperate whim. "I want you to close your eyes and remember our honeymoon. That evening we shared after we walked through the park and saw the temple leaning out over the water.

Paris was so 'devastatingly beautiful,' I remember you saying. Full of old paths, exactly like how you'd imagined. A city to sing you to sleep. Do you remember what I said to you after?"

Eyes shut, she nodded.

"I remember like it just happened. You said: 'Now that we've found one another, we'll live a whole and devastatingly beautiful life together.' Every day was beautiful because it was a day spent discovering new paths together." Her twisted lips were replaced with an achingly familiar, perfect bow. "We were so young and newly in love then."

Now. It had to be now.

Stop, Vole willed the universe. *I want everything to stop.*

And it did.

Saturday, June 20, 2015
Rosabella Memorial Hospital, Dorset, Ontario
8:45 p.m. eastern time

Vole had never been inside a hospital room that didn't have machines beeping and gasping. The sudden silence was eerie. He felt unwelcome. Like a visitor who'd stumbled into the wrong room.

How is she? Did it work on her too? He couldn't bring himself to examine Bay to verify. Instead, he glanced down at his wrist. According to his watch, it was quarter to nine.

Vole got to his feet and stepped into the hallway, and—

"Watch out!" he cried, stumbling into a stopped cart; a blue pen and three plastic pill bottles flew into the air.

Unexpectedly, the airborne items slowed their climb. Came to a halt. Dropped slowly to the floor, making barely a sound upon landing.

Each item he'd sent flying had changed course midflight instead of continuing its foregone trajectory. The strange motion defied everything Vole learned in high school physics.

"Fascinating," he murmured.

Vole picked up the pen. Chucked it at the wall. It never made impact. The pen simply left his hand, slowed to a halt—no more than half a meter in front of him—and dropped quietly.

"Fascinating!"

He bent to pick up the pill bottles and discovered a nurse lying on the ground, hidden by the cart.

"Crap," Vole swore, looking down at the fallen man. "I didn't mean to do that."

The nurse lay on his side in an unnatural position. Both his arms were extended out in front of him, and his scissor-spread legs formed a wide V.

"Excuse me," Vole said as he pulled the man's body up and positioned him in a seated position against the wall. "I, um, hope you're comfortable."

He expected the nurse to make a sound. Not a single grunt of surprise or cry of dismay rang out. A chill took Vole.

What if the nurse knows? he wondered. *What if he remembers everything when he wakes up?*

But he's not asleep.

He's awake right now.

Maybe he's watching me and seeing everything I do. Vole's bones turned to winter at the thought.

"Hello! Can you see me, Mr. Nurse?" There was no response. Goose pimples emerged all over Vole's body.

Despite his misgivings, he crouched down and examined the man's face as though it were a map. It held as many spots, crevices, and bumps as any other face he'd seen.

The rest of the man's body felt alive too. His neck was warm to the touch, but there was no pulse or evidence of breath. His eyes were alert. Shining and intelligent. Despite being folded at the waist and seated on the floor, his entire form seemed taut. The nurse appeared ready to lunge, and no matter how many times Vole tried to set the nurse's erect leg flat on the ground (he managed to make the man's extended arms stay by his side), it wouldn't budge. It remained stuck, up in the air.

Vole pinched the man on the arm—not so hard he'd cause a bruise, but with enough effort to make a person squeal.

Nothing happened.

"CAN YOU HEAR ME?" Vole hollered into his ear. "HELLO?"

Still nothing.

"Fascinating," Vole muttered. "I'm sorry about all this. I needed to know, you see . . . and, um, watch yourself. Try to be careful with your leg. Don't want to knock anyone over by accident."

Vole cleared his throat and got to his feet. His eyes never left the nurse's face. He kept waiting for the man to shout suddenly for security and accuse Vole of doing something inappropriate and weird.

The moment never came.

Silence reigned.

Vole took care not to bump into anyone after that. Making his way around people was difficult to do. It was harder than making his way through a crowd with someplace to go. Usually, when people go places, they give off signals, subtle clues that reveal the direction and speed they're moving. Rapid processing of so much tiny detail allows a crowd to be fluid, and individuals within can flow with the group to get where they each need to be. Flow is something people understand, inherently. Perhaps because the world's in a perpetual state of motion. Walking between stopped bodies was like having to weave through a silent forest.

A hospital isn't intended to be a comfortable or easy environment. Being inside one was like being stuck in a traffic jam on the 401, or the Don Valley Parkway, or any road in the world for that matter. It was a place of in between. Of wasting time. People who felt completely comfortable in a hospital were either too far gone or demented, in Vole's opinion. It made him especially squeamish when he caught sight of a patient in their bed or when his gaze locked onto a somber-faced family member who waited, troubled and barely human, at a loved one's bedside. That was the problem with hospitals. People were only there because they had no other choice.

In the end, it didn't take long for Vole to become accustomed to crossing boldly in front of unseeing eyes (so he came to tell himself). Curiosity became his guide. For the first time in his life, Vole felt comfortable walking through a hospital. It occurred to him he was too far gone, and probably quite demented.

The farther Vole got from the oncology ward, the less depressing things became. The tableau of grim and suffering faces transformed to contain flashes of joy. Air he passed through shifted to include some new quality to it. *What is that?* Vole wondered. Construction bird cutouts and pastel-colored greeting cards came to decorate the walls around him. Light softened. Vole pushed open double doors and entered the maternity ward.

Two hospital employees were seated behind the front desk. Their necks were bent as they each worked on separate tasks. Vole nodded at them out of habit, and he obeyed the posted instructions by rubbing two pumps of alcohol-based sanitizer into his hands. "Just in case," he told himself.

The sticky liquid coated his hands. Vole questioned whether it would absorb into his skin. It did, but it didn't smell like what he was used to. He imagined a permanent residue, and rubbed his palms against his pants. Two smears appeared but didn't fade.

When he discovered the infant, tucked into the elbow crook of a young woman who sat next to the sleeping mother's bed, he almost reached out to take the babe.

"Bay, look," Vole said instead, though she wasn't there with him. "He looks the same as William did."

Half expecting Bay to poke her head around the corner and tell him to stop making the baby cry *(Will, would you please tell your father he shouldn't touch someone else's infant?)*, Vole looked up. His eye caught the clock mounted to the wall in the hallway outside. It read quarter to nine.

"I'm coming, honeybee."

Vole bid goodbye to the small family and left to make his way back to Bay's bedside in the oncology ward. On his way, he noticed a gentle-faced nurse. She held a hand in hers, ever tender, as she checked beneath a wrapping. *Toothpick arm draped in elephant skin*, Vole thought. *That will be me one day.*

But not Bay.

The longing looks of a boy, hooded eyes ringed in purple, chased him through the halls. A heavy glance shared between two people dressed in scrubs, silver-green, made him cry; a gentle brush of fingertips stole away his breath. Hallway after hallway, Vole counted the small beds tucked away inside small rooms and left alone the lonely ghosts fast asleep within.

It could have taken him minutes, it could have taken him days—as he made his way back to Bay's bedside, every clock he passed showed the same time. Quarter to nine. Quarter to nine. Quarter to nine.

When Vole made it back to Bay, it was with great relief that he discovered her eyes closed, face aglow with the warm light of nostalgia as she remembered their time together in Paris. She looked the same as she did back then, and Vole wondered if more was happening than he knew. *Although, I don't know much about anything, do I?*

They honeymooned in France. It took all his savings to take them there. *You were born with pennies in your pockets*, his mother would say (often followed in later years by, *Snapping Bay up and marrying her so quick was the smartest thing you ever did*).

For as long as Vole could remember, he'd been a conservative spender. Money was hard earned; every coin was precious. It was lunacy to drop it all on a single trip. But Bay did something to him—she turned him into a lusting lunatic. When it came to matters of the heart, Vole would turn to his father's single piece of emotional advice. A child's lumpy memory polished into crystal over time: *A roof over your head and a good woman in your bed*, the mantra went, as he pulled Vole's mother in for an embrace. *All a man needs. Know your numbers, know your heart. Nothing else is up to you. Nothing else matters.*

Vole wanted Bay, and Bay wanted Paris. Nothing else was up to him and nothing else mattered. To Paris they went. Their locked eyes glistened wide and blissful the entire time. They kissed each other's necks and nibbled each other's lobes; they visited the Eiffel Tower to pay worship to one another beneath its wrought iron steeple. They grasped each other's hands—with care, because his right one was still tender from being so recently healed—and traced each other's flesh with the tips of their tongues. They blushed crimson as they gloated about the secret they'd found in one another, and they strolled languidly through Parc des Buttes-Chaumont. When they gazed upon the Temple de la Sibylle together, Bay sung of their next trip, where they would go to Italy to see the original. Vole's vow to do exactly that flew from his mouth and danced circles around their heads. He promised her the world because the world felt his to offer.

Four months after they returned home from Paris they learned they were pregnant with their first child. Reality showed its hand, drawing their fairy tale beginning to a close. They bought a house they could barely afford with money Bay's parents needed but loaned them anyway. They moved in and learned Bay wouldn't be carrying the infant to term. A blessing of the worst kind, because shortly thereafter, lending rates peaked. Borrowers nationwide suffered. For many people in similar situations, barely affordable became unaffordable, and payments everywhere were missed. The number of defaulted mortgages rose higher, and higher still. Downsizing happened; countrywide layoffs began. Those families whose livelihood lay in manufacturing and construction were impacted the most. Ontario families were hit the hardest.

It wasn't easy being in the business of money at the time. No one could get a loan. Businesses that had been in people's families for generations closed their doors and boarded up their windows, and bankruptcy ran rampant. Vole told each penniless person who came to see him about a loan to come back in six months. "If I can help you then, I will." Loaves of air for the starving.

Bay was his rock through it all. She rarely asked for anything. If she ever felt like she was missing out, or he wasn't delivering on his vows, she never spoke to him about it. Instead, she maintained her list of broken dreams in silence.

"I didn't know what I was doing," Vole moaned. "I never knew what I was doing."

When he was too spent to do anything but wipe salty moisture from his face and take deep, ragged breaths, he made another promise. One he would keep.

"It's not too late, honeybee. I can still make it right."

What he didn't say out loud (for fear of Bay hearing and knowing), was he doubted his ability to make it up to her. Not because she was unforgiving—on the contrary, Bay had the most forgiving nature—but because he never shared with her all the facts. The life Bay led wasn't the one she chose for herself; it was the one he chose for them.

"There wasn't any time to explain," he whispered.

Becoming tired, Vole checked his watch. It was still quarter to nine. He stowed Bay's belongings inside William's old diaper bag, which also held her medication.

Every time they were admitted to the hospital they brought all of Bay's medicine with them. If they didn't, they were told, doctors might miss some important detail. Where they were going, he would need her medication and schedule. He couldn't afford to miss a single important detail.

With the burgeoning bag slung over his shoulder, Vole lifted Bay into his arms. She felt more like a doll than a woman. Her body was lighter than when they got married, more than three decades ago.

Yesterday, the thought would have made his throat ache. Today, he was overcome with gratitude. Their time together wasn't coming to an end. In a way, it was beginning.

FIVE

Saturday, June 20, 2015
Rosabella Memorial Hospital, Dorset, Ontario
8:45 p.m. eastern time

AFTER PUTTING BAY in the front seat of their Sebring and snapping her seat belt into place, he found the car's engine wouldn't start.

A nearby ambulance caught Vole's eye. He walked over to it and yanked open the driver's-side door. "I'm sorry," he said to the driver, who happened to be looking in his direction, but at something behind him.

Over his shoulder, silhouetted against the sunset and stuck midair, was a soaring flight of geese arranged in a near-perfect wedge. Blended streaks of hot pink and tangerine-orange filled the sky. It was exactly the sort of summer sunset he and Bay loved to become lost in.

As far back as he could recall, he'd never seen a wedge of geese without hearing an errant honk or flapping of wings first. It must have happened, he was sure of it, but no occurrence other than this one stood out from memory. *No doubt they're practicing for the migration south this winter,* he mused. *It is a helluva long way to go for such a short time.*

Humbled by the enormity of their journey, and sure the goose was an evolutionary dead end because of it, Vole turned back to face the driver. He leaned across her lap to check if keys were still in the ambulance's ignition—they were. Not seeing any way around it, Vole maneuvered the driver's right leg. Placed her foot on the throttle. Applied downward force to her knee.

Her foot pressed down on the gas pedal, but the pedal didn't budge. The ambulance made no sound.

Vole pushed down harder on the woman's knee, pumped her foot into the pedal. "Go! Go! Go!" he demanded. "The gas must be going someplace!" The ambulance remained stock-still.

"So," he grunted in dismay. "Nothing makes sense, and it appears as though we'll be walking everywhere we go." No one responded. "Good grief! Is there really no one else listening?"

Vole found an empty wheelchair near the hospital entrance and developed a new plan. He pushed the chair to where Bay sat in the Sebring and locked its wheels in place. He lifted her from the car and placed her in the wheelchair. *Note to self,* he thought. *When we get back home, write down what I take and where it's from.* Bay would want him to, and what would William think if his father became a thief? *I'll make amends someday. Although, I may be getting ahead of myself. At the rate I'm moving, I'll die of old age long before Bay does!*

"Hrrrm," he said aloud. "Best not joke about that." Not that he found it an amusing thought in the first place. "And not because I'm superstitious or anything."

With Bay clipped into the wheelchair and the bag holding her medication on her lap, Vole was ready.

"Hold on tight," he advised.

He pumped his elbows and prepared to push forward on the chair's handles. "Onward!" he cried, and he grunted as a sudden jolt made his teeth crack hard together. Sheepish and smarting because he forgot he'd locked the wheels, he unlocked the chair's brakes and gave it another heave. This time the chair propelled forward with such unexpected thrust that Vole stumbled to catch it.

"I knew you were on the light side, honeybee, but I didn't think you were weightless!"

Any natural friction seemed to have vanished, which was peculiar. If anything, the air felt denser. Vole had anticipated more resistance. *How is this happening? What is happening? Why does pushing Bay take such little effort?*

Confounded, Vole continued to push Bay along. He took up both lanes of the hospital driveway and thought to himself, *I don't need to take the sidewalk either!* The roads were empty at that time of night. *It'll be better for Bay's bones*, he told himself.

He passed by the dark panes of nearby shop windows and noticed how everything appeared closed. It was the type of small town Dorset was. That, at least, remained unchanged and expected.

Above him, the sky remained unchanged, which was far from expected. At quarter to nine, the sun was only twenty minutes away from setting. It hung in the sky and smoldered. It didn't move the entire way home. Not the tiniest bit.

Saturday, June 20, 2015
Gibbons residence, Dorset, Ontario
8:45 p.m. eastern time

By the time Vole made it home, he was exhausted. Somewhere between the hospital and their house, the weight of his circumstances began to burden him. Now, their front door was more of a pain than usual to open. Not because it was more difficult than usual to do, but because the wood's surface, punished from exposure, made Vole regret never installing a new storm door.

"I should've taken better care of it," he said, addressing the summer-lean squirrel with a feathery gray tail. It sat perched on the maple tree that grew tall and thick next to their house. "It never seemed important enough to replace," he continued. "Storm doors are expensive! Especially this one. It's a custom height.

"Stop looking at me like that, squirrel. I bet there's a lot you'd redo too!"

It didn't bat an eye.

Inside the house, Vole looked to where Jock should've been sitting, waiting for the door to open.

Jock wasn't there. "Jock!" he called out, though he knew better than to expect a nail-clicking response. "Jocko! Where are you, boy?"

He placed Bay down on the couch and went to look for the dog. It took a while to hunt the schnauzer down. When he did, Vole let out a cackle.

"You rascal!" he accused. "I've often wondered what you got up to while you had the house to yourself." Jock had nestled himself beneath the blankets of their bed and was using Bay's pillow as his own. The way the sheet fell, Jock may as well have been wearing a lace sleeping cap. "The look suits you, you big bad wolf," Vole joked. "Wait until your human mum hears about this." Bay probably already knew of Jock's antics, he realized, and there was still much to be done. He put it from his mind.

Vole stepped into their small office, once William's bedroom. He turned on their computer. Waited. The monitor remained dark. He pressed the button again. Waited. Nothing happened.

"Oh *no*."

Vole checked to see if his phone was still connected to the internet. The screen was dark. Was the device still on? He couldn't tell. He thought it was glowing the smallest bit, but maybe his eyes were playing tricks. It felt flimsy and artificial in his hands. Like a toy. He'd never bought into touchscreen technology, much to William's chagrin, and was still using an old Blackberry, much to Bay's amusement. Regardless of what sort of toy it was—whether it was a Blackberry, an iPhone, Android, or hunk of meteor rock—Vole was loath to discover no amount of touching or pressing could get his device to make a single sound or change a single screen.

"Back to the Stone Age we go," he muttered. "I suppose I'll need to think like our ancestors did. Sort of."

Giving up on motorized vehicles, electronics, and the World Wide Web, Vole carried a pen and notepad to the living room and sat down on the couch next to where he'd left Bay. "I could use your help here, honeybee," he said. "You're the one who thinks of everything I don't." Vole imagined her small smile deepening the littlest bit and was heartened.

It didn't take long for him to fill three pages of his notepad. Inventories of what he would need and where he could get it all. *Big Ticket Items* was the first list. A bicycle. The right type (something durable with good tires). A boat. Also the right type (he underlined it twice). A trailer. A hitch (he made note to come back to it later because the hitch might need a list of its own). A bicycle emergency kit. A medical emergency kit. A boat emergency kit. Water filters. Purification tablets (hundreds, no, *thousands*). Desalination pump (as many as he could find—"A pretty penny," Vole muttered, and he made another underline and added an asterisk to it and wrote at the bottom of the page, *To research*). At the bottom of that list, he wrote another list. The bicycle seat must be comfortable. It must have many gears. Tires that could withstand gravel and pavement. Strong, sturdy shocks.

When his first rush of ideas subsided, Vole remembered he hadn't eaten since . . . some amount of time ago. He was hungry, and he was unsure how much time had passed since he arrived home from the hospital.

I should make a list for those items too.

He started another list. This one for additional items, items Bay would have prompted him to think about. Vole would need to keep track of the passage of time. The days that went by. Sunglasses, a hat, comfortable shoes, durable socks, appropriate clothing, and so on and so forth. That list grew and grew. On it, he added things like road maps, books about plants, books about animals, blank journals, and pens.

When it was complete, he made another, more precious list. A list of the things Bay would want and need to have with her.

By the time Vole took another break, he'd filled twenty-three pages of his notepad with sketches, lists of items he would need to collect, and lists of needs he must tend to. Bay would be proud of the masterpiece. He wished he could share it with her.

"Aha!" Vole exclaimed and laughed at how ridiculous he sounded. What was happening to him? "My dearest Bay," he continued. "You told me I should keep a diary, and I told you I'd one day try keeping a journal. This isn't exactly a diary or a journal, or anything else either of us ever thought about for that matter, but I will write to you, as though you are my journal, and I'll do it every day, and when we're back together, I'll share every experience with you. I won't leave anything out. Would you like that?"

He imagined her smile deepen.

"It's a deal!"

Swept up in the moment, Vole gave Bay a full kiss on the lips. His stomach tightened and he recoiled in response. Romantic intimacy without Bay's knowledge of it felt, well, the opposite of romantic. The sensation sobered him. It frightened him. He gave up on planning and gave into his stomach-rumbling hunger instead.

As Vole prepared himself a sliced ham and cheese sandwich, he thought about Toronto. Dorset wouldn't have a quarter of what he needed. How was he to get to the city?

He would bike there!

It must've been longer since he last ate than he thought for his mind to be so erratic and sluggish. Vole would take his bicycle to Toronto where he would find what he needed. *I can't possibly carry it all. I may as well put it together there.*

How in the world will I pay for everything?

Vole sensed an avalanche looming. If he didn't soon rest he'd get buried forever. His belly was full, and for once, time was on his side.

He scooped Bay into his arms and carried her to where Jock lay asleep on her pillow. Vole laid her down next to the dog and covered her to keep her warm. He stripped down to his boxers and slipped under the covers next to her. Wrapped his arm around her sharp shoulders, and—like he had every other night for most of their lives—fell fast asleep.

The first thing Vole did when he woke was replace the storm door. From the basement of their house, he withdrew a brand-new door, free of rust and with glass intact. The door was good quality, bought ages ago in an end-of-season clearance sale, but it was too short for their tall frame. Once the rosy blush of having scored a great deal dissipated, Vole berated himself for making an airhead decision and stowed the storm door away in darkness to deal with another day.

The door wouldn't fit without modification. Vole removed its hinges and spaced them correctly before screwing them back in place. He nailed to the bottom a skirt made of wood doweling and rubber gasket—bits and pieces he'd collected over the years from doing his own household repairs.

"Judge me all you want," Vole told the squirrel, who looked on with shining eyes from its tree-trunk perch, "but mark my words. The next time I open this storm cover, the wood beneath won't have aged a single day! Stormy weather be damned. You remember that, squirrel, when you find yourself huddled and wet inside your leaky hole, eyeing up my nice dry wood!"

If the neighborhood squirrels hadn't eaten half his fence away, Vole might resent them less. As it was, his grouchy neighbor, Harold, refused to pay for his half of repairs, and Vole refused to pay for the entire project. The wood fence between their properties had been chewed and splintering for years. It would likely remain that way forever.

"Bloody squirrels," Vole muttered as he hand-tightened all the screws, careful not to strip any of them. "You're cute, but Harold's right about one thing. You're annoying as all hell."

With the door in place, and after making sure Bay was still safe and tucked away in bed with Jock to guard over her, Vole set out for Toronto. Like before, what should have caused him physical exertion came easy and felt exhilarating. "It's like I'm cycling down a slight slope," he marveled, "and there's a whisper of tailwind at my back, giving me a push."

Vole pedaled faster, and he was rewarded with the sensation of slipping down an oil-slicked slide. Why couldn't it have been so easy on all those long, aching rides with Harold? (It nearly killed him trying to keep up with the old coot, and he never would have if Bay hadn't insisted it was good for his health.)

"Maybe the time of night has something to do with it," he said, still trying to make sense of things. "The sun is still setting, after all. On second thought, that doesn't make any sense.

"What if I'm experiencing some sort of alternate dimension? Or a memory? Perhaps this is a shadow of what's real." Those ideas didn't make sense either. "Or perhaps the air feels dense when I'm standing in one spot because I'm under lots of pressure. All of Earth's forces, caught midmotion, press down on me when I'm not moving. Yes, of course. All those forces are pressing down on me because I'm in the way of them. When I move, I slip between. If I keep myself moving, I'll have an easier time of it.

"Though, it's all impossible," he continued to himself. "Time is infinite. Space is infinite. There is no going *between* forces. If anything, I'm proving it right now. Infinite complexity exists between moments of infinite complexity. Have I stopped time? Or have I simply entered a similar-looking world running parallel, no, orthogonal, to our own? Back to it being an alternate dimension, then. If that were the case, wouldn't the car have started? What about gravity? When I bump or drop something that's frozen in time, it moves, but not normally. Isn't gravity linked to time?" So it went. After not much time spent ruminating, Vole stopped trying to make sense of it and simply accepted it for what it was: impossible.

It took approximately one full day to get to the city, but it was impossible for Vole to know exactly how much time passed. Not without counting every single second. There were too many distractions to keep counting seconds for long. He couldn't help but stop every time he encountered something new: tapered seeds flying through the air, front-to-back like tiny train cars; a butterfly, periwinkle blue, floating overtop a glass windshield, not touching it, though car and butterfly were in head-on collision. A burning sun, hanging, in the same spot in the sky, never falling, never rising. The moon, shy, ever peeking out from behind nighttime's veil.

Utter silence.

Humming helped when the quiet became unbearable. Vole hummed all the songs he and Bay used to hum together. But even their favorite songs wore thin eventually. The dark realization accompanied him as he rode into downtown Toronto.

When he arrived at the busy intersection of King Street West and Spadina Avenue, he stopped. Got off his bike. Stood there. Watched.

There were so many cars and so many people. The streets were busy but nothing bustled.

"Hello!" he called out.

The crowd of statues waiting to clamber onto the next streetcar ignored him.

Every step Vole took carried him into a new cloud of scent—a burst of someone's shampoo; air that had whooshed up through a street grate, dry and hot from the subway tunnels below. A warm and savory aroma, a hot dog stand, made his mouth water; rotten garbage had spent all day in the summer sun and made his stomach roil. Underlying it all were the heavy notes of sewage and sweat.

Everywhere he looked was someone different. Eyeglasses and eyes, scalps and scarves; headphones and hats, sandals and socks; wheelchairs and walking sticks, the barefoot and broken. Every single person stood out for reasons all their own. Every single person was exactly the same. Still. Except for him.

"Can anybody hear me?" Vole shouted. "IS ANYONE OUT THERE?"

It was an absurd question to ask, much less shout in public. Vole was the one who was stuck. *He* couldn't hear anybody else around him. To everyone else, the world was the same. Not the other way around.

"Fine," Vole compromised, as though someone was listening. "I can't hear you, and you can't hear me. We're both impacted, and neither of us is wrong. We both have a right to be here." He was lying. He'd been feeling like an imposter ever since time had stopped for everyone but him. He was as ordinary as anyone else. What right did he have to be so different?

Itchy and agitated, Vole leaned his bicycle against the outside wall of a liquor store. Went inside. Found a bottle of fine whisky. Left cash for it at the counter. Was about to cross the street when he decided instead to take a freshly cooked sausage from a recent buyer. Vole put five dollars in the man's hand where the sausage had been and crossed the street to a tall redbrick building. He found a fire escape he could climb. Carried his bottle and sausage to the top. Took a seat on the roof, and looked south toward the water.

Boats with glowing sails filled the Toronto harbor, a glittering lake as large as any sea. Rippled lines behind each vessel were predictable and soothing. From so far away, Vole could pretend nothing was different. He imagined the petulant cry of feasting gulls, the clank and whir of streetcars, and distant voices, murmurs, carried along by the wind.

"Ah," Vole sighed, cracking open the twelve-year-old bottle of Gibson's he'd brought with him. He'd never paid so much for a drink before. "Summer. Second only to autumn. This is your season, honeybee." If only Bay could be there with him to enjoy it.

Vole sat there, sipping between generous bites, and felt nearly normal.

To the east was the CN Tower, a knobby needle that poked up into the sky. North was home, and west was where the evening sun hung low. His path took him west. It was a sight he'd better get used to.

He stared westward until his vision blurred and he couldn't take it anymore. Glancing down at the street below, he waited until the spots in his vision cleared. When he could see again, he was struck by how the world, at such a far distance, resembled a wax museum.

"Marie Tussaud," Vole muttered, taking a deep swig from the bottle. He recalled the time he told William they had no money for him to visit Madame Tussauds in New York with the rest of his class. William was sixteen at the time, and it had been a difficult year for the family. "You ain't got nothing on Vole Gibbons."

Two city pigeons in a rare romantic embrace caught Vole's eye, and he remembered he wasn't supposed to be there. He climbed back down the staircase and continued on his way. Something was troubling him. A question he brought with him all the way from home, *How will I pay for everything on my list?* remained unanswered. Vole wasn't a thief. He didn't want to steal anything, but he wasn't about to restart time just to make the credit machines work. Wasting Bay's remaining minutes for the sake of his morality wasn't an option. On top of it all, he didn't want anyone to get into trouble for his actions; although, truth be told, all that seemed to matter much less to him now.

In the end, Vole resolved to find an open store, and he would take only what he needed. Not a single thing more. He'd write it all down in his book. It would be like keeping a ledger. He spent his whole life practicing self-restraint and good ledger keeping, he was sure he would have no trouble keeping himself to the basics of both now.

When Vole arrived at his destination—a nationwide outdoor and sporting goods retailer—and took in all the unsupervised possibilities, he was forced to confront that belief. Which was difficult to do, because it had been with him his entire life.

What's the purpose of self-restraint in a world of infinite opportunity? he wondered. *What if holding yourself back doesn't matter? What if people* should *do whatever they want, so long as it gets them their happily ever after?*

His world shook under the weight of the question.

SIX

Saturday, June 20, 2015
Toronto, Ontario
8:45 p.m. eastern time
1 sleep since

SECONDS LATER, "YOU dummy," Vole muttered. "Happiness isn't achieved by getting what you want all the time. Happiness only happens when you feel like you've earned the right to it. Self-restraint matters because nothing would work otherwise. Laws exist for this reason . . . and the police too! Without consequences and rules and police, we'd all behave like children. It would be anarchy!

"Hmm. I think you've had enough to drink for one day."

Vole turned to consider the store. It was closing soon and there were few people about. It was a fortunate thing, because if Vole had to climb up and down the stairs with his arms full, while also having to weave around time-stopped bodies, he would have wanted to pile everyone together like pick-up sticks. Ever since taking the hot dog from the man's motionless hand, warm fingertips against smooth skin, Vole resolved not to interfere with any more lives. Not directly, at least. (He couldn't bear the thought of a stranger touching him without his permission, or worse, without his knowledge of it.) Moving anyone was strictly off limits.

The thought probably would have occurred to him sooner, but he was still getting used to managing his schedule without the help of a changing sky. It made eating at the proper intervals difficult to do. Vole hadn't realized how hungry he'd become until he arrived downtown and smelled the hot dog cart. *Hunger brings out the airhead in you,* Bay often said, and she was right.

First thing was first. Vole needed to make sure the store had sufficient food and water. He had no idea how long he'd be there, though he suspected he would need to stay more than one night.

The staff kitchen fridge was stocked, full of leftover takeout and half-eaten lunches. A large cooler, three quarters full, stood in the corner; a full refill tank was on the floor next to it.

With food and water secured, Vole walked methodically through each of the aisles and the stock room. Checked the inventory against his lists, and made notes so he could come back more easily to items later.

The store sold things Vole had no idea existed. He'd never conceived of such variety before. There were snowshoes for infants and first aid kits for giants. Sporty underpants with parallel stretches of fine netting to keep his most sensitive parts in place, and watches that could keep time in environments as extreme as the deep ocean floor or inside an erupting volcano. (Those were most interesting to Vole because every time display in the store read 8:45 p.m.) The store also stocked hundreds of long, skinny tubes that contained gels and baby food–like substances—synthetic compounds nutritionally dense enough to provide enough sustenance for weeks. If you could imagine it, and it might be needed outside, the store carried it.

Vole set about collecting items and tabulating totals inside his journal. He'd pick one thing up, drop it off in the center of the store, take note of its price, calculate a new running total, and move on to his next list item. Over and over, he passed by two young employees caught tickling each other behind the checkout counter instead of doing their jobs. Every time, Vole made sure to say, "Hi there," "Sorry about all this," and, "Um, thank you for your help."

Having collected everything on his list except for two things, Vole allowed himself a break. Out of habit, he checked his watch. It read quarter to nine. *Good.* Strangely, he wasn't tired despite having already had such a long day. Rather than force sleep, he decided to get to what he'd been looking forward to most: choosing his bicycle. The second last remaining thing on his list.

At first, Vole approached the back section of the store with reverence and awe. It was where all the bicycle equipment was kept. After taking in the glinting metal and matte rubber splendor, he dove into assessing every single one with rigor.

After much humming and hawing, flicking and dinging, sitting and bouncing, poking and pulling, Vole decided on a best-of-breed cyclocross—one reliable enough for smooth roads and rough terrain—that could be fitted with a bicycle trailer via a hitch attached to its back axle. The bicycle had a seal-gray aluminum frame with thin purple lettering spread across it. It was perfect. He'd considered a road bike, the style of bicycle he was accustomed to, but the seats were all too pointy, and the tires weren't as hardy as he imagined they'd need to be. The bicycle he settled on had a gear setup that looked like it belonged on a spaceship and great big treads that belonged on a tanker. It looked solid enough to withstand the apocalypse, which, in the end, is why he decided it was the one he wanted most.

Historically, Vole avoided such expensive-looking stores. They were too complicated. The world had spun out of control, left him in the dust, and he still couldn't imagine ever needing a quarter of what the store provided. More than that, he never wanted to look too closely at new bicycles. What if he fell in love with one he couldn't afford? Besides, he'd told himself, his built-to-last road bike had a lot of life left in it. It was going to last forever.

Now, looking at modern bicycles with all the widgets he could fantasize about—and then some—Vole found he wasn't seized by unrequited love. The experience served as a stark reminder of how quickly the world was changing around him.

A big yawn took him. *I'll get the rest of what I need when I wake up, tomorrow,* he thought. Before lying down on his sleeping bag and mat, he called out good night. Good night to the two flirts behind the counter, and good night to the only other customer in the store (she stood, back to Vole, inspecting the most extreme climbing gear he'd ever seen). Before he could close his eyes, there was something he needed to do. Vole pulled out his journal and began to write.

> *Dear Bay,*
>
> *I wish I could speak with you. There's so much I want to talk about. I've been thinking a lot about Will, trying to figure out what to tell him. I've already wasted twelve pages writing nonsense. I think I'll wait until we're ready to go. Write down what I must at the last minute, my last minute, before we leave.*
>
> *Does waiting make me weak?*
>
> *My love. I miss you more than ever, now, at this moment. I've become spoiled, being able to*

embrace you, letting your soothing presence carry me into sleep.

I can't wait to hear your voice.

Until tomorrow,
Vole

He shut his journal.

"You're going to embarrass yourself," he said as he placed his journal under the pillow. Letter writing. Romance. What was he thinking? Bay teased him frequently about being a sap, but Vole knew he was far from being a letter-writing romantic. He was an avid reader, but his own words came out contrived and cheesy on paper. The only letters he'd written in recent years were notes to clients, updating them on the bank's performance, but those he wasn't responsible for making up. He copied the words the head office sent him and signed each letter with royal blue ink to make it more personal.

What will Bay think of me? He wondered. *What does she think of me now?* Vole pulled his sleeping bag over his head. Closed his eyes.

Tried to fall asleep.

Overhead fluorescent couldn't be turned off, and it felt like the young woman inspecting climbing gear was watching him out of the corner of her eye. Silence where there should have been clanks and chatter unsettled him. Vole tossed and turned for what felt like hours, before deciding to go search for the perfect boat instead of sleeping.

The boat he needed was specific, and he knew exactly the type he was looking for. It needed to have ample seating—for four, preferably five, even six, depending on the design of the vessel—and space at the back, like a platform. It needed a tall canopy. To be light weight. Not too big or bulky. Something he could pull and lift and that wasn't made of wood. It needed to be pedal powered.

Luxurious pedal boats topped with solar panels and furnished with built-in coolers stood out like crown jewels in the harbor. He fantasized about using one, but he couldn't afford such finery, or the extra weight (he doubted his ability to tow a heavy vessel, though the atmosphere had become like an oiled slide).

The perfect boat was hidden, deep within the field of docked ships that sprouted along Toronto's winding waterfront. It was a five-seater pedal boat with a platform at the front, on which one person could sit perpendicular to two, side-by-side, low-back seats. In the footwells were foot pedals mounted to a crankshaft. In addition, the pedal boat featured two more seats, long ones, facing the back. These extended into another platform, this one long and at the back of the boat.

The family-of-five pedal boat was exactly what he needed, with one small problem: it was a personal vessel, not one of the fancy store models. Its owner, or the person Vole presumed was its owner, was standing next to its trailer on the dock.

Vole dreaded this might happen. It was much worse taking something from a person than it was from a store.

"At least I'm not an airhead all the time, honeybee," he said to himself.

Prior to leaving Dorset, Vole collected all the cash he and Bay kept in their house. It was their emergency, emergency fund. These days, no one carried cash with them, so the minute a person needed it, they never had any available. The Gibbons kept cash handy, and Vole brought it all with him to the city. "Just in case," he'd muttered while summing the precious rainbow of slippery bills. The money amounted to twelve hundred dollars. He'd carried it with him in an envelope tucked into his waistband, because his right pocket held his wallet, and his left his keys.

I could use one of those waist bags. The ones that clip and can be tightened, Vole thought as he pulled the sweat-dampened envelope from his waistband. *A fanny pack!*

"*Oh no*," he groaned aloud. "I want a *fanny pack*. It's finally happened, honeybee. I've become *old*."

In a burst of strength, Vole yanked the boat from the water. "I can still do that, at least!" Taking the envelope containing all their cash, Vole placed it in the pocket of the likely owner. With a dry mouth, he wished the envelope luck—another thing he never would have done before—and exhaled. "I'm sorry," he whispered. Took a deep breath to clear his thoughts and turned to his next problem: the small matter of getting the boat from the dock to the store.

"I suppose I'll have to tow it there myself."

It wasn't easy to pull the boat onto its trailer, and it wasn't easy to navigate it through the city. If time had stopped any earlier in the day, the streets would have been too packed with cars for him to make it through; any later and there would have been too many party-seeking pedestrians to skirt around. Vole picked a careful path through it all but was unfamiliar with his surroundings. He stopped frequently to regain his bearings, usually after catching sight of himself in a storefront glass window. He was a thick-waisted, graying man in beige shorts and white sports socks pulled up over his shins, slowly towing a pedal boat along behind him. If only the silent statues of people he passed by could talk. What would they say? Would they criticize him? Help him?

I don't think they're thinking about much, Vole mused. *Probably regretting what they ate for dinner. Bad mutton, maybe. No doubt someone would be recording me. Bearing witness is a big part of exciting living these days, isn't it? Hah! I've been a stand-up passenger all my life, and look where that's gotten me.* Worried he was becoming preachy—someone William would lament over—Vole cast his mind to the road ahead.

It was a slow journey back to the store. The second his head touched down on the synthetic fiber camping pillow that could be compressed to the size of a nut, he was fast asleep.

Saturday, June 20, 2015
Toronto, Ontario
8:45 p.m. eastern time
2 sleeps since

The wrench slipped from Vole's fingers and clattered to the sidewalk. "Best-of-breed technology my ass," he muttered, rubbing his hands together to massage out another painful sting.

Attaching the bicycle trailer to his bicycle was supposed to be a simple task. The hitch was an adaptable and universal system. It was made to work out-of-the-box, with any bike; but Vole couldn't get either tongue to latch properly, which meant neither arm would sit in its proper place.

"If I didn't know any better," Vole grumbled, brimming with frustration. "I'd say the fancy new universal tow mechanism doesn't work with the fancy new bike. I'll show you *fancy*, you rotten, stinkin', fancy piece of . . ."

Mutter, mutter, mutter.

Everything else had worked. Securing the pedal boat to its trailer had required few steps. Ratchet straps and bungee cords fixed the boat in place. Removing the bicycle trailer's two wheels and securing the wheel-less platform beneath the pedal boat's trailer had also been straightforward. The bicycle trailer's platform was slightly lower than the pedal boat's, so it slid beneath to make for a snug fit. Vole used bolts with steel fasteners he sourced from a nearby hardware store to secure the frames together. The job required enlarging existing holes with a hand file and hammering thick metal chains through tight places, but, overall, it was a simple task. Attaching the bicycle trailer to the bicycle, however, was not.

The universal hitch was too small, or the rear axle too large. It was a problem no amount of jury-rigging could reliably solve.

"Aren't there universal standards these universal widgets have to comply with?" he complained. "Maybe I'm going about this all wrong." Vole checked the hitch's instruction booklet once more. Perhaps he was complicating things. What other, simpler option did he have? Motors didn't work. He couldn't transfer flame or generate a spark. Pushing Bay in a wheelchair, simple though it seemed, was a far worse option. No, he had to try harder. Think harder. Figure out some way to make this work.

Maybe it's not meant to be.

The thought made him start.

"Meant to be? Destiny? *Fate?* Hmm. You know better," he ridiculed himself. Vole wished he'd left to find coffee sooner. "You'll think of something. You're not the first to have figured out a way."

The idea of pulling a pedal boat behind his bicycle occurred to him back at the house, before he left for Toronto. There was an article he'd read, long ago, well before all this happened, that stayed with him. It had been about an adventurous couple, a quirky do-it-yourself pair who lived somewhere in northern Québec. They'd made a custom bicycle hitch to tow their pedal boat to a pond nearby.

Vole recalled vividly the clip accompanying the article. It was too long and not high quality, despite the times. The video showed a young child, giggling, as her mother took her on a rickety ride around the block. Their laughter, a chorus of play, made him wonder what it would have been like to raise a daughter.

At the time, Vole thought, it was hard enough to raise a son.

Looking back, Vole knew he didn't have any of the same materials the YouTube family used, nor any way of welding, but he could improvise. Between the mega outdoor retailer and the nearby hardware store, he could find what he needed to take a bicycle trailer—removed carefully from the store display—and fasten it to a pedal boat's trailer. Vole would tow Bay behind him in a boat. A boat he'd have to use one day.

"Well then," he muttered, eyeing up the new bike. "I suppose there's no point in fixing it if it ain't broke."

Vole ditched the fancy cyclocross and wheeled his weathered road bike over to his work station. He maneuvered his bike so each arm of the bicycle trailer hitch was positioned on either side of his rear wheel. Then he placed the holes of each tongue over the back axle. Slid them into place. Cranked top nuts to fasten the tongues using a wrench. They fastened perfectly.

"Hah!" he exclaimed. "I knew it would work." *And it's a good thing too,* Vole mused. *I'd probably be lost if I got stuck somewhere and had to repair it. All those gears! At least with mine I know how to repair every single part.*

Perversely, it pleased him an extraordinary amount to use his own bike. Vole was raised to repair things to death.

New purchases were a big deal back when he was a kid. They remained a big deal his entire life.

"Things are different now," he said to himself before retrieving a pair of scissors to snip apart a waterproof tent. He took the tent's pieces and hung them down from the boat's canopy to create vertical walls that could be rolled up or left hanging. He added cushions, pillows, and safety straps to the pedal boat's two main seats. On the front platform (where a person could lounge comfortably, perpendicular to the two people pedaling), he bolted down two squat containers to hold tools—like clamps, rope, wire, and pliers—and an extra sleeping pad.

Vole found two rain barrels in the nearby hardware store and installed them side by side at the back (rolled, one by one). Each could hold 120 liters of water. From his calculations, he'd need, at minimum, six liters of water a day to survive. With both barrels full, he could last a period of forty days without a top up, and that wasn't considering the bottled water he'd turn to along the way.

"I think that'll do for now," he muttered to himself, refusing to think about towing 240 kilograms of water, on top of everything else he'd packed so densely, behind him. *What if Bay needs to drink water too?* The worry nagged.

Immediately behind the front two seats and in front of the rain barrels, in the narrow space that remained between, he bolted down skinny containers lining the boat's two parallel sides. These he packed with medical supplies, vitamins, calorie-rich food, items for water purification, and Bay's medication. On top of the containers, he built two stacked shelves by lashing together tent poles with nylon rope. These he joined with the top of the canopy. The shelves would hold important books, maps, and his journals. He made sure the appropriate fixings held everything in place and took a step back to evaluate his handiwork.

Vole chuckled.

"Who needs to buy a heated garage when you can make a floating hotel?" And then, "All right, so it's more like a junk boat than a hotel, but, honeybee, I swear, this thing weighs more than our brick house."

An unexpected burst of nerves covered his body in cold sweat.

"Almost there," he muttered. "But not done yet."

There was only one thing left to do. Back to the hardware store he went. Vole returned with a can of blue spray paint. Sea Foam, the color was called.

Bay's middle name was Margaret. She was born Baylotta Margaret Groening (a name she groaned a lot about). With big sweeping strokes, Vole wrote *Molly*, the only derivative of Margaret that made Bay smile instead of frown, in cursive on both sides of the boat. He tried to make his writing beautiful like Bay's, but it came out looking more like William's first grade practice work. Finally, the pedaling pontoon was transformed into a luxurious litter fit for his queen.

Vole checked his watch. It was still quarter to nine.

"I suppose I'm done," he said. "Hang on, honeybee. I'm coming home."

Before departing, Vole made sure every single thing he used and amount it cost was recorded in the ledger. He put everything he'd collected in excess back in its proper place. Recycled what empty packaging he could. Crammed the rest into black disposal bags he found in the kitchen, and threw them into a dumpster in an alley nearby. He maneuvered *Molly* onto the street. Checked one last time to make sure everything was solid and secure, and set off.

He moved slowly at first, wobbling wide before falling into a steady rhythm, but Vole soon discovered his titanic load wasn't difficult to tow. Not at all. In fact, at times he wondered if it was there and found himself checking over his shoulder.

"Side mirrors," he told himself. "I need side mirrors."

Following a nail-biting near-collision with two police officers on horseback, Vole was free and clear of downtown. Back on the highway, he remembered the traffic jam he encountered on the way—unusual for 8:45 p.m. at night, and partly why it took so long to reach Toronto—and so got off at an early exit. Took country roads. Stopped once to relieve himself in a roadside bush. After an indeterminate number of hours, Vole found himself back home. He parked his modified bicycle and newly acquired pedal boat in their driveway.

"Would you look at that," he said to the gray squirrel who was still there, waiting for only a squirrel knew what. "I'm coming home to a brilliant sunset."

At that moment, all Vole wanted was to see a different sky.

Once inside, fatigue overtook him. In all the time he'd been away, he'd slept only once. Vole flattened himself out next to Bay and Jock, who both lay exactly where he left them. He touched Bay's cheek. She was still warm. Still smiling. Her eyes were still closed.

Vole's tight stomach eased as though a tangled and thorny knot came undone. "I'm home, honeybee." He sighed and melted into a deep sleep.

When he woke up the first time, Vole was unsure how much time had passed, though it didn't matter because it was still quarter to nine. He fell back asleep. Two more times he woke up and went back to sleep. Tomorrow, whenever tomorrow was, he and Bay would leave. Before they did, he'd have to decide what he was going to do about William.

SEVEN

May 1985

"BEING A FATHER isn't easy," Mr. McKinsey said. He was a man whose suit jacket slipped frequently from round shoulders, and whose too-large dress pant bottoms were constantly unhemmed. "It takes a lot out of a man. Steals his sleep and turns his wife against him. Kicks his killer instinct into overdrive, if you know what I mean. A baby triggers that in a man, the instinct to serve and protect.

"You're a father now, Vole. Take it from another—that's no small thing. You've changed. I can see it in your work. You deserve this promotion. You take your job seriously and you're a good, hard-working family man. You've earned this, and it's only right I'm the one giving it to you."

To be clear, Vole wasn't receiving a promotion. Not really. He'd been acting as the regional bank's assistant branch manager since the fall of 1982—two-and-a-half years prior. Five-year-fixed-rate mortgages just peaked, and at the time, everyone blamed the banks. "You're stealing from the poor!" a mother of four once accused Vole, whose eyes blinked slow and wide from behind the counter. Vole couldn't blame her.

No one anywhere knew what would happen from one day to the next. On top of confusion and black moods, the branch had been thrown into a state. Tickets weren't being audited and client interactions were suffering. Vole started going over the memos and tickets, and he audited the cash book himself. He began helping the other tellers get by, and he took on a lot of what his boss should have been doing. Never one to complain about what he couldn't control, he'd been operating as Mr. McKinsey's unofficial right-hand man ever since.

"It's about time he makes good on at least one of his promises," Bay griped when Vole told her he was being granted the title. "He's only been gassing about it for years! You're being recognized because you've earned it. It comes at a good time too."

The wage increase Vole would receive alongside his title change wasn't much, but it would help. With Bay not working to take care of the baby, their shoestring budget got shorter.

A lull formed as Vole thought about his and Bay's recent conversation.

"Do you have any questions?" Mr. McKinsey asked.

Vole shifted in his seat. Acknowledgment was the first step to recognition and reward. Right?

"Will you be announcing it to the team?" he asked.

"And disrupt everybody's day?"

Vole nodded. "Right. Of course," he replied. "Wouldn't want to do that."

Mr. McKinsey didn't like having it known he needed help. Most who worked at the bank had been there as long as Vole and thought of him as the assistant branch manager already. He was only being promoted now because head office was making changes to performance targets, and Mr. McKinsey didn't want to be the only one responsible for any misses.

"Anything else?" Mr. McKinsey asked.

"Will I have new responsibilities?"

"Nope. Just the same old accountabilities. You'll be held to those goals we discussed, obviously. Last chance for questions."

"You mentioned the possibility of changes to compensation. Is that still . . . ?"

Mr. McKinsey made a show of smacking his broad forehead with his marshmallow hand. It produced a gooey sound: wet meat slapping.

"How could I have forgotten! You won't be working Saturdays anymore. Although, it *has* been what sets us apart from the Big Five. Don't worry. I've already taken care of it. Nancy will supervise the shift. The girl needs an opportunity to play Boss every once in a while, or else she mopes. I know opening and closing on Saturdays has been a sticking point between you and the missus since we first started doing it. From now on, your schedule will be Monday to Friday, nine to five. What a blessing."

"Great," Vole said after a moment. "But, um, can I expect a raise?"

"Oh." Mr. McKinsey sat back in his chair. "Well now." A frown came over his face. "The thing is, Vole, there's no budget to offer you more money. Your annual review is on the calendar. How about we reopen the conversation then.

"Cheer up, eh? You got out of working Saturdays! Now you can spend quality time at home with your little family. That what life's all about, isn't it?" He checked the wall clock. "Time's up. I'm meeting with Mr. Maxim this afternoon. Thank God for the big fish. Without them, the world's oceans would dry right up. Give your lovely wife my best, would you?"

"Of course."

Later that evening, following William's evening feed, Vole told Bay about his conversation with Mr. McKinsey.

"He's not going to announce it?" Bay railed, sitting up straight in their bed. "That man. I swear, if the regional manager wasn't his cousin, you'd be branch manager. It's not fair."

"I'll never manage a branch, honeybee."

"You should!"

"I don't have a degree."

"So? You're way smarter than he is. A fat stupid pig would make a better bank manager than him."

"*It matters.*"

Bay fixed him with a look.

Before, when it was the two of them, she would have relented; she would have said her fat stupid pig reference had no bearing on what she thought about Vole. She would have told him everything was going to be all right.

"He's not all bad," Vole defended, his stomach tight.

"What are you talking about? He's the worst! A total hypocrite. When's the last time he's seen his kids? Four years, isn't it? I know, I know. It's none of my business. I feel for his ex-wife, you know?" Bay paused to take a generous gulp of water. Breastfeeding was thirsty work. "At least you'll get paid more now. It'll help cover all the diapers the kid's ripping through, and formula, once he's ready for it. Oh, and you'll be here all weekend to help clean and do Monday prep! I'm happy about that.

"One thing I forgot to mention, earlier," she continued. "Mom took another spill. I think we're going to have to consider long-term care. I know it's expensive, but I'm worried about her being on her own during the day while Dad's working."

Vole wanted to cry.

"Of course, honeybee," he said.

Bay looked at him and her face changed. She wrapped her arms around him.

"*Shhh,*" she said. "We've got this. It'll be all right."

"Isn't it an awful lot, all the time?" he asked into her shoulder. He breathed deep, drawing in her scent.

An unexpected aspect of bustling family life were all the smells that came with it. Most of them were bad, and Vole tried to avoid them, but some of them—like William's freshly wiped skin and Bay's sweet swelling breast—offered comfort.

"That's what dreams are for," she said, breathing into his hair. "If not today then tomorrow, or when we're both wrinkly and old—the kid should be able to take care of himself by then—we'll be able to do what we want. We'll take long trips and go on walks by the ocean. Spend our days chasing the best sunsets in the world. We'll get there, one day. We have to keep moving forward."

The baby began to cry.

"I'll get him," Vole offered. Bay moved to the rocking chair and prepared herself to nurse. "Shush," Vole murmured as he picked William up from his cradle. Neither he nor Bay had red hair, but their son's soft scalp was covered in the lightest thatch of flame. *Is this love, true love, I wonder?*

After the baby had been fed, burped, and changed, they lay down together again. In the past, they would have each stayed up. They would have talked more about their days or read side by side in silence—the deep and calm kind of silence, simple and uncomplicated. Life was different then. Now, each spent for reasons of their own, they surrendered to the dark and daydreamed of a good night's rest.

But the night *was* good, if not yet restful. The air was at its freshest. Bay had left a window open. A tingling breeze blew over them. She breathed in. He felt her body swell and fall. Swell and fall. Big, undulating breaths far too full for sleep.

Her quiet voice filled the room.

"Do you think we'll ever go back?"

"Hmm? Back where?"

"To Europe."

Vole thought about boarding a plane and flying far away to a place he'd already been to. "Not until Will's older," he said, turned off by the stress of foreign travel.

"I don't mean *now*. In the future. Next year, maybe."

He sighed. Turned on his side to face away.

"Not so soon. Wouldn't you rather go up north, anyway? Rent a small cottage on a lake somewhere?" They'd talked about this before. "Sunsets over Georgian Bay are the best in the entire world. I read it in the paper. We have a paradise in our own backyard. Plus, staying in the province is much more affordable. Less time spent traveling, more time spent relaxing."

Travel wasn't in the budget, and retirement was a lifetime away. It depressed him to think their time to be free together was so far from reach.

Vole took Bay's silence for sleep.

Broodish thoughts occupied him as he drifted in and out of troubled darkness. Inadequacy and disappointment haunted him. He'd only told Bay half the story. He couldn't admit to her he wasn't getting a pay raise. What would she think of him? Of his job? His boss? Vole managed their household finances; he knew exactly how much they'd struggle if her mother's health worsened. Maybe he'd pick up another job. A weekend one.

Though he'd never admit to it, Saturday was the one day he'd been looking forward to lately. All the other days had become so . . . much.

EIGHT

Saturday, June 20, 2015
Gibbons residence, Dorset, Ontario
8:45 p.m. eastern time
5 sleeps since

>   *Dear Bay,*
>   *I have a confession to make. I broke into Harold's garage yesterday. That's not all. My confession is I've dreamed of breaking into Harold's garage, and when I did, it felt good. Really stinkin' good.*
>   *Harold's garage is the first place I've ever broken into. I should say that. I had good reason to, I swear. See, we were all set to leave. You were wrapped up and belted in. Jock was next to you (I couldn't take away your chance to see him again), when I noticed I hadn't packed my good wrenches. If Molly fell apart or if you were injured—though I'm not sure you can be, but more on that another time—from a bolt coming loose, I don't know*

what I'd do. Lose my mind, probably (if I haven't already).

After searching everywhere (I went to the attic too, and you know how much I hate going up there) and coming up empty-handed, I remembered I'd lent it to Harold.

I didn't break into Harold's looking to steal. I went searching for my own wrench set.

Harold's garage is magnificent. It's more like art than the Louvre. I understand now why he was protective of it, never wanting any of the neighbors to accidentally wander in. Did you know he has saws with teeth of all different sizes? He's got drills and a welding station, right next to a wood-working station. The whole building must be soundproof. If I'd known about it, I may have skipped my trip to Toronto altogether!

I'm joking, I wouldn't want to impoverish the man. (Though he is a good-for-nothing jerk.)

I know you don't like it when I call people names, and I know you'd say, "Harold has his redeeming moments," but sometimes he deserves a lot worse than name-calling. Wait until you learn where I found my wrench set.

It was buried beneath a pile of leaky garbage. Garbage!

All his tools were elevated off the ground and neatly kept—not to mention there was an altar, built for his prized carbon fiber frame road bike. You recall the one he lorded over me during our last ride together? All of it, pristine, except for what was mine. I had to wipe my set off, and it still stinks! I don't know why he bothered with *mine when no doubt he has his own much nicer set. Disrespectful. I shouldn't have expected anything else from the crotchety old goat.*

All this work has made me more patient. I'm stronger than I was before. I've begun to feel my muscles again, and I think I'm almost prepared. I wish we were going on this adventure together. You're with me, technically, but you're also not. What if I fail? I'm not taking you to the first place on your list of twelve. I've had to reorder all the places to make this work. Please don't be disappointed.

The point of this letter is to let you know we're leaving soon, later today; tomorrow at the latest. Not that my eyes would register any difference between the two. I measure the passage of time, the accumulation of days, by counting sleeps. It's not foolproof, not by a long shot, but you'd be the first to say I have a reliable internal clock, and I hope that holds true. Without the sun's progress to measure time, I have no other way of knowing the difference between yesterday and today.

Until tomorrow,
Vole

Vole didn't bother mentioning he unplugged each of Harold's machines and switched around the contents of his meticulously organized and strictly labelled drawers.

"Too bad I won't be here," Vole chuckled to himself as he imagined the explosive display of sputtering anger that was sure to result. "But as a friendly neighbor and conscientious citizen, it's the least I can do."

Near ready, he locked up their house. Pinned *Molly*'s tent flaps back to keep a clear view of Bay and Jock. "You've got the best seats in the house," he told them. There were no other seats for them to occupy.

With no tasks remaining, Vole turned his gaze to their red-brick bungalow. It blazed bright in the evening sun, as though to sear itself into his memory as he said goodbye. For most of his life Vole had never been one to cry. When he learned Bay was sick, a switch inside him flipped. Now there was no one in the world to see or hear him, tears flowed freely down his cheeks.

What's happening to me? he wondered, again, and wiped tear-dampened hands on his black bicycle shorts. Vole tried to remember what their house looked like when it was new. He couldn't. His memories had been supplanted by this one: A glaring sun, casting its gaze down onto the sum of their life. Sometimes he found he couldn't look away. Sometimes, like now, it made his insides quake.

Vole turned to face the road ahead.

"Onward!" he exclaimed. Pushed his foot down. "Good grief..."

Molly rattled slowly into motion. The water in his rain barrel tanks moved like sludge from side to side and made gentle slapping noises, as though a full-out slosh was too enthusiastic. As he gained what he imagined must be something like momentum, Vole discovered it was no more difficult to tow *Molly* fully loaded than it was for him to cycle to Toronto. The constant motion would get tiring, but the additional weight of his load didn't drag, and cycling up hills didn't cause him added strain.

"Fascinating," he murmured, significantly relieved and disbelieving. "Everyone buckled in?"

They were off!

He followed the road west out of Dorset while nodding goodbye to the people and places he had known his entire life. He passed by the conservation area, one of his favorite spots, where he, Bay, and William had whittled away late afternoons and crisp mornings, until William had gotten old enough to whittle away lazy summer months there by himself. *Black mud leeches and tadpole frogs,* Vole reminisced. *It certainly didn't seem so simple back then.*

Vole began to hum, then sing.

It's a long way to Tipperary,
It's a long way to go.
It's a long way to Tipperary,
To the sweetest girl I know!
Goodbye Piccadilly,
Farewell Leicester Square!
It's a long way to Tipperary,
But my heart's right there.

He had never been to Tipperary or Leicester Square. He didn't know if they were real places, though he suspected they were. His mother used to sing those words to herself. Vole recalled her voice wafting down from above as she pinned his father's good shirt, collar splayed and primed for pressing, on the clothesline. The sun burned hottest on days like that. "The best way to keep your whites white," she would tell him when she caught him spying, trying to make friends with the grasshoppers and worms, "is to dry them outside. There's no better bleach than sunlight."

Vole hadn't heard the song since he was a boy, and he was pleased his mind had conjured it. It seemed a fitting tune for the journey ahead and maybe, just maybe, he would discover a place called Tipperary.

It wasn't long before Vole had no breath to spare for singing. Soon, his labored grunts and *Molly*'s horse-carriage rattle became the only sounds on an otherwise silent road.

NINE

Saturday, June 20, 2015
Purple Hill Township, Ontario
8:45 p.m. eastern time
6 sleeps since

VOLE WASN'T LATE for anything. No one had any expectations of him. He didn't feel rushed, and he could take his time weaving between cars. Food and water could be found in most places, and he carried with him a full stock of supplies.

All his boyhood fears about surviving in the wilderness on his own, about surviving on his own without money, melted away. All the fears he'd formed with age, fears of people taking advantage, of violence without cause or warning, faded. He had no predator. No enemies. No bosses to answer to.

No dangerous storms rolling in.

Is this absolute freedom? Vole wondered. *Or some new sort of prison?*

Over and over, the same worries cycled through his mind. He worried about Bay, and making sure she was content and clean and comfortable. He worried about keeping her safe, but there she was behind him—alive and safe. She couldn't disappear while he was watching over her.

Vole glanced back over his shoulder and narrowly missed crashing into the back of a halted motorcyclist.

"How could I have forgotten about side mirrors?" he groaned, heart in mouth.

A familiar retail sign, red and white and green, glowed in the distance. It was the beckoning promise of reasonably priced added safety.

He rolled into the parking lot, climbed off his bicycle seat, and waddled bowlegged into the store. When he came back out, he was carrying two plastic shopping bags, stretched and bursting, filled to their translucent limits. The first line item he recorded in his journal read: *Canadian Tire, Purple Hill Township, Bicycle rear view mirror, 2, $7.99+HST, CAD*. Store name, Location, Item, Quantity, Price, Tax (if applicable), Currency. No matter how much distance he covered, or how many times he slept, he borrowed every item on the same date: Saturday, June 20, 2015.

Vole collected all the water purification tablets the store kept in stock. "Just in case," he'd told himself. Just in case the many he'd packed aboard *Molly* ran out (there were fifty tablets per box, and he'd borrowed almost two hundred boxes from the store in Toronto). He didn't know for how long he'd be relying on them, but since discovering that water didn't come shooting out of any spout, no matter how far he cranked any valve handle, he couldn't be sure where he'd next refill, and there was no guarantee he would find water when he needed it next.

One could leave Canada and enter the United States by crossing over the Blue Water Bridge, a long cantilever structure made of steel trusses that spanned both banks of the St. Clair River. It was one of the busiest border crossings in the entire country, and Vole had been dreading it. Borders made Vole antsy. Traffic got backed up. Tensions ran high. Friendly officers became brusque and imposing on the turn of a dime—one more of many reasons, he supposed, why he and Bay hadn't traveled much.

"How hard can it be, really?" he asked himself. "Sure, there are lots of cars and curbs, but I'm the only one who's *moving*. This should be a piece of cake!"

Self-encouragement rang false to his own ears.

The mouth of the bridge was guarded by a long line of patrol booths. The booths were squat. They sat side by side with gaps in between. Yellow gates and red lights barred impatient drivers from passing through when they shouldn't. Vole needed to get to the other side. To do that, he had to find a way through all the cars and one of the booths.

Each booth contained a vehicle, followed by a long queue. He considered trying to squeeze his bike and *Molly* through, but after inspecting every gap between cars, and after scraping his leg against a sharp license plate edge for the fourth time, he resolved to find another way to the other side.

"I guess we can boat across. Better to test *Molly* over a river before . . ." Vole's words tapered off as he noticed where oversized vehicles, transport trucks and diggers, crossed in a lane separate and to the right. He hesitated. It was backed up there too. The line of trucks stretched farther into the distance than any of the car lanes.

He walked over, just in case.

Long gears and heavy loads had worked in his favor. There was a broad gap between the driver whose turn it was to approach the border guard and the one who passed through. A concrete berm rose to divide the large vehicle lane from the other lanes, but it was partial. It stopped short, leaving enough space for Vole to creep around and follow along beside.

A plain white transport with tire flaps caked in mud came into view at the same time a vile smell took over the air. Bile rose. It smelled like rank manure combined with exhaust and burned fuel. With no kind wind to take it away, the entire area was covered in an unavoidable stench.

Vole covered his mouth and nose with his shirt. The smell clung to the inside of his throat. He left Bay briefly to step inside the duty-free shop and returned with a black bandana tied around his face. He tied another around Bay's face, and covered Jock's head with the blanket he'd laid across Bay's lap.

It was a tight squeeze between the concrete berm and transport truck. The pedal boat's trailer wheel scraped and left a dark rubber stain on the concrete behind them. Something caught his eye. He ducked, barely fast enough to avoid colliding face first into a glob of gum and spit that arced down from the driver's window above. Time must have stopped as soon as the driver spat it out because it was frozen midair. If he were to flick it, it would fly a short distance before falling slowly to the ground, like the pill bottles at the hospital. When Vole realized the glob, because of the height it hung at, would likely hit *Molly*, or much worse, *Bay*, he had no choice but to swipe it down out of the air.

Towering signs, digital and pixelated, greeted him on the other side. Glowing yellow words directed him to stay in his lane and Vole enjoyed ignoring their instructions. Looking in the distance, he mentally traced a path through the cars. *I have a better chance taking the shoulder,* he decided. Distracted by the length of the structure stretched out in front of him, Vole was ill prepared for his right pedal to give out.

He grunted and fell forward into his handlebars. Sharp pain flashed across his ribs, and the world tipped sideways. He stuck his right foot out to catch himself, almost too late.

Countless seconds passed as he waited for his pounding heart to return to its normal pace—sending Bay tumbling was one of his greatest fears.

When he bent to inspect what had happened, he was rueful. He'd been careful and thorough when preparing for their trip; how could he have forgotten about his warped spindle?

The mechanical injury happened when Vole crashed his bicycle into a bush with twisted and woody branches. The pedal wobbled, but he'd become used to it. It never concerned him because he and Bay kept an annual CAA membership. If anything happened on the road, say he got stranded, he'd call for a pickup and fix the bike when he got home. (It was a buttoned-up solution: no up-front cash, he'd get as much use out of the part as possible, and he'd make use of a service he was already paying good money for. Harold razzed him for not having proper clip pedals, but Vole didn't ride frequently enough to justify the upgrade; and deep down he got intense satisfaction out of foiling Harold.) But the old rules didn't apply anymore, and Vole regretted not having thought of it sooner. His right pedal had finally given out, the spindle was bent at a severe angle, and the damage was done. He needed a new pedal.

Every muscle in Vole's body groaned as he got to a stand from a crouch. He was sure his bruises had grown roots, that they'd come to stay on his ivory bones. His body wasn't used to so much constant motion, and before all this, his joints creaked from underuse.

Vole rotated his shoulders. Stretched his sore sides. Winced, and looked around.

Somewhat predictably there were no bicycle repair shops in sight; and it was quarter to nine, which meant there wouldn't be many shops open. He would have to leave and explore the city. Not the one he came from—the stench he passed through was enough to deter a turd farmer—but Port Huron, the blinking city on the American side of the river.

It doesn't make sense to bring Bay on a short foot trip, he decided. *Not without my bicycle to help tow.*

Wasting no time, Vole donned his backpack (he kept it filled with what he considered to be three days of supplies), and clipped around his waist the fanny pack he usually kept hidden.

"To be clear," he told Bay, "this isn't a fashion statement. It's practical." He turned to address the dog. "Jock, don't you dare move. You watch over her. If anything weird happens, wake up immediately and bite anyone who comes near. I'll be back soon."

Vole turned to leave, but he couldn't bring himself to lift a foot.

"Dammit," he swore. He looked up at the sky. Glowing strips of pink and orange beat down. The sun, low and red, remained steady and unchanging. "I swear, universe, not that I think you're listening, but if you are, you better keep her safe. If something happens while I'm gone, I'll, I'll . . . I'll hate you! And I'll tell everyone you're out to screw them over!"

With only weak threats in his arsenal—what could someone in his position do to take revenge on the cosmos?—and no other choice, Vole turned his back to the sky.

It was gut-wrenching to leave Bay behind in a foreign place. What if someone else was out there? What if he wasn't the only one? What if it wasn't safe to leave Bay alone?

As Vole put more distance between them, he decided he'd need to *believe* he was alone. "It won't work otherwise," he explained, pragmatic as ever. "None of this makes sense anyway. If everything gets mucked up and time starts while I'm gone, there's no safer place for them to be."

Vole failed to convince himself.

"Good grief," he grumbled. "Stop torturing yourself, man. You have no choice but to have a bit of faith." And then, "Hah, faith! Never before in all my life," he grumbled louder. "Bay's not going to let this one go, that's for sure."

Eventually, Vole came upon a bike shop, but it was closed. Taking things from closed stores seemed far worse than taking things from open ones. Vole wasn't worried about getting into trouble, rather, he feared he'd be swallowed up by the surrounding silence unless he imposed some sound thinking on himself. He'd already started recording his *Rules to Live by When Time Is Stopped* in the front of his journal. *Do Not Enter Places that Appear Deliberately Locked* was already on the list, because breaking in involved breaking other people's things, and that didn't sit right with him. (The only exception he'd allow himself was with Harold, who was hardly a blameless victim, in Vole's opinion.)

Vole walked the highway south from Port Huron, down past Marysville until he saw signs for New Baltimore. Time passed, but only for Vole. He trod on. He ate a protein bar, an apple, and sipped on water as he walked. He slept when he got tired. Every time he woke, he added one more day to his catalogue of passing days. It was difficult to know how long and short his days were because every time he tried to count the seconds, he'd get to a thousand and become distracted by a new thought and forget what he was doing or where he was in his count. Tens of thousands of seconds passed by, but he never knew for how many minutes or hours he was awake.

His strides were slow. Despite being able to move quickly with minimal effort, whether he was walking or cycling, Vole found the mental effort required to keep a fast and regular pace to be exhausting. Everything he did, he did at a snail's pace. Every sensation he experienced, he savored and pondered. Walking felt like stretching. It was a welcome break from cycling. It allowed him to move his legs and ankles in different ways. It worked other muscles, ones he'd forgotten completely about in late adulthood, and it gave rest to the sore spot between his legs from the pressing bicycle seat. (The bicycle shorts he wore were heavily padded, but not even a down-filled pillow chair could protect the underside of a man's scrotum from a bicycle seat forever, and his was tender and out of practice.)

The farther south he traveled, the more everything changed. It was a gradual transformation. Open fields gave way to sprawling neighborhoods, which gave way to tight interconnected ones.

The roads back home were dirt, gravel, or patchwork-paved tar. Roadwork never stopped in Ontario. There were signs posted, reminding local inhabitants provincial tax dollars were being responsibly spent to keep their roads flat and clean. These roads were different. Sun-bleached concrete surfaces speckled with more potholes and pits than smooth sections. He had to watch where he placed his feet for fear of turning an ankle or incurring some other ruinous injury.

Lawns changed from green-grass lots with pink flamingoes to wild gardens of weeds, tall and unruly. Some plants threatened to tear houses down to their foundations, they'd become so overgrown and scrappy.

For every hardship Vole endured, he knew someone else in the world had endured harder; but life was life, and the love he felt for his family trumped everyone else's needs and pains and desires, or so he'd told himself.

Industries growing and collapsing, urban sprawl and transformed inner cities, racial tensions coming to a boil—these were big topics his parents griped quietly about until he became old enough to question them. By the time Vole was grown, he'd learned to focus only on the state of his own small affairs. The bank and Bay had told him what he needed to know about the changing state of the world. It had been enough.

Unlike the houses and commercial buildings in Dorset, the buildings he passed were in shambles. Some were in varying stages of collapse. Some were partially burned and others had slashes of cruel spray paint cutting up the walls that still stood.

Where is everybody?

As though something unseen was paying his thoughts attention, he turned a corner and saw a group of people in the distance. They were standing beneath the awning of a corner store. Silhouettes, hats pulled down over their faces, made them all the same. Four of them stood close and hunched together, as though they'd been caught in a single loping swagger. A cloud of dense smoke was caught in the air above their heads. The setting sun glowed pale red behind them, and the air took on a metallic tang.

He shivered and continued. As he walked alongside a dark car with dark windows, he glanced inside.

Vole's body became flushed, and he had to look away from what he saw within.

Who was this car's driver, and what did she intend to do with such an angry-looking gun? Guns, weapons, violence . . . they were all too frightening and foreign for him. Was he supposed to step in and make matters right? What did *right* mean? Who was he to make such a call?

What should I do? he agonized. *What would you do, honeybee?* Vole couldn't be sure about any of it.

He wasn't sure it was a real gun.

Vole turned away. Kept walking up and down streets, as though he were back in Toronto, taking stock of a thief's paradise. Vole perused the streets until he found a bicycle repair shop built into the side of a residence. It was on a lane, skinny and private, marked with a sign to indicate one-way traffic only.

A semidetached townhouse stood next door to the shop. Though it was approaching late in the evening, a handful of children sat on the front lawn, a grass quilt of greens and browns. Backs straight and bellies tucked, the children had arranged themselves in a closed ring. Each child gripped the hand of the one who sat next, and they all had their eyes shut tight (except for one, who Vole surmised to be the ringleader; she held one eye shut, but through a crack in the other, a spark gleamed). A volcano of toys spewed in the center of their circle. Plush toys, torn and muddied from recent play, spilled like lava overtop of plastic robots and rag dolls in ruffles, the likes of which Vole hadn't seen in years.

The children's faces, young sculptures of anticipation, reminded Vole of how William used to get when Lawrence was over for a visit; when building a solid block fortress, two arm lengths wide and spread over a cardboard plain, was the only sure path to survival. *Let me show you,* he could almost hear one young boy with stained knees, William, tell the other, Lawrence, as their game of make-believe reached its messy climax. *All you need to do is pour vinegar on top of the baking soda and shake it up real good. Everything'll explode. The blocks'll hold up the mess. It's why we glued them together, to fill in the blanks. My dad says, the more impenetrable the surface, the stronger it'll be.*

The residence-turned-bicycle-shop beckoned Vole with a wash of artificial light. He left the children to their play. The store had the replacement pedal he needed. He took two, a left and a right one. *Just in case,* he thought to himself.

Vole knew, so far, happy coincidences had helped to shape his path forward. Ever since he'd come into the ability to stop time he'd been lucky. Or, now that he was looking for opportunity and seeking meaning, was he finding fortune? Is that how these things worked?

But luck wasn't a real thing. Nothing could cast a spell and grant him more opportunities than someone else. Magic wasn't real. God didn't exist. These were facts he knew. Or he thought he knew, until recently, when everything he knew to be true got turned upside down and flipped inside out.

Was he lucky?

What did it mean if he was?

No matter the answer, Vole didn't want to believe something or someone was looking out for him, arranging happenstance to be just so. Already, so soon into his journey, he sensed he'd be tending to his own anchors in a slippery sea. Vole couldn't rely on there being a higher power who had his best interests at heart because he might come to expect a helping hand. Bay's life was on the line. He couldn't come to rely on gestures of help from something as ephemeral, as fickle, as faith. He had to believe everything happening to him was random and unaccounted for, or else he'd lose focus.

But, then, wasn't he telling himself to keep faith in his chosen beliefs?

The loop never let up, and no answers came. He stopped thinking.

He turned off the residential street and came upon a local bar. It was built into the side of a tall building made from gray stone blocks. They appeared to be weeping green and black, moss and mildew. A metal plaque, proudly stamped, was mounted to the stone outside. It informed him the establishment dated back to 1958, the same year he was born.

A brass bell, the size of his hand, marked the bar's doorway. The door was propped open. The room beyond was inviting. It glowed with an orange light.

When he peered inside, curious and thirsty, Vole saw all manner of people. They were smiling and holding drinks high in the air. Heavy scents of booze and sweat filled his nose. Emanating heat remained caught in the entranceway where he stood. He could almost hear the peals of laughter he was passing between, and it gave him the distinct sense of watching a friend rising from a deep sleep.

When he turned to leave, he kicked the doorframe with the tip of his toe, bruising it. It was difficult for him to admit his shoes needed replacing, but when he saw he'd bloodied his nail, he ducked into a gently used clothing store (his big toe tore through his shoe-top, many months back). Vole selected a used pair of trainers that fit especially well.

"Hmm," he muttered. Wiggled his toes. Winced. The blinking clerk paid him no mind. "I think my feet must be growing."

The detour had been a tiring one. Vole slept three times since leaving Bay, and he was anxious to return to her. He left the city center. Vole allowed himself one stop before returning to find Bay and Jock exactly as he left them. He leaped into replacing his bike pedal. Not pausing to rest, Vole continued south, putting as much distance between Bay and the border crossing as quickly as he could. Questions nipped at his heels as he considered all he'd seen in a few short days. Confusion drove him forward, farther and farther, onward his legs, circles spinning.

That person had a gun.
I'd done nothing about a gun.
Why must people want guns?
What should I have done?
What would you have done?

TEN

Saturday, June 20, 2015
Somewhere in Michigan, USA
8:45 p.m. eastern time
22 sleeps since

VOLE WAS LESS troubled in the countryside. City traffic was harsh, and throughout his life he'd sought to avoid wafts of engine exhaust, never liking how the chemical taint made his lungs feel. Tractors and cows and sleepy farmhouses with red-painted roofs, however, made him smile. The sights warmed him to pass by. He adored how uncluttered the countryside seemed. As William once informed him (with the full surety of a scientist, ten years of age), a person's natural need for sleep, their circadian rhythm, is set by Earth's turning face; but in the absence of an orbit, Vole found he still preferred the countryside to cities, for the simple fact that sprawling fields were empty of people.

But in moments of extreme fatigue (when his legs became too much like wood to lift, and rest clouded his thoughts but refused to take hold), he imagined his body as the planet, round and absolute, turning its shoulder to the sun. Often the trick worked and he could fall asleep. Though, still, sleep only came over him when his eyes were covered, and the sun was blotted out.

There was something else William once told him about daylight and sleep, some other important fact, but he couldn't remember what it was.

Cheeeruuup, cheeeruuup, cheeruuup, he imagined. Was he thinking of crickets? Or frogs? He and William would debate nature's sounds. With every passing moment, it became more difficult to recall the exact notes, or to imagine what arguments William would use to make his case. Goldfinches. Grouse. The throaty lowing of a mourning dove. What did each sound like?

Vole had trouble remembering once-familiar animal sounds too.

What he didn't think he could ever forget, and what he missed most of all in nature, was being approached by a stubborn wind and the wan greeting of a full-faced moon.

"I'm sorry, honeybee," Vole muttered beneath his breath. Like his legs, his thoughts spun. Round and round they went. He was sorry they waited to travel instead of actually traveling. He was sorry he hadn't tried harder. Why didn't he do more when he had the chance? He was sorry she was sick. Why couldn't it be him? It was Bay's dream to travel the world, and here he was, living her dream. If only he'd been less complacent. Less fearful.

If only we'd made every decision together, like we should have.

The roots of Vole's guilt reached deep. Unbeknownst to them in their youth, their years together accumulated quickly; and those layers covered up many apologies, both big and small, all unspoken, left dormant.

"I'm sorry," Vole whispered, again and again, as he tried to spin his legs faster. "I never meant to lie."

They slept under the open sky, often in a field beside a roadside stop. "I like to be civilized," he reasoned with himself as he borrowed the toilet. It was confounding his body still worked that way. "Isn't my waste evidence? Digestion is a chemical process, like breathing. Processes take place over time. Somehow, time is still passing, though I'm the only one who appears to know it. What'll happen to, you know, all the stuff my body has produced, when time restarts?" Without William or Bay there to debate it with, the fate of his feces seemed unimportant. Vole didn't dwell on the topic long.

Common outdoor nuisances, like condensation and bug bites, didn't bother him. The temperature stayed as constant as the sun, and bugs were as time-stopped as everything else. He took great pleasure in passing by clouds of mosquitoes and black flies as they hung impotent in the air. "You're not sucking any of this blood," he would cackle. "Not today!" and pass slowly by with glee.

Every time he readied for sleep, he would leave Jock in *Molly* and carry Bay down to place her on the foam camping mattress next to him. He liked writing to her as she lay next to him. Oftentimes, when he was done writing, he'd turn to one of the novels he kept with him, tucked in a shelf on the boat, to lull himself nearer to sleep. Occasionally he'd review the list of things he took from different places, but not often because it unsettled him. He would never be able to pay it all back at the rate he was going. What piqued him most of all was realizing his desire to pay it all back decreased the farther west he got.

Vole followed a path that would eventually take them north of Detroit, south of Chicago, across the middle of Iowa, Nebraska, and Wyoming. They were to cross the American Midwest.

The longer he spent on the road, the less he talked out loud. By day fifty-one the conversations he maintained inside his head faded. Vole forgot the need to hum. Days passed in silence. He began to refer to silence as stillness. The word *silence* made the world remote and lifeless, which it wasn't. Air he passed through, thick with heat and pollen, throbbed and pulsed. It oozed with life, though nothing moved to prove it. There may have been no breeze, but the wind he sliced through remembered what it was like to blow.

As the world of in between stretched on forever before his handlebars and wheel, and as the twisted muscle around his spine became hard and corded from remaining in one position, days blended—but they didn't blur. They did the opposite of blur. The scenes he passed by were crystalline in clarity. They blended into a single profound moment. It occurred to him that maybe he was dead, or perhaps he was caught in his own dream, or some other dreamer's dream. Perhaps his entire life was imagined, and he was the momentary spark of a dying synapse; his memories a flash of chemical fiction.

Am I sleeping? he found himself wondering, one day, when he was especially tired, *or wide awake?*

I find it difficult to tell.

The day stretches.

The flutter of a leaf, flicking wings overhead; clouds drifting, a shadow sliding. If only. None of these slight changes exist to excite my peripheries. In all this, it's hard to know I'm not stuck in one spot, imagining my motion into existence, caught up in whether I can really modify the passage of time, or if I've dreamed it all.

Part of me aches to run a test.

What if I restart time, and from there I learn I can never repeat the process? What if I try, and learn I can't do it?

What would become of Bay then?

Vole shook his head. Two droplets of sweat flung from his nose, sailed through the air, slowed, drifted to the pavement behind him.

Whether I'm awake or sleeping, whether this life is real or not, doesn't matter...
   None of it matters.
   One thing matters...
   Ever onward.

Saturday, June 20, 2015
West of Oskaloosa, Iowa
7:45 p.m. local; 8:45 p.m. eastern time
87 sleeps since

   When city roads became jammed with cars, Vole took country roads. The path he followed then was winding. Tall bluffs and humidity gave way to dry fields of gold, and the ever-setting sun crept marginally higher in the sky. Vole donned darker sunglasses. He shed his shirt and tucked it beneath his hat to provide more shade. His exposed skin was pale and then turned pink, then brown, and then a deep red-brown. The air grew hotter. At times it was difficult to take air into his chest. There was never one consistent temperature. He experienced the sky's fluctuating thermals in distinct layers, not as one blended breeze; and when, at some point, he outpaced a train, he wrote about it to Bay.
   She'll remind me to tell William, he thought to himself. *One day I'll tell William.*
   Birds kept him company. They hung in the air beside him as he pedaled past—feathers of white and black with pointed yellow beaks, poised in midflight. They were caught flitting around the landscape, as though the road he passed over was

a path through their playground. When he felt the urge, he would stop to look closer and study them, but despite his itching fingers, never touched one. *Don't Touch Wild Birds and Other Living Creatures* was another rule on his list.

Vole took a break to relieve himself and was caught unaware by a field mouse stuck in place mid lurk in the brush beyond the road. He jumped, shouted out loud; he let loose another shout, louder, as his own voice startled him more. It was the first time words had passed his lips in thirty-one sleeps.

Later that evening, with his tongue already loosened by the rodent's impenetrable stare, he read the letter he wrote to Bay out loud for her.

> *Dear Bay,*
>
> *You would've loved today. As I sat in an icy stream that should have been burbling around me (the water's surface looked especially glassy as it was caught, cascading over rocks), I met someone. A turtle with two red splotches on its cheeks! Similar to the one Will found at the lake. He begged us to keep it. Do you remember?*
>
> *I would've touched it—the turtle, that is. It was sitting on a rock with its eyes closed and mouth open wide. I wanted to run my fingers along its shell to experience its gleaming texture. It looked made of rubber, and I wanted to prove to myself it wasn't. I didn't touch the turtle, though, because I've learned my lesson.*
>
> *I haven't shared that story with you yet. The one where I learned my lesson. I was too ashamed to write it down at the time. Now, I see no valid point in keeping it secret.*

I was passing by the woods of a rifle club—moving slower than usual because the back spasms that were plaguing me two weeks prior had returned—when I saw something.

I parked Molly *immediately in front of a bright red roadster. (After discovering* Molly *rolls down the slightest of slopes when left unattended—although not far before coming to a full stop—I try to be careful with where I leave you. Annoyingly, the handbrake I fitted the boat trailer with works only some of the time.) A smiling woman who looked to be about your age drove the car. The roadster's convertible top was down and her windows were lowered. Her joy was obvious. She reminded me of you.*

I stepped to the edge of the forest. Parted the branches to look closer at what my passing eye caught glimpse of.

Before I knew any different, I found my hands wrapped around the soft-as-clouds body of a baby finch. It hung head down, like a downy torpedo shooting through the air, aimed at the ground below.

As soon as my hands closed around its small form I regretted my nerve. I had no choice but to carry the fledgling back to its nest in a nearby tree, where I placed it next to its gray-and-white siblings, all silent and milky eyed. The one I put back was different than the rest. Its triangle mouth wasn't agape. Its beak was shut tight in what I imagine must have been gritty terror. What will the mother do when she returns to the scent of my interfering touch? Will she throw the hatchling from her nest, force it to relive its fatal plummet?

Such a simple thing. I wish I knew how to take it back.

All I see are shadows in the trees. Do you love me still? I ask you often, but it's because I don't hear you say it. I've gone almost a quarter of a year without hearing you say those words, and I miss them.

I miss you dearly.

Until tomorrow,
Vole

Vole couldn't tell if his words sounded pensive or pathetic, though he could tell he was becoming drawn out and grave. To his rested ears his voice sounded comical compared to the stillness around him. It grated on his nerves. Hearing it left him hollow, maybe because it drew attention to what he couldn't say. He felt uncomfortable knowing he could interfere so directly without anyone else's knowledge of it; and he was uncomfortable recalling how, before he found the bird, he'd stared deeply into the driver's happy face.

Why did she, this stranger, get to rejoice in a surge of vitality, when, at the exact same moment, Bay suffered the rapid drain of it?

He shut his journal. Placed it beneath his pillow. He would need to start another new one soon and his pen was almost out of ink.

When Vole slept that night, black bandana tied over his eyes, he dreamed of life back home. He dreamed the family was back together. William was becoming a young man and Jock was a pup. Bay was healthy.

Or was she?

In his dream she looked thin, pale, as though the sun never touched her cheeks. She looked the same as she did now, because, somehow, riding into the rays of the constant sun brought no color to her. Dirt never clung to her skin, or to Jock's fur. Bay's hair never grew or lightened. Their body temperatures never changed.

As days passed, only Vole changed. His hair grew long, and his breath turned sour when he didn't brush his teeth. His nails needed regular trimming, and his body stank when he went too long without washing.

Vole's dream turned into a nightmare, as they often did. It ended with him waking up in a sweat. He got up to relieve

himself, not needing to open his eyes as he did, because he'd already spent such a long time absorbed in his surroundings prior to rest.

Oh damn, he remembered in a sleepy fog, *I forgot to brush my teeth,* and passed back into a fitful sleep.

Saturday, June 20, 2015
South of Omaha, Nebraska
7:45 p.m. local; 8:45 p.m. eastern time
212 sleeps since

> *Dear Bay,*
>
> *The sun looks like nothing. Have you ever noticed? When I stare into its center, all I see is nothing. When I look away from it, a round void of nothingness travels with me and pulls everything into it. Sometimes it grows so large a void is all I see. Sometimes it consumes you.*
>
> *I close my eyes and it's there. Open them again, and yes, it's there too. Yellow, white, blue; throbbing pulsing growing red. How does the view of it hold such sway when all I see is nothing? My legs somehow keep turning. Hypnotized and slow, I slide between the layers of this melting cake. I think I'll cover my face and rest for a while.*
>
> *Until tomorrow,*
> *Vole*

ELEVEN

Saturday, June 20, 2015
Somewhere in Nebraska
7:45 p.m. local; 8:45 p.m. eastern time
238 sleeps since

THE LANDSCAPE WAS slow and rolling and gave the impression of being flat. Rare silhouettes of farmhouses and wind vanes gave the horizon a pleasing texture. A cloak of sunlight lay over dusty tractor paths and seeding fields, as though the land lay beneath a halo. Vole would never have known they were crossing state lines if it weren't for the sign telling him they had reached Nebraska . . . the good life.

Vole didn't cycle far during his first days in Nebraska. With increasing frequency, he found himself stopping to climb off his bicycle seat and stand completely still. Standing still helped him to keep moving. When he was stopped completely, he became a part of the stillness around him. It helped him feel closer to Bay, and when, after a time, his stomach grumbled or his bladder seized, he was reminded of his purpose and found himself able to keep going. But, as rejuvenating as those moments could be, he knew he needed to be careful. *Don't stay too long,* came his own silent warning. *Or you'll get stuck, and you'll forget, and disappear, and all this will be for nothing.*

It was during a moment of self-imposed stillness when Vole saw the funnel cloud in the distance for the first time. "A tornado is the worst kind of enemy," his father told him once, "because you're powerless against it in a way that steals all your fight. It hasn't a care in the world for your wife or children."

The serpentine cloud turned the distant sky black and gray and a little green. He got closer to it and the layers of air around him changed. It was hot, cool, and hot again. The atmosphere took on an excited charge. A similar excitement crackled inside him. He wondered what the tornado would be like up close. Would he be able to touch it? Pass through its walls unharmed and pierce its eye? What would he find inside?

Or maybe it would be impenetrable and fierce, like how it appeared in that movie. What was the title? He couldn't remember. The one where dairy cows were caught up in the turmoil, tossed around like gumballs in a vending machine. What was it? It was one of young William's favorites . . .

Vole wracked his brain to try and remember. He could only recall Nora, his favorite radio host, naming all the different types of tornadoes in a low and soothing voice. It wasn't long ago, but he couldn't recall her list. The one he spotted was thin and severe looking, twisting tight at the bottom like a coil of rope. Like that movie. What was it called, again?

As Vole's excitement grew, so too did his trepidation. Though nothing could have prepared him for what he'd find in an unnamed town just outside of Kearney.

Saturday, June 20, 2015
Just outside of Kearney, Nebraska
7:45 p.m. local; 8:45 p.m. eastern time
238 sleeps since

Vole didn't know the name of the community they'd rolled into because there were no signs left standing to tell him. Everything had been flattened. Bare foundations and piles of rubble appeared where houses, schools, and public buildings once stood. The remnants of a torn flag—red and white and blue—stuck out from beneath one of the mounds. Entire trees, and the splintered remains of others, were strewn across his path.

People must have been warned far enough in advance because no one was there. Everyone had fled. Only eyes, feline and round with fear, shone back from beneath broken buildings.

Cats, Vole thought. *Good luck, little ones. Where will you go after this? Will your families come back to find you?* Vole couldn't help but think of Jock.

Where structures once rose, boards lay stacked on top of boards, wrecked drapes, and torn furniture. Vole considered the pieces of wood he dragged to the side of the road as he cleared a path. Some pieces were old. Carefully polished. Well taken care of. Family heirlooms, he suspected, and his heart grew heavier inside his chest. His suspicions grew stronger when he found a glossy oak box. It once held silver kitchenware. It lay crumpled and broken among everything else. *What devastation,* he thought, *what unfortunate waste.*

After he cleared a path wide enough to pass through, he got back on his bicycle. Began to pedal them away. Got fifty meters before coming to a wheel-grinding halt.

A hand, fingers curled, each digit tiny and soft, stuck into the air near the top of what was once a home.

Vole closed his eyes. Drew a million electric molecules into his lungs. Instead of energizing him, the latent charge drained him further.

"Don't look," he whispered to Bay. "Make sure she doesn't look," he murmured to Jock.

Vole slid off his bicycle seat and lurched forward, legs leaden. Both hands trembled as he began the climb to the pile's top. His grip kept slipping. It was a slow scramble. He took great care not to disturb the precarious pile. The child might still be alive.

If she were, he would do whatever it took to make sure she stayed alive. Vole dreaded to think about what that might mean for Bay. He didn't want to waste any of her precious seconds. Would bringing a child with them on their adventure be a mistake? Could he drop the youngster off in a hospital? Surely hospital staff would notice and take charge when clocks began their steady march forward.

Healthcare is different here. You're not in Canada, anymore, remember...

Vole lifted a brittle piece of window frame. Broken ceiling tiles surrounded the pale arm; it stuck out from beneath ruin. When he saw the body it was attached to, he let out a resounding *Whoop!*

"It's nothing, Bay!" Vole shouted. "It's *nothing*! A doll! It's a *doll!*"

From where he stood, Vole could see the snaking path of destruction the tornado left in its wake. He traced it with his eyes until he reached where the funnel cloud pulled at its constraints, begging to continue on its terrible way. He threw his hands up into the sky and opened his throat.

"IT'S NOTHING! *NOTHING!* BAY, IT'S NOTHING!" And then, cackling, "*TWISTER!* THE MOVIE IS *TWISTER!*"

He skidded down the rubble heap. Leaped onto his bicycle. Pedaled with renewed vigor. Vole pedaled the hardest he'd ever pedaled.

Go from here.

The thought filled his mind, drowned out the rattle of the boat's trailer behind him.

I need to get her far away.

They passed by people in their cars. Some were headed in the wrong direction. He screamed at them as he blew past. "YOU'RE GOING THE WRONG WAY! DON'T YOU SEE?"

For all Vole's power of observation, he was powerless to make them see. No one heard him. No one paid him any mind.

Vole didn't stop cycling until the state of Nebraska was behind them. They had four states left to get through, including their destination, and he didn't want to waste a moment more.

TWELVE

Saturday, June 20, 2015
Somewhere south of Reno, Nevada
5:45 p.m. local; 8:45 p.m. eastern time
340 sleeps since

BEASTS OF ALL types hid within the rugged hills of Nevada, a short way south of Reno. Deer with antlers, broad and branched, loped toward a pool of water. Antelope with white bottoms leaped from sounds he could only guess at. Everywhere he least expected, donkeys, burros, the color of soot. They were solemn creatures who seemed to be at ease in a timeless world. To Vole, the sturdy misfits were most alarming. He swore their eyes followed his every move.

When he came across a herd of horses in a wood fence enclosure, he knew he was getting close. He was further reassured when he encountered a different herd being chased by a helicopter in the sky, though it pained him to witness. When at last he came upon the valley and herd that waited within, he knew the first leg of their journey had come to an end.

Every wild horse gleamed like a polished pebble at the bottom of a clear stream. There was an amber-colored horse—it reminded him of Bay. There were sand-colored ones, ivory ones, and ones with broad pale splotches marking their chocolate-brown bodies.

"I found it!" he exclaimed, giddy with relief. "You'll get to see where the wild mustangs roam across the hills of Nevada!" Then, becoming dubious, "Well, I think these are mustangs." He paused. "Good grief. A wild horse is a wild horse, isn't it?"

Dear Bay,

I washed my body in someone else's bath. Clipped my hair and cut my beard. My teeth are brushed, and I remembered to floss. I have nothing left to do but wake you. This whole time I've never been more frightened than I am right now.

I'll describe to you the scene so when you read this, you'll see it how I see it. We're at the flat edge of a deep valley. Cascading down the valley's walls are tufts of dying grass and crumbling dirt. You're lying on top of a green wool blanket, and your head is resting on a clean feather pillow. Your lovely toes and peekaboo smile are pointed up toward the sky. Stretched cotton batting lays in streaks across the sun's surface. The shadows the clouds cast are generous. Soothing. Aloe vera across my burned skin; freshly whipped cream on my tongue. (As I civilized myself I found, gradually, such thoughts and sensations came back to me.)

The sun's higher than it was back home. It looks as though it will set in two hours. Darkness falls at a different time here, and the time zone we've come to is three hours off our own. I share these facts because I know you'll ask to hear them. Please don't let them clutter your mind. You shouldn't concern yourself with how much time has passed, or has yet to. Time doesn't matter. Not when we're together. It was never supposed to. It shouldn't ever again.

I've missed you, honeybee.

I'm crying now, again, so I'll keep on. It's warm outside, though we can see snowcapped mountains in the distance. I've spread a blanket over your legs. Rested your hands over top. I don't know what the wind will do, but I don't want it to blow your cover away. Chasing it would take me away from you.

On the ground, to your right, is water to drink. I poured it from a bottle into a glass to make you feel at home. It's at room temperature so you don't get chilled. I remember how the sicker you became the more quickly your temperature dropped. All the while I still ran hot. I still prefer ice in my water.

I don't think I've told you this yet, but when time is stopped, ice is special. It does what it shouldn't (like many things). It stays whole and unmelting until I place a piece on my tongue, then it vanishes, and my mouth floods with ice-cold water. I imagine it must be what a spring melt is to a parched riverbed. If only you could be so refreshed.

I was telling you about the scene, so that we may remember it the same way. Next to your water *is your medicine. I looked back through the charts I brought with us from the hospital to make sure I prepared everything right. I've kept your medicine stowed away this whole time, made sure each bottle stayed free of smudges. I remember, now, how much I resent their smooth touch in my palm.*

I've prepared a selection of snacks for you to eat, though I know you won't be hungry. Warm butter and creamed honey spread over fresh bread. A wedge of sharp cheddar. Sliced apples, crisp and juicy. I brought along two tarts from a bakery we passed by. I think they're peach. There wasn't any sign posted and my crude palate hasn't improved any. I'll leave it to you to decide. (You'll be happy to know I didn't forget Jock. I've left a royal treat next to his cozy body. When he wakes up, it'll be the first thing he notices.)

Now for the truth, the real reason I'm darting around these pages like a headless chicken, writing whatever comes to mind. I don't know if I can wake you up. What if all this is the grand delusion of a madman, and I'm locked away somewhere, undergoing clinical trials and psychiatric treatments?

Do you love me still?

I look over at you as I write the question. You're smiling at me. You must still love me if you're still smiling.

Can you believe it? Tomorrow has finally come.

Vole

Throughout his life, Vole had never once considered the United States of America to be exotic. The United States was like Canada. Canada was portly and kind. It wasn't lithe and dangerous. It wasn't an exotic country. The two nations seemed more alike than not, despite the differences he knew existed between them. The place where Vole now found himself was distant and vastly different than home, and it was exotic.

This was his opportunity to prove to Bay he understood what she desired: to see past exotic. To take in the world with eyes that had seen beyond Dorset. Somehow, he'd been given a second chance to show her he was as right for her as she was for him.

Given a second chance by whom?

It wasn't the first time the question occurred to him, but Vole didn't know how to come up with the right answer. He wasn't a spiritual person. He was the opposite of spiritual. Vole valued tradition, and he believed religious sentiment served an important purpose in many people's lives. He and Bay never spoke much about God with William, other than in an informational sense—though they'd gotten him baptized at Bay's request—and their son never showed much interest beyond his childhood belief that Santa Claus was Jesus Christ's regional manager, and they worked together at The World Bank, which was a thing, but not nearly the thing William thought it was at the time. Bay held faith in something, but Vole could never tell what was stronger: her belief in God or her belief in playing devil's advocate.

Despite it all, at various points throughout his life, Vole questioned the existence of God, or something like it. He questioned when Bay crashed into his car at the red light (they agreed, years after the fact, Bay was at fault for the collision); and, again, after their second miscarriage, when it seemed like nothing would feel right ever again. He questioned once more when William was born. Every time his conclusion was the same: *Human beings exist because of geological time frames. We evolved from primordial sludge. Our presence demonstrates the immense power of evolution, which happens over time, a known constant, like gravity.*

"Immense *divine* power," Bay would tease whenever the discussion came up.

"Divine? In the way you're talking about? Not possible. Only you're divine, honeybee."

Bay's lips would curve. *To each their own*, her ready laugh would say, and he would agree there was no God.

But this time was different than all those other times. What provoked him was more than good fortune at finding a new pedal, or bicycle tire, or pair of snug-fitting shoes, all when he needed them most. All of a sudden, his journey seemed too absurd, too spectacular, for him to be the only one to witness it.

"Universe," Vole said. "If you're listening to me, you better not tell Bay how long I went without taking a proper bath. And, while I'm at it . . . you, um . . . better never tell her, well, you know, um . . ." He petered out before sputtering, "Oh, for the love of—This is ridiculous. I'm an adult. Bay doesn't need to know about any of that sort of thing. Okay?!" Vole kicked at a nearby tuft of grass with his foot. No drifting cloud of dust resulted. "And you know what else, universe? Screw you! Screw you for making everything so damned confusing. You could have done something. Anything! You could've written a goddamned instruction manual or boo—*Oh.*"

Sensing he'd gone beyond his depth once more, Vole stopped delaying and went back to worrying about starting time again.

He scanned over everything once more, checking for imperfections. *Molly* was off to the side, out of the way of their view. The simple picnic he prepared looked delectable, though he was too anxious to be hungry. Bay was a vision. Her mind was still in Paris, caught in a daydream he'd asked her to recall only a second before. She looked as though she belonged on the green blanket, smiling up into the sky, oblivious to the magnificent horses waiting for her in the valley below.

"I hope this is everything you dreamed it would be," he said with a sigh and caught himself looking over everything once more.

Vole exhaled all the air from his lungs. Flapped his cheeks to relax his face. Pulled out a folded piece of paper he typically kept in his fanny pack, but after bathing and dressing, had placed inside his pocket. It was a sheet torn from one of his journals. On it were words Vole wrote for Bay the day he left Dorset. He hadn't read them since.

He closed his eyes. Opened his eyes. Glanced down at his wristwatch. Was relieved it still said quarter to nine. Took one more deep breath and stopped thinking.

"Go," he whispered.

The loudest thing Vole heard in the suffocating clamor that followed was a resounding click. It was the sound of the minute hand on his watch moving from 8:45 p.m. to 8:46 p.m.

THIRTEEN

December 1990

THE GIBBONS LOOKED forward to Christmas. Especially five-year-old William, who was coming to understand it was his parents' most generous time of year. In the weeks preceding, they would bake shortbread together, watch movies, and sing off-key jingles in loud, warbly voices. Every Christmas Eve morning, before heading to the same house Vole grew up in to spend the day playing card games, they would drink homemade eggnog out of special clay mugs and go for long walks in the crisp wintry air. It was modest—gifts were few though rich with good intention—and to the Gibbons, it was exactly the best thing.

That year, William would spend Christmas Eve at his grandparents to give his parents the rare chance to be alone together on an important day, but the boy had a condition. Vole had to handwrite a letter to Santa Claus explaining the extraordinary circumstances, to ensure that Santa didn't bring his gifts to the wrong house.

The boy volunteered to supervise the important project. He dictated Vole's written instructions and redrew Vole's hand-drawn map. He added his private wish list of presents to the envelope, licked the stamp, and dropped the letter into the mailbox himself.

With the critical task behind him, William became a cyclone, spinning and squealing, blowing in circles from room to room, overcome by the thrill of adventure and newfound responsibility.

"A sleepover! A sleepover!" he chanted. "I'm having a sleepover!"

William threw himself into packing for his first solo sleepover—something Vole had been looking forward to, but hadn't the time to think much about.

"Happy anniversary," Vole said when he and Bay were alone and back at home together. "So. Will's having a sleepover."

"Tell me about it," Bay replied and sipped eggnog from her mottled mug. "I didn't hear it enough times before we left." They sat across from each other at their small dining room table. "How quickly that happened. Doesn't it feel strange to you without him here? Like we're playing hooky, or putting off something. . ."

She glanced over to where they kept their washer and dryer.

Vole covered Bay's hand with his own.

"The dirt's not going anywhere, honeybee. Don't think about it. I'll do it this weekend. Tonight is ours. How do you want to celebrate?"

"I was thinking, I'd love to make it an early night."

Bay spent her days doing different things than Vole. She took care of William and a pair of twins from their neighborhood, and she worked part time at a small spa in town where she tidied up, did paperwork, and made sure visitors were tended to.

"I'm tired too," Vole said. "But shouldn't we do something a bit more exciting?"

While he hadn't spared much thought for this evening, all his brief fantasies involved something more titillating than an early night of rest.

"We could watch a movie?"

"Hmm."

"Vole..."

"You're right. I should have planned something. I'm sorry."

"I didn't say that."

"Want to go out for a drink?"

"It's after 9:00 p.m. on Christmas Eve. Nowhere is open right now."

"We have some leftover rum from your cousin's birthday. Do you want some in your eggnog?"

"Vole..." Bay regarded him with soulful eyes. "Sweetheart, I'm tired. How about we close our eyes and listen to music."

"Of course."

He put on one of their favorite albums. Began to sway on his feet.

"Come on," he said. "Dance with me a little."

Vole held her against him. Their bellies touched and chests pressed tight. Slowly, she came to rest her head against his neck. Leaned into him. He hummed, low notes she knew well, and they melted into one. They stayed together, bodies vertical and glued, as music filled them. They swayed. They breathed. They remembered.

"I missed this," Vole sighed. "I'd like to take you someplace nice."

"I'd like that," Bay murmured.

They fell quiet.

"Why are you crying?" Vole asked when he noticed. "Is something wrong?"

"I don't know."

They kept dancing.

"I got you something," he said, remembering. "A surprise."

"Oh?"

They stopped swaying. He left and returned with a small silver box. Placed it in her palm.

"Happy anniversary."

"Hold on," she said. "I got you something too." She returned with a paper-wrapped package.

"You first," he said.

Inside the silver box were two velvet beads, pink ocean pearls, perfectly polished. Bay blinked. Wiped traces of moisture away from her eyes.

"They're *lovely*."

"I noticed you haven't worn earrings since Will dropped the ones your mother gave you down the storm drain."

"Thank you," she said, sliding thin gold bars into her pierced lobes. "Your turn. Open what I got you."

Inside the paper wrapping was a silver tie clip and matching business card holder, both engraved with his initials.

"I thought you could use them for work."

"I will. They're perfect. A perfect pair."

They looked at each other, and Bay began to laugh.

"Happy anniversary, you old sap," Bay said. "I love you." They kissed. Before long she pulled back. "Next year let's go somewhere nice instead of getting each other gifts. Okay?"

"Done. I'd like to make you dinner sometime. I haven't in a while."

She leaned into him.

"Hold me," she said.

They watched a movie they both knew well and fell asleep on their small couch. As they lay cramped together, before sleep came over them, they talked in a way they hadn't in months. They kissed before drifting off. When they woke the next morning, they kissed again. William would be in first grade soon. Bay would stop babysitting the twins and go back to working full time. It was the dawn of a new year and change was in the air. Things promised to be . . . less.

Two weeks into January, Bay's mother stumbled and broke her hip. "She refuses to go into a nursing home alone," Bay told Vole, "but she needs round-the-clock care. Dad won't go with her. I've agreed to volunteer at the home half the week. It's the only way she'll go. I'll see about increasing my hours at the spa."

"Of course."

Later that spring, Bay's father had his first of three heart attacks. He stopped working after. The Gibbons stretched themselves thinner to support him too.

Then Vole heard a rumor. One of the Big Five banks of Canada would purchase the regional bank where he worked. Mr. McKinsey promised to make good on a pay raise, until federal budget deficits caught up. Wages were frozen. The Toronto housing market dropped a quarter, everything dropped with it, and there was no acquisition and no pay raise.

Vole's annual bonus barely helped cover his mother-in-law's care and his father-in-law's living expenses. There wasn't much left over, but what extra they squeezed, they saved. The garage needed work. The basement did too. The ceiling in William's bedroom closet was falling in. Their son needed a good education. They couldn't work forever. The future promised to be expensive, and every little bit helped.

By the time the caroling choir came knocking on the Gibbons' door for the last time—already, by then, door-to-door singers belonged to a sepia past—it was as though their magical moment of holiday peace the year before never happened.

Five years later, in May 1995, the rumors came true. One of the Big Five acquired the Ontario regional bank where Vole worked, and Mr. McKinsey wasn't part of the deal.

"Congratulations," Marc Rodrigo, the new regional manager, said. "You've been elected to step in as branch manager. Our pay bands are different than what you're accustomed to. After making some adjustments to account for your lack of education and lack of formal senior managerial experience, we decided that we won't be issuing you a pay increase. However, there will be growth opportunities, and as it stands, we won't be level-setting. Welcome to the team, Gibbons!"

Bay was livid when he told her.

"They don't deserve your loyalty," she insisted. "They're taking advantage of you again! They can't keep expecting you to take on more if they don't compensate you properly."

"It's different this time. There's a new bonus structure in place, and I'm on a much better compensation plan. I have to stick it out. You never know what could happen. Before there was a ceiling. Now they tell me this branch could expand, or I could be offered a better location."

"It's just—at what point is enough, enough? I hate how they take advantage of you. You're too nice."

"I hear what you're saying, honeybee, but things are changing. I should at least wait and see what this new management team is like. They're the fastest growing bank in Canada. This is the big leagues. They must know what they're doing."

"Whatever makes you happy."

Vole was grateful for her understanding. "You're lucky you're not being canned too," Nancy had told him in the staff room following the announcement. "Everyone in management usually gets fired. They could have ripped you right out. Given someone else who's been here as long the job. Lots of people don't get the opportunities they deserve. Wonder why they kept you."

Nancy wasn't someone Vole enjoyed debating with, so he said nothing. He didn't question his new manager's motives, like how he didn't question William's decision to quit hockey. William never liked the sport. They kept him in it for the sake of Bay's father, but the boy knew his own mind. Plus, he was eleven years old and growing quickly. Equipment and ice time was expensive. There were lots of other, cheaper sports, like soccer and track and field, William was into. It seemed like a smart decision to Vole, and Bay respected William's wishes. She never mentioned how she felt about it. Vole never thought to ask. After her father passed away following his third and final massive heart attack, she avoided driving in the winter, and never brought up the game up again.

FOURTEEN

Saturday, June 20, 2015
South of Reno, Nevada
5:57 p.m. local; 8:57 p.m. eastern time
340 sleeps since

"LOOK AT ME," Bay's soft voice commanded when Vole finished reading his letter aloud.

Jock looked up from chewing his bone. The dog's tongue was watermelon pink and covered in slobber; it hung ignominiously from his mouth. Somehow, the dog didn't notice he wasn't at home, and Vole wondered at his aging friend's state of mind.

Jock's tongue flicked out to lick Vole's hand.

"Please look at me," Bay implored.

Vole looked up from the creased paper. It trembled in his hands. Her eyes were luminous, thin face vibrant.

"Would you please kiss me, already?"

Vole didn't move.

"I've missed you," his voice crackled. "What do you think of it here? Is it what you hoped it would be like?" *Are you angry, do you hate me? I took something from you—for the last time, I promise—when I carried you away sleeping.*

She didn't glance to the side, nor did her steady stare flinch.

"Honestly? I think you should kiss me."

The slowly rising, ever-sinking sun had left him chapped, but he thought about this moment, every day, and he dreamed about how it might go. As hopeful as a teen, he drank water and moisturized his cracked lips in the weeks preceding.

Gentle, Vole kissed her.

Bay surprised him. She placed her hand behind his head and pressed his mouth into hers. Vole leaned into her kiss and was met with more interest; Bay's tongue slipped from her mouth into his. She sought his depths, drew him out, teased him.

They pulled away, breathless, before laughing like two knock-kneed lovers caught necking at the year-end student ball.

Bay started to cough.

She didn't stop until she couldn't continue, because her chest was too weak to spasm. Vole held her trembling body against his. They fell into solemn silence, finding comfort in each other's quiet presence. It was the kind of moment Vole fantasized about sharing with her, despite what loomed between them.

"I never knew it would be like this," Bay said, more breeze than voice.

Nothing could have prepared either of them. The blazing sun had seared away the clouds around it, and its molten rays poured down into the valley they sat above. Distant mountaintops punctuated the horizon. A sharp wind blew over them, carrying with it the scent of animal sweat. The horses smelled pure and strong, like gods.

The wild and free horses were what Bay had desired to see. There were young ones in the herd, colts whose knees folded as they ran in tight circles. Hooves thumped hard against the earth, as, in twos and threes, stallions were seized by the desire to gallop and toss. Chuffs and whinnies floated up over the crest. Sounds of unrestrained play made the Gibbons wistful. Bay pointed out her favorites—the two-toned ones Vole knew she would love the most—and she sighed, over and over.

Bay turned to look at him, and Vole was transported back to when she laid eyes on the river Seine in France for the first time. It was at night. City lights and dramatic arches painted rippled scenes across the river's porcelain surface.

"How did you do it?" Bay asked, drawing a close to his reverie.

"*Molly.*"

Bay rose to her feet. Vole jumped to his.

"Let me carry you," he insisted. "You shouldn't be walking."

She shot him a look. "The least I can do is walk myself over. Molly, did you say? You couldn't have chosen a different name? One that's less . . . womanly?"

Vole looked chagrined. She gave a small smile and moved toward the boat.

"It looks reliable and study," she told him. "The name suits. I adore it. Promise me one thing, though. Promise me you won't start referring to *it* as a *she*—" She faltered, and Vole rushed to Bay's side. He helped her over to where *Molly* was parked.

"It's incredible," she murmured.

Vole's gaze traced hers, and he imagined what it must be like seeing the boat for the first time.

Its body glowed white beneath a layer of dust, and its canopy, somehow, was still bright blue. The front two seats were lined with Bay's pillows. He'd taken two matching yellow-and-white ones from their house.

There was a period in Michigan when, for a time, Vole was obsessed with keeping Bay safe. During this period, he strapped safety pads to her kneecaps and placed a support pillow around her neck. He also replaced the seat belts he added in Toronto with five-point harnesses, and for Jock, he installed a special safety harness that clipped around the dog's narrow chest.

At another point during his lonely ride, he secured a canoe paddle to each side of the boat, and he fitted a clear plastic screen to the top of the canopy, which could be pulled down over the front of the boat and secured in place.

"Is that your bike?" Bay exclaimed.

Vole nodded. "It didn't originally come with mirrors."

"You don't say." He blushed. "You towed all *that*, using *that* little hitch?"

"Yes, well, you see . . ." He began to describe how simple things they took for granted, like physics and natural law, didn't apply when time was stopped, and the bicycle hitch, which by all rights should strain to tow more than its four-hundred-and-fifty-kilogram limit, appeared to have no trouble at all.

"It works," he said. "Though I don't suggest you try it."

Bay opened her mouth to say something more, but demurred.

"I was going to ask how you're doing all this," she explained when Vole looked at her in question. "Climbing hills the size of mountains, crossing stretches of land as big as the sea—are you sure you didn't teleport?

"I must be hallucinating all this . . . If this isn't a wild hallucination, it's still the same: magical. Unbelievably wonderful, and then I look at you, and I worry. Where is my husband? I see a wiry man whose once-dark hair is growing gray, making its steady way toward white. Your hands are becoming claws."

She was right. As his fingers grew calloused and his knuckles became round, he'd taken to wearing his wedding ring on a shoelace around his neck. "You limp when you walk," she continued. "Don't try to deny it. I saw when you moved past me, and you arch your back more frequently than a cat in heat. How are you managing? What can I do?"

Vole worried that she might get angry. He thought she might demand he take her back home. He worried she would deny him the chance to carry her around the world, or worse, what if she didn't believe him? He never once considered she'd be concerned for him or want to help.

"Take your time, honeybee. Enjoy the moment. Nothing else."

"What does Will think about all this?"

"W-well," he stammered, caught off guard. "The thing is . . ." He hadn't told William anything. He'd thought about trying, many times in fact, but each time he imagined scenarios in which he told their son the truth, William became too upset or too involved, and the problem too difficult to work around.

Bay's eyes grew round.

"Oh. Well. Hmm. I suppose there's not much we can do about it right now, is there?"

"You're not worried?"

"You bet your damned socks I'm worried! But, on the other hand, what is there to worry about? It's only us, here and now, baby." She winked at him.

This was a different Bay. This wasn't the defeated woman he found lying in bed in room 1221 at Rosabella Memorial Hospital. Nor was it the quietly content woman he'd become accustomed to in recent years. It was the Bay who set his broken arm in a parking lot; the goofy and bold woman who denied culpability to a stranger for fear of rising premiums (it turns out she'd just gotten her license at the time); the one who challenged him ceaselessly to keep up.

Or had so much time gone by he was misremembering it all? *Was she always this way?*

Or perhaps theirs was a different story altogether.

"Oh!" he exclaimed, remembering something else. "I have something for you."

"There's *more?*"

Vole guided Bay back to the green blanket. They sat down. Paused to watch an eagle soar across the sky in front of them. The raptor focused its eye on Jock, but the dog was oblivious. Gnawing on his prize kept him preoccupied. Once the bird flew out of sight, Vole handed Bay his journals; two were already filled with letters he'd written to her over the year, and he was almost halfway through all the pages of his third.

"What's this?" she asked.

Bay opened the first of the three journals. Tucked inside, under the cover, was her list of wonders. Vole knew it by heart. She ran her fingers over it, and he shivered. She turned the page and let her eyes wander over his words. She looked to the next page, and the next page. She stopped when she'd read as much as she could.

"How could you ever think I'd stop loving you?" she asked, voice thick.

Vole didn't answer. They interlocked hands and watched as the sun sunk lower and lower in the sky. Horses grazed until they'd had their fill and then moved on to find water. Within two hours of opening her eyes and taking a breath for the first time in three hundred and forty sleeps, Bay drifted off with her head resting against Vole.

He checked his watch. It was 10:50 p.m. back home. Bay needed rest, and if Vole was going to fulfill the next item on her list, he needed to make sure they didn't sleep through the night.

Gently, he lifted Bay's head. Was careful not to wake her. Set her down. Her parted lips beckoned, and he remembered the kiss they'd shared earlier in the evening. He couldn't stop himself from brushing his lips against hers once more before. . .

Vole began to count down in his head: *three, two, one* . . .

"Stop," and everything relaxed into stillness.

FIFTEEN

Saturday, June 20, 2015
South of Reno, Nevada
7:50 p.m. local; 10:50 p.m. eastern time
340 sleeps since

THE NEXT PLACE on Bay's list was the Grand Canyon. A stone skip away compared to the trip he just made, and, though it was now setting, Vole was looking forward to having the constant sun at his back instead of in his face.

On his way south, Vole stopped at a fuel station to use the facilities and refill his supply of water. In the restroom, Vole turned his back to the man washing his hands at the sink, and when it came time for Vole to wash his hands, he apologized to the stranger for having to stand close.

"My apologies," Vole muttered, and cupped his hands at the bottom of the stream of water that poured down from the tap head. He kept his hands cupped and raised them, collecting water as he did. When he used up the entire stream, he entered the food mart. (Both his water barrels were half full—he depleted them equally for balance—and, as he discovered in Nevada, opportunities to find water changed with the landscape.)

Inside the food mart, he picked up two boxes of straws and seventeen four-liter jugs of water (Vole sometimes used straws to suck water from hard-to-reach places) and emptied all seventeen four-liter jugs into his barrels. Still fifty liters short, Vole took as many two-liter bottles as he could find and emptied those into his rain barrels too. He took three water purification tablets and crushed them into a fine powder.

"Just in case," he muttered, though he preferred to save the tablets for when he filled his barrels from natural sources. "You can never be too sure."

He dropped the powder into the top of the first rain barrel and swirled vigorously. Unless he crushed them first, the tablets would plunk in and float whole. When he crushed them into powder and agitated the water, they dissolved.

"Well, the water appears to absorb the powder," Vole muttered, comforted only by the fact that ice, in specific circumstances, still melted. And he hadn't died from gastroenteritis or a severe waterborne pathogen, yet.

The farther south he got, the more traffic he encountered, and the weightier the air inside his chest became. He kept to the road's shoulder, taking care to avoid vultures and strips of burst tire rubber. Vehicles blended. The people inside the vehicles blended. There was such monotony, he barely noticed when something differed slightly.

"Look up," he begged silent passengers. "Look up and see who's there with you. Talk to each other. Look. Really *look*."

Nobody listened, but he was used to that.

Vole made frequent stops, despite his anxiety about Bay's safety, which had returned in full force. He would crouch to the ground and squint at his tires. Pinch them. Appraise their tread and hairline cracks with a critical eye. He would lubricate his bicycle chain, and lubricate it some more, before checking everything over again. For a reason he couldn't pinpoint, the stakes seemed higher than ever.

When Vole made camp, he propped Bay up in a seated position and told her about his day. He laid dinner out in front of them as though they were sharing a meal. When his supper consisted of chips and dried pepperoni sticks from a gas station, he would turn away from her as he ate. Sometimes he would talk and talk to Bay and not bother with food at all.

Like with many changes he sensed were coming, Vole knew he was approaching Las Vegas because of the air. He would have preferred to avoid the city altogether but a bad accident forced him to take a different, longer route. A sticky smell lined his nostrils in oily residue. Billboards gleamed through layers of dust in the evening sun; dusk hid ugly tears and transformed empty slogans into tangible fantasies designed to lure.

Vole didn't stop to camp until the city grew small behind him. Guilt flooded as he considered its gauzy halo in his bicycle mirrors. *I'm leaving lots of money behind.* He felt ashamed for thinking it. None of it was his, and what good would having all the money in the world do? He kept going.

Saturday, June 20, 2015
Hoover Dam, Nevada
7:50 p.m. local; 10:50 p.m. eastern time
350 sleeps since

Upon reaching the Hoover Dam, Vole decided to take the bypass. It appeared shorter than the road over the dam; and looking out over the scene, he was struck.

The dam gaped before them, a yawning chasm with a thin strip of water at the bottom, black and impenetrable. On the other side of the dam wall, the full weight of the Colorado River bore down. He imagined white water spewing through cracks in the dam and crashing down its face, a hundred thousand white mares bearing down all at once; it stole his breath away.

The effort required to blast through such quantities of natural stone, as with the number of human deaths it took to accomplish, made history books. The dam was a testament to the past, a time when taming the west was the wildest adventure; a time when governments could draw a struggling nation back from the brink with a brick-and-mortar feat. With computer software being the new frontier—he'd heard William's wild theories on many occasions—what in the world would governments build to rally a depressive nation?

At least computers can't kill so many young and strong workers, Vole thought, but the fine hair covering his body raised as he considered the sort of trouble all the young and strong workers faced today. One more chilling notion to add to an infinite pile, his sole companion in an otherwise empty room.

Vole wasn't the only tourist to take a stroll along the walkway that ran parallel to the road bridge. Others had stopped to appreciate how the day's remaining light looked, skimming off surrounding peaks. The dam itself was dark. Vole found himself wishing he could see it earlier in the day. He imagined it would light up like the moon. A wave of nostalgia washed over him. Vole's eyes became awash with tears. He would've been happy to share this experience with William, too, if only it seemed worth seeking sooner.

Then Vole did something he rarely did. He walked up to the people around him. He didn't avoid their eyes and pretend ignorance. Instead, he breathed deeply their wide array of smells. He considered touching their hands as he looked into their faces.

Are you warm? Alive? Here?

White, brown, pale, dark.

Blind, all of them.

What do you think you're seeing?

A slender young man dressed in slacks and an untucked shirt claimed Vole's attention. A brown leather camera bag hung across the front of his body; a camera hung about his neck. The lens cap was on. Vole didn't know whether the man put it back on, or if he hadn't taken it off in the first place.

At first, Vole was struck. Here was someone like him—someone who wanted to stop and become a part of the view rather than get caught up in the need to capture its unstoppable passing.

At second glance, Vole realized he might be wrong. The man was staring off to the side, fascinated by something Vole couldn't see.

Vole moved to stand next to him. Traced his gaze. Heart swelled. "It would seem we do share something precious in common," Vole murmured.

The young man was watching an older man. Vole suspected, having observed the photographer's face at length, he was watching the person he loved most in all the world; without a doubt, his lover.

But maybe Vole was reading too deeply into the scene. Maybe he was projecting his own deep-rooted desires of companionship. Like with everything else, he couldn't be sure. The problem was he had no way of knowing what recently occurred, and what would happen next. Everything was kept secret. Face value was everything.

Perhaps it was simple. Perhaps the man was showing simple concern for a simple bond. His brother, a cousin, a friend.

Maybe the riveting subject was a stranger in need of help. Or maybe the man didn't care for anyone at all but himself.

Vole doubted it all. He knew if it were him standing there, and it were Bay who was stretched out over the side, face lit like a sun-soaked daisy, loose hair waltzing with a breeze, he would be watching her in that same transfixed way.

"I suppose it's simple no matter how you consider it," Vole muttered.

Overcome by the desire to give the man back his privacy, Vole left to be near Bay. Before he did, he whispered, "Goodbye," and, "Good luck," and, "I'm sorry."

As he approached his bicycle, he imagined Bay watching him with a longing face. Vole felt at peace. Fell back into silence.

His seat cushion was badly cracked, and his left knee popped and snapped whenever he bent it. His joints had seen younger days, and he still had a very long road ahead.

SIXTEEN

Saturday, June 20, 2015
Grand Canyon, Arizona
7:50 p.m. local; 10:50 p.m. eastern time
354 sleeps since

THE PATH, SPOTTED with shrubs, was as wide as Vole was tall, and it followed the canyon's edge, which was curving and to his right. On the left, a wall of dirt rose as the path's slope dropped farther down and away from him. At the end of the path, which couldn't be seen from where Vole was standing, was a fat thicket of leafless and snarled branches. Beyond the thicket was an alcove. It was sheltered from view by rocks, red and jutting, and needle-covered trees. The air smelled of pine and clovers.

Looking down, to his right, Vole expected to see water rushing, carving away dirt and rock, driving the great divide deeper into the earth; but the canyon below was bone dry.

Drops of sweat beaded his brow as he considered the bottomless plummet.

"Don't look down," he muttered. Body pressed tight against the wall of dirt that rose to his left, Vole took a step forward while pushing the bicycle alongside his right. *Molly* rattled. His eyes flicked to the bicycle's side mirrors as Bay swayed in her harness. Vole squeezed his handlebars in dismay; bloodless knuckles flexed and blanched. He forced his lungs to drink deep. Exhaled. Took another slow step, pushed his bicycle, *Molly* rattled, Bay swayed, his eyes flicked, and they crept forward along the narrow route. "Look straight ahead. Point your eyes in the direction you want to go. Whatever you do, don't look down."

It paralyzed him to imagine his tired legs buckling. He took frequent pauses. Vole became sticky and slick. Little black insects, no bigger than a pinhead, clung unknowing to his skin as he walked through a suspended burst of them. When it became almost too much, he considered turning back, moving backward along the path; but he recalled Bay's lifelong desire to spend an evening sleeping beneath the same sky the Grand Canyon took its rest beneath. With such thoughts on his mind, he mustered the courage to keep pushing.

One long, agonizing moment later, he rolled them to the safety of the alcove. He promptly fell asleep.

When Vole woke, he was ravenous. After eating the last of his jerky, he left Bay and Jock behind to source what they'd need to spend a cool night in the desert together.

When he returned, as before, he laid down a blanket. Rolled out a thick pad. Brought thermal covers and thick layers for Bay to wear before they nestled in close to one another. It seemed ludicrous to prepare for chilliness when he'd become accustomed to summer's stifle, and he grew excited at the prospect of night passing around him.

He laid a telescope, small enough to be held in one hand, on Bay's side of the sleeping pad. It rested next to a pile of books about constellations and stars he borrowed from the same tourist shop. He'd prepared a buffet for her too. An assortment of things they rarely ate at home, collected from nearby restaurants. There was lemon water, a selection of salty meats, fresh cheeses, recently baked bread with seasoned oil to dip it in, and spreads that smelled of garlic. He'd found a fish-and-chips stand. It stood at the center of the most mouthwatering aroma. He brought some battered and fried fish back too. For the morning, he readied a pile of fresh fruit and picked up a piece of rawhide for Jock. Everything he took he added to his ledger, which was now long enough to require its own journal.

With Bay's appetites taken into account, it was time for Vole to clean himself. Attached to a nearby hotel was a saltwater swimming pool. At first, Vole was embarrassed to be stripping down in front of sun-soaked families, soiling the water with his sweat. After slipping in, his inhibitions were wiped away—the sensation of water, warm and still, was like the finest spun silk washcloth drawn across his skin.

Vole climbed out of the pool, jumped back in, sank a bit, stopped sinking; he hung, suspended, below the surface. He blew air out his lungs and watched in awe as clear, oblong shapes glittered like crystal and grew out from his nose. They hung in the water around him. His finger passed through a large bubble and it split in two, but neither raced to the surface. The glittering orbs stayed suspended and sparkling there with him. Unless he kicked his legs and moved his arms, he would float indefinitely.

"Nonsense and more nonsense," he muttered to himself when he got out, marveling at the secret he'd discovered.

The last item he needed was buried in one of the containers in the back of *Molly*. His old Blackberry. He fished it out. Tossed it up and down. Tested the weight of it in his hands. Put it aside, and started time.

"It's ringing!" When was the last time he heard a phone ring?

"Shhh," Bay giggled. "You're being too loud. It's supposed to ring. What did you expect?"

Vole hadn't meant to shout, but he'd grown frenzied thinking about speaking with William again. He hadn't heard his son's voice in—

"It's his answering machine," Vole hissed in a panic when the telltale click sounded over the line.

"So leave a message," Bay hissed back.

Right.

"William! [pause] Will. Hi. [pause] It's, um, your father. I wanted to tell you . . ." What? What could he possibly say to his son over a voice message that wouldn't result in William insisting he drop everything and see a shrink? The glass of wine Vole finished was slowing his already muddied thoughts. " . . . Uh, to tell you I love you. Your mother and I are well. She sends Gina her love. We both do. We love you, son. [pause] Be safe." Vole hung up, feeling much older than he had a few moments ago.

"Well?" Bay asked.

"Well, what?"

"What was it like?"

What was it like to hear a recording of his son's voice, tinny and distant, for the first time in over a year? It made him miss the real William. He didn't want some digital rendering. It made him feel like they were worlds apart.

"It was good. I think."

"You *think?*"

Bay swatted him lightly on the arm, and Vole caught her. Pulled her close against him. The sun had already dipped below the horizon, and the heavens were about to reveal themselves.

"Look," Vole said. He pointed to the sky above. Already it held more winking stars in it than India ink. Pink and purple blended into deep, diamond-speckled night. Bay sighed. Her eyes shone brighter than the stars themselves.

She lay back. Put the telescope to her eye. Breathed Vole's name.

This is bliss, he thought to himself.

"The Milky Way is up there," she said. "What if there are other people out there, looking down the same way we're looking up at them? Think about it! Wouldn't it be sensational?"

Vole said nothing. He'd already spent too much time thinking about that—and every other sensational thought under the sun. All he wanted was to observe Bay. The way she lifted her chin. Smiled by lifting only one side of her mouth. She became lost in her joy and her smile become so brilliant her face emitted its own shining light.

You're a star, he thought to himself about Bay. *My beacon in the sky.*

She looked frail and small, bundled up in blankets and warm wool; she wore a toque the same color as *Molly*'s canopy. He loved the way toques, especially blue ones, looked on her.

Vole noticed she was watching him watch her.

"I can't help it," he defended against her stare. "You're divine!" Vole saw his compliments and attention were having an unintended effect on her. "What's wrong?" he asked as her glow dimmed.

"Nothing." She shook her head. "Everything."

"What do you mean?"

"Why now? Why all this," her arms swept the air in front of her. "*Now?* I don't understand. I don't want our life to end.

I feel like it just started. I can't—" She began to hiccough, or gasp, he couldn't tell by the shake of her shoulders.

"Please don't cry," he pleaded. "I'm sorry. I didn't mean—"

Bay cut off his words by rising from the blanket and placing her lips on his. When she pulled back her eyes were unreadable.

"Don't you dare be sorry!" she insisted. "This is all I need. You can turn around now, Vole. You can go home! You've given me all I hoped I would ever come to know, and more. *You have nothing to be sorry for.* Don't you understand?"

You're wrong, he thought to himself. There was a lot for him to be sorry for. To make up for. She was the one who didn't understand. How could she?

Jock chose to remind them it was past time for his last walk of the evening. The dog stretched and shook before climbing onto Vole's lap and finding his face with his tongue. Vole scratched Jock all over before hooking him to his leash. He didn't worry about Jock disappearing, the dog never strayed far from Bay, but he was old and set in his ways. Jock wouldn't relieve himself without having a leash attached to his collar. Vole obliged, and he allowed himself to be transported back to a different life where walking Jock was a regular activity done four times a day, on a small street, in a small town, in quiet southern Ontario.

When he got back to their campsite, Bay was sleeping. Often she'd be awake, laughing and smiling; then he'd glance away and turn back to discover she'd dozed off. He stroked her hair while she snored. Lifted the blankets to let Jock burrow beneath them, now he knew it's what the dog wanted all along, and lay down to consider the sky above.

Vole's thoughts turned quickly back to earlier in the evening. When Bay first woke, she wanted to know everything that transpired since they last saw each other. She was astonished to learn what was a blink for her was weeks for him. While he spoke, she regarded him like he was a stranger, and it pained him to see. When he asked why, she said she didn't know. "This must be what it's like for parents who don't see their kids for years at a time," she tried to explain, and he thought of Mr. McKinsey. "Every time they do, they find their baby's become a new version of the same person. It's strange."

Vole asked her about Nevada, about why it remained on her list. She recounted a movie about wild mustangs, and the actor in it—a dashing cowboy—was her first fluttering crush. The untamed wildlands of Nevada seized her imagination then, and never once let go. Vole was perturbed to hear about Bay's cowboy fantasy, but she reassured him he was the only cowboy who occupied her dreams.

When he thought about trapping wild mustangs, he didn't think he was capable of it. "I hate to disappoint you," he told her, "but I think I'm much more like Charles Darwin than I am John Wayne."

Bay laughed and said, "Bay much prefers Vole to either Charles or John," and he was satisfied.

A dusty gust reminded him things were moving. Vole checked his watch. It was past 1:00 a.m. eastern time.

He woke Bay gently. She sat up and smiled at him. Her cheeks looked fuller than they had earlier that day. If Vole didn't know Bay was sick, he never would have guessed.

She took her medicine. Asked him to tell her a story. He began to talk, and talk, and talk. As much as Vole desired a breeze blowing over his body while he slept, he didn't want to waste any second of their time together by sleeping through it. Besides, he thought to himself, what he missed wasn't nighttime breezes as a category; he missed the specific wind they got back home as they lay together in bed, and he found he was willing to wait for that. Somewhere along the way he learned a new kind of patience. He talked about that too.

Bay went in and out of sleep as he spoke. He told her about the paw prints, as big as two of his hands, found overlooking a stream in Nebraska. Bear prints, he was sure at the time, because they were broad and large. When he saw the cougar and her cubs who made them, he remembered again how little he knew. He told her about the nightmares that kept him awake at night when he was alone. Visions of swirling darkness following him wherever he went, and of being held back, unable to race in and save her and William from a tornado as it bore down on their home. "But you don't like cats," she murmured, barely awake, when he told her his nightmares often contained lost and lonely cats too.

His words took him down paths he hadn't explored since leaving Dorset. As he recalled his old life, he forgot he was the person who lived it. It didn't matter to him Mr. McKinsey never invited Vole to his goodbye party, and never wrote him the recommendation letter he promised. It didn't matter that Nancy complained about him to head office, and told them he was unqualified to be branch manager. Their ongoing basement renovations that snowballed in time and expense, setting them back far more than he budgeted for, no longer made his stomach churn. He didn't worry about how William and Gina, his son's confidante-turned-lover, would end up. It was enough for him to know they were in love.

Vole entertained Bay's slumbering ear until the cool sapphire night grew warm. The world grew brighter and brighter, and he talked faster and faster, as though his stories might keep the sun from appearing over the horizon's crest.

With great reluctance, Vole checked his wristwatch. It was almost 8:00 a.m. back home. Here, the sun would rise above the horizon in fifteen minutes, and the next day would begin in a blinding flash of yellow and gold.

Vole woke Bay. Her eyes found his.

"Good morning," she said. It was morning's waking sigh, the same one he'd woken to every morning for decades, and to him, the sound was exquisite.

"Watermelon?" he managed to say.

She took the piece of watermelon he held between his fingers between her lips, and she sucked it into her mouth. Velvety warmth on his fingertips surprised him. He hadn't been expecting such soft heat, and it sent a shock through his body that left him quivering.

Bay seemed oblivious to the effect she had on him while she chewed. He kept distracted by thinking it was good she had an appetite.

"Ish delishus," she said, mouth full. He smiled, now only a bit flustered, and agreed. Jock poked his head out from under the blanket, curious to see what they were eating.

"Hello, little wolf!" Bay greeted and scratched under his chin. He closed his eyes, stretched his neck, and leaned into her hand. "It's good to see you too."

Vole watched as Bay gave into temptation. She fell silent and stood. Blankets tumbled off her and pooled on the ground. He moved to take her elbow, but she waved him away.

Full of strength and confidence, the likes of which he hadn't seen since before her first collapse, Bay walked to the edge of the canyon. Wrapped her arms around her body, and basked in daytime's glory as dawn transformed the landscape yet again. Vole half expected a nymph flying on the back of a winged dragon to appear—anything to confirm his suspicions that what they had was truly magical—but no such sign appeared, and soon enough, magic faded as his watch hands ticked ever forward.

Bay began to wheeze, then cough. Vole ran over to where she was seated on the ground and helped her back to their nest. He stayed glued to her side until the coughing fit passed.

When it subsided, she looked at him with frightened eyes. Despair brought new pallor to her cheeks. She held out her hand to show him her palm. Flecks of spittle, the gloss and hue of rubies, speckled her tissue-paper skin, and the barest waft of iron rose to meet his nose.

"My stomach . . ." she whispered.

"What is it, honeybee?"

"It hurts."

"Is it bad?"

"It feels off."

Vole didn't know what she meant, yet he knew exactly what she meant. He checked his watch: 8:43 a.m. Tourists, many awake by now, would soon find them. It was almost time. He held her close. Rocked her. Raised his arm behind her head to where she couldn't see and watched as the second hand traveled in a circle. The moment the minute hand moved into position, 8:45 a.m., he told time to stop, and it did.

Sunday, June 21, 2015
Grand Canyon, Arizona
5:45 a.m. local; 8:45 a.m. eastern time
355 sleeps since

Once again alone with nothing but nagging doubts for company, the remaining nine-tenths of Vole's journey loomed over him. The Hoover Dam over an ant, and he was the ant. He turned quickly to the daunting task of preparing to leave, and noticed a big problem.

Bay and Jock were watching him.

At first, happiness blazed through him; but when he realized neither was attentive, that both their eyes were stuck open for the coming eternity, his thrill turned to dread. Vole had no idea what effect the constant sun might have on their eyeballs. What if they became dried out?

What if it meant Bay could *see*?

Briefly, he considered trying to shut her eyelids, like how he'd seen actors do in movies when confronted with a corpse, but the thought revolted him. He told himself he was overreacting. There were ample instances for him to refer to where her state defied all reason—she never got darker, for one. Her fair skin seemed to repel dirt while he became nut-brown from absorbing it.

Unsure of what he should do, Vole resolved to find her and Jock sunglasses as soon as he was finished packing up. "That won't solve my problem," he said out loud to Bay. "What if you're paying attention to what I'm up to?" He didn't like knowing Bay was watching his every move. Vole wasn't certain she would approve of who he was becoming.

Putting his Blackberry away, its bright screen caught his attention. Somehow, they'd missed a call from William. Time must have stopped shortly after the notification came through. According to the time stamp, they'd been awake when their son called.

How had they missed it?

Vole vowed to play it when he and Bay were together again, and then, like with everything else less pressing than the lonely task ahead, he let it slip from his mind.

He started down the road leading from South Rim and didn't look back. Vole was embarking on the longest leg yet, and he had no notion of what he'd encounter. It was all new territory. He would continue south through the United States, pass through Mexico, and keep going through Central America until he reached South America. He would cross into Colombia from Panama and continue down the west coast of the continent, passing through Ecuador, Peru, Chile, until he reached Argentina. He was taking Bay to the south, as far south as they could go, to the ancient land of fire. A place known as Tierra del Fuego. He was taking Bay to look out over the world's edge.

"How will you get to where we're going next?" she asked as they lay gazing up at the stars, a few short hours before he'd stopped time again. They long since gave up on trying to identify any constellations.

"A day at a time," he answered. He refused to confirm with her his next destination, preferring to keep it as much of a surprise as their circumstances would allow.

"Will you do something for me?" she asked, full of concern for his safety. "Will you please wear a helmet?"

SEVENTEEN

April 1998

NORA WAS STILL Vole's favorite radio host. He listened to her husky voice every day and looked forward to the evening program she hosted. Nora played the best crooning classics, and her pun-filled jokes were amusing. If she told a zinger, he'd share it with William and Bay over dinner.

This time, however, when Nora's throaty chuckle sounded out following a real belly-jiggler, Vole turned the volume down. He was too preoccupied to pay attention to what she was saying, and it was distracting to try and listen.

Arriving home, he pulled into the driveway and parked beneath the overhang that jutted out from the side of their house. It offered cover from rain and snow, if not dry heated comfort. Their long-term plan was to enclose the structure, turn it into a real garage, but time was never on their side.

Vole paused before going inside the house. Hand hovering over the doorknob, he glanced up at bare hinges where spots of rust were beginning to show. Last summer he removed the original storm door, stripping the screws in the process. It had been a frustrating job, but the door never closed properly to begin with. After William ripped through its screen with his hockey stick and shattered the glass, it became an eyesore.

At the time, he told Bay their main entrance was sheltered enough by surrounding trees, because it was, and it didn't rain enough to warrant buying a new one, he'd explained. They never bothered replacing it. She hadn't brought it up since.

"What are you looking at?" he asked a young brown squirrel that sat tall on a branch, watching him. He found their little black eyes to be shrewd and judging. "You critters are too nosy for your own good!"

The squirrel chattered and moved its bushy tail up and down, becoming the picture of indignation. It raced up the trunk and disappeared into the green canopy above.

When Vole stepped inside and called out, silence answered.

"Will?" he tried again. Bay told him she would drop William off at the house after picking him up from school, but she had to go right back to work afterward. He didn't expect her to be home. Vole called out her name anyway. "Bay? William?"

Vole dropped his briefcase on the floor. Hung his spring jacket in the small closet next to the door. He filled a tall glass with milk and took down the bag of chocolate fudge cookies from the top shelf of the pantry. *Out of sight, out of mind.* "Yeah, right," he muttered as he took two out, changed his mind, and took a third cookie. He placed one in his mouth and carried the others in his hand, and he walked down the hall to William's bedroom. The door was closed. Vole knocked lightly, careful not to spill the drink.

"Will?" he said. "You in there?"

No reply. He knocked again.

"Will?"

"What?" came the muted reply.

"Can I come in?"

Silence.

Vole opened the door. The overhead light was off. William's Toronto Maple Leafs lamp, a gift from the boy's late grandfather, sat on the corner of his small work desk. It glowed a muted blue, casting dim light onto a pile of paper on the table. Every sheet lay decorated in blue-penned doodles—rockets and flowers, among other indecipherable shapes.

William lay on his single bed, staring up at the white stucco ceiling. A magazine lay spread, spine bent and compressed, next to his pillow. The floor was clear of clutter, but there was a pile of clothing and papers that the swinging bedroom door had pushed together.

"Hi," Vole said. William didn't respond. "I brought you a snack. Dinner will be late. It's you and me tonight."

"Okay." It was a dull, noncommittal word for the usually enthusiastic boy.

William sat up as Vole stepped into the room and handed his son two cookies and the glass of milk. William's eyes widened, but he didn't crack a smile. Treats—like double chocolate fudge cookies—were rare, and usually saved for holidays and birthdays. These were left over from Vole's fortieth birthday party. At his request, Bay had put them on a lonely shelf in the tall pantry to help him forget they were there. The strategy hadn't been working, and his gradually expanding waistline was proof.

"Scoot over," Vole commanded. He plopped down next to William, who sat weary on his bed. "Want to tell me what happened?"

William put one of the cookies in his mouth, whole, and shook his head. His copper-colored hair, pressed flat from his ball cap, fell into his eyes.

"I'm going to ask you a few questions. All right?"

No answer.

"So," Vole continued. "Why did you think it was okay to leave school property?" William kept chewing. "Did you know you were going against the rules?" This time William looked up at him through limp bangs as though he'd grown horns. "Okay, okay. You knew it was against the rules. Why'd you do it? Were you trying to make your mother and me upset?"

William's face crumpled. His fair neck turned the color of beets.

"No," he said with a sniff. Ate the second cookie. Drank down his glass of milk.

"What were you doing in the forest?" Vole asked.

William mumbled.

"I can't hear you."

"We weren't trying to hurt anyone," William mumbled again, the slightest bit louder. "Lawrence said it would be better if we did it outside. We didn't think anyone would find us in the forest."

"And you listened to him?" William gave a miserable nod. "Where did you get the money to buy them in the first place?"

The boy's lips pinched tight together.

"William . . ."

Vole considered his son a friend and hated being reminded otherwise. He tried to remember what his father had said to him when he got into serious trouble, but he couldn't remember a single useful thing.

Slowly, bit by bit, Vole tugged all the important details out of William. He learned Lawrence paid an older boy for three roman candles and a box of fire crackers. Five students, four boys and one girl, left school property at lunch by climbing over the back fence. They went to set them off in the forest. They got caught by the lunch monitor before any wicks were lit, but it was too late. Lines were drawn and sides were taken.

William and Lawrence got suspended, and the other three kids got off with afterschool detention.

"You're on thin ice," Vole told William before he left to prepare dinner. "Grounded until we say you're not. No TV, no computer, no fun."

"Whatever."

Bay didn't get back to the house until after William went to sleep.

"You should have waited for me before talking to him," she admonished as she and Vole sat side by side in bed. Her eyebrows were pulled together and her normally generous lips were pursed; Vole recognized his son's fearsome frown in Bay's features. *He definitely gets it from her.*

"Those types of conversations are best had when we're together," she continued, interrupting his thoughts.

"Honeybee, I'm telling you, waiting would have made it worse. You should've seen him. He was miserable."

"I asked you to wait," she insisted. "You said you would."

"I wanted to, but when I got home, he wasn't doing anything. He closed himself up in his room. What was I supposed to do? Ignore him all night? Not a chance. Anyway, these types of things are best handled in the moment."

"Bullshit," she snapped. "You should have waited!" Her face flushed—William also got his fair, clear skin from Bay—and she stretched her neck from side to side. "Oh, God. It's been such a long day. First Ronnie called in sick, and then one of the nurses called because Mom banged her knee badly. When I got the call to pick up William, I was eating for the first time all day, but the cab company took forever to come and get me."

"Call me sooner next time, especially if I have the car. I can get out of meetings for a family emergency. It's better than you taking a cab." He pulled her against him and kissed the top of her head. "I'll come with you this weekend to visit your mother. I'm sorry I haven't gone with you in a while."

They fell quiet.

"Did he say why he went along with it?" Bay asked into the still room.

"I didn't press too hard."

"See?" she insisted, pulling back to stare Vole in the face. "You should have waited! If I'd been there, we would've gotten to that part. If they started a forest fire, who knows what could've happened? He was a Boy Scout, dammit! He knows better."

Vole tried to pull Bay back against him but she resisted. He sighed.

"He was going along with Lawrence. You know what that kid's like. At least Will insisted they do it in the clearing next to the pond. He didn't let any of the other kids handle them. He tried to be safe, honeybee. They were having fun. He knows better now."

"He knew better before."

"No one got hurt, and this is the first time he's ever done something like this."

"That we know of!"

She was right, Vole knew, but William was a gentle boy with a kind heart. He was the type to save bumblebees from drowning, or a slow turtle from getting run over on the road. He wasn't dishonest. His greatest fault was his loyalty, and if Lawrence insisted something was a good idea . . . Well, William wasn't going to let his best friend do something dangerous on his own. Especially not when there was a girl to impress.

"Shit," Vole said.

"What?"

"What should we do about Sonia's party? Should we let him go?"

Bay shifted her weight and rested her head on top of his chest. Their son had been looking forward to his classmate's birthday for weeks. All his friends were going, and they'd already formed teams for laser tag. The birthday girl chose him to be on her team.

After a long moment, "I don't know. What do you think?"

"I think . . . crap," he swore again. "I think we should let him go. Show him we trust him still."

"Though he's suspended?"

A pause.

"He's a good kid," he said.

"Should we be thinking about moving?" It wasn't the first time Bay was bringing it up.

"Why would we? Where would we go?"

"Somewhere there's more people. The school is so small here. Everybody knows everybody, and if William gets in with a bad crowd . . ."

Her unspoken worry was of Lawrence McCarthy, William's childhood best friend. Bay didn't have anything against the boy, but he came from a family with three older kids who were all going wild. She worried about the household's growing influence over their impressionable son.

Vole shook his head.

"Transplanting a small-town boy into the big city before high school won't make his life any easier or stop him from getting into trouble. It'll do the opposite."

"Well, we should encourage him to invite his friends over instead of going to their houses."

"If you say so, honeybee," Vole agreed.

Silence took them.

"Can you pop out tomorrow afternoon to grab Mom's medicine from the pharmacy?" Bay asked, suddenly remembering one more thing. "It'll be hard for me to get away."

"My last meeting of the day finishes at three. I'll swing by afterwards."

The sound of their breathing filled the room.

"How did things go with Nancy today?" Bay asked, breaking the spell once more. "Did she have anything to say about the new system administrator?"

"Oh, you know how these things are," Vole evaded. Ever since taking over the branch, it had been one technology and personnel issue after another, and thinking about everything—and everyone—at work, on top of everything else, gave him acid reflux. "The same."

"I see."

"I don't think you need to worry too much about Will, honeybee. He's a good kid."

"I can't help worrying."

"Of course."

It wasn't until over an hour later, when Vole lost himself in his bedside mystery, tattered and creased from use, he slid sideways into sleep.

The next day, when he rushed into the pharmacy and turned out empty pockets, Vole remembered the prescription was still at home. It was on the counter where Bay had left it for him. Vole could visualize it. Clear typeface on white-and-blue paper, lying on their salmon-pink countertop, right next to a list of things he was supposed to pick up from the store, which he'd also forgotten. Leaving the office midday agitated him, which in turn made him forgetful. Getting William to his old sitter's had been a major distraction. (Vole agreed with Bay: William should be supervised during his suspension, not because they didn't trust him, but to reinforce an important point.)

"Shit," he grunted, standing at the counter. The pharmacist glared. Vole apologized and left.

He would have raced home to get the prescription, if he hadn't locked his keys inside the car.

"Shit!"

The pharmacy was down the street from their house. Vole jogged home. When he arrived, breathless, he muddied his fingers retrieving the spare house key they kept hidden under a special rock in their back garden. He used it to unlock the side door.

Inside, his senses were immediately soaked in a savory bath of rich beef stew. Bay had prepared it in the slow cooker. The stew was for later, so, in the kitchen, he jammed a soft slice of bread into his mouth to soak up hungry saliva. He put Bay's list and his mother-in-law's prescription into his pocket and grabbed the extra set of car keys from a kitchen drawer.

It was already quarter to four, and he needed to get back to the bank. Dirt under his fingernails from the garden caught his attention. *I can't go to the office with black soil under my nails.* He'd be in violation of their polished dress code.

Vole went to the restroom to apply more deodorant and relieve himself before scrubbing his hands clean. He was stepping out when he heard two familiar young voices.

He opened his mouth to call out—*why was William not with the sitter?*—but something about their creeping tones made him pause. He stayed silent in the hallway and listened.

"See?" came Lawrence's pitchy and all-knowing voice. It rang clear in the tight quarters of the small bungalow. "I told you she'd leave a message. Come on, let's listen."

The drone of a dial tone filled the kitchen. Buttons beeped. The answering machine rang out. *You have one new message,* it said through a thin layer of static. A beep sounded, another button pushed. Vole's stomach tightened when he recognized the voice that rang out.

"This is Principal Waverly calling to speak with William's parents, Vole and Bay Gibbons—"

"Delete it!" Lawrence hissed over the recording.

"No! I mean . . ." William mumbled. "I don't think I should."

The recording continued, "I'm calling to discuss your son. Could you please call me back as soon as you get this? We've recently discovered he's been—"

Foreboding words were cut short by a loud digital beep, followed by a recorded confirmation that the message had been deleted.

"Lawrence!" William exclaimed. "What did you do?!"

"What?" Lawrence's pitchy voice broke. "You can't get in trouble if your parents don't find out. Come on. Let's go to the plaza."

There was a pause and some shuffling; clothing rustled and feet scuffed the laminate floor.

"Okay . . ." William agreed, sounding dubious. "I can't be late, though. Or else I'm seriously dead this time."

"Whatever, man. Take a chill pill. You worry too damned much."

Their voices faded and the door shut. The lock slid back into place, and the boys, oblivious to Vole's presence, went on with their day.

Know your numbers, know your heart.
All there is to it.

Vole stepped out from the dark hallway into the lit kitchen. The lid on the slow cooker rattled as the stew surpassed its previous boil; its smell grew suddenly too rich, making his stomach queasy. He looked over at the phone. It was mounted against the wall above their counter. The dull red plastic lay lifeless where a bright light had previously blinked. He pushed the button.

You have no new messages.

He sat down at the small dining room table, rested his head in his arms, and looked at his watch.

"*Shit.*"

It was after 4:00 p.m. Vole was late for work.

EIGHTEEN

Sunday, June 21, 2015
Calexico, California
5:45 a.m. local; 8:45 a.m. eastern time
360 sleeps since

LIKE MOST PLACES outside of Ontario, Mexico was somewhere Vole had never been. The country was long and thin at the southern tip, shaped like the twister he encountered on the plains of Nebraska, but that was all he knew about the country before he reached its border. Well, he knew Mexicans spoke Spanish, but to him Spanish was a foreign language he knew little about.

Vole was to cross the border at a place called Calexico, into a place called Mexicali. The countries were separated by a metal barrier that loomed red and impenetrable and stretched high into the sky.

"Good grief," he muttered to himself as he stood before the barrier. "It must be at least ten stories!" Passage through was guarded by a long multilane patrol booth and uniformed officers carrying tasers and clubs. "Border crossings," Vole continued. "I hate stinkin' border crossings."

To get to the crossing point, he followed road signs pointing him to the International Border of Calexico-Mexicali. The lanes were wide enough that he could cycle between cars, and in one instance, when he passed over a pair of train rails that followed the border's lateral path, he hopped the curb and balanced carefully on the concrete shoulder, never taking his eye off Bay in the right-side mirror.

The road leading up to the border was twisting and unpredictable. Vole didn't know what to expect from one corner to the next. Around one corner he discovered a restaurant. Beyond the next, another tall metal barricade. Around the next, a multistory shopping center. Until, finally, he rounded a corner and found himself in a paved area full of cars, waiting to cross to Mexicali, arranged in long rows, brake lights lit up like strings of Christmas lights.

He couldn't tell from looking at the faces he passed by whether folks were angry at the temperature or bored by it. It was early in the morning. The day's full heat had yet to mount, but the promise of it threatened.

Hands and elbows poked out windows. A child, head capped in tight curls, had hefted the top half of her body out a car's backseat window, and she was pointing up at something Vole couldn't see.

There was something about cycling past countless full cars that made Vole feel particularly adventurous. Of all the things he'd done, nothing made him feel as criminal and naughty as cutting in front of a long line of people. "You're so Canadian," Bay teased when he described the thrill of cutting lines to her. He didn't know what she meant by it, but Vole laughed along anyway. Her face was fresh and full, like the moon, framed by the jewelled skies of a passing desert night.

The thought of Bay, alive and well, teasing him, left him aching, and he found himself grow impatient in the nascent heat.

Vole turned his attention back to the border crossing. The third booth from the left was empty. The next car was slow to take its turn. Its driver wasn't looking forward; he'd turned his upper body around to look at a child seated behind him in a car seat. Short sausage legs extended straight out, and the child's face was tomato red in silent anger.

"Good luck with that," Vole said to the distraught driver and crept past him to take his spot in line.

A white-and-red striped metal bar blocked his way forward. Vole struggled to lift it with his arms. He resorted to rolling over a garbage bin to use as a prop, and he passed beneath. The entire time he pretended to ignore the officer who stood, arms crossed, nearby. When Vole cycled past her, he didn't look long enough to verify whether she carried a gun.

Weapons frightened him, and he was tired of the hot, underlying tension that filled the air. Already, though it was early in the morning, he knew the sun's warmth would grow difficult for him to bear.

Mexico frightened him in a way the United States didn't, he realized. He tried to deny what he sensed stirring within him, knowing Bay wouldn't approve. *You can't judge what you don't know*, he remembered her saying, a lesson they preached earnestly to William. The air felt foreign in Mexico; it felt charged—not with the electricity of a storm, but with a mysterious human energy, like everyone was in the same pot of boiling water, about to bubble over. Vole didn't think he was imagining it, and found himself looking back at Bay in his mirrors frequently.

They followed the main corridor south as he took them the long way to Hermosillo. Tall, freshly painted buildings gave way to short, worn ones. The roadway became dusty. A heavy pollen began to pepper the air he passed through—*Perhaps*, he thought, *the promise of lush vegetation to come.* Something smelled fragrant and floral and scratched differently at his throat.

The more distance he put between them and the border, the better and less frightened he felt.

"Stinkin' borders," he muttered, taking in the changes to his surroundings with a looser chest.

Vole passed through Hermosillo, a tableau like any other, where ritzy neighborhoods marked by shining buildings and flashy new cars abutted the most decrepit neighborhoods, marked by shabby buildings and beat-up old cars. In both the most luxurious and Spartan of places, Vole was coming to understand, there were people who looked happy and there were people who didn't. With all the world's tensions at standstill, everyone was all the same. Vole cycled out of the city none the wiser.

Sunday, June 21, 2015
San Carlos Nuevo Guaymas, Sonora, Mexico
5:45 a.m. local; 8:45 a.m. eastern time
370 sleeps since

For most of his adult life, Vole discounted the ocean. "What's amazing about a giant salty bath?" he asked Bay whenever the topic of tropical travel came up. "Our lakes are more than enough, honeybee. They're beautiful and as big as any sea. Besides, the fish are smaller and—pardon my French—they shit less. Will won't puke or drown from drinking down a wave, and in fresh water there's little chance something will kill him." Stories about coral and microscopic flesh-eating bacteria frightened him. Bay, not having spent any time exploring the ocean before, didn't have any experience to draw on to help her suggest otherwise, and gradually they stopped talking about it.

Since discovering the ocean, Vole had become enamored of it. Its vastness did something to him. It compelled him to collect fleeting moments in a way he'd never done before. He began sharing his experiences with Bay through rough illustrations instead of with words. Certain scenes wouldn't let him rest until he'd dreamed about them a thousand times over—a seabird with its talon caught in the mouth of a slick silver fish, droplets fanning out in a diamond net; churning white and turquoise waves, hanging on the precipice, threatening to spill over like a tossed drink; and colorless creatures, like polished silica in the sand, safe in muddy slip.

On painfully quiet days, the days he felt especially agitated, Vole would step slowly across the sand. Drag a toe along the surface of a beach-kissing swell. He would wade, a gradual submerging, by parting peels of liquid with his ankles, calves, and thighs, until he was surrounded by cool open water up to his waist. He'd breathe deep the sharp saltiness surrounding him, and every space within him became filled. He would slow his breathing and let his sight stretch into the distance. Then he'd close his eyes. Sink down until nothing of him remained above the surface, and float.

Slowly, bit by bit, he would let go.

Memory faded until it disappeared altogether, and everything transformed. The world became covered by water. He became one more molecule. He let himself be, exactly how he was supposed to be, and nothing more. He became still.

The ocean made Vole want to break one of the rules he lived by. He would stay submerged, hip deep, and follow a sandbar until he spotted a school, an eel, or a starfish in the water, and he would get close. He'd allow his fingers to touch what he'd found. If he was unsure what type of creature he'd come upon—like when he saw a dark shape, long and spotted and with fins—he would simply look. (It was a whale shark, he later discovered, flipping through the pages of *Life in Baja*, a book for tourists hoping to catch a glimpse of Jurassic worlds through oval glass). With others, the more predictable creatures—fish in a pond like any other—he felt it was acceptable to run his fingers along their curving backs and sloping heads. *They won't mind,* he told himself. *They won't know any different.* Latent energy beneath scaled bodies reminded him this wasn't forever; his fears of being trapped were held at bay in exchange for a fleeting touch. It made him feel human and temporary again, so he made the exception and broke his rule.

Vole left the alluring waters and scraggly palms of Sonora behind him. He was looking forward to finding a remote villa, craving a snooze on a plush outdoor couch.

The newly paved road they followed snaked through a small town with a name he couldn't pronounce. On the other side of the town was a river. It drained into the ocean. Vole stopped pedaling and stood on the road-bridge to look out at the riverbank, lush and green. The view reminded him of back home, and he found it to be a comforting sight.

The river disappeared into the distance; its rippled chrome surface merged with the same sky it reflected. On the southern side of the bank, where tall grass grew thickest, Vole's wandering gaze registered a surprising sight.

"Hey!" he cried out in pleasure, filling the quiet skies. "Hey you!"

He ran to the waist-high metal rail and leaned over.

"Look, Bay! Jock!" he shouted. "Over there!"

There, caught in an achingly familiar silhouette—broad wings stretched wide and long necks reaching into the sky—was a flock of Canadian Geese. Vole could almost hear their rude honks and angry hisses inside his mind.

"Why are you so far from home this early in the season?" Vole asked, not bothering to wipe trailing moisture from his cheeks; he counted twenty-seven black-and-brown round bodies through tearful eyes. "Never mind me. I'm passing through. You birds had it right the whole time."

NINETEEN

Sunday, June 21, 2015
A road in Mexico, Mexico
5:45 a.m. local; 8:45 a.m. eastern time
372 sleeps since

> Dear Bay,
>   If a man exists, but no one is around to verify his heart still beats, is he truly alive?
>   Remind me to ask Will, one day. I'd like to hear what he has to say. I've come to believe a life where no one spares you a thought is a lifeless one, not that it applies to me in this alternate state. But, the trouble is, the longer I go in this state, the more people become like ghosts. In the end we're all just memories, haunts of the mind, one way or another.
>   I question every body and thing I encounter, except for you and Jocko. You two have been with me from the start, and I think you're the only reason why I still think I'm alive.

I'm tired. On some days writing is more difficult to do than on others. In that, it's exactly like cycling.

Imagine if I were an extrovert, like your father? Good grief.

Until tomorrow,
Vole

Sunday, June 21, 2015
Guerrero Province
7:45 a.m. local; 8:45 a.m. eastern time
531 sleeps since

A man, frowning and slouched, was seated on a plastic crate outside his cinder block home. The crate bowed beneath his weight. Wooden shutters hung askew over a window cut in the shape of a square. The shutters looked well-used, as though they'd survived a fire, perhaps a hurricane, maybe both, prior to being installed there. A dog with piano key ribs lay curled on the dirt, half a meter from the man's flexed seat. A train of black flies rested along the beast's spine. Its fur was the same color as the dust he lay on, and from between his legs spilled the largest set of testicles Vole had ever seen.

The frown dominating the man's entire being wasn't aimed at the dog, or the dog's generous endowment. It was aimed across the packed dirt road to where a neighbor, Vole presumed, was setting pots outside to dry in the sun.

The neighbor was wearing a yellow-and-black patterned shirt and a vibrant skirt. She was ignoring the man who scowled darkly at her from the other side of the road.

For the first time, Vole found himself missing Harold.

The moment stuck with him, and he made sure to tell Bay about it that evening. He told her about the dog ("Imagine if we'd let Jocko's grow so big; he'd be a quintaped!"), and about the man who frowned furiously at the woman who lived across the dirt road. "It's not healthy to harbor such resentment," he told her, thinking Harold may have discovered his upside-down garage by then. "There's too much in life to let yourself get stuck in a moment of anger or jealousy. Not that I have to tell you. You're quicker to the core than me."

He stopped talking and instead wrote to her about what he found when he ventured on foot to a nearby town.

The town was a modest one. More like a village. It was no more than a handful of concrete huts with shadow-block windows, and it wasn't far from where he'd left Bay. Which was a good thing, because he had no choice but to walk there. Vole had broken his bike. His front wheel had gotten caught in a narrow divot in the road and bent as a result. It was nothing short of a miracle Vole discovered a new wheel in the village he'd come to, and that, too, was being generous; the rim was already pitting, some of the spokes were already broken, and the wheel's rubber surface appeared cracked like a peppercorn.

When he found the wheel, it was alone. There was no rusty frame or scattered parts nearby to suggest it once belonged to a whole bicycle; and there was no one around looking to claim ownership of the orphaned tire. He found it, and only it, leaning against the side of a peach-painted building, and the building itself was empty.

Long past the point of dwelling on the fortunes of his finds, Vole instead considered the excessive loneliness of the place. *Where has everyone disappeared to?* he wondered as he passed between buildings; he hadn't seen a single still soul in days.

On his way back to Bay, Vole stumbled on the path—a narrow strip of dirt following the rise of a steep mound to his right.

The path was marked by a dark wedge of shadow, a dark doorway into a grass sea, tall and bone-dry. His feet led him to it, because, for the first time since leaving home, he felt bored.

Vole walked the shadowy path as it snaked up the hill; surrounded by tall dry blades, he felt steeped in warm grassy odors. He climbed and climbed until he came to an abrupt stop. The soil strip he'd been following ended, and in front of him rose a wall of grass with no way through. He could tell he was close to the summit, and it annoyed him to be stopped short.

Dissatisfied, Vole parted the wall of grass with his arms and stepped forward. He couldn't say what drove him to continue, only he felt driven to do it. As he came within arm's reach of the summit, the grass changed. It grew less dense and more feathery. A clearing emerged beyond the final fringe.

He stepped into it.

In the center of the clearing stood the remains of an ancient building. A church, Vole knew, because he'd seen churches like it before. The church had fallen mostly to ruin. Only the front façade remained intact. Walls behind it were crumbling to the ground. Pious worshippers, for one reason or another, must have discarded the place. Now nature was eagerly reclaiming what was left as its own, and it was nature, not piety, that spirited Vole's breath away.

A piercing light, hot enough to make his mouth dry, shone through the chipped stone doorway. *What lies beyond?* Vole wondered. The light was bright and pure. He believed, for an instant, he'd found the sun.

Vole stepped through the doorway with reverence; the light's intensity never dissipated or became less vibrant. Glow filled his vision. He stepped forward and back through the light, over and over, moving his face against rays, vivid and invisible.

He held his hands high and watched as they became absorbed and disappeared. He couldn't stand in the light for long because it throbbed with heat, or the memory of it, anyway. He took breaks and came back to the doorway when he felt ready.

Before long, Vole found himself nude, swaying his hips back and forth through the light, delighting in how it cleansed everywhere on his body it touched.

Vole never did find out what made the light inside the church. He didn't want to ruin the mystery of the moment by learning it was something mundane, like a shattered mirror or broken pane of glass caught in reflection as the sun's angle struck it. Vole wanted to preserve the magic of it, and maybe allow himself to believe such experiences happened for a reason. If he could believe that, he could believe all the discomfort and pain he was putting his body through, all the years of seeing Bay but not hearing her voice or being able to touch her as he wanted, were happening because they were meant to happen.

It was the first experience Vole couldn't make himself write about. Instead, he wrote to Bay about the abandoned tire in the abandoned town near the abandoned church, and he hoped her open eyes weren't watching his collusion to withhold the truth.

He learned that day not all experiences can be shared. Not because they seemed too private or holy, but because being present when they occurred was the only way they could be known.

It didn't take long to repair his bike (he'd replaced his tire and inner tubes multiple times since leaving Dorset, and was familiar with the motions). The wheel was small and would wear quickly. He would replace it with a proper size and do a proper tune-up at the next proper town. Vole promised Bay, who continued to watch all his movements, it would be the last tire he twisted from negligence.

Sunday, June 21, 2015
Darién Gap, Panama
7:45 a.m. local; 8:45 a.m. eastern time
1,364 sleeps since

Central America was a land meant to be frozen in time. There was so much going on, so much nuance to take in. Without being stopped still it was impossible to absorb it all. Yet, nothing absorbed Vole more than the range of hues he saw in the open sky.

At first, Vole thought it was a pretty cloud in the distance. As he got closer, he realized he was looking at a rainbow coated in mist, and not a cloud at all. After that, the colorful arch never dissipated. It expanded. It grew to encompass everything around him. Vole thought at some point he would pass through it, or under it, and it would disappear into the tableau, but the psychedelic sky followed him wherever he went.

Colorful haze infused the air he breathed; the air became as potent and intoxicating as the full-bodied richness it contained. It painted his skin with shimmering sweat. He hadn't ever heard of pink, opalescent and rich, that could fill a thousand kilometers of sky; but he assumed it had to do with light refracting off droplets in the humid air, or something sensible like that.

Green, blue, yellow, orange; orange, yellow, green, blue, violet. Red.

Threads, scintillating, wrapped rainbows round his head, snuck inside his brain and lay siege to his thoughts.

Sense twisted and split like hairs. The dark corners those splintered thoughts took him to frightened and confused him, but he kept thinking; he didn't want to stop thinking; he couldn't stop thinking. His mind swung, thought to thought, like a pendulum; and in tight circles, a spinning wheel, threads spooling and unspooling.

Gradually, Vole lost sight of his ability to think nothing of everything, which had been his last remaining crutch. To be clear, it wasn't that Vole abandoned all reason; it was reason that drifted slowly away from him.

What if Bay were to get injured? Would she see it coming? Know who was to blame?

What color were the leaves he passed by? Green or yellow or blue?

What was it like for all those people who were caught for eternity in their final throes—their last moment alive; their first moment in death—while he cycled the world's nations for love? Or was it for pride?

What went on in the shaded space between colors; didn't they bleed too?

What would happen if he were to commit murder? Bear witness to murder? Take his own life?

Would any of it be possible to do?

There was only one way to find out.

And how was Bay's skin supposed to look? What was natural? Was she naturally such a chameleon?

He didn't know any of it. He couldn't think straight. Everything was jumbled, a kaleidoscope on its side, turned over and over. At times, the only thing he remembered was the yellow sun, because only it didn't shine green; but then, it too began to shine with what he imagined to be a toxic hue.

Vole's mind didn't halt its endless spiral until, soaked in the salty sum of his confusion, he stopped pedaling and stood in front of a metal fence more forbidding than any border crossing. Sweat dribbled down into his eyes. The way forward was guarded by men wearing black military uniforms and hats with short brims pulled down over their faces. They wore machine guns draped over their shoulders as casually as Bay once draped a purse over hers.

"What is this?" Vole whispered.

The spectrum of voices inside him stayed stubbornly silent.

The road he was following through Panama led him to a park, the Darién Gap. Vole expected to pass through. Seeing the impassable border in front of him and what lay on the other side—tangled black jungle and no way through—he realized he'd made a terrible mistake.

"Bay," he wheezed, staring deep into her eyes in his bicycle's right-side mirror. When did she remove her sunglasses? *Honey brown*, he thought to himself. *Her eyes are golden brown like honey; skin buttery and soft like cream.* "My honeybee," he croaked, not recognizing his own voice.

If only she would blink.

Vole stumbled and threw back his head. Shouted Bay's name up into the sky, desperate for anything, even one of the machine guns, to answer back.

When no answer came, his shoulders slumped, and he crumpled to the ground beside his bicycle.

Eyes closed.

Kaleidoscope eyes are my kaleidoscope skies—it was his last fragmented thought before all the colors around him converged into one final color, black, and the encroaching darkness absorbed him.

Vole fell into a silent, heavy slumber.

When he woke the next day—or was it the following week? he couldn't tell—Vole immediately sensed something was different than before.

Something fixed had *moved*.

TWENTY

April 1998 (continued)

"—AND WHAT DID I say about going to the plaza with Lawrence?" Bay demanded. William, red and shamefaced, mumbled he was sorry, and he shouldn't have gone because he wasn't allowed to.

"That's not what I said," Bay retorted. "I mean, *yes*, I did say so—because you're not allowed to go anywhere right now, much less leave the sitter's early—but *before*, I said, 'You need to ask permission to go to the plaza with your friends!'" William's hunch became more pronounced. "We want to trust you," she continued, "but you're making it difficult right now. We don't like you being at the plaza after school when the older kids are outside smoking. I especially don't like it when Mrs. Chatham calls to tell me my son is ruining public property with his skateboard, like we'd raised some sort of inconsiderate, idiotic hooligan!"

"I'm sorry," William mumbled. His puffy cheeks were streaked with tears. "Can I go now?" He sniffed. "Please?"

Bay exhaled, loudly.

"Yes, but—Don't do it again. We need to know we can trust you. Do you understand?"

William nodded, then scuttled down to the basement where they kept their family computer, the Intel Pentium Processor.

When Vole arrived home from work, late, due to his earlier mishap with the car keys, Bay was already there with William. He walked in on their dramatic exchange but didn't want to interrupt.

"He's allowed back on the computer?" Vole asked once the scene was done, surprised Bay hadn't disallowed their son from going downstairs. They regarded the computer as a critical investment into William's future, but William only wanted the machine to play games. "Since when?"

"I should've discussed it with you first," she admitted, resigned. "But I didn't know what else to do. I thought maybe I came down too hard yesterday when I picked him up from school, and he was suffering because of it? I'm not sure. He's acting strange. I think he's starting to have mood swings. He's at that age . . .

"When I told him Mrs. Chatham called, he began bawling his eyes out. I hadn't gotten to the point where he was in trouble before he started crying. I thought some time on the computer might cheer him up." She paused and looked thoughtful. "Did he say anything to you when you talked last night? Or afterward?"

Vole steeled himself to deliver the disappointing news about their son, but from his cavernous belly came a lion's roar.

"Hungry?" Bay asked before he could say anything. She lifted the lid off the simmering beef stew to add more broth. Predictably, Vole's mouth filled with saliva. Somehow, the stew smelled more delicious than before. "Dinner will be ready soon," she said. "It's going to be good. This has been on all day."

"I know," Vole said as he moved to join her in the kitchen where the tantalizing smell was strongest. "I came by the house this afternoon to pick up your mom's prescription because I left it on the counter—No, it's okay," he cut off her sympathetic murmurs. "It wasn't a hassle. It was my own stupid mistake." He cleared his throat. "Speaking of stupid mistakes, Bay . . ."

Vole prepared to launch into his unhappy story about locking his keys in the car, which forced him to use their spare key from the garden, which put him in the position to overhear their son being dishonest, when William poked his head around the doorway.

"How long till dinner?" the boy chirped.

"You've got thirty minutes," Bay said.

"After that your butt's up here, helping to set the table!" Vole added, though he could tell Bay was relieved William didn't seem scared of them anymore.

William vanished back downstairs.

"What about mistakes?" Bay asked. "I was thinking I'd get washed up before dinner. Do you mind?"

"Go bathe, smelly wench! But not before I get a proper *hello*."

Vole wrapped her in his arms and hugged tight. Kissed her on the cheek. Maybe he would talk to William while Bay was washing up. With her mother's rapidly deteriorating health, she had enough on her plate.

Vole didn't talk to William while Bay was washing up. Despite the earlier turmoil, both Bay and William were in relaxed, happy moods. Why weigh down a light evening with heavy conversation? Vole decided to wait and discuss it with Bay after dinner.

He didn't bring it up after dinner either. Long after William went to bed, Vole didn't tell Bay what happened.

The next day went smoothly. William went to a different sitter's house for the second day of his three-day suspension, and Vole didn't leave anything important on the counter. Everything fell back to normal. The answering machine incident passed to distant memory, and soon Vole barely remembered he'd witnessed anything ugly in the first place.

Until, that is, Principal Waverly called again and left another voicemail.

When William and Vole were both home that evening, Bay gathered them together. Not uttering a single word, she played the recording for them to listen to.

Seconds in, Vole noticed his son's face lose all its blood and turn paper white. *It probably matches mine,* he thought as his own jaw clenched in distress.

"This is Principal Waverly calling," the serious I-really-mean-business-this-time voice rang out. "I need to speak with William's parents. Again. He's escalating. He's been caught helping other students cheat on their homework assignments. We need to discuss consequences."

When the recording was over, Bay hung up the receiver. She stared at the top of William's head, which hung to his chest. No one said a word.

Then, "I didn't cheat," William whispered into the quiet. "I was *helping*."

Vole ran his hands down his thighs and back up again and stood.

"Go to your room," he ordered, "and stay there. Your mother and I need to talk."

"But," William protested. "I didn't—"

"*Now*, William!" Bay commanded.

The boy gave a loud sniff and slid down from his chair. He trudged to his bedroom and shut the door behind him with stubborn force.

Bay took Vole's hand in hers. Confusion spread across her hurt face.

"What do we do?" she asked in a low voice. "I'm in shock. I don't want to believe it. He's a cheater. If he does this sort of thing in high school . . . He can't! Plagiarism is a serious offense. He has to go to university. We can't let him get away with it. This is important, Vole. This is his *future*."

"I know, honeybee."

Something about the tone of his voice made her jerk away from him and stare hard.

"What do you mean, *you know*?" she demanded, eyes narrow. "Why aren't you surprised by this?"

"I-I guess I knew something was up. I mean, he's a sensitive kid. I can tell when something's up with him.

"We're getting ahead of ourselves. We don't know what happened yet. We should find out what he did, from him, before speaking with the school."

"Hmm."

"Maybe he didn't do anything too bad."

Since William's dishonesty came to light, it shamed Vole to realize he conspired to keep it in the dark. His parents taught him better; the least he could do was try and do the same for his son. For Bay. They both deserved better from him.

"Will you talk to him?" Bay asked, softening. "I think I'm too upset right now. I'm worried I could say something . . . bad."

Vole turned to go meet William.

"Hold on," she said, grabbing hold of his arm. "Wait." She took a deep breath. "If I can't face this head on, what good am

I? We're partners. It's important we do the big important things together. Present a strong, unified front. I'm coming with you."

"Of course."

It was a hollow victory for them both.

TWENTY-ONE

Sunday, June 21, 2015
Gulf of Panama
7:45 a.m. local; 8:45 a.m. eastern time
1,496 sleeps since[1]

>   *Dear Bay,*
>   *You shouldn't spare a single thought for the pages I tore from this book. We're both much better off without them.*
>   *Now, and I don't want to be one to point fingers or anything, but you should know my extended silence is all Jock's fault. That's right, you should blame the dog.*
>   *See, as I took you and Jock away from the tangled boundary, I whispered to him, Do you notice what I notice? And his eyes, still sparkling from having smelled things no small-town beast is born intended to smell, sparked. A single stoic*

---

1   Vole's best guess was that he'd spent 132 nights in Panama, most of which went unaccounted for in his memories.

flash was all it took; he confirmed what I already knew deep in my heart was right.

We were being followed.

With fingers like icicles and a fluttering pulse, I took roads into the jungle. We went to the places where trees grow on top of trees. I was trying to throw our stalker off our scent. Who, I wondered. I obsessed. Who could this unwelcome shadow be?

Every time I thought I'd taken a route tangled enough to confuse the hunter, I'd sense a presence. Catch a glimpse. Every time I looked at the dog, his eyes shone. I saw it too, they seemed to say. Don't you worry about her. I'm ready. I'll be ready.

I had to protect you. I became the hunter. I tracked our shadow like a hound tracks a hare. I found myself on my hands and knees, pinching at something soft and mottled I'd found beneath a log. Someone other than me walked there before the log fell, the tracks told me. Who had it been? When were the tracks laid? Why hadn't I found who'd laid them yet?

A shadow slithered by. Alerted, my eyes flicked, and I saw the figure, our shadow, with clarity. His head cocked to the side. He was watching us.

I shrieked and he vanished. I pedaled the roads around Panama once, twice, and for a third time, seeking the sneak's lair. (As I write this, my chest heaves. I'm ashamed to admit to doing violating, unspeakable things during this time. I'm sorry, honeybee, but no one's private spaces remained unturned. I broke every rule of conduct I'd diligently lived by in my search for what I believed to be a young boy, no older than six or seven, with a terrible visage—featureless, except for two smoking pits where his young eyes once were.)

Something slippery in the vines reached out to catch me. What is it, I asked Jock, eyeing up the shadows. Do you think it's him?

I gave you stern instructions not to move, and I left Molly in the road. I carried with me, in the bag clipped about my waist, a small cosmetics mirror. I used it to watch you with my back turned.

As soon as I stepped away from you, an orchestra of snares let loose inside my chest. I thought I might explode! But I continued. I had to.

I parted dense greenery that lay beyond the roadside and ventured into the forest beyond. A swarm of thirsty flies appeared in the air in front of me. I swatted them down and out of my way. A flower stem stood tall like a tree and blocked my path; its unique tone and shape made me pause. The color and texture of the bloom was like sun-kissed flesh. It was round, bloated—a toad's throat. I pushed the flower aside, too, and found myself stepping into a new, hot smell. It was cloying and rank (my eyes tear at the memory).

Death's breath—it couldn't have been anything else— stunk of rot and gore, and it filled my nose, my head, and I gagged. I spat. I wiped my eyes, and I looked up.

Two round yellow marbles shone back, framing a gaze as unforgiving as the sun. Fear, visceral and stark, glued my throat shut, and my fingers and toes curled. Go, my every cell screamed. Go from here. Go to her. Go, go, go!

But I didn't go.
I couldn't.
My joints seized, my muscles locked. I was hypnotized by the deep and absorbing stare of a fearsome predator, one whose caustic breath was more stunning than the scorpion I stepped on in Arizona; and whose demeanor was more terrible than the cougar I faced in Nebraska.

Spinning and dizzy and locked in one place, I stared into the beast's eyes, clear and all-seeing, trained on my every move, and a reflection formed. In its bottomless mirror, I saw a face. This is what I've been chasing—the thought floated in, sounded out like a gong, reverberated; a maze fortress, unseen and unwelcome inside me, crumbled in a single instant.

Clarity, at long last, was mine again.

Here he was, the foul-breathed culprit, the ghost who haunted me. My reflection, still visible in the ochre sheen of the jaguar's smoldering orbs, blinked, and I was set free.

It took a real monster, real fear, to break open my imaginary prison, or so I surmised. What other conclusion could I have come to? I'm only a beast: human and fallible.

The jaguar lolled on a thick branch above my head. Back in control of my limbs, I touched it to verify. Yes, unmoving and quiet, queer; but flesh and blood, like me, like you, like Jocko. Its mouth hung open in unsung laughter, sinister, as though it derived pleasure from how deep and single-minded my predicament ran. A thick drop of saliva dangled from its jaw. The force of my exhalation made it tremble and drop slowly to the ground.

I backed away. Returned to you. Touched your hair, breathed you in, looked into your eyes.

Your gaze smoldered too, but with a different heat. One I needed and craved, but had strayed far from knowing. Your eyes, fixed on something distant and invisible to me, told me what I already knew—I needed to get out from beneath the rainbow sky.

I rode to the coast where I prepared for my first water crossing (ladled water from an open cistern into my rain barrels, restocked my supply of dried fruit and cured pork, tightened loose bolts on my bicycle and the boat trailer, realigned my wheels, inflated my tires, the list continues), where I find myself now, writing to you from the sea for the first time, sitting next to you in Molly.

Because the border between Colombia and Panama is impenetrable, I'm pedaling us across Panama Bay toward the gulf, where I will follow the coastline until I reach Ecuador.

To have those sticky webs lifted!

Panama was . . .

It was suffocating me. It held unparalleled beauty in every speck of delicious detail. The soil bled with life. It was too much to take in. It was all too much.

Seeing you next to me, your eyes pointed forward and a pixie smile dusting your lips, is exactly what I need. Simplicity. I can almost fool myself into believing we're vacationing up north. Soon we'll see loons settle on the water in front of *us. Jocko's here, as of course he would be on our vacation.*

I know we're far from home. Our lake is much calmer than the water here, and everything smells of brine and blooms. Back home, up north, everything smells like rainfall, fresh spruce, and soil. I miss it. I miss you.

Traveling across water is different than on land. Here, on the water, a cold beer in hand—yes, you read my words right—I can lean back in my seat. Stretch my shoulders and neck. When I pause and stop rotating my knees, I don't need to worry about tipping over or being taken away on a current. Ah, another thing. There aren't any currents pushing me in one direction or another; only soft surface peaks caught in memory of the direction they were pulling. I glide across the surface, leaving a breadcrumb trail of split splashes in my wake. The water provides less resistance than the roads we've been taking. It's like nothing else, and I find words fail me.

I warned you once before I was distilling into a poet. I worry by the time I see you, only the essence of me will be left—I'm joking. I'm tired of haunting myself. Perception plays tricks on me. I'll let be.

Until tomorrow,
Vole

Vole knew he lost time. Most of what had happened he couldn't recall, and the rest he was too embarrassed to mention.

The pages he'd removed from his book were stained with smudges of mud and blood. They contained broken words, shards of words, sliced phrases with hints of bleakness that would never again leave him completely alone. He knew he must have left all those marks on all those pages because he recognized his lopsided script, and every letter began the same way, *Dear Bay*, but the memory of it all was gone.

There was no point in telling her about the scratches and infections that had formed on his arms and legs, gained, no doubt, from tearing into festering logs and ignoring the soft rotting creatures within.

When his consciousness emerged from lunacy, befuddled and disbelieving, he'd been shocked to see the swollen, turned-out edges of his wounds. He raced to find liquids and creams to cleanse them. When he lanced the worst of his putrid cuts—taut skin, puckered and pink, stretched across his shin—a scent emerged, eggy and sweet, like baked meringues. It made him gag and spit bile.

Eating had become a strange affair and hindrance during that time. He'd become thin as a result; his body was barely his own. When he caught sight of himself in the drug store's mirrors, he stopped and stared, fascinated and appalled. Matting, thick with dirt and moss, clung to his scalp and face, and he realized it was his hair and beard. Sharp bones jutted out on either side of his hips, and his limbs resembled saplings. Somehow, he'd chipped the tip off his left incisor. He was grateful not to have lost any teeth.

"No, you don't need to know, honeybee," Vole muttered, and slid his tongue over the sharp edge of his broken tooth. He reveled in the smooth, clean feel of it. When he first came to, his mouth was coated in a layer of fuzz as padded as the undergrowth he'd been sleeping on.

Vole stopped pedaling the boat as he remembered putting something hard and brown into his mouth. He'd bit down viciously; a flash of recalled pain made him shiver.

He recalled suddenly something else flickering and quick.

Go from here, he remembered feeling compelled when he encountered the feral cat.

Go to her.

Go—the impulse had come over him with such strength he'd included it in his letter to Bay. But, excluded from his written account, because he was only recalling it now, another swift thing happened immediately after.

Vole's tongue turned to ash at the new recollection.

Was the sensation of the world lurching into motion, the moment after he thought *Go* with such force, something imagined? Had he, in a brief and broken instant, done the unthinkable, and provoked time into motion for a split second?

Go, he'd thought. *Bring her near and back to life.*

Vole shook his head to clear away the webs. His stomach felt like a boulder. It was terrible to think about, but he couldn't remember what happened. Not clearly. Madness was murky. Recalling what went on was like looking up at the sky from the bottom of a pond coated in scum. Darkened water and ripples obfuscated everything above.

No matter how hard Vole wrung his horrified memories for more, accuracy and detail evaded him, and he couldn't tell if the shine in Bay's eyes was a shade darker than it had been before his descent. Perhaps her eyes were unchanged and they were always so wide and open.

Or was it as he feared, and had his life flashed before her eyes? What had she been looking at? What did Bay see?

"Selfish, foolish, man."

His arms were covered with goose pimples; Vole rubbed warmth into them and sat back down. When he didn't know himself, talking out loud was thoughtless and easy. Since regaining lucidity, he felt like he was addressing a stranger.

"What's wrong with you?"

What shamed him most was how close he'd come to the brink. What would have happened to Bay and Jock if he never came back? Or went too far? Unlike Bay, he was getting old; and he was alone in a world that had its dangers. What would have become of them?

He turned to Jocko.

"I'm sorry for pinning the blame on you, little wolf. I'll, um, try and make it up to you with a tasty treat next time. Speaking of next time, I should tell you, I'm not looking to you for guidance anymore. From now on, there'll be no more second-guessing. It is what it is, and that's all there is too it.

"No point in overthinking things."

The entire time leading up to his first water crossing, Vole worried about it, though he tried not to. He tried to keep the thought of it tucked away, locked deep in the furthest reaches of his mind. He was fearful of what those worries, dark and bottomless like the ocean itself, might do to him.

The problem was the trailer. It was too heavy and awkward to tow behind him in *Molly*, and it was too cumbersome to mount on top of the boat's canopy. He worried his muscles, especially in their emaciated state, would fail him. Experience showed that while time was stopped, rust didn't form. He wasn't worried about the frame weakening from corrosion. He was worried about lifting bulky metal out of water, and about Bay's body getting dunked in the cool gulf.

Seeing no way around it, Vole did the simplest thing he could think of: he changed as little as possible. He made sure *Molly* was securely fastened to the trailer, that the boat's rudder and rudder rod column remained unencumbered, and detached his bicycle from the hitch. After removing the hitch arm (so it didn't stick out from the trailer like a two-prong proboscis), he mounted his bicycle to the back of the boat, making sure it was raised above the water line. He secured plastic floats to either side of *Molly* for added buoyancy and surface area.

When he was ready to disembark, he rolled the trailer, *Molly* attached to its top, into the water, and began to pedal. Progress was slow. Every time Vole inched up the surface of a swell and back down it on the other side, he worried they might fall over headfirst, or *Molly*'s tall and heavy form might tip on its side, or his bicycle might topple off, or the fastenings he used to secure the trailer to the boat would snap.

For all its dangers, the ocean was a safe place. There were no storms he needed to pass through. No waves too tall to surmount. He didn't need to consider his bicycle tire popping, or think about his chain getting caught. Space between boats was wide enough that he could navigate between. Seabirds, motionless, were easy to avoid and duck under. His bicycle almost tipped backward when he pedaled alongside the crest of a wave to avoid its severe drop; but he managed to correct the boat's angle in time, refasten the loosened strap, and continue on his way.

Sunday, June 21, 2015
Illescas Peninsula, Peru
7:45 a.m. local; 8:45 a.m. eastern time
1,680 sleeps since

Vole never made it to Ecuador. When he landed on the shores of Peru, he didn't know he was so far south. South, in his mind, was where heat grew. In truth, the deep south, south of the equator, was where heat vanished. Perhaps the cool air is what seduced him into taking Bay farther south than he'd originally intended. Respite from heat was difficult for him to abandon, and the farther from the equator he got, the more refreshed he felt.

Everything changed when he reached the desert. The Atacama had a lot in common with the sand hills in Nebraska, the Mojave Desert in Nevada, and the Sonoran Desert in Mexico. Flat land with little change between monumental mounds of dirt; endless, ever-hazy skies; and air infused with rippling heat. There were distinct differences too. The sand hills were covered in yellow-green fields; the Sonoran Desert was a sea of dunes with grass clumps scattered; the Mojave Desert was empty; and the Atacama Desert was barren.

Still, Vole was more at ease in desolation than he was in cities or dense forests. If anyone asked before he left, he would have predicted deserts as being most difficult to cross. He would've been wrong. Subsistence, it turns out, wasn't the hardest part of survival in the world he'd come to know. Hardest was not being able to see the road ahead, and getting caught up in all the complication people introduced to a landscape. He abhorred intimacy interrupted more than he hated anger and violence. He could never be sure of what he'd stumbled into.

But there was nothing harder, nothing more taxing on his spirit, than feeling eyes fall on him from every corner of the world; in those moments it was a matter of time before he convinced himself that someone, somewhere, was observing him. What then? His was a simple mission. Vole didn't think he could survive having to account for anyone else.

The Atacama was the driest desert in all the world. The lowliest microbes struggled to survive there. The books he looked at (since leaving Central America, Vole never once passed a book shop without stopping) showed him photographs of sun-bleached animal skulls strewn across plates of burnished dirt; dirt from a planet closer to the sun than Earth.

Being close to the sun was exactly the reason for the Atacama's extreme aridity (he learned from one of his books), but Vole found no solace from the fact as he crossed it, cycling slowly for a short time, until forced to seek protection. Despite the air temperature being moderate, without shade or a sweeping breeze, his body turned into a brazier beneath the sun's unrelenting watch.

The road he followed turned prehistoric and parched. The ground was packed. It felt like stone beneath his wheels, and chunks of dry earth were hard like boulders. Vole tightened fastenings frequently; he worried about the impact such a tooth-rattling surface might be having on Bay's moth-eaten bones.

When his legs refused to turn in one more circle, he gave in and broke another rule. He found salvation inside a Daewoo station wagon, the likes of which he'd never seen in North America. He opened the back passenger-side door. Cool air inside made him swoon. It was one of those moments when he questioned whether having rules in the first place was such a good idea.

Sunday, June 21, 2015
San Carlos de Bariloche, Río Negro, Argentina
9:45 a.m. local; 8:45 a.m. eastern time
2,282 sleeps since

The baked mud abated as Vole turned inland and continued south. As he traced the curving spine of the Andes, green returned to the land and the temperature dropped. It reached ten degrees centigrade and crept lower the farther south he got. Though that was the case, no matter how frequently he checked, Bay's skin never cooled and Jock's nose never dried. He developed a nagging cough. Vole had grown used to filling his lungs with hot air. Making the adjustment to cold weakened them. Despite this, he was grateful for the change. He grew up accustomed to every month bringing a different climate, and the unrelenting heat had begun to wear him down long ago.

An ice-cold prick on Vole's cheek jolted him out of his thoughts about back home. Did he imagine it?

No, he couldn't have because—there it was again!

He stopped cycling and walked cautiously forward with his fingers spread in front of him. When Vole was sure of what he'd found, he picked up speed and began to run.

He soon found himself grinning, leaping through a flurry of snow. A dusty habit formed in another life, he stuck out his tongue and lifted his face to the sky.

Bursting with laughter, he spun in circles. Looked up at all the snowflakes frozen in the air above his head. Became mesmerized by their frozen dance. *This must be what it's like out there*, he thought, imagining the snowflakes were stars suspended in the sky beyond Earth's atmosphere. He remembered Bay's wonder at seeing the Milky Way, and his eyes overflowed, tears showered and flashed like comets, and he let himself remember how much he missed her.

He stopped spinning.

In front of his nose was a single fat white snowflake. The longer he stared, the more he was convinced: the snowflake held as much detail in it as the world around him did.

Vole let go of the breath he didn't realize he'd been holding and immediately regretted his decision as the snowflake in front of him disappeared along with its neighboring brothers and sisters. A hole, a deep negative space, appeared where his hot breath touched the delicate flecks of ice.

He turned around and looked back the way he came. In the galaxy of snow behind him, like a tunnel dug through a bank of snow, he could see the twisted path he took to get to the middle of the flurry.

Inspired, Vole stuck his arms out on either side and began to spin them round and round. He turned to face the direction they were headed and ran, spinning his arms in wide circles. Vole ran from one end of the mini blizzard to the other and back. Snowflakes melted at his touch. Rivulets formed on his face; drops flew from his chin. Vole kept at it until he'd tunneled a way through the snowfall.

He took his time leading Bay through. Imagined her gasps of delight behind him and let himself believe he felt the warmth of her beaming smile as her open eyes glistened and took in the splendor of their winter wonderland.

"It's like when we met, honeybee," he said, then whispered, "*Soon*," as he continued down his path to Tierra del Fuego, the land at the end of the world. "It won't be long, now. We'll be back together soon."

TWENTY-TWO

May 2001

"THERE SHOULD BE a school for parents," Vole complained as he turned the car toward the driver examination center. "One with exams and trials. If you pass, you're allowed to have a kid. If you fail, you've got to redo it, or hand yourself over to the government for sterilization. It could be a provincial thing."

Bay looked up from the book she was reading in the front passenger seat.

"Not only is that a disgusting proposition," she said, "but it's also impractical."

"Oh?"

"Think about our birthrate. It would plummet. Besides, we could never afford the taxes required to run a program like that, and it would have to be a federally funded program because the other provinces wouldn't go for it otherwise." She paused a moment to think. "Also, insurance would cost a fortune. Regretted sterilizations would happen all the time. It would be a mess."

"I don't know about that, honeybee," Vole countered. "If you add up how much it costs to fix all the bent signs, broken windows, and knocked-over trees caused by mismanaged kids—not to mention court appointments and all those expensive legal fees—it would probably add up to less. I bet we'd see massive tax savings. In fact, this might be what Canada needs! Obligatory parenting school and voluntary sterilization."

"You're sick," she accused. Vole looked over to check that Bay was still smiling. She was the only one he could joke about such things to.

"Will's going to be a great driver," she told him, sensing which worry his insensitive and unorthodox suggestion had sprung from. "He'll be driving laps around you in no time."

"Not literally, I hope."

"God no, not literally."

She went back to reading her book.

Normally, Vole was the relaxed one in such circumstances. This time was different. There was a lot to consider. Driving was an important life skill. They'd bought a brand-new car. Up to this point, they'd been a single-car household with two drivers. When William turned sixteen, that number bumped up to three; and Vole's slow-growth career at the bank seemed to be taking a turn. It was time for a change.

Vole and Bay had already discussed their plan with William. Their son would practice driving using their old Mercury, and when he passed his driver's exam, the Mercury would be his. The new Infiniti was off limits. Totally okay, he assured them, because he'd have his own car! It was by far the most generous gift they'd ever given their son (aside from the savings account they'd set up to pay for his university education, but they regarded those as obligatory measures this day and age). They were as excited to be giving the car to him as he was to receive it. All William needed was to pass his test and not get into any trouble, and the car was his.

The Gibbons promised William that once he obtained his learner's permit, they would take him on his first lesson. At first, Bay wanted to be the one in the driver's seat, but Vole insisted that would be an affront to the age-old, father-son institution of taming horsepower. She rolled her eyes and called him a sexist, but relented, probably because it gave her time to read her book.

The Gibbons waited in a parking spot outside the glass window of the examination center until William came outside.

"Uh-oh," Vole said, alerting Bay. "It doesn't look good."

William's shoulders were slumped.

"Oh dear," Bay said.

William loped over to their car and pulled open the back door. He didn't say anything or look at either of his parents as he buckled himself in.

"So," Vole began, eyeing his son in the rearview mirror, trying to catch his gaze. "How'd it go?"

William mumbled something and looked out his window.

"You can write it again next week," Bay said. "There's no limit to the number of times you can try."

William lifted his head and caught Vole's eye in the mirror's reflection.

"Now why would I do that," he asked, a slow smile spreading across his face, "when I PASSED?!"

He began to hoot and shake Bay's chair from the backseat. Both his parents laughed, not entirely happy at having been fooled by their son. "You two are so *gullible*," he continued, laughing and flapping around his temporary paper license. "I can't believe you'd think I failed!"

"*Har-har*," Bay said to quiet him down, though Vole could tell she was relieved. "Congratulations, kid. You're well on your way to having a full set of adult responsibilities."

"Do you know what that means?" Vole asked.

"Dad!" William complained. "Do you have to make everything so serious? Don't be glum, chum."

They drove to the nearby coffee shop.

"We'll be back in an hour," Vole said as Bay stepped out and William took the front passenger seat. "So long as he doesn't do anything that makes me kill him."

William groaned and told them not to worry, and no infanticide would be necessary.

"You mean filicide," Bay corrected him. "And you better be joking . . ." But her threat was made in good humor, and she was smiling as she waved them goodbye.

Later, over dinner, William thanked his parents again for the lesson and for promising him the Mercury. He began twirling his spaghetti round his fork and cleared his throat.

"So," he started. "When can I drive your car, Dad?"

Vole's head jerked up. Bay groaned William's name. The Infiniti wasn't yet two weeks old, and they'd made it clear it wasn't a toy for their son to play with.

"I just want to try it," William wheedled.

"That's why we let you ride passenger," Vole said. "So you can try out the front window and seat belts."

"Dad!"

"Isn't the Mercury enough for you?" Bay asked. "Why do you need to use your father's car too?"

"I just want to try it!" William repeated. "Never mind. You don't get it. Forget I asked. Can I be excused?" He pushed himself away from the table, chair legs scraping along the floor.

"You haven't finished—" Vole began, but Bay surprised him by placing her hand on top of his leg under the table. He fell quiet.

"Listen to me, William. Your dad and I need to hear you say you understand. Under no circumstances should you drive the Infiniti. It's important to us you acknowledge where we stand on this. I'm not joking."

William glared at his parents and threw his hands in the air.

"Whatever! It was a hypothetical question! You two make such a big deal out of every little thing. I won't touch the Infiniti. *Don't worry.*" He loped away from the dinner table toward the basement. Before disappearing downstairs to twiddle around on the new computer the Gibbons' bought to help him stay ahead in school, William said, "Lawrence and I are partners on a physics project. Can I go to his house to work on it? I'll be back by ten thirty."

Vole and Bay exchanged a glance. It was the first they were hearing about it.

"What's the project about?" Vole asked.

"*Physics.*"

"Hmm. Do you need a drive?"

"I'll ride over."

"All right, but be careful coming home in the dark."

With William downstairs, Vole looked over at Bay.

"I don't think we need to worry," he said. In truth, he was as shocked as Bay to learn William expected to drive the new car. He knew it would come up eventually, but their son finished his exam that same morning. "You remember what it was like when you learned to drive."

"My parents didn't give me a car."

"Like I said, you remember what it was like when you learned to drive. The world was different then, honeybee."

"Don't patronize me," Bay snapped. She looked immediately contrite. "It's not your fault. I shouldn't have said that. I worry we're spoiling him too much."

Piqued, Vole reminded her they didn't have to give William the Mercury. "We could have traded it in and saved the money. That's what I wanted. You pushed for keeping both."

Bay got to her feet.

"I don't understand. I thought he'd be happy," she said as she began clearing away the dishes. "I thought it would be enough. I remember how much having freedom meant to me. I saved for a bicycle and rode the bus by myself. Oh God," she groaned. "You're right. Things are different now.

"Remember when my parents offered to help us with the house? I thought I'd die from shock, and I was *grateful.* They'd never done anything like that before. Though if they knew Mom was sick at the time, they wouldn't have."

"And we wouldn't have accepted their help . . ."

"Yes, yes. I guess I don't remember ever wanting *more*, you know?"

Vole helped Bay load the dishwasher.

"I hate to break it to you, honeybee," he said, trying hard to modulate his voice. Whenever the topic of Bay's late mother came up he had to be watchful of what he said. "But given inflation, we'll probably have to help him when he's ready to buy a house too. Which reminds me. Did I tell you we've had to hire another mortgage specialist? Their salaries are getting expensive."

She fixed him with a glare and tossed him a clean cloth to wipe the table.

"I have no problem helping our son. He deserves whatever opportunities we can afford him. My problem is he doesn't understand how much help we've given him.

"But," she sighed, "that's on us. Not him. And no, you didn't tell me about the mortgage specialist. Exciting. I'm happy for you."

She didn't sound excited or happy for him.

Bay worried they'd sheltered William too much. Because William was an only child, he was the sole recipient of their parental efforts. To teach him some responsibility she insisted he work part time at the pharmacy.

Vole didn't see it the same way, having grown up a loner in a small town himself. He had no siblings either. Bay had a sister, but she'd be the first to say Eloise knew nothing about responsibility—not that Eloise was ever a topic of conversation.

"Give him time," Vole insisted, coming up behind Bay. He placed long arms on either side of her and held her against the counter.

Ignoring his sudden nearby presence, she plugged in the kettle to make tea.

"He's getting good grades and doesn't do drugs," Vole continued, kissing her neck from behind. "What more could we ask for?"

She turned around to face him. Placed her hands on his shoulders. Leaned back against the counter's edge.

"A little respect, maybe?" she suggested.

"From a sixteen-year-old? He *is* respectful. He knows when not to swear. Really, Bay. I think you're being too hard on him."

"Fine," she capitulated. "Our baby got his driver's license today. I'm allowed to worry about his wellbeing."

"Of course," Vole replied, placing his hands on her waist and smiling. "But what about me?" he teased. "Aren't you the littlest bit worried about my wellbeing?"

She flashed her teeth, and he rejoiced in having succeeded in lightening her mood.

"Yes," she said. "But as I'm sure you'll recall, I'm not your mother."

Bay ducked under his amorous arms and took to the couch to finish reading her book.

As Vole tried to find sleep, he felt his mind slipping back to work. Bay pushed for them to get a second car because his professional image mattered to others, though it didn't matter much to him. Bay never intended to drive the Infiniti, much preferring to walk or be driven, but she knew what having it meant to everyone else.

"They'll never offer you a better branch if you keep driving the Mercury," she insisted in the months leading up to William's sixteenth birthday.

"But we don't need another car," he'd insisted right back. "I'd rather run the Mercury into the ground than buy new. A new car depreciates so fast, it'll make you spin."

"We can get a lease and trade it in after a few years."

"There's no way we're getting a brand-new vehicle."

"Vole, dear, go get yourself a new car. I don't care how you do it, as long as it's legal, but I won't let you drive the Mercury into the ground. When was the last time you spent money on yourself for something nice?"

"We haven't closed the garage in yet."

"Screw the garage. Maybe if you have a car nice enough to look after, we'll get to closing it in."

He'd compromised on a four-speed automatic luxury sedan he believed would hold value over time, but he'd grumbled at the needless expense the entire time they were shopping. Vole knew Bay was right, though. It wasn't enough to wear a suit and tie anymore. The make of his suit and tie had begun to matter too—something Bay noticed when he hadn't.

At some point in recent months, all his favorite dress shirts and suit jackets had been replaced with newer, more stylish cuts. His stomach roiled as he considered modern markup on new, good-quality clothing.

With Vole's new upgraded appearance and new upgraded car came new upgraded attention. The first day he pulled into his parking spot with the gleaming Infiniti, everyone made it their business to bring it up in conversation. Marc Rodrigo, his boss, commented on it during their daily meeting, though Vole hadn't mentioned it to him.

"Tire Slayer!" Marc addressed him over the line. "How are the new wheels treating you?"

"Oh, um, good. It rides much smoother. Brilliant suspension."

"Tell me again: what model is it?"

"The Infiniti."

"i30, right?"

"Correct."

"What year?"

"Um, it's this year's. Brand new."

"New! How about that! Great to see you treating yourself. What's it rocking under the hood?"

"Pardon me?"

"How many brake horsepower is the engine?"

"Oh. Two hundred and thirty."

"Damn, Gibbons! A sweet machine. I thought it was only two hundred and twenty-seven."

"Right, you're right, I'm sorry, it's two hundred and twenty-seven."

Vole hung up feeling like a moron. He knew the exact number, and he liked talking about mechanical things, but he'd never talked about cars with his boss before. Tire Slayer? What language was the man speaking? But everyone knew Marc was a serious car guy. He drove a red Porsche to all his meetings. A Porsche! Why would he pay attention to Vole's four-door family sedan?

Vole had no clue getting a new car would garner such buzz, but what surprised him most of all was how he'd already become accustomed to it.

When he mentioned what was happening at work to Bay, she told him people cared because it was *new*. It helped it was luxurious looking too.

"It's a good thing," she said. "It means they've noticed you. You've talked about moving to a bigger branch for ages. This is part of it. Now, if you start talking about kitchen renovations, people will know you mean *business*."

"Of course."

It made sense they'd want someone who was ambitious. A bigger branch meant more prestige and better pay. Upward growth was the desired norm. Taking charge of his image, changing how he was perceived, demonstrated Vole was willing to work for upward growth. Being a man with ambition made people who would have otherwise ignored him take note. Like Alice Trafalgar, the new mortgage specialist.

"Don't be an idiot," Vole muttered to himself as he rolled over in bed. "She's a professional. She doesn't mean anything by it."

He tried to strike the image of Alice watching him from his mind's eye. Not even night's persistent darkness could dim the tone of her lipstick, nor could he pretend he hadn't seen her blue eyes regarding him from overtop her computer monitor. She hadn't said anything, but she raised her eyebrow, which gave Vole the distinct impression he'd been asked a big question—to which he blushed in response.

"You're not encouraging anything," he told himself, repeating Bay's words: "It's all a part of it."

He tossed onto his other side. Reached his arm around to hold Bay close against him. As he drifted into troubled sleep, he wasn't sure what *part* he was referring to—or what exactly *it* was.

The following day, Vole agreed to take William out on a practice drive after dinner. While sitting in the parking lot, as he prepared to back into a spot, William tried to strike a deal with his dad.

"When I start driving school," William proposed, "you should let me drive the Infiniti."

"We'll see what your mother says about that. Now pay attention. Eyes forward. Both hands on the wheel. See where the lines appear in your side mirrors? This is the angle you want to ease between them."

Vole never brought up the possibility of William driving the Infinity with Bay. Timing was never right, and ever since he'd begun working longer hours to oversee the implementation of their new backend system, they'd been arguing more. When Bay mentioned that he seemed distant and preoccupied, he told her it was *part of it*.

"Marc is throwing more at me all the time," he explained. "It's got to be a good sign."

"Yes, I suppose. You do still want this, right?"

"Of course."

When Bay came to him later that week, nose swollen and cherry red, demanding to know why he hadn't told her he'd given William permission to drive the Infiniti, he defended himself.

"I didn't agree to anything! I told him that you and I needed to talk about it."

"Why didn't we?"

"Why didn't we *what?*"

"Talk about it! What's wrong, Vole? Why do I feel like we're living on two different planets, lately? Will is *driving*. We can't check out. You know what he's like. Once he gets an idea in his head, he goes for it. He thinks he's got your permission to try the Infiniti. I told him he must be mistaken, but he got upset . . ." She shrugged. "We both did."

"Bay," he exhaled. "Tell me again. Why shouldn't he be allowed to drive the Infiniti?"

It was a reckless question, but in that tired moment Vole forgot all the reasons why they were hell-bent on keeping the new car away from their son. Though it was his idea to begin with.

"I don't believe you," Bay accused. "Will just started driving. He's a teenager, for Christ's sake. He needs *rules,* Vole. Don't you care about any of this?"

"I don't appreciate these accusations, honeybee." Vole struggled to keep his voice level. "I was forgetful, and I'm sorry, but I don't think you should be blaming me for anything else. I didn't tell Will he has our permission to drive the new car—if he told you that, he's lying."

It was scary to consider their son had played them off each other with such skill.

Bay sniffled into the cold quiet between them. "I'm not—" she began. "I'm not trying to attack you. There must have been a misunderstanding. Could you please speak with him? I tried, and we had words, and he won't listen to me right now.

"He thinks you're going to take him out, but it's important we stick with our original plan. After he's graduated driving school, after he's passed his road test, he can try the new car. Not a moment before. Vole? Talk to me. Do you still agree with our plan?"

"I'll talk to him."

Vole found William in his bedroom. When he described the misunderstanding, and explained to William he must wait to try the new car, William begged and pleaded to have a chance sooner.

Before long, Vole relented.

"Fine, fine!" he agreed. Guilt stirred deep in his gut, but it was slow and lazy. Easily ignored. There were some things that went on between a father and his son no one else, not even Bay, could appreciate. "I'll take you this weekend, but you have to promise me you won't tell your mother."

"Like I'd want her to find out about this. Thanks, Dad. This is awesome!"

Furtive intentions drew them tighter together. The morning driving lesson turned into a special afternoon, and a giddy evening after that. It formed a precious memory, a gem to last, that each would come to treasure, though neither knew it yet.

Bay never found out about their secret, and soon, after a few short days, Vole felt as though he hadn't done anything wrong in keeping it from her.

TWENTY-THREE

May 2001 (continued)

VOLE NEEDED TO attend a conference in Winnipeg the week following William's secret driving lesson. He was looking forward to spending some time away from home, though he denied that's why he was bullish on going. When he bid Bay goodbye at the airport, he didn't notice she was more subdued than her usual self.

The first day of the conference was long, as first days often are. It didn't help he'd forgotten his card holder in his car back home. The loss nagged because it was the same card holder Bay gave him for their anniversary, years ago, and he brought it with him whenever he travelled.

Despite missing his favorite token, his spirits were high. New products promising unprecedented returns were announced, following an encouraging keynote that cast an optimistic light on the state of Canada's growing economy.

Typically, after a day spent socializing at a work conference, Vole would decompress by having one drink alone at the hotel bar before retiring to his room. This time, he found himself sitting at the hotel bar next to Alice, the new mortgage specialist, long after everyone else went to bed.

They were getting to know one another.

"You didn't!" she gasped in appalled laughter as Vole recounted the time he nearly blew a passing crow to smithereens with a roman candle. William was nine years old at the time, and Vole was making good on his promise to show him how roman candles worked in exchange for the boy's solemn vow to never handle fireworks without an adult present.

"Weren't you worried he'd do something dangerous?" she asked once she'd caught her breath. "Every single time my kids learned something new, they'd test it out the first chance they got. If they'd gotten their hands on fireworks, they would have blown each other's faces off! Brave man. What did your wife have to say about it?"

"It wasn't like that at all," he explained, his words coming out gurgled. "Will's a good kid. He's real smart. He gets it. Safety first! It was—"

What had it been like? Why was he having trouble recalling Bay's reaction?

"Your turn," he suggested, regretting his last cocktail, regretting a gnawing bleakness that was emerging inside him—he couldn't recall Bay's reaction because he never told Bay about the incident. It would have made her livid. Hadn't William been suspended for bringing fireworks onto school property only a short time after? "What's been your biggest parenting screw-up to date?"

Alice had two children she shared with their father—now her ex-husband—and her current struggles involved her new partner. Vole felt badly for her.

As Alice was answering his question, they were interrupted. The hotel concierge tapped Vole lightly on the shoulder.

"Mr. Gibbons?"

"S'me . . ."

"Would you please come with me, sir?"

"Wha' for?"

Did the concierge's eyes flit briefly at Alice, or was the alcohol interfering with his vision now too?

Vole couldn't tell.

"A personal matter, sir," the hotel staff person replied.

Vole wasn't sure why he felt embarrassed, or why he was disappointed to have their conversation cut short.

Alice held up her near-empty drink.

"I'll finish this and call it a night. It's an early start tomorrow. We can pick things back up another time."

"Thanks for the—" He hiccoughed, burped, and blushed harder. "Um, talk. I think you'll have no problems fitting in at the office. Yes, you're fine—I mean, you'll be fine."

Face hot, Vole followed the concierge. He tried not to sway as he walked, but the room was lopsided and the floor must have been playing tricks on him, because he kept stumbling over his own two feet.

A different staff member handed him a phone receiver when he reached the front desk. Vole fumbled with it before holding it tight against his ear. He rested his elbows on the cold countertop. Leaned into them for support. Breathed hard into the mouthpiece.

This is strange, isn't it, to receive a phone call at the front desk late at night.

"H'llo?" he mumbled.

"Vole?" came Bay's voice, audibly distressed. All fuzzy thoughts about Alice's lingering looks dissipated, and adrenaline sharpened what alcohol had dulled.

Bay was crying.

"I-I tried your room," she stammered.

"*What's wrong?*"

"It's William," she replied, voice tight with tears. "He's had an accident, and now he's—they've taken him to the hospital!"

"*What!* Is he okay?!"

"Y-yes—" Bay began, but her words dissolved. "He'll be okay . . . a-a broken leg—"

"*What happened?*"

"—and s-some bruises. He's sorry. But, Vole, dear, the car . . ."

"What about the car?"

"It's done. Totaled."

"Huh?"

He'd never heard Bay use such language before. Did she know what that meant? What did she mean, *totaled?*

"What happened?" he asked again.

Between shaky breaths, Bay explained how William asked if Lawrence could stay overnight to work on their school physics project. She'd agreed, though it was a school night, because it meant he would be home instead of somewhere else. She had no idea the boys were waiting for her to fall asleep. When she went to bed, she suspected nothing. It wasn't until the police came knocking on the front door, shortly after midnight, she realized William wasn't home.

"They sn-snuck out to t-take a joy ride in the country. William lost c-control and ran off the road. When the car r-rolled . . ."

"Shit," Vole breathed.

Will could have killed someone.

Our son could have died.

"It's a miracle they're safe," she concluded.

"I'm coming home."

A pause.

"I-I don't think you need to." She sniffed. "I'm fine. Nobody got badly hurt, thank God. The car isn't going anywhere. I'll tell you what the insurance company says. I had to talk to you . . ."

"You shouldn't have to deal with this on your own, honeybee. I'll see you tomorrow. I'll cab home from the airport."

"I understand if you stay. It's only one more night. We'll get through it."

They hung up. Vole went to his room, where he vomited into the toilet bowl before passing out on his hotel bed.

The next morning, Vole logged into his email to find the airline's phone number. A new note from Bay was at the top of his inbox. She repeated that he should stick to his original travel plans—*It's not worth the extra airline charges to change your flight*—and since it was only one more night, and his head was pounding, and he hadn't been so dehydrated in years, he agreed.

Vole called first thing in the morning to speak with William.

"I'm sorry, Dad," William wept. "I didn't mean to."

"Your mother and I are happy you're alive."

"I'm sorry."

After the day's sessions ended he told everyone he felt sick to his stomach (food poisoning from the fish, he said), and he retired to his room.

Sunday, June 21, 2015
Tierra del Fuego Province
9:45 a.m. local; 8:45 a.m. eastern time
2,837 sleeps since

> *Dear Bay,*
> *I haven't been sleeping well. Before I elaborate, I want to share a story.*

I was cycling along a lonely road like any other when, from behind the wide base of a snow-topped peak, appeared a lodge with bright windows. I could taste particles of salt and grease on the air, molecules wafted down from its kitchen to the road on what was once a brisk midmorning breeze. Tantalized by the savory taste, I went to the building intent on food and a bath. Something out front caught my attention. I stalled outside the door.

They were seated on a long bench, which rested against the lodge's log exterior. Each young woman held a mug between bare hands, and by the way they sat in each other's presence, I believed they considered themselves close sisters. The scene was unexpected and simple. Two teens with black ponytails and a single red scarf between them to share sat serene, soaking in the view.

After admiring and wondering about their austere solemnity for a time, I noticed something on the bench between them. An unclaimed thermos. I couldn't help myself from reacting with curiosity. I reached out and twisted its lid and sucked the scent up into my nose.

Nostrils flared with appreciation. The thermos contained coffee, fresh and hot; and it was seasoned to perfection. Nutty and rich and a little too cooked. Exactly the same blend as what we'd get from Timmie's back home. My mouth flooded with anticipation.

It's not mine to take, I reminded myself, and it seemed too personal a violation. Our time

together was approaching, and I was reminded of the person I strive to be for you.
I put the lid back and put it from my mind. I went inside.
It was a pretty building, but I've seen what humans make and call pretty before. I went to where they kept tubes of toothpaste and clean laundry. I washed with hot water I found waiting in the kitchen sink. I ate pan-fried fish and scallops and drank fizzy water with lemon. I took with me all the whole fruit I could find.
When I stepped back outside, feeling fresher than I had in months, I couldn't stop myself. I wanted the thermos.
I snatched it from the bench, ran down the front steps, threw my pack and bags into the back of the boat, and cycled us away like a madman.
I beelined to the lake I'd found—the one made entirely of turquoise glass. I didn't stop to celebrate my victory (and record what I'd borrowed, including the thermos) until the lodge passed out of my mirrors, the ocean opened before me, and my pulse settled to its normal pace.
I emptied the thermos and for a short time was transported back to Ontario. Of all the wonders we've witnessed, there haven't been any so deserving of my constant attention as this place. We've stumbled upon the last unspoiled child of the universe. What's most remarkable is here, time never went one direction or another. Everything is. Stillness is the way of life. That's the truth of it.

It's time I tell you the truth behind why I haven't been sleeping. The real reason. Not my jacked-up, caffeinated excuse.

Tomorrow has come again, and I must restart time. Is this what being nervous feels like? I don't remember.

I love you, honeybee.

Vole

He put down his pen and rubbed his hands together. The cold made his growing knuckles ache and his creaky knees creakier. Though he regained some of the weight he lost, he was still skinnier than when he saw her last; and his hair and beard were both long and ragged. He made sure to trim his fingernails and clean behind his ears, but he couldn't bring himself to cut away all the extra hair on his head and face. It kept him warm in the chilly air, and he'd become accustomed to it. He doubted he'd be himself without it. In compromise, he trimmed his beard into a civilized bush that would make William proud, and he pulled his hair back. He secured it in place with an elastic band and tucked it beneath a warm winter hat.

Vole patted Jock on the head—the only animal he let himself be familiar with—and went inside the cabin.

He'd found the abandoned building at the end of a road that ran parallel to the Beagle Channel, on the Argentine side. It was a musty structure, not a notable place, but it was surrounded by a sweeping vista. Vole's jaw grew lax and his mouth fell open when he discovered the scene. There were mountains, distant and remote, but they appeared near and alive. He felt he could pluck them with his fingers from the horizon; the ocean, glittering and stretching, was a sea of jewels that went on and on, this way and that way, frozen in motion.

Vole readied the cabin for Bay before starting time again. He cleaned the cabin's floors, wiped away dust from its surfaces. Brought his preparations inside.

The place they'd come to was north of the continent's tip—but barely north, if he was to believe his small-scale paper map. Any farther south and it would be too cold for Bay, but as he looked out the door into the wilderness beyond, he didn't think she'd be disappointed.

What will she see when she looks at me this time?

His mind flicked through the years, and he was reminded of when he would look over Bay's shoulder as she flipped through William's photos on the computer.

"I'm getting old," he muttered out loud.

Vole knew he looked and sounded different than before. In the space between moments he'd aged, grown harder, more worn. The grooves and jagged lines on his arms had scars. He wondered whether the way he regarded Bay would be any different, or were the transformations within him too nuanced to notice?

When the world shuddered into motion and her eyes refocused, a sharp gasp escaped her. Expressions of disbelief and sorrow wrestled for ownership over her face.

"Oh, Vole . . ." she exhaled, reaching to cup his face in her palm. Her eyes searched his. "You foolish, foolish man. What on earth have you done to yourself?"

"Please tell me you wore a helmet!"

While Vole admitted to never once wearing a helmet, he was spared having to admit they couldn't stay long in Tierra del Fuego. Bay knew the air temperature was too cold for her body to withstand for long, and Jock was panting as though he'd run a race. Bay's recent coughing fit remained top of mind, and she complained of her head being sore and her chest feeling tight.

Though, soon, she was between laughter and tears as he made light of some of his most dire experiences. Her concern turned to horror as she stared into his face and traced swollen knuckles with her fingertips.

"What about these?" she asked, trying to push his sleeve up his arm to take a closer look at the scars hinted at beneath.

Vole stilled her seeking hands. She leaned back and looked out at snowcapped peaks instead. They drank in the sight of water, endless and deep, winking at the mountain's base. Bay ran her hands along the steps of the cabin where they sat, exploring its grain with her fingertips in the same way she'd tried to do with Vole's arm, and she drew tight the blanket about her shoulders.

"What have we done?" she whispered and turned back to him, eyes as glassy as the turquoise lake he'd found in the mountains. "We can't keep going. We can stay and live here!"

Her words rang false.

She began to ask questions again, one after the next, and he struggled to catch them all: How long have you been cycling? Did you put *Molly* in the water? How many kilometers is that? Wasn't it too difficult to get over the Andes?

What did you do to your *teeth*?

The words he responded with were deliberate, chosen with care, and she teased him about getting slow in his old age.

When he coughed, a rattling hack she'd never heard before, she begged him to stop. Vole shook his head. He couldn't stop. There was still much to atone for, much she still didn't know.

They sat with their heads leaned against one another. Their fingers knit while Jock chewed on the piece of dried beaver Vole saved for him. When Vole asked if Bay would like to have any of the rabbit stew he'd collected from a cozy café in the distant town of Ushuaia, she said she wasn't hungry.

She watched as he spooned some into his own mouth.

"What are you doing when you move your lips like that?" she asked with a start.

Vole hadn't known he was moving his lips.

"I think I must be saying *goodbye*, and *thank you*."

"To the rabbit?"

He paused to consider her question.

"Yes. To the rabbit, in this instance, but I suppose it's meant for all things I eat."

"Vole!" she exclaimed, eyes wide. "Do you believe in *God*?"

Jock looked up from his chewing, disturbed by the force of Bay's question.

"I don't think so," Vole responded after a lengthy pause. "At least, not in the way you're thinking . . . When I think about my love for you, what my fears have driven me to do, I can't help but believe our lives are influenced by unseen forces. Not seen by my eyes, at any rate. These forces don't originate in our minds, or perhaps they do as chemicals in the brain, I don't know. The mind is where their seeds take root and flourish.

"If the whispers I know exist inside me are God, then yes . . . Though, all things considered, I don't think that's God. I think it's part of being human. I think it's being alive . . . but being alive doesn't make me entitled to understand why, or who, or what our purpose may be, or if there is one. There's so much I'll never understand. My limitations aren't evidence enough for faith in God, in anything, really, if that makes any sense."

He shrugged. Swallowed another spoonful of stew. It was the longest speech he'd made in a long time, and it tired him.

"I don't think I have enough perspective to decide," he said with an air of finality. "I've stopped thinking about it."

Thinking about God took him to the brink, and there, in the vortex on the other side, he feared he'd lose control of the only thing he had left: time with Bay—a resource far too precious to risk. He'd already done it once, restarted time for a flash when he lost control in madness, or so he thought, though Bay denied it when he asked. Like with everything else, he would never know for sure.

She watched him through shining eyes.

"I know you, but I don't know you," she said.

"I don't know myself anymore."

"I think you know yourself well."

It was impossible to know yourself in a world where everything you thought was true could dissolve away with a single command from a single man.

"Don't give up on me, honeybee," he pleaded. "We'll get there, you'll see. We still have time."

Her smile faded, taking the light away with it; the skies around them grew dark.

"Get *where*? I don't know where I'm going to be, one moment to the next. I close my eyes, and when I open them, you've lived a lifetime without me. I don't get the chance to miss you until it's too late!" Anguish made her voice grow hoarse and his throat constricted in response. "I'm completely torn," she continued. "Can't you see? Every moment we have together, I feel like the sun. You're orbiting me, worshipping me. I can see it in the way you move around me, the way you look at me. You're telling me the kinds of stories I've never dreamed of. It's only this way because of what you go through when I'm not looking." Her whole body was shaking. Vole pulled her to rest against him. "It's not fair!" she cried out, muffled, into his chest. "Why is this happening? What do we do next? Why can't I stay here with you?"

Her words stiffened Vole's resolve.

"Bay," he whispered into her hair, "*honeybee.*"

She looked up at him.

His face leaned toward hers, as though drawn by the gravity of his sun, and his lips touched the places on her cheeks where falling tears flashed.

When there were no more drops left to whisk away, he moved salted lips to hers and explored her mouth with his own in the way he longed to do, every minute of every day, for the past six years.

Bay's breathing grew heavy. When their tongues met, he felt warmth spread through his body, anchoring in his core.

Vole shifted his weight and lifted himself above her to lay her gently down on the wood. His lips trailed from her lips, to her chin, to the delicate hollow of her throat.

He would've moved farther down, if she hadn't let out a pained groan.

"Did I hurt you?" Vole asked, pulling back, suddenly cold with fear. "Is it your stomach again?"

"My head," came her strained reply.

He got to his knees. Cradled her head in his lap.

Bay held her eyes shut. Her face was white as snow; but after not much time, a flush—pale blossoms in early spring—returned to her.

When she opened her eyes, they were clear.

She smiled.

"Is it too late to try again?"

Bay realized what she'd said after the words left her lips. It *was* too late. Her skin was already too cold, and it was almost quarter to one in the afternoon back home, which meant they had already spent too many minutes together.

Bay's smile collapsed. "It feels so short," she whispered. "I know it's supposed to be this way, but I hate it. How can I keep up?"

"We'll see each other soon," he said to console her, but that only made her more upset because it wasn't true for him.

Vole told her they would be stopping in Paris on the way to their next destination. He told her he'd take them back to the park to see if their names were still chiseled into the tree behind the tower.

Her face brightened, and Vole knew he'd succeeded in distracting her. He was glad, because he couldn't bear to think of leaving her in such a sad state.

Jock trotted over to put his head in Bay's lap, and she laughed lightly at his burp, loud and pungent.

Vole stopped time. Sudden silence was deafening. He hadn't waited for Bay's laughter to subside, because then she would look at him and realize the moment was upon them. He wanted her to have as much joy in her life as possible, and having her smile keep him company as he crossed the Atlantic made it seem almost possible to do.

Vole didn't realize he'd forgotten to do the one thing he promised himself they would do together, until after the world went still. They were supposed to have listened to the voice message William left on his phone. When he remembered, Vole felt bad about it, and he vowed they would listen to it at the next opportunity. He was looking forward to it very much.

But something nagged at him. A heavy thought, an insidious doubt. It had been a long time since he'd seen his son, and on some days, Vole wondered if William was real.

TWENTY-FOUR

Sunday, June 21, 2015
Río Gallegos
1:45 p.m. local; 12:45 p.m. eastern time
2,837 sleeps since

VOLE DIDN'T SPEAK as he prepared *Molly*. He didn't say a word as he cycled back the way he came, until he reached Río Gallegos, where he stayed a few sleeps before continuing up the continent, along the east coast. He found books about the provinces of Argentina, Uruguay, and Brazil. He collected enough supplies to get to their next stop, where he refuelled with enough supplies to get to their next stop after that.

He never said good morning, good afternoon, or good night to Jock. He didn't make a single peep. Not even when the forest around him turned back to jungle, and the dripping moss turned weighty and emerald, did he make a sound.

Air became hot again. It contained moisture and Vole found himself covered in a permanent slick. He would catch himself longing after every body of water he passed by. *Forget and be still,* the rippled pools called out to him, *remember what it is to belong.*

Ever since his time with Bay at the edge of the world, he hadn't wanted to dally in any single spot, much less seek solace. Seeing himself through Bay's eyes left him disturbed. While the rest of the world wasn't aging, he was, and one day, he'd run out of time just like everybody else.

Sunday, June 21, 2015
Border between Argentina and Brazil
1:45 p.m. local; 12:45 p.m. eastern time
3,230 sleeps since

It was midday, somewhere near the border of Santa Catarina and Rio Grande do Sul in Brazil, when Vole gave in and stopped to go for a swim. (When he turned inland at Buenos Aires, many sleeps prior, he unwittingly cycled too far west and ended up on a road that followed the east coast of the country from hundreds of kilometers inland.)

The river he'd come to was like any other except in one remarkable way. Where most rivers had two rising earthen banks on either long side, this one had one rising bank and one severe drop into a short waterfall. The waterfall extended alongside the river, far into the distance.

Vole found himself drawn to the river's defiant asymmetry, and he couldn't stop himself from getting closer and diving in.

Wearing nothing more than his wedding band strung about his neck, he slid fearlessly into what should have been turbulent water at the base of the falls. He swam with broad lazy strokes under its silent curtain, reveling in cool liquid sliding against hot, naked skin. Vole drank in the sight of jumping drops and launching streams, appreciating their sparkle without any of the raucous drama that usually accompanied such an exuberant rush. He took a deep breath and swam down, headfirst, through murky depths. When his chest began to burn and his ears to ache, and he still hadn't touched sand, he turned around and pulled himself back up.

"It doesn't have a bottom," he gasped as his head shot through the water's surface. Vole found reason to break his recent, long-held silence. "Why doesn't it have a bottom?"

Inspired, he approached the waterfall. His fingers passed effortlessly through the chilly veil. Beneath, he found hard rocks. When he swiped his arm across the tall cascade, clearing it away, he discovered the rock face beneath was sloped. Chipped and roughened holds looked strong enough to support his weight. He tested this theory and the rocks held fast.

Up the falls he went, grabbing on to edges behind the water curtain. Where his arms and legs passed through, gaps in the pour remained.

"Watch this, honeybee," he grunted as he climbed, careful to protect soft genitals from knocking against rough protrusions. Bay and Jock sat waiting in *Molly* on the road, far from where he'd come to. "I'm going to cannonball into the shortest longest waterfall you've ever seen!" It was one more thing he'd write about to Bay. She'd remind him to share the story with William later.

It was a slippery struggle to the top, which was approximately five meters up from the base. By the time Vole pulled himself over, his arms trembled with effort.

Where the cascade curved down over the river's lateral ledge, vegetation grew, creating mounds. The plants were lush and verdant, and in many cases, more slippery than the stones.

From his high vantage, Vole could see the colorful bodies of hikers through the surrounding bush—specks of blue and pink and yellow popping out from green shadow. He'd become used to passing by people without stopping, and it surprised him to remember he wasn't the only person alive in the landscape. It occurred to him he was standing in clear view of anyone with two working eyes.

"Hey!" he called out to the tourists, waving both his arms, gyrating his hips back and forth and side to side. "Why don't you give this a try!"

Bubbling with enthusiasm, Vole readied himself to jump. He settled into a comfortable stance by placing his right foot on a stone jutty and his left foot on one of the roughened rocks. Something hard poked into his calloused sole on the left side, and he winced before adjusting his weight. He bent his knees and cocked his arms and—

His left foot slipped without warning.

Vole cried out as his leg shot out from beneath him, and he fell, crashing down onto stones. The water offered minimal cushion; his skin ripped against the stone's jagged surface and a sharp pain shot up through his backside. His right arm snapped out to grab on to a branch or stone to steady himself. His hand closed on a sapling instead. It snapped under his sudden force. Vole's upper body contorted and he floundered, desperate to gain purchase on the grit.

A sensation that felt suspiciously like the slowing of time—a thought Vole knew he couldn't consider at length without inviting demons down upon him—came over him, and his entire left side scraped as his balance tipped, and he tumbled over the cusp of the falls.

Vole tucked his chin and covered his head with both arms as he fell. He never saw the crevice his flailing left foot found, so he never knew what caused searing pain to shoot through his ankle as the weight of his body yanked it free. Grunts and cries rang out, piercing the silence, and his crashing tumble ended with him cannonballing into the water at the base of the falls.

He didn't sink far down. Without his arms and legs working to propel him, he hung, suspended, a few meters below the water's surface. Vole let the water's silence soothe him. It hurt too much to move, though he knew he was in shock and would perish if he stayed forever.

A burning need surged through him all at once, and with an urgency unlike any other, Vole flailed his arms and jerked his right leg back and forth. He scrambled to the surface like a maimed frog. Fear he wouldn't make the short distance drove him to move quickly, and he leaped to the surface with a gasping shout.

Once he'd regained his breath, Vole began to curse in earnest.

"Shit! Dammit! God dammit. What is wrong with me? *Why the hell did I have to go and do that?!*"

June 2001 (continued)

In time, the euphoric appreciation of William's survival diminished, and the depressing reality of Damage Done set in. Vole's brand new i30 was a write-off. Insurance wouldn't help them recuperate the loss. Now, William was up nine demerit points on his driving record, his driver's license had been suspended, and he was tens of thousands of dollars in debt. He wasn't old enough to own a credit card.

How? How had this happened? How had Vole failed his son? He'd been at a hotel bar, blushing over cocktails and empty stories, at the same moment his son almost died, and Bay was alone in the immediate aftermath to cope. What did that say about him?

Vole threw himself into work. His already long days became longer, and his typical patience was nowhere to be found. He developed new reports and experimental training programs; programs that required work to be done outside of standard operating hours. Bay distanced herself from him, filling her time with other things she rarely discussed. William tiptoed around both parents as carefully as he could on two metal crutches.

After the prescribed six weeks passed, Bay took William back to the hospital to get his leg cast removed. She dropped Vole off at the bank on the way. She said nothing about it being Saturday, and Vole was too preoccupied to notice silence was the new norm between them.

A few hours later, after the bank closed (it closed by 3:00 p.m. on Saturdays, which was why Vole liked going in on weekends), Bay broke Vole's concentration by knocking loudly on his office window.

"Bay!" he exclaimed when he unlocked the front door to let her inside. "What can I do for you, honeybee?"

"*We need to talk.*"

"We do?"

Despite the bank's apparent emptiness, they marched forward in charged silence. Vole wasn't sure what they needed to talk about, especially in such privacy, but he was certain it wasn't going to be fun.

When they were behind his closed office door, Bay turned to him.

"You lied to me," she accused.

"Huh?"

Bay repeated the conversation she'd had with William while they were at the hospital, waiting to have his cast removed. She'd been explaining to their son Vole's standoffishness and recent distraction was due to increased pressures at work, and in his guilt-ridden and bitter confusion, their adolescent son revealed the truth: Vole had given him a secret driving lesson in the new car prior to his crash.

"So?" Vole demanded, his own temper rising, his own wounds feeling scratched at and salted. "I don't see how that has any bearing on Will's accident. He lied about his intentions. He stole the car. He crashed it."

"And *you* led by example. I don't get you. You're so busy, tending to your own needs, your boss's needs, your employees' needs, you've completely forgotten about your own family's needs. We need you, Vole. *I needed you.* How could you do this to me? To our son?"

Drops spilled from her eyes and tumbled down her cheeks.

"I don't understand where this is coming from," Vole said, entreating her to be reasonable. Why was she angry? He could understand if she blamed him for not coming home the moment he learned what happened, or if she thought he did a bad thing by getting the car in the first place, but the reason he worked hard was them. His family. It's what she encouraged. It's what she wanted. "I've always been here for you. I'm busy working hard, for *us*. You don't understand how stressful my job is. I have *responsibilities* to these people. My employees have families relying on them, and they rely on me in turn."

"Is this about the New York thing Will asked to go on?"

Bay stared at him. Wiped her cheeks. Looked away.

"No," she sighed. "It's not about the school trip to New York City."

"Good, because there won't be any money to send him to New York, so he can look at fancy wax museums and eat fancy food with his friends! There won't be any money for fancy things until he pays us back for the damage he did! You were right about one thing, honeybee. We've spoiled him. He's entirely too entitled. It's time the kid grows up and learns some responsibility."

Bay's slackened face tightened with renewed anger.

"You have no right to blame him. This is *your* fault, not his!" Vole stepped back, startled by her renewed blaze. "If you had acted with a little integrity, he would have known better, but no. You had to go behind my back. You had to show him authority can be laughed at, as long as authority doesn't know it's being made the fool. Yes, he felt entitled! What did you expect, sending him mixed messages like that? He's a teenager, *a child,* for Christ's sake. We need to work *together* to teach him."

"Honeybee—"

"Don't you dare patronize me. We'd agreed on how we would parent. A unified front. A partnership. Together. Our son almost got himself and his best friend *killed*, and that's on you. I won't stand being lied to. I didn't sign up for that." She tossed the keys to the Mercury on the table. "Take these. I'm going to walk home."

"Bay. Please don't leave like this—"

She turned, yanked open the door, and slammed it shut behind her.

In the absolute vacuum that followed, Vole fell back into his chair. He closed his eyes and placed his head on his desk.

Several long minutes later, a gentle tapping sounded.

He said nothing, didn't lift a finger, but the door creaked open anyway.

"Excuse me," came Alice's voice.

Vole looked up. Cleared his throat. He didn't realize anyone else, especially she, was in the office.

"Hi."

"It's only us here," she assured him. "I locked the front door after she left. I couldn't help but overhear what happened."

"Um . . ."

"I've been here all day and could use a break. What about you? Grab a pint at the pub with me?"

I should go home . . .

Bay's heated words rang out in his otherwise thoughtless head.

My family needs me.

"A pint sounds perfect."

TWENTY-FIVE

Sunday, June 21, 2015
Border between Argentina and Brazil
1:45 p.m. local; 12:45 p.m. eastern time
3,230 sleeps since

VOLE'S LEFT ANKLE had swelled to the size of a grapefruit and was starting to mottle. Shooting pain consumed his left foot and leg when he tried to wiggle his toes. Whether the ankle was sprained or broken, he didn't know, but he feared the worst.

He glanced up at the spot in the sky he could count on; the sun was a glowing ball of white beneath a blanket of gray.

"What am I going to do if I can't move?" he moaned, arching his back and wincing at how sore his muscles already felt.

The sun had nothing to say.

Vole heaved himself off the ground. Crawled over to where he'd left his clothing and fanny pack—he never left *Molly* without it—and carefully pulled on his shorts and faded cotton shirt. He reached into his fanny pack and removed a small bottle, plastic and white.

It rattled as he tapped two pale pills into his palm.

"The case calls for it," he muttered, and swallowed them down. Ever since crossing Central America, he kept a modest collection of medical supplies on hand at all times.

With his pack slung over his shoulder—he'd taken to wearing it across his chest on some days—he crawled slowly back to Bay. His left foot dragged painfully behind him in the dirt.

When he got to the boat, he turned his head to the side because he couldn't look Bay in the face. He pulled himself into his seat with great care. Moving at a glacial pace, he swung his two legs over the middle steering column to face the back of the boat. He removed a clear bag from a container to his right side. The bag contained cleansing wipes and sterilizing lotions.

Vole washed and dressed the scrapes he could reach, and he slathered what he could onto his stinging back. Bare flesh was red and swollen where his body scraped along the sharp rocks, and he knew the bruises on his left haunch and hip, already forming, penetrated deep. They would be rich in color and long-lasting.

When he felt as ready as he'd ever be, he slid back into his seat and faced forward, like Bay (who he continued to ignore), and extended his left leg out in front of him.

The mottled grapefruit joint was swollen, and tenderness extended to both sides of the bone. Rotating it was impossible. He gripped above his left knee, a hand on each side of his leg, and maneuvered his foot, with great care, to gain a better vantage.

"Good grief," he muttered, squinted, blinked. "What have you done to yourself?"

He tried again to move his toes, but a stabbing pain took his breath away. Vole reached his arm back behind him and rummaged around in the same container as before.

"A*ha*!"

Fingers latched on to another bag. This one contained ice instead of lotions and disinfectants. The ice was what remained of the supply and helped cool him as he crossed the Atacama, before he gave up and turned inland to continue south on more forgiving roads. Only bits of the ice melted in Tierra del Fuego. He took what was left and wrapped it in his bandana.

Careful not to jar his already aching bones, Vole placed the cold package on the outside of his left ankle and let his head fall back.

"What am I going to do?" he muttered. Finally, he turned to Bay. "What would *you* do?" and then, "Forgive me, honeybee."

Vole sat there until he fell asleep. When he woke, it was because the ice slipped. His injury didn't look any better, and his swollen toes were itchy and tomato red. He stretched his neck from side to side and sat up to reach for the sleeping bag he kept in *Molly*.

Pain exploded throughout his body, making him cry out. He retracted and forced his clenched muscles to relax.

After a moment, he eased himself out of the boat, right leg first.

Standing one foot on the ground, Vole unhooked a canoe paddle from its mount on the outside of the boat. He used it, blade down, like a walking stick, and began to hop. After every hop, he stopped and prepared for the next jarring jump. By the time he got his sleeping pad and sleeping bag laid out—the thought of sleeping on the ground without either, in that state, was enough to make his mouth sweat—Vole's body was shaking and slick all over. Eyes stung. His pits and limbs felt clammy; his core, cold.

With the last of his strength, Vole set a bottle of carbonated water and two baked cheese rolls down next to his fanny pack, which he'd stocked with more antibiotics from *Molly*. (After

Panama, he never went anywhere without those either.) He lay down, propped his foot, and fell into uncertain darkness.

Nightmares assailed him. Half aware, he cried out against his attackers—voices in twisting shadow—and begged them to leave him be. "You don't know what you're doing," his own voice came hurtling at him from out of the darkness. Amber orbs, all the crystal shades of honey, bore into him, unrelenting, like the sun; her smooth face cracked—the floor of an ancient lakebed—and fell to pieces. "Who do you think I am?" she demanded, while he cried and dissolved, and tearfully tried to reassemble Bay's scattered parts.

When blessed oblivion took him, he was too exhausted to know anyone. Not Jock, not Bay, not William, not himself.

Days passed as Vole came in and out of sleep. Sometimes he woke cold. Sometimes he woke hot. Every time he woke shaking and with aches, he made sure to drink a bit of water, eat a bite of bread, and swallow down a pill. He didn't know if what he was taking would help. How could he? But he hadn't any choice because there were no hospitals to check into, no doctors or health-care practitioners to guide him. All he had were the books stored in *Molly*, but those reference materials were far away from his sleeping mat, and he hadn't the energy to retrieve them.

One of the times Vole woke, he found the gray light of day to be less offensive, and he cared he could smell his own stink. He looked down and saw all the toes on his left foot were pink and still attached, something he'd feared wasn't the case in his feverish state. Closer inspection revealed his ankle had adopted a new layer of color—yellowish green—and the inside swelling was reduced. The outside was still big and nasty looking, but when he dared try wiggle his toes, they moved (though the motion greeted him with a mixture of lancing pain and joy).

Seized by the desire to move, Vole balanced himself on his knees. With the canoe paddle gripped tight between his two hands, he pulled himself to a slow one-footed stand. The other foot, his left, he kept raised by holding a right-angled bend in his knee.

"I need a cast," Vole stated out loud. "One of those air thingamajiggers they gave to Will after cutting his plaster off."

"All I need is to find one . . ."

He looked around. A forest loomed, dark and dense behind the riverbed he fell from. It towered above the wall of water framing the river's lateral side. A trail marking his upward climb remained clear, a black crack splitting the pale curtain. Everywhere he looked, all around, rugged hills and tangled jungle looked back.

His injured ankle began to throb, as though repelled by the notion of the jungle and a weight-bearing cast. His leg grew hot and rebellious. He became dizzy and sat to raise his leg again and catch his breath. He took another painkiller. Realized his supply was running low and recalled the tight scatter of buildings he passed before turning onto the road that led him to the falls.

Without another word, Vole dragged himself along the ground back to where Bay sat in the boat. He took care to avoid the areas he'd soiled in fever-addled wakefulness and pulled himself to a one-footed stand using the trailer and boat as supports.

"Jocko," he addressed the dog on Bay's lap. "You look after her. I'll be back soon. I've got to take care of a few things."

Vole assembled a pack of supplies and retrieved the canoe paddle. Leaning heavily on it, he hopped slowly on his right foot, down the dirt road, away from Bay. Every ten steps or so, he stopped to rest and raise his leg.

"Don't hold your breath," he muttered when he became frustrated. "This may take all day."

When his focus slipped, he would misplace the canoe blade or misjudge his landing, and a paralyzing shock would ripple throughout his body. When he lost his balance, the toes of his left foot would dip and come into contact with the ground. Pain would shoot through his leg and up his spine, and his teeth would chatter. He'd be forced to sit down and wait for his vision to clear while his body trembled.

Eventually, Vole reached the cluster of small buildings. Close up he saw they were more like huts. Seven moldy plywood plank structures with corrugated metal roofs, all topped with chicken wire, and all without windows. He approached the one closest to him, and, with great effort, hopped up the rotting front stairs to the door.

A map, torn, was tacked to the door, and beneath it, a faded piece of paper that stuck like glue to the ridged wood surface. The door was locked shut with a rusted deadbolt. A padlock the size of Vole's fist held the deadbolt in place. He pulled at the lock until welts formed on the tips of his fingers, but it wouldn't budge. He checked the remaining six structures. They were all the same.

Broken glass decorated the steps and platform outside the largest of the buildings, the last he'd come to. Vole fell to his knees in the muddy mess of shards, not caring if they cut into his skin; dark gleaming spots marked his fall. *I'll have to clean my mess before I go,* he thought, before he passed out on the wood.

When he woke, his eyes focused on a motionless train of back-to-front ants, russet chitin gleaming like armor. He considered the industrious insects, ready for anything, next to his nose.

"Why can't I be more like you?" he gusted, displacing a few with his breath.

After mindlessly eating a number of them (ever since Panama, the crunch of ants and their delicate flavor reminded him of his favorite bran cereal from back home), Vole tended to the cuts and blisters that formed on his hand from the chafing canoe paddle. He wrapped his hand in cloth, ate a pink-fleshed guava, thought wistfully about tender cooked Canadian bacon, and continued hobbling eastward.

After another silent and dragging day of lopsided travel, he came upon an abandoned fuel station. There weren't any cars in sight and the jungle was closing in on the space. The station's metal signpost was rusted and knocked over. What remained of the plastic sign was a mess, and there were sharp shards scattered nearby and half buried in dirt.

Closer examination revealed the pay station to be locked from the inside. Through the grimy front window, he could see there were shelves, still intact and partially stocked, within.

Vole sat down on the ground to muster his energy. When he felt ready, he assembled a pile of fist-sized boulders, collected slowly from under nearby brush, and began a methodical assault against the front glass window. He pounded it up close, holding on to the corner of the building for balance. Every hit sounded out like a gunshot. Vole was long past the point where he expected a fleeing response from disturbed wildlife. The only sounds accompanying sharp cracks of glass were his sobs of effort.

When spiderweb cracks looked ready for breaking, Vole jabbed the blade of his canoe paddle through the flexed center of it. A flurry of glistening slivers rained slowly to the ground.

Vole was surprised to discover he was weeping. He sniffed and blew his nose on his shirt.

"Rules are made to be broken," he whispered, and he wrapped his forearm in cloth before reaching in and unlocking the door.

Inside, the linoleum floor was covered in a blanket of leaves and twigs. It smelled animalistic, like the jungle outside. A broken plastic container that once held dried meat was affixed to the wall, and plastic packages of salted nuts hung beneath.

A small Coca-Cola fridge stood in the corner by the door. The fridge wasn't on, though it still held a few drinks. Vole tugged open its door. It took some effort to accomplish because the seal was stuck shut by some sticky residue turned to glue.

The air inside the fridge smelled sour and dank, but the bottles of water inside were sealed. They looked all right. He drank one down.

Behind the counter was another closed door. He limped toward it. Twigs and dried leaves snapped beneath his right foot and left crutch. *Snap, crackle, pop.* He was careful not to mislay the canoe blade.

Vole crept under the counter and jiggled the knob of the door on the other side. It turned, but barely. Taking a deep breath, he cranked the knob and pushed. It scraped open, creating a gap wide enough to fit his head through.

A wall of stench greeted him and he gagged. The smell would have wafted if only there was a breeze, but there wasn't, and the world remained silent, except for Vole's retching.

Once he'd collected himself, he pried open the door with his paddle and squeezed into the back room, no bigger than a closet.

A toilet, porcelain bowl cracked in half, sat in the tight corner. Above the toilet, on shelves threatening to collapse, were cartons of cigarettes, deeply molded; wrapped chocolate bars; and three yellowing rolls of toilet paper.

"Good grief," he muttered. "What's a man got to do for some aspirin around here?"

He limped out of the small room, grateful to leave its smell behind. Piles of spotted receipt paper sat on a head-high shelf to his left. He rifled aimlessly through the sheaves.

Not finding what he sought, Vole ducked back under the counter into the main entrance. From their slim metal hooks plugged into the wall, he took down air fresheners and individually wrapped products, most of which he didn't recognize. The cellophane wrappings were dusty, but particles didn't clog the air. Dirt clung to his fingers and, he assumed, dropped slowly to the floor.

The abandoned station hadn't enough inventory stocked to keep Vole preoccupied for long. When he ran out of packages to peer at, he slumped to the ground. His canoe paddle clattered to the floor next to him. Crushed glass and sticks poked into his backside, but he didn't care. Hungry and dejected, he opened a bag of mixed nuts he'd knocked to the ground in his search. He began to eat them; they were chewy and stale. One by one, he ground them into a sticky paste before swallowing, while he stared at the mess he'd made.

"Wait a minute," he said. "What's that?"

Pushed to the back of the top front display shelf was a single, dusty carton. He hadn't been able to see it before—not from his previous vantage, hobbled and leaning down from above.

Vole reached in and yanked, dislodging the thin cardboard box from where it was caught. When he saw what the carton contained, he cried out in relief. Painkillers—tiny pills wrapped in pairs—tubes of petroleum lubricant, and what looked to be anti-itch cream.

"I knew it would be here!" Though he knew nothing of the sort. The only knowledge he could claim was a sense of neutral expectation; the pills would be there, or they wouldn't. Beyond that, all he could do was prepare for the unknown and hope for the best outcome for all, including himself.

So far, on this journey—throughout his entire life, he'd come to realize—he'd been excessively fortunate; he tried not to dwell on it for fear of tarnishing good fortune's glimmering effect. Sobering consideration was known to leave a dark stain on beautiful things. All he could do was believe that believing in nothing was most right, while hoping for the best, and doing his best, and wishing the best on others; all he could do was embrace the journey and persevere. Nothing more was his to lay claim to. Nothing less would do.

Vole promptly removed all the packaging, grumbled a bit about how they weren't as strong as the last painkillers he'd scavenged, and placed fifty-four pills—twenty-seven packs of two—into a small bag he crammed inside his pack.

"Onward," he muttered once he'd finished, before passing out on the musty floor.

Sunday, June 21, 2015
Border between Argentina and Brazil
1:45 p.m. local; 12:45 p.m. eastern time
3,240 sleeps since

Vole left Bay and Jock alone for one more day while he readied himself for the return journey. Having eaten the food he brought with him, he collected all the supplies he could carry in his pack. Like the gas pumps outside, his supply of wealth went dry long ago. Before departing, he tidied his mess and scrawled *thank you* on a piece of spotted paper.

When he made it back to Bay, he didn't dare tell her what he'd done, nor did he write to her. He went straight to sleep.

He woke corpse stiff, and his ankle didn't look any better. The pain had dulled, which he told himself was a good sign, but every time he put the smallest amount of weight on the joint, his chest seized, and the cough he'd grown accustomed to flared up and made him shake.

As days passed, his scratches grew scabs. Battered muscles stopped aching. Purple bruises turned completely green and then yellow. His scabs became itchy and dry and sloughed off. He never ventured far from Bay. It wasn't long before Vole visited every building and habitat within five square kilometers in search of useful supplies.

While Vole healed, the world remained unchanged: the sun never moved, the clouds never thickened, and the wind never blew them away. Every ringing sound was of Vole's own making. Food turned to dust in his mouth, and visits to his latrine sickened him. How long it took for his old bones to mend, Vole could only guess. He stopped counting his sleeps because he slept so often, and he ran out of things to write about. As his body weakened from misuse—except for his right leg, which stayed wiry and strong—his ankle healed.

When the swelling reduced enough for Vole to assess damage, he determined the joint would never be the same again. His left foot flopped from side-to-side, and when he put pressure or weight on it at the wrong angle, it collapsed beneath him and became swollen and painful all over again. A dull pain on the outside edge of his foot remained constant and never diminished.

When Vole's need to depart outgrew his discomfort, he continued the journey north. His left leg did little, relying on his right foot to push down on the pedal and pull back up with hooked toes.

In the first sizeable town he came to, Vole found a store that sold things like crutches, bandages, and plastic braces. He slid tight sleeves over both knees and wrapped his ankle in cloth tape. He found a sports medicine book, written in Portuguese. Following illustrated instructions, Vole managed to get the angles of the tape right. With his ankle taped, he could put weight on his left foot without it buckling beneath him.

The pace Vole set was the slowest he'd set yet. He lost all his calluses and most of his muscle; the damp heat made his bicycle seat's chafing almost unbearable. He pushed on and pushed discomfort from his mind. Focused on the way forward, Vole didn't notice the gray above him turn black. The sun vanished.

Heavy rain began outside of Salvador. Vole stopped on the storm's threshold. Where he stood, the air was humid but there were no rain drops. A meter in front of him, though, extended an endless curtain of rain.

Drops, plump and juicy, gray like the light around him, were caught in the air midtumble. Vole touched one. It burst and coated his fingertip in gentle dampness. He poked his head into the downpour. When he pulled back out, his face was glistening and wet.

"Dear desert," he muttered to himself, blinked, wiped an arm across his face. "How I miss thee." Though barren and endless, deserts were simple and uncluttered and *dry*.

Vole had yet to use the windshield he fitted *Molly* with in the beginning, so he experienced a momentary thrill when he pulled it down and latched it into place. He donned a pair of nonprescription glasses (which he'd relieved from a store somewhere along the way), and kept on.

They struggled through the storm. The mud-slick roads were slippery, and his rotating wheels never produced a dirty spray; the water seemed to move aside and cling. Every raindrop his face, his arms, his torso came in contact with felt like a finger poke and made a small slapping sound. Soon Vole was consumed by the light pitter-patter of a monsoon.

When he needed a rest, he'd get off his bicycle and swing his arms to clear away the drops. Cold water pooled around his feet and ankles. When he needed a break he would dry off seated next to Bay in *Molly*.

A scar, luminescent and thin in the dark sky above—a crackle of electricity—accompanied him most of the way. The skies were gloomy, the sun nowhere to be seen. Lightning became his primary light source. Sometimes, through the dense rain, he could smell woodsmoke.

Vole wondered whether the lightning had struck a tall tree, and for a time was consumed by the thought of encountering a forest fire.

He never did find out what fuel burned so hot tropical rain couldn't quench it, and the skies above him became clear again by the time he reached Porto de Cabedelo in João Pessoa.

Vole arrived before noon, local time. Sun-kissed beach goers rested on the sand, opposite the port. Some people were swimming, luscious in their pleasure, while others lay on flat boards in the motionless wash. Others were seated on rusted chairs in front of rusted tables beneath a tattered canopy, caught in time, whittling away their quiet day in peace.

Vole planned on setting off, but he was tired. A slow idle, brought by the beachcombers nearby, had worn off on him. He found himself serene and dawdling, and he poked around shops as though he were vacationing there with Bay.

Movement in a narrow display mirror at a sunglasses shop caught his eye. *Who in the world . . . ?* he wondered, and leaned in close.

A bearded scarecrow with reams of gray and white hair stared back at him.

"Good grief!" he exclaimed. "What a sorry sight I am! Well, at least I've still got all my teeth." Vole cut his hair and shaved off his beard and felt younger than he had in years.

TWENTY-SIX

Sunday, June 21, 2015
Porto de Cabedelo, João Pessoa, Brazil
1:45 p.m. local; 12:45 p.m. eastern time
3,581 sleeps since[2]

THE OCEAN'S DANGERS drove Vole to deep and early consideration—followed by deep and early denial—because of how real and terrifying those dangers were. Hurricane winds and electric storms, tumultuous night squalls and towering waves—each circumstance spelled sure death for a pedal boat at sea.

But screaming squalls were pieces of a pattern Vole had fallen out of, symptoms of monumental movement that took place over time. Time, in the traditional sense, was something Vole had the luxury of being without. The dangers that stole Vole's sleep weren't of winds, screeching and malevolent. Steep drops over big waves worried him. As did running out of food and fresh water and having to relieve himself so near to Bay.

---

[2] Vole estimated he'd spent more than three months recovering, and he moved slowly after that.

If she were fully aware, it would be different. Being married for decades meant they'd been through many urgent scenarios together, and urgent scenarios left little room for modesty. What troubled him was doing immodest things in front of her while she was in *that* state. Because, no matter how long Vole thought about or ignored his situation, he'd never *know* for sure.

What if Bay could see him? Hear him? *Smell* him?

What if, with the regular passage of time, she was taking in nearly imperceptible detail, the sort of detail that's present in every single snowflake? Vole could behold infinite complexity in a single snowflake, all the while never comprehending it. Perhaps, in her current state, Bay could too, but in the seconds that passed instead of in flecks of ice.

Other than all that, heavy rain bothered him intensely, and navigation was a constant concern. He hadn't thought about navigational charts since leaving Toronto, and back then crossing the ocean was too daunting and deep to consider lightly.

When Vole considered Toronto, it was with tight pain in his chest. He didn't yearn after it or miss being close to downtown. A city was a city was a city. What lanced him was if he were to ask Bay, she'd say he was there hours ago. She would never understand. She'd never know what it was like to live alone in the stretching expanse between blinks.

In stark contrast to Toronto, Porto de Cabedelo was an industrial and concreted place. The port was long, and along its length was a line of buildings, squat and beige. Steel containment units rose up from the pier into the sky behind; they towered above the dock like monoliths over the people.

It wasn't like any tourist destination he'd ever been to before, and Vole was shocked to discover a seven-story expedition vessel, built for stormy ocean crossings, anchored off the pier. The ship's gangway was extended. He walked up the platform and into the ship.

Vole stepped into a room, a convergence of multiple hallways. In the room's center was a winding staircase lined with mirrors. The staircase connected all seven floors. Public areas of the ship consisted of a stage, a dining hall, a library, and a teak wood observation deck. Vole found blueprints framed and posted to the walls in the captain's bridge, and from them he learned the ship was equipped to hold under two hundred passengers, including staff.

"Now that's a *boat*," he observed as he walked around the bridge and peered out the front glass.

A seabird sitting on the deck rail with its head tucked under its wing caught Vole's eye.

"You've got the right idea," Vole said. The bird wasn't moving, but Vole could tell it was at ease with the ship's pending voyage into the unknown. "I could learn a thing or two from you."

He turned away from the window and inspected an electronic map displayed on a flat, upward-facing monitor. The map had a white background. Blue and red rings outlined high- and low-pressure systems, and small matching arrows indicated real-time wind speed. It highlighted which weather systems brought torrential rain and sky-high waves and which could be sailed through and safely ignored.

Next to the monitor was a stack of printouts, showing older versions of the same information. "Fascinating," he muttered as he fingered through the papers. Speaking to no one in particular, "Here's a riddle: I'll do anything for it, though it's my greatest enemy. It's a part of me, yet I'm never aware it's there. I take it for granted, but it's what I fear being without the most. Every life form requires it for survival. What is it?"

Out of habit, Vole made a mental note to write the answer in his next letter to Bay. Though it had been a while since Vole wrote her a letter or drew her a picture. He feared the moment would pass from memory before he got the chance. Thoughts didn't flow to his hand as they once did. "It's a compounding issue," Vole said out loud in explanation. "We're doing this together, but I'm the only one making memories. It's a lonely life to admit to in writing, you see."

But there was a different, real reason behind his long drought of words: Bay would never get to read them all. His letters were a handcrafted illusion. Vole wasn't extending her life or giving them more time to make new memories together. Bay was dying, still, and she didn't have enough waking hours left to read all his words. It was pointless to bother writing the riddle's answer down for her to read later, because she'd never get to it.

The ocean stretched endless, was without bottom, and he feared it would absorb him.

"Time," he whispered. "I'll do anything for more time." He sighed. "Water, too, I suppose. Two right answers, then. It wasn't a good riddle, anyway."

After that, Vole stopped trying to improve his mood. He lost count of the number of ships he boarded. The small ones without an extended gangway he jumped carefully into or boarded by jury-rigging a platform with nearby planks. If a ship was too tall, or anchored too far from the dock, he'd study it from the outside and imagine all the ways he could scale up its side. "Good information to know," he told himself. "If I come across a similar ship out there in the wild, knowing how to find a way in is essential." He paused. "I hope I find a good pair of water shoes in all this."

The weather charts and instruments all began to look familiar, and Vole knew he'd seen enough. He had the information he needed. Most desirable were the grainy satellite images providing snapshots of current conditions—weather systems, pressure changes, other vessels, islands; but that information was delivered in real time, stored in electronic form, displayed on hefty steel monitors too heavy to carry with him. Plus, they were bolted down to the ship's metal floor.

Vole developed a plan.

Four of the ships he'd boarded kept paper logbooks; he went back and copied each of their most recent entries. He hand-traced the images he wanted from the monitors onto sheets of paper.

If time were to start, if the readouts were to change, he'd be in trouble. As long as everything continued to stay the same, the way he'd come to believe it should, he'd find a way to keep going.

"Onward," he said to Bay as he unloaded a bulging bag and an armful of papers into *Molly*. How much time passed since he arrived at the port, he couldn't say. Bay still sat tall and forward looking. "Ever onward."

Sunday, June 21, 2015
Atlantic Ocean, approximately 5°17.60'S, 33° 30.0'W
2:45 p.m. local; 12:45 p.m. eastern time
3,631 sleeps since

"'The sky had changed from clear, sunny cold, to driving sleet and mist. Wrapping myself in my shaggy jacket of the cloth called bearskin, I fought my way against the stubborn storm. Entering, I found a small congregation of sailors and sailors' wives and widows. A muffled silence reigned, only broken at times by the shrieks of the storm.' Shrieks of the storm. Imagine that! It gives me goosebumps to think about. Oh! Here's another one, honeybee. You'll like this one. 'The wind increased to a howl; the waves dashed their bucklers together; the whole squall roared, forked, and crackled around us like a white fire upon the prairie, in which, unconsumed, we were burning; immortal in the jaws of death!'"

"'*Immortal in the jaws of death.*'"

As the last words left his lips and he fell silent, Vole looked up from the book and stilled his legs. The boat stopped moving. Small splashing sounds were swallowed up by silence. Water, endless and molten, extended into the distance on every side. Foamy peaks, mostly small, punctuated the rippled surface, but they didn't fall away or change in size. The ocean air was chilly. Sun shone down on them in a steady wink. The sky was mostly clear.

He looked over at Bay. Steeply angled sunglasses with black lenses protected her eyes from the sun's perpetual glare off the water's surface. Jock was at her feet, dried strip of beaver still wet inside his mouth. They each, woman and dog, had on life vests, and Bay's harness held her upright, as though she were alert and present, though it was obvious to Vole she was neither.

"I could never captain a real ship," Vole said with a sigh, breaking the heavy quiet. He put aside the account of Captain Ahab's lust for revenge. "The sea monster ripped the poor man's leg clean off from the knee down! If that happened to me, well, I don't know what I'd do. I couldn't cauterize it easily, not being at sea and with fire being the way it is. I suppose I'd have to sew myself up . . ."

A shudder coursed through him.

I could never, he thought, though he knew if he had no other choice, he'd have to reconsider.

The book was one of two English-language novels he found in a tiny disheveled library, nestled in a small village. The other book had all its pages glued together and the cover scratched out. He couldn't discern its title, though he suspected it was a duplicate copy.

Vole left two novels of his own, both mysteries and each a favorite (one for its swarthy protagonist; the other for its satisfying and predictable ending), in exchange for the intact book, *Moby Dick*, which he brought with him to read at sea. "A little context goes a long way," he'd told himself at the time, thinking of what little he knew about survival on open water. "Maybe it'll give me some perspective. Thank you, and goodbye, little library. Good luck."

Now, at sea, the days wore on; they would continue to, with or without Melville's added perspective. Vole had read the novel three times already. It didn't change anything. His path forward stayed the same, and the book described a different sort of ocean, anyway.

Up the backside of a swell. Over its frothy crest, down its charging slope. Up the backside of a swell, over its frothy crest, down its charging slope.

When Vole had done as much pedaling as he could and couldn't hold open his drooping eyelids any longer, he assumed he'd done a hard day's work and prepared for sleep. When he woke, everything was the same as when his eyes first shut, and he'd mark down another new dawn. That pattern, and his appetite, helped guide him forward through listlessness. (Much to his perpetual disappointment, he kept to 1,800 calories a day in dehydrated fruit, bars, fitness gels, and high-calorie nut paste.)

"It would appear, honeybee," he said one morning after swallowing down a multivitamin tablet, "time is relative, my math skills fall short without a calculator, and the food here is atrocious.

"One more thing." They were traveling abysmally slow and it depressed him. "We're tiptoeing backward to Africa."

But when Vole came upon Fernando de Noronha, the volcanic island reserve of the Brazilian Atlantic Islands, his black mood dissipated. The Brazilian Atlantic Islands served as a point of reference. They gave him new information. The islands were approximately five hundred kilometers from the port he'd departed from, and he counted twenty-one days to get there.

When he disembarked and pulled his precious cargo to safety on the beach, Vole found the sand to be fine and compact. It felt like polished marble beneath his bare soles. Farther up the beach, where the ground became dry and white, ground silica and shell poured from between his fingers and toes, and he told Jocko his entire life was a dream.

More like a nightmare than a dream, he thought after, though he didn't say it out loud.

As Vole washed and lay afloat in a salt water pool veined with gold and lapis blue, his mind didn't empty. He didn't dissolve away and become one with water and light. He became filled with thoughts of home, and of William, but mostly of Bay, who sat next to him but was caught up in a different moment, living out a different story, and was missing one more extraordinary thing. It was one more memory they wouldn't share.

TWENTY-SEVEN

Sunday, June 21, 2015
Atlantic Ocean, approximately 6° 54.0'S, 23° 18.0'W
3:45 p.m. local; 12:45 p.m. eastern time
3,702 sleeps since

Dear Bay,
 Can you smell the sparks peppering the air? The skies here are beyond gloomy. Distant clouds are the darkest they've ever been. I can see the cotton ball boundary where they turn from ash gray to coal black. Peaks in the water, once turquoise, have deepened to sapphire, and white foam appears where the waves ahead get choppy. The weather system is near enough I can see it, but far enough away I can say, "There's a storm brewing over yonder!" and point from a safe distance.
 The storm is a ferocious-looking thing. It's been twirling slowly here, stewing the entire time we've been squeezing seconds from minutes. Now that it's come into its own, I'm here to witness the

brink of climax. What will it be like in action? I'm happy we won't be here to find out.

Onward we go. Pedal, pedal, pedal. Overtop millions of fish. Pedal, pedal, pedal.

You're wearing the most adorable rain hat. Your hood is pulled tight. All I can see of you is your sublime face. The air has become saturated with water. Beads of drizzle hang in the air. There, I've pulled down and latched the tent walls and windscreen. We'll be protected as we chug through these wet bedazzled skies.

The waves are getting large now—

"Dammit," Vole complained, tapping his pen against his leg, grumbling something about of all the laws, it would be Murphy's Law, wouldn't it. He willed the pen to have flowing ink, pressed the tip into his page, pressed down harder—gouged a colorless hole in the paper.

"Dammit!"

At least one more letter, he'd convinced himself, *because no one knows what could happen. You just never know.* To his disappointment, he forgot his pen had little ink left in its chamber. Recently, all he'd used it for was to keep tally and he'd forgotten to bring an extra.

"I shouldn't have gone so long without eating," he said, agreeing with what Bay's voice was telling him inside his head. "If I'd eaten something sooner, I would have remembered."

Resigned, hungry, Vole put his eighth letter-writing journal aside. He ignored the pangs shooting from his empty gut, not ready to squeeze another saccharine gel pack—liberated from one of the many survival-themed stores he'd ransacked—into his mouth.

"Air pressure must be different here," he muttered, turning away from the hungry echoes inside him, addressing instead an ache that lashed out to seize his left ankle. He rubbed it, absentmindedly.

The storm, the one he was writing about to Bay, was in front and to his left. He'd turned away from it, turned south, to go around its tremendous eye. The current he climbed over had been flowing northwest, against him, and every large swell he encountered had its own spitting crest. Vole approached each wave from its tapered side and pedaled across the broad swell until he found where it blended peacefully with the mounting next, which he climbed the same as the last.

"It's like sailing down a river with rapids, or like sailing through a sea of moguls," he said out loud, thinking of William's last tearful encounter with the hateful, icy mounds.

William never forgave Vole for leading him ignorantly down a black diamond hill, speckled with moguls. At the time, Vole thought it was an easy way for the young boy to learn a hard lesson. William was sensitive; all the youngster needed was a helpful nudge now and again to toughen up. What else was a father for, if not to impart lessons of weakness and strength? Bay insisted good parenting was about seizing the teachable moments.

"What were you thinking?" Bay accused when she found out what happened. "He's not some buddy from school you can push around and pull pranks on. He's a ten-year-old boy. He's never been down anything more wicked than a blue before! *He could've broken his neck.*"

It was the last time they drove to Collingwood to go skiing as a family.

"I despise moguls," Vole muttered as the boat's nose dipped to follow the downward slope of the wave he summited, water as cold as the Blue Mountain's winter breath. Neither Bay's nor

Jock's bodies adapted naturally to the steep change in incline; they stayed mannequin stiff as he pedaled them forward down its slope, unaware of what danger they could be sliding into. "Damned suicide humps."

The quiet route he took through the waves brought him farther south than he wanted. He zigzagged and took detours to avoid severe drops and rain, which he'd also grown to dislike. Unfortunately, some squalls couldn't be avoided, and the cold, drab weeks it took to get through them dragged on.

Vole kept his teeth clean. Trimmed his hair, beard, and nails regularly. His face stayed dark, and he ate as little as he could get away with. His arms stayed strong, and his hands became callused from treating seawater.

Making seawater potable was consistent and steady work. He pumped it by hand to remove harmful pathogens and excess salt. The desalinator he relied on was the first of three handheld units he'd carried all the way from Toronto. With every pump, water was sucked from the ocean through a tube, skinny and plastic, and passed through a membrane encased in a black metal box. The water was deposited into a bottle he drank from directly or used to fill his rain barrels.

"I'll do whatever it takes to avoid drinking my own urine," he vowed to Jock. "Because at the end of the day, there's only one difference between us, little wolf. I draw the line at yellow snow, and you . . . well, you eat crap." He cleared his throat and glanced over at Bay. "Pardon my French."

Broad distances of boredom yawned between ships. There were few he passed he could board—the occasional yacht, fishing trawler, sailboat, cargo ship, or, most occasional of all, vessels with their gangway or pilot ladder extended—and many he passed he couldn't fathom a way into. Oftentimes, their sides grew too tall out of the water, or their slick hulls had no grips for him to hold. Every time Vole came across a ship he could board, he boarded it. In between, because he couldn't count seconds to pass the time, Vole counted the frozen wildlife he passed instead.

He spotted 1,398 sea birds ("Fried albatross probably tastes like fried chicken," he told Jock, wistfully); 241 gray-skinned dolphins ("Eyes like burros," he muttered, skirting past); 78 humpback whales (each with dozens of barnacles glommed onto their faces; he became weepy when he looked too long); 54 sea lions (like Jock from a distance, but up close a wild nightmare); 687 sea turtles ("They're not at all like what you see in the cartoons," he told Bay); and 1,078 other fish and marble-eyed creatures ("A naturalist's dream," he said, cackling, "in the most unnatural circumstances. Naturally, that would be the case. Haha!").

When he came across an expedition ship—not unlike the one he boarded at the port he departed from—Vole was inspired. A rubber excursion vessel, launched from an extended platform, sat on the water next to where the ship's cold metal stern kissed the ocean's frigid swell.

He pedaled them around, in a circle, up to the raft's side. He reached out to take the boat's mooring rope from the excursion leader's hands. Without her boat, she looked absurd. She stood, leaning out and stretched, precariously, over open water. Vole broke one of his rules and repositioned her to keep her from toppling into the ocean the moment time started.

After apologizing for his intrusion, he tied the empty rubber raft to the back of *Molly*'s trailer; he tied a second rope to the raft's opposite end. The tail of the second rope he tied to the pedal boat's canopy, at a spot within easy reach. When he needed to access the raft, he pulled it over the water, around to his side of the boat.

Using the pieces of an emergency shelter, a handy resource he'd scavenged from the big ship, Vole installed a canopy above the raft. The raft became a bedroom. Their bedroom. He laid down blankets and pillows, also removed from the ship; then, with the raft tied parallel and tight against Bay's side of the pedal boat, Vole unclasped her racecar harness and lifted her gently from her seat. He climbed into the raft with Bay in his arms.

Neither boat rocked beneath his movements. Neither boat stood completely still either. They each moved, the smallest amount, constantly beneath his soles. Trying to keep balance, despite his focus, made him feverish with concern over dropping Bay.

Coated in his own slick, he laid Bay down beneath the shade. Vole lay down by her side. He took a deep and shaky breath, let Bay's calm overtake him, and fell asleep.

Sunday, June 21, 2015
Atlantic Ocean, approximately 14° 36.0'N, 24° 54.0'W
3:45 p.m. local; 12:45 p.m. eastern time
4,103 sleeps since

Vole slept 401 times beneath the canopy, next to Bay; and when he wasn't sleeping beneath it, he was napping in his seat, next to Bay. He was in the middle of what he believed was an afternoon daydream, his legs moved up and down without any thought, when a loud sound rang out.

Instantly alert, he cried out and leaped to his feet. Rocks, sharp and black and all around, poked barely through what had been churning water.

"How did I miss those?" he agonized, heart racing from the boat's loud scrape against rocks. "Why did I have to nod off like . . ."

Eyes flicked to the distant horizon; Vole lifted binoculars from his chest to his face and stared hard through the long lenses.

"Bay!" he shouted, disbelief coloring a voice that caught from underuse. "Bay! Jock! I think we've made it!"

Vole pored over the maps he'd brought with him from Brazil. (It wasn't strange to him that he hadn't needed a compass—he wasn't convinced one would work, though in the end he had forgotten to try—because the sun never moved. When there wasn't any fog or mist to block his view, he could look back and see their zigzagging route behind him; their trail stood out like a snail's struggle through the sand.)

"Yes, yes, yes!" he exclaimed, crumpling the precious papers in his excitement. "That must be it! It's got to be. We've made it to Cape Verde!"

Vole tore off his hat, pointed his arm and finger at the horizon, and cried, "Land ho!"

A strange feeling settled over him.

The ocean's dangers were elemental. Reasonable and simple, like those of the desert. Land carried people, and people made everything complicated. Cities overwhelmed him. They reminded him of how complicated human living had become.

Vole sat back down and took them on their way.

Sharp smells, salt and seaweed, hung in the air and grew more sour as he approached the shore. Surrounding boats increased in number as they decreased in size. Waste and refuse, two smells he'd become familiar with in the most intimate way, overpowered the ocean's wild and natural oxygen. He encountered other smells, spicy and fragrant, none he recognized, and despite himself, Vole found their newness tantalizing. It wasn't long before anticipation mounted alongside his trepidation.

He didn't disembark at Cape Verde, and although his destination was nearby, he didn't disembark there either. Short buildings lined the Mauritanian coast, and taller ones towered behind. Above that, blue sky, empty and expansive.

"Another new continent," he breathed, staring through his binoculars at all the people, places, things. Everyone was going somewhere. No one was going anywhere. There were so many people. "Did you ever once think, honeybee . . . ?"

Not ready to pick his way through a packed crowd of sweaty statues and craving fresh water instead of the tinny tasting liquid he forced through his third and final hand pump, Vole pedaled up to a fishing boat, its faded blue underside covered in dripping streaks of rust and algae.

A ladder, dripping with emerald slime, hung down from the edge of the boat. He climbed up its slick rungs and slid over the crusted rail, balancing on the ball of his right foot when he touched down on the deck.

Vole smelled danger before he saw it. Chemical traces of anger and fear hung in the air. He'd become attuned to such subtle scents, having walked through countless bursts, many of which should have been carried away on a breeze or sunken down to become part of the earth. His nostrils flared in recognition. The air here reminded him of something he'd encountered before.

But what?

Vole stood still. Closed his eyes. Breathed deeply. Mentally traced his journey back.

It was there, in front of him. It didn't take long to pin down. A hot cloud of blood and gore that had sunk down from above. The air on board smelled like one who deals in death, death's breath the exhaled fumes of a blood-hungry carnivore from the jungles of Panama. Or, perhaps what he smelled was his own fear, but he didn't think that was it.

"You should probably go," Vole muttered to himself. He glanced down to where Bay and Jock sat waiting for his return, though they didn't know it. *"Go Around Foul Smells (Especially Jaguar Breath)* is at the top of your list of rules."

But he couldn't leave, and it was for the same reason he couldn't stop his journey until it was over, whenever that happened to be. He owed it to Bay, to the entire world, to take it all in. Because with his power came responsibility. How could he expect Bay, anyone, to understand? His quest to become the person she thought she married transformed him into someone she'd never known. Vole had been shown a world where the only danger worth fearing was himself. Only Vole had the ability to do something wrong or make a mistake. There was no one else around to blame. To turn his face and look away was to introduce poison into purity, fear into paradise, and he didn't have the right.

Vole quaked, but he didn't leave. Instead, he sniffed the air like a starving jungle cat, and he followed his nose down into the belly of the ship.

A single lit bulb illuminated a single room that held a sparse collection of vertical metal beams, painted blue-gray. The only furniture he could see was a foldout table, aluminum and round, dented badly, somehow standing on three bent legs. On the table's tilted surface was a small bowl, brimming with spent cigarettes and white ash.

The hot room stank like rotten fish and ocean slime.

Stifled, he climbed back up toward sunlight. Walked a circle around the trawler. Took in stains on the synthetic green carpet and wood surface. Everything was worn from salt, footsteps, time, and he realized he was looking at blood on the deck.

"Fish bleed red, don't they?" he croaked around his leaping heart. He did another lap of the main deck but found no one. "What am I looking for?" he muttered. "Am I here to conduct a witch hunt? What do I hope to find?" But he couldn't deny the fear he smelled in the air, still. He stayed and kept searching.

When he finished circling, he stepped into the captain's bridge. The smell grew stronger. A plastic panel, peeling, marked a poorly concealed compartment on the wall behind the captain's desk.

He tugged its corner, pulled it free, and found, resting within, dozens of black guns the length of his arm. They were stacked on toppled boxes overflowing with bullets. Unlike everything else he'd encountered aboard the trawler, the ammunition was clean and new. It gleamed, polished black and bronze.

Vole let go of the panel as though it burst into flame.

A pistol, alone, asleep on its side—metallic tang and cigarette smoke cloying—split red leather of the front passenger seat of a black car, round edges dipped in chrome; a tightlipped driver with clouded eyes and rainbow-tipped claws gripping the wheel. Who are you, driver? Where are you going? What target fills your focus red?

"I remember," the words escaped on Vole's breath. "How could I forget?"

It was the first gun he'd seen since he was a young boy. Back when he'd left Canada and crossed into the United States, a man grown, all he'd wanted was to fix a broken bicycle pedal. What he'd found was the unspoken promise of violence. He'd panicked and fled back to Bay.

"Guns are why all those babies have their futures rewritten as orphans," his mother once told him. He recalled watching her fingers, bone white, press into her throat as she denied herself tears. She was a weepy pacifist; his father, a die-hard keeper of the peace.

"A pity. A damned pity," Vole muttered, heart pounding.

Then he caught sight of something else. A small, familiar shape beneath the desk.

He dropped to his knees, pulled back the mold-spotted curtain, and lost his breath. It was a child. *A boy*, he thought, though he couldn't be sure.

"Good grief," Vole whispered.

After a time, he dropped the curtain and straightened. Walked out of the cabin. Leaned over the rail. Vomited over the side of the vessel. He didn't want to stay there any longer, but what was he to do? Leave the child alone, surrounded by artifacts of war? Stark reminders of violence and pain. What would he do if it were William?

It wasn't William. He didn't know the boy's story. Vole didn't know anything about the situation. Passing judgment made him squirm. What if the boy had a brother, or sister, or the missing crew was his family, and taking him away only made the situation worse? What if the boy was a stowaway, and the life he was running from was inconceivably bleaker? What if the cache had been taken from evildoers and was on its way to be disposed of?

Vole spun fantasies in his head but all of them ended in the tragedy of firearms in the presence of innocents, and none of them gave him the answers he needed.

"What should I do?" he whispered. He wished Bay were there with him, but he was grateful she wasn't. Vole wouldn't wish this on anyone.

He couldn't leave having done nothing. Not like last time. He removed his journal and a pen from his pack. The pen held red ink, which was new to him. He'd retrieved it from a different ship he'd boarded somewhere else along the way, and he hoped it held enough deep color for his purpose.

After deliberating for some time, Vole tore a piece of paper from his book and began to write: *I happened to be passing through when I saw you. I didn't want to interfere because you look as though you're up to something important. Whatever <u>you</u> think is important, you should do. Should you ever think it important enough to come find me, you can, and I want you to. More impossible things have happened.*

There was no way to know whether the boy could read the words, and if he could, whether he would, but Vole rolled the paper and slipped the tiny tube into the boy's fist. Vole violated his rules a bit more, and he kissed the boy on the forehead.

"Good luck," he whispered. "May you find yours."

Before disembarking, Vole collected all the guns and ammunition he could find. He dropped it all overboard, far from where he'd left Bay and Jock in *Molly*. The weapons landed on the water with barely a splash. They sank down and hung beneath the water's surface. When time ticked once again, the glittering black pile would plummet and disappear from view forever.

Back in the pedal boat, Vole found his thirst had fled. He savored the bitterness of bile in his throat as he pedaled away. Glancing back over his shoulder, he noticed text he hadn't seen before on the side of the trawler. He was surprised to recognize the script.

Vole raised his binoculars to his eyes. *The Truant*, it said, and beneath, in smaller cursive, *World's Finest Fish*.

He let loose a heavy sigh and steered them toward land.

Sunday, June 21, 2015
Nouakchott, Mauritania
4:45 p.m. local; 12:45 p.m. eastern time
4,115 sleeps since

Vole was sad to part ways with their bedroom raft. He'd grown fond of its luxury and of the closeness it enabled between him and Bay. He left it on the beach, a busy place covered in nets, buoys, and household clutter, with a note, *In need of a new home, please take.* Then he checked the pedal boat's trailer wheels. Secured the hitch to his bike's rear axle. Tightened the trailer's nylon straps. Pinched his bicycle tires and replaced both tubes, and filled his rain barrels with water from a hotel fountain. After dressing Bay and himself in wispy layers of loose-fitting clothes, peony petals of cloth, and after visiting every bookstore he could find, Vole departed.

He led them north through Mauritania, the Western Sahara, and Morocco.

The desert was desolate. Dry. The only sounds to be heard were of his grunts and coughs, the rattle of *Molly* over rocks, and the slight slap of brown-tinted water sliding around in the two rain barrels.

Grunt, cough, rattle, slap.

Sand, like the world's quiet, stretched as far as his senses could perceive.

Hot air stifled without the ocean's neutralizing breath to blow away pools of it. Heat mirages cloaked everything in a lasting rippled haze, and when Vole looked down at the dirt beneath his turning wheel, he saw his tire slice through the glimmer like it was jelly.

Heat, steady, pressed against his chest and ears. At times it was unbearable, and he begged the skies to release a wind.

Clear blue barely changed overhead and the late afternoon sun barely moved. Vole felt like he was crossing the ocean again; infrequent lorries and fuel stations (empty of fuel and closed to customers) were islands of paradise in a sea of dust.

They cut through Marrakesh on their way to Tangier, but they didn't cross the Strait of Gibraltar there. He continued cycling them east, toward beckoning green hills. Crumbly roads rose and dropped. They crossed to Spain from Belyounech, a small and colorful community nestled along the curving coast.

They continued, pedaling up through Spain.

North of Madrid, the skies were clouded and the air burned less. Vole itched to take Bay straight to the United Kingdom, where she needed to be next, but he'd made a promise. It didn't matter she'd never know whether he kept it or not.

The castles and pastures of Southern France began to clog with cars and modern infrastructure, and Vole knew they would pass through the suburbs of Paris soon. It surprised him to discover cities bothered him less than before. Perhaps he'd become used to not seeing people to the same degree they were blind to him. Or perhaps it was because he had returned to Europe, a place he'd been to before, a place that resembled home.

Whatever the reason, by the time he was on L'Aquitaine—the longest motorway in France, which led directly to the heart of Paris—he was lighthearted and optimistic.

"This is it, honeybee," he said. "And you said you didn't think we'd ever make it back here."

Had she said that?

Or were the words his own?

When he recognized the first of many landmarks, his pulse quickened and leg rotations gained speed. He was looking forward to retracing the steps he and Bay had made thirty-five—or was it forty-three? He couldn't be sure—years ago.

TWENTY-EIGHT

Sunday, June 21, 2015
Paris, France
6:45 p.m. local; 12:45 p.m. eastern time
4,207 sleeps since

ON ONE HAND, Vole felt like nothing about Paris was any different. On the other, nothing about it felt the same. He was extremely tempted to wake Bay to discuss the topic, but he remembered how she'd clutched her stomach. He boxed his longing away and continued.

Vole picked their way through a maze of people and cars until he reached Saint-Denis, a suburb located a few kilometers north of the city center. Upon arriving, he discovered their hotel had been converted into offices with white walls, and there was now a popular café on the ground floor. The only part of the building he recognized was its façade.

There was a lasting and subtle appeal in the façade's ornate arches. He looked closer. The stone's looming familiarity did something to him. Standing on the sidewalk, in front of what was once a honeymooner's dream hotel, Vole cast his mind far back, until he'd gone back in time, and the singsong echoes of Bay's delight filled his head.

Making her laugh and smile was his life's only mission then. When had that changed? Had he changed? Or had he never known what made her happy in the first place?

Sadness swept him and made him languid. Without a single ounce of rush, Vole cycled Bay around the city streets using a rickshaw taxi he borrowed. Slowly, absentmindedly, he remembered what it was like to stroll back and forth across the same street, every street they came to, stopping to look through every shop window, forcing people to move around them for a change. He recalled how they'd handfed each other sculpted chocolates and sweet cakes topped with savory cream. He recalled late mornings and the essence of coffee—dark liquid strong enough to fell a horse, served in porcelain cups the size of thimbles. He remembered how they'd each commented on the unforgettable weather they were having, speaking secretly of each other's dewy smiles and sunshine kisses.

They'd made love every day for ten days straight, and for another ten when they got back home.

"Maybe not *ten* days," Vole admitted to himself. "Why did that have to change too?"

Vole grew warm as he glanced back at Bay, who sat smiling behind him. He remembered how she looked, sleek as a seal with her new bob cut, lilac lace and ivory curves on rumpled sheets, body languid after a morning of rolling around beneath them.

Did she still remember that morning too?

The smile on her face told him she did.

He followed an invisible path. It wound between tall buildings and took abrupt left and right turns and crossed at the most thoughtless junctures. Vole followed it all the way to Parc des Buttes-Chaumont, where he searched for the tree they once claimed as their own. He found that, like their hotel, the landscape was transformed. Their tree was gone. Bulldozed or torn up from its roots, it was hard to say. Some restoration work had been done on the tower, and he suspected the removal happened then. He was disappointed, but what was he to expect? As time passed, things changed. When time stood still . . .

"Well, that remains to be seen, doesn't it?" Vole said, becoming frightened by the thought.

Soon after he discovered their tree was gone, they left Paris. The city's magic was a shadow of what it had been before. His memories of their time together were what made Paris precious. Alone, the city held little for him.

He pedaled vigorously. Vole was anxious to make new memories. Ones Bay would remember too.

June 2001 (continued)

After two pints each, Vole left Alice at the pub.

"I don't know why I'm comfortable telling you this," she'd said, "but I trust you for some reason. I think it's because you're a good guy. Will you help me? You must understand how hard it is to break into the ranks, the 'old boys' club,' and I want to manage a branch one day. I've got the skills for it."

All she'd wanted was to discuss her career. The undercurrents he'd felt tugging weren't trying to drag him under. He'd been a fool to mistake her interest in him for anything more than professional. Though he'd never had any intention of acting on his suspicion and was relieved to discover the truth, he was ashamed to have found the unsolicited attention thrilling.

"A bloody fool," he muttered, scuffing the bottoms of his polished leather shoes against the sidewalk.

More than anything, Vole wanted to go home, but he didn't feel welcome there. Aimless legs carried him around town instead, and he found himself at the conservation area. He stayed there, sitting on William's favorite boulder, as the sun dipped lower and lower in the sky. The lower the sun got, the more like the emptying sky he felt. It was the first time Vole went unaccounted for at family dinner.

In the end, a sunless sky drew him home. Dusky pink clouds accompanied him on his walk. Dusk also happened to be when Harold checked on his advanced web of sprinklers and hoses—a complex network he referred to as *The System*—for any apparent weaknesses.

"Everything in The System has a proper place," Harold chortled when he saw Vole seated on the front steps of the Gibbons' house. His back was bent from coiling a heavy rubber hose around one arm; spiderwebs spread across the aging man's sagging face. "But those damned squirrels take liberties and move things!"

"Those damned squirrels," Vole replied, sensing from Harold's gleaming squint the churlish man was out for blood.

Harold's eyes grew narrow. Sly. His jowls, leftover on his neck from when he was a much fatter man, trembled with what Vole imagined to be cruel anticipation.

"How are things going with you, Banker Man?" he wheedled. "Talked to a friend from the force after I saw cruisers parked outside your house the other night. Is that boy of yours doing hard time for what he did? Reckless son of a gun . . ."

"Did I ever tell you I golf with Lawrence's old man, Joe McCarthy? I like golfing with Joe. You should come with us sometime. He's a good talker. You've gotta hear some of his stories! Anyway, he tells me he's gonna keep both boys out of trouble. It's about time someone takes charge, if you ask me. It's like I said about raising sons: Never stop working them to the bone, or else they'll never stop working to bone." He let loose another evil-sounding chuckle. "To be a young stallion again!"

"None of that's true, Harold," Vole said. "And my son isn't a criminal. Or a . . . stallion."

"Hard times for young bucks these days. Hard times. You tell me if you ever need to blow off steam. I know the place."

Evil wink.

"Of course."

"And don't stand me up on our next ride. You're getting fat. Bay's going to leave you if you get fat."

Harold chortled once more and vanished into his meticulously kept, two-story home—a building fortified with animal traps and pest poison.

If Bay hadn't insisted he stay on good terms with their neighbors, especially Harold, who lived closest, Vole would have gladly helped the suburban creatures in their torment of the man.

"What a tool," Vole muttered and leaned back against the hard concrete step. "What a godforsaken tool."

"An oblivious blowhard at the best of times," Bay agreed, startling him with her quiet voice. He hadn't realized she'd come outside and had missed her standing near the unruly bushes next to their house. "But he has his moments. Besides, we can't pick our neighbors . . ."

"So instead we pick our fights," he said, finishing her thought.

"Exactly."

She walked over to where he was sitting. Took a seat on the lower step. Laid her head against the side of his knee and breathed deeply.

They sat still together for a long time.

Bay was the one to break the silence: "Harold wasn't lying."

Vole sniffed. "Harold's always lying."

"He likes to exaggerate. I spoke with Joe McCarthy this evening. He's going to hire Will and Lawrence to work in his odd jobs business this summer. He's got enough work, and they can take on his smaller projects, maybe help manage them. I think it's a good idea."

"If you say so, honeybee."

"Vole . . ." She gripped his forearm and forced him to look at her. "I'm sorry I lost my temper."

She could tell when he was spinning.

"I'm sorry," he insisted in a choking way. "It was my fault. You were right to be angry."

She sighed. "Yes."

Vole's throat became too tight for him to talk. He coughed; taut cords slackened. "Bay," he implored. "I have no idea what I was thinking."

She sighed again. "You weren't thinking about what was best for the family—you were thinking about what was best for you."

What could he do but agree?

"I've thought a lot about this promotion you're chasing," she continued when it became clear he had nothing more to offer. "The added stress of it is driving me bonkers, but I think it's positive. I think you need a change. You must be bored of doing the same old thing with the same old people, every day." She bit her lip, something she did when she was about to say something he might not like. "Are you bored of doing the same old thing every day with me too?"

Vole reached down to pull her up next to him; he hugged her tight against his body.

"Never ever *ever* will I get bored of you," he said, pressing his lips against her neck. "You're the most interesting person in the entire world. Please don't think I could ever get bored of you. I'm sorry. I was being a jerk."

Again she sighed, but a different note this time.

"Can you promise me one thing?"

"Whatever you need."

"No more lies," she pleaded. "I can't handle not trusting you. It's too much."

"Oh, honeybee. I'll always be honest with you."

"I hate it when we argue."

"Me too, hon—" His stomach, loose after weeks of being snarled tight, unleashed the most familiar growl.

Bay laughed. "Am I at risk of getting eaten alive?"

Sheepishly, "I had a pint, but nothing to eat."

"The pub! That's where you were hiding."

"For a bit. It was too crowded. I went to the conservation area."

"Lucky for you, I'm a conservationist who specializes in saving leftovers, and, conveniently, I've kept the fried chicken warm."

Vole's throat constricted once more. She knew exactly what he needed.

He held her against him and breathed deep the scent of her.

"I love you," Vole whispered.

"I love you too, you old sap," Bay answered back.

Respecting the value of hard work was ingrained too deep inside Vole for him to take William's mistake lightly, and it wasn't a topic Vole knew how to talk about. Such a momentous waste of money hurt him on a level he couldn't put in words, and no one, not even Bay, could help him sort it out. Though there was much he didn't understand, Vole understood people made mistakes, and some lessons came at a cost; he knew he should be grateful the price in this case wasn't anything too dear.

William continued to save for repayment, but they resolved in secret to let him keep his money. Still, whenever the topic came up, Vole struggled. His folly put his son's life in danger, and Lawrence's life—another man's son—in danger too. He would never forgive himself for that.

They stopped sharing small jokes. William stopped seeking him out for advice, and Vole stopped being the one William came to for permission. A muted, near begrudging respect formed between them. Never again did they collapse into fits of laughter; and never again did they conspire to keep anything from Bay.

TWENTY-NINE

Sunday, June 21, 2015
Moor of Rannoch, Scotland
5:45 p.m. local; 12:45 p.m. eastern time
4,248 sleeps since

LUMPY FORMS EMERGED on the distant skyline. They rose from the Earth to form mountains that grew craggy as Vole ventured deeper into northern Scotland. Cool air became crisp and sweet with pollen. Feathery thatches of brown seed gave shelter to glittering black eyes, and not for the first time—nor the last—Vole wondered whether the hidden beasts he passed saw more than their dumb silence let on.

The gray strip of pavement he was following ended at a set of train tracks that crossed the road in front of him. The tracks stretched out on either side, then vanished, swallowed by a surrounding ocean of full grass. The tracks marked a boundary. On one side, the side he'd come from: touring country. On the other, where he was headed: wilderness.

The road continued on the other side of the tracks, but it became awash in sharp stones and gravel and dropped quickly out of sight as it snaked down between two enormous hills.

Around him, on the rising green hills, Vole saw dots of pink and canary yellow speckling the slopes. He was drawn to the blossoms.

Vole's most recent selection of books included one about moor plants and animals. It said heather had yet to reach full bloom in June. The flowers were most likely tormentils and rhododendrons. Or were they marsh violets? He had trouble remembering without the pages in front of him, and he knew Harold would be disappointed. Vole didn't care to learn the names of everything he saw—he cared only to see.

In the faraway distance the road reappeared. It hugged the banking slope of one of the hills until it faded from sight over the crest, ending at the base of a gray sky.

Vole shivered. Drew his jacket tight around his shoulders. It wasn't cold—he guessed it was about fifteen degrees centigrade—but the early evening sun burned shy behind clouds, and the air seeped a kind of moisture that soaked through his clothing and clung to his bones.

"Mist," he said to Bay as he led them over the railway tracks and bid rueful goodbye to smooth pavement. "Where's all the creeping mist to go along with this primordial scene?" He took in her familiar and unchanging expression in his bicycle's right mirror (she was wearing that adorable toque again), and told her to hang on tight.

Vole soon found the birthplace of mist. It emerged from grass marshes and collected over bogs of lichen and moss. The roads he encountered were low and soft. He thought them to be pond bottoms, and when he got stuck, which happened with annoying frequency, he had to free his bicycle and trailer from mud. On more than one occasion, he lay down books—Vole didn't bother keeping the one about plants—so the trailer's slick wheels could gain purchase. When that happened, the canopy would sway and Vole found himself eyeing up the chest harnesses he installed back in Michigan. "Without those," he huffed to Bay and Jock between mighty heaves, "you two might be treading this swamp with me! There better not be any leeches in here . . ."

Bay dreamed of one day visiting the moors. That much, Vole knew. Though, he couldn't recall when she first brought it up. He thought she must have told him about a specific thirst that could only be quenched by sipping scotch, looking out over the birthplace of mist itself; yes, that must have been the time. They'd sat down to share a drink, William was young and in bed, and she'd been feeling sentimental.

"This silvery vapor," Vole whispered as he split a ground-hugging cloud in two with his front wheel, only now recalling Bay's hot passion behind cool words. "You were right, honeybee. Clouds are born here. Though I do find the silence makes it eerie."

Rannoch Moor was west of Loch Rannoch, which was a small lake compared to the Great Lakes. It had low banks covered in grass all around.

Vole scoured those banks, going deeper inland, searched for the place he knew would make Bay's spirits soar. When he found an unused, single-room cottage, built from stone with a wood swing out front, Vole knew he found it.

He walked himself back to a hotel, high on a hill they cycled past earlier the same day. Vole wanted to be refined for Bay this time, but he was having difficulty remembering what being a gentleman meant, and he doubted he ever was one. How did he look, back when they first met? Not sophisticated or refined, in his opinion.

After cleaning his hair and skin with water he collected from a spitting shower head, and rinsing in cold rainwater from the cistern outside, Vole set about finding a change of clothes. He sourced an outfit from an orange and brown suitcase behind the hotel's front counter. The near jack-o'-lantern pattern reminded him of when William dyed all his copper hair black.

"Oh my God," Bay exclaimed when she saw the dramatic hairstyle. "Please tell me that's not permanent. The dye's going to go straight to your brain!"

"Re*lax*. I'm only doing it to impress all the girls."

Chuckling at the memory of William's glibness, Vole checked himself in the mirror. Little of his hair remained dark brown, and the gray was becoming lighter with every passing day. He cut it short, as best he could, in the style Bay liked most. His teeth were clean and vibrant in a tanned face. Thin lines fanned out from his eyes. They'd always been there but had grown deeper and more plentiful since he left home, though his wrinkles were far from Harold's tortured chasms. Freshly shaved, a thin white line on his chin was visible, but it was an old scar; his clothing masked the new ones he'd earned on the rest of his body. He wore a gray wool vest over a yellow button-down shirt with long sleeves. Bay told him his tanned hands were her favorite part of summer, and he thought the pastel tone contrasted favorably with his skin. On his legs he wore dark trousers and a belt around his waist. *Maybe never a gentleman*, he thought to himself, *but I can try and look the part.*

"I'm only doing it to impress all the girls, honeybee," he joked to himself, then went to the hotel bar in search of scotch.

The bottle he needed was kept in a locked cabinet behind the bar. Vole borrowed the keys—found strung about the wrist of the bartender—to get inside.

He muttered an apology to no one in particular as he liberated the gleaming bottle from its glass shelf. It was three quarters full and weighed heavy in his hand. "So this is what eighteen years—fifteen of those stewing in a bourbon oak barrel—feels like. I bet this will last eighteen minutes with Bay!"

The joke sobered him. He moved on.

When Vole added the bottle to his list of things he borrowed from places all over the world, it was with appreciation. At first, the list burned into him like the sun, never letting him forget it was there. As he traveled south through the Americas, he found the list increasingly helpful. He looked forward to keeping it. Whenever he wrote down one of his secret thefts, he removed the burden of it from his shoulders. In a way, the list was his release. He hoped the letters he wrote to Bay would be that, but once he understood she would never get to read them, he avoided looking at where they sat in *Molly*.

"Maybe I should throw all the letters in the garbage," he suggested.

Bay said nothing. Not even in his head.

Vole swept the cottage floor faster, driven by the thought of Bay and a velvet kiss shared at the world's edge. The blushing memory had become rosier since his time in Paris, and his lips tingled.

The broom slipped from Vole's hands for a third time and clattered to the floor.

"I suppose it's time," he said to calm his fraught nerves. "It must be time."

As Vole welcomed motion and chaos anew, the sound of Bay's laughter—the exact notes he imagined every day since leaving Tierra del Fuego—filled him. Her song was a soothing balm spread over an aching sting.

"Oh!" Bay exclaimed, looking around in wonderment and running her hands over her body, taking in the clean clothes she wore. "Did it happen again? Where are we now?"

She went to the door.

"Are we *here*?"

Vole walked over to Bay. Handed her a glass of scotch.

It was early evening and a gusting wind blew away the cloud cover overhead. Though the wind's assault, welcome as it was, wasn't directed at him, Vole's skin tingled and he felt bruised beneath its blustery touch. It could have been the mildest wind and it would have made his skin feel as fresh and tender.

The smells carrying past his nose were subtle and brief. They seemed nothing like the invisible bursts, dense and consistent, that went on forever in a time-stopped world. The air he breathed in now felt airy, nonexistent.

He watched, saying nothing, as the sky above them opened further. It teased with the promise of a brilliant sunset to come. Insects sang, and wave after wave of alien sound crashed into Vole's ears. Animal calls assailed him. A brown bird with sharp wings and a pointed beak dove down, and soared up, and flew out of sight; his heart beat like a drum.

Where should I look, he wondered, struggling to keep up with all the activity. A feverish energy overtook him. *There's so much to see.*

Bay turned and her steady regard held him. Whatever she saw must have made her happy because she threw her hands up into the air, sending liquid gold splashing, and wrapped him in her arms.

He embraced her back.

"Vole," she breathed. "You're crying."

Startled, "I hadn't realized," he said, and wiped his cheeks. "How . . . ?"

"It doesn't matter." He brought his lips to her forehead.

"Did you make it to Paris?" she asked.

"We did."

"What was it like? Was it different? Is our tree still there?"

He poured her another glass of scotch. She sipped and sighed as it lit fire to her veins.

Bay wasn't supposed to have alcohol. Not in her condition, or with the medication she was on. He wasn't about to deny her this. She seemed healthier than she had been in the months preceding their departure. The headache she felt moments before had passed, and neither was going to bring it up.

They moved to sit outside on the wooden swing. Strong metal chains kept the bench suspended, though they squeaked and groaned under their weight.

Vole described what it was like in Paris. He told her it wasn't the same, but it was still lovely. He talked about the memories that returned to him while he stood there, in front of their old hotel; and she interrupted him excitedly to add her own memories, ones he'd never heard her admit to before but made his own recollections much clearer.

The whole time they talked, her fingers moved back and forth along his arm, and she never once looked away. He wondered whether she cared about the moors anymore.

A natural lull formed between them. Into the quiet he asked a question, one he'd been carrying with him since they left home.

"Why didn't you tell me you kept a real list of wonders?"

She shrugged and took a sip.

"It wasn't important," she answered.

Vole sat up straight.

"What do you mean?" he asked. It was her list of dreams. It must be important.

"I don't mean to say it wasn't *important*, it was less important than what we had at home. We were building a life together. We had William. I wanted to spend as much time at home with him as I could, to help take care of our family. I guess . . . my priorities changed." She shrugged once more.

Was it as simple as that?

"But you kept it up. You added to it, and you scratched places from it. It was a list you maintained, and you never told me about it."

Hurt colored his voice. For the first time, he realized how much it pained him to discover she'd kept something from him.

They were a partnership. A unified front. The big things they discussed together. It's what they promised each other; and while she never once strayed, he'd reneged, time and time again, and now, hadn't the courage to set things right.

A twisting sickness he knew all too well seized his stomach.

Bay leaned into him and ran her fingers through his hair.

"It's always lists with you," she murmured.

"With *me*?"

She nodded.

"But you were the one keeping lists around the house!" Now Vole was confused. Had he done it again? Had he been wrong about everything, all this time? Was all this unimportant to her?

Bay held both of his hands in hers, held his gaze with her own.

"There is the list, and there are lists. I keep lists around the house because you need them. If you were going shopping, I'd give you a list of what we needed, because without it you'd forget something and blame yourself. If there were phone numbers you needed, I would add them to a list to help you find them, because if you couldn't, you'd berate yourself for not being more organized." She raised his hands to her lips. "You're hard on yourself. I saw how I could help you. I kept my list of wonders because I've had one since I was a little girl. I would've kept scratching out places until there was only one left if it meant I could dream about going there one day with you.

"The magic of somewhere, like here, means nothing if I can't share it with you."

That's why Paris seemed lackluster. Not because it was changed, or because the tree was gone, but because he couldn't share it with Bay. Life together. Memories together. Time spent *together*. That's why he must take this journey. It was their last chance to spend time together.

Vole did what he'd been burning to do since he first heard her laughter. He lifted her from the wood swing and carried her to the air mattress bed he'd set up on the floor inside the little cottage. He lay her down flat on her back in comfort, and he kissed her.

Scotch on her lips was intoxicating. Her arms reached around his body and she pulled him closer. Breathing grew ragged as he felt her soft fingers free his shirt from his waistband, and reach up beneath.

It was the first time he felt her touch in ten years.

Blood rushed through his body, filling his head with a pounding beat. Soft breaths quickened as he kissed a trail down her neck to her collarbone, a place he dreamed of paying a visit to with his lips ever since she stopped him short the last time. He'd selected the shirt he fitted her with because of its softness, but now he was undoing its buttons, slowly, one by one, he wondered if his subconscious guided his hand.

For every button Vole undid, he kissed a newly exposed place on her body. When her shirt was completely open, he looked down at her, saw her amber eyes had become dark like molasses, lips red like raspberries.

Vole undid the string holding her flannel pajama bottoms in place.

"I can't—" she began but stopped short when her pants slid to the floor. "Will you . . . ?"

He knew what she was asking of him, though the words wouldn't come.

"Yes." His reply strained against his throat, and she smiled in a way only Bay could smile. He removed the rest of his clothing until he wore only boxers.

They were both almost nude.

She reached out, tentative, shy; touched his chest, stomach, arms.

"You're strong," she murmured. "You're changing so quickly."

He looked down at himself and saw muscles where years before there was time-ripened skin. It was strange to be growing strong when most people born the same year were weakening. He felt frightened. Butterfly wings beat steady inside him, and he became more unsure of himself than he was their first time lying together. He began to wonder whether Bay found him attractive anymore.

When her searching fingers worked their way down from his stomach to the waistband of his boxers, he felt his insecurities melt away. When her fingers slipped lower, his mind became empty of everything but her.

They made love on the moors of Scotland.

He was gentle, like he promised, making sure to take his time teasing and touching, first with his fingertips and then with his mouth. By the time he lost himself within her, she'd already cried out once, arching her back and pushing against him in a way she hadn't done since their honeymoon.

After some time, Vole began to cry.

"You have no idea how much I missed you," he said. "How much I needed this."

"Oh, I have an idea."

"Bay," he said, seized by a compulsion he didn't sense coming. "I need to tell you something."

Then Jock, having finished his most recent treat, put his paws up on the bed and pressed his cold nose into Vole's face. Despite the dog's beaver-musk breath, Vole nuzzled Jock's head. "I almost forgot about you," he said to the dog.

"I almost forgot we could do that," Bay said before shutting her eyes and humming a song he recognized.

"I wasn't sure we would be able to."

"I had hoped," she replied in a sleepy voice. "What do you need to tell me?"

Vole remembered something else he had to tell her too. He reached down to the floor. "We have voicemail," he said.

He didn't recognize William's speech at first. Not until the recording played for many seconds did the cadence of their son's voice become familiar again.

"Hi, Dad. Thanks for calling. The doctor phoned. He wondered if we'd spoken. He told me to be in touch. Here I am. Being in touch. Are we still on for lunch this Wednesday? If you could let Mom know I called that'd be great. Thanks, Pops."

Thanks, Pops.

That was it.

They replayed it, over and over, clinking glasses and sipping scotch to congratulate each other on a job well done. They giggled over how mortified William would be if he knew they listened to his voicemail while lying naked, mooning over each other in bed.

August 2001

On a Thursday afternoon in August, months after William's accident, Vole received a phone call from his boss, Marc Rodrigo.

"Gibbons"—Marc stopped referring to Vole as Tire Slayer after the i30 vanished and word got around—"I'm not going to waste your time. You're too smart for that. I'll cut to the chase.

"You know there's been a lot of talk surrounding who's going to head up the Etobicoke branch. It's been a long time coming, and a lot of good people were considered for the role."

"It's a popular location."

"You're telling me! It's got the highest teller productivity in the country, least amount of customer churn, and they get huge points for diversity. Women flock to that branch like cows to a bull. I don't think they've had to fire anyone in half a decade! It's a damned sexy location to manage. Damned sexy."

"I, uh, couldn't have said it any better myself."

"Can you handle a sexy location like that, Gibbons? The pressure will be high. Next year's targets are high. The respect you'll get for nailing high targets is high. Everything about it is a high. It's a high, sexy-as-hell location.

"So I ask again, Gibbons. Can you handle—can you *tame*—a branch like Etobicoke?"

"Um, yes, of course."

Pause.

Marc cleared his throat.

"Keeping your cards close to your chest, eh? I like that about you.

"You know the London branch? It's exactly like the Etobicoke branch, only better. It has limitless potential. All it needs is an experienced leader to bring out that potential. I want you to be the one to do it.

"It's time to show us what you're made of, Gibbons, in London. The London branch needs you."

"So, um, I'm not getting Etobicoke."

"Bernard's got a copy of the offer on his desk. Take it home. Look it over. Get back to me. You won't be disappointed. This is a big opportunity. It's real. I know it's real, because it's exactly the same opportunity I got, and look where I am today. It's *your* opportunity to lose, Gibbons."

Vole, not sure Marc was done, let the silence between them linger.

"Absolutely," he jumped in, a few seconds too late. "Do I tell you my answer on Monday?"

Giving people the weekend to consider was standard courtesy at the bank.

"I was hoping to hear from you tomorrow. We're fighting multiple timelines here. But, if you need more time . . ."

"Tomorrow isn't a problem. I can't say it enough, Marc. Thank you for this opportunity. Like you said, it's been a long time coming. I'm ready."

"We'll have you back to being a Tire Slayer in no time. *Vroom-vroom!* Go get 'em, Gibbons!"

The dial tone buzzed.

"*Vroom-vroom?*" Vole muttered, placing the receiver in its cradle. "Good grief."

He picked up the documents Bernard, the office administrator, had prepared for him. Bernard winked and made an odd stretchy face when he handed the envelope over, and Vole knew he'd snooped. *How many people know already?*

Vole took the envelope back to his office. Put it down on his desk. Picked it up. Put it down, picked it back up again, and opened it.

They were offering him the London branch to manage. He hadn't realized Lorna was moving on from the London branch. The London branch. That's how Marc said it, and Vole thought it sounded proper and worldly. London was a city with distinguished banking history. Vole liked that too. It wasn't as big or celebrated as Etobicoke, but it was still a performant and growing location.

Finally, he'd been granted access to the ladder. Now all he had left to do was climb up to the next rung.

After how long he'd worked at the bank, Vole had become something of a legend. The uneducated worker bee whose time and efforts paid off. It was a proud part of his image and the bank's regional heritage. Maybe that's why they were offering him a twenty-five percent increase to his on-target earnings to relocate, plus a stipend for the first year to help cover the cost of settling into a new home. Their household expenses would wind down when William went to school. With such a generous offer, they might do all the work they wanted done to their home.

But why would they? There'd be no point. They'd be in London. Bay would have to get a new job in a new city. London had a big population; air quality and road rage would be worse than in Dorset. They'd have to make new friends.

They'd save more money. William would have access to more and better services in London. He'd get exposed to city living before applying to university. It might help soften the devastating blow of not being allowed to keep his license. When he moved out, which would happen in a few short years, Vole and Bay would be alone together. Didn't they want to be alone together somewhere more exciting than Dorset?

There was an airport in London. Maybe they'd use it to go places when they retired.

Maybe, before he and Bay retired into full-time cottage life on the lake, he'd get to drive a Porsche. Maybe he'd retire as a regional manager, one who called employees by their last names and made chummy jokes. *Tire Slayer.* Maybe, when he took Bay on exciting London city dates, he would roll up in his shiny red convertible, and she would have on lipstick the same apple-red shade, and she'd swoon into the front passenger seat.

"Absurd," Vole muttered, rubbing his forehead as he considered Bay swooning. "Not the lipstick part. I like that. The part about becoming a giant—excuse my French—*asshole.*"

He put the job offer back in the envelope.

"Well, one thing's for certain. Bay's going to be happy."

As though saying her name out loud cast a spell over him, Vole began to imagine what Bay would think about the offer.

She'd be proud of him—she was always proud of him—and she'd be supportive. She was always supportive, but would she be happy?

She encouraged him to grow and challenge himself. Moving to a bigger city for William was important to her. It pained her when they denied their son something because they couldn't easily afford it (though William was growing into a good-natured young man who never held his disappointment against either of them for long). Plus, Bay deserved a better house. London had much better houses. Yes. Bay would be happy with the offer.

Without a doubt, she'd want him to take it.

THIRTY

August 2001 (continued)

VOLE TOOK BAY out to dinner to tell her the life-altering news. They went to their favorite French restaurant on Main Street. It was the third, fourth, or fifth time a European chef tried to set up shop in the same location, and they joked about the ghost in the back who haunted the soup ladles and burned all the buns.

"It must be haunted," Bay giggled. "There's no other reason why restaurants would always fail. The chefs here are doomed from the start!"

"Obviously the building is haunted," Vole agreed, feeling more relaxed in what felt like years. "Cheers, honeybee." He clinked her glass and smiled. "To ghosts."

"Cheers." She sipped her wine, keeping her eyes locked on his. "You're in a mood," she observed. "Anything specific? Or happy our son hasn't broken a bone, destroyed a vehicle, or caused a devastating explosion in recent months? At this rate, he might live long enough to go to university."

"Our little darling has matured, hasn't he?"

"Speaking honestly, I think he has. I think the car accident scared the living crap out of him. I'm surprised he stopped going to see the psychiatrist."

"Really?"

Bay laughed.

"You're right. Those appointments were awful. He put on a brave face, at least. I'm proud of him. He kept his marks up despite being depressed. He's already thinking seriously about what school to go to. I think the crash gave him some much-needed perspective. Don't you think?"

"I do so think, honeybee."

They fell silent.

"Why are you looking at me like that?" she demanded after a time.

"Like what?"

"You know what I'm talking about."

Vole was mesmerized, caught, absorbed by how the restaurant's low light filled her eyes, as though they glowed from the inside out. He loved her eyes. A rich amber tone, exactly the color of his favorite, sticky, tongue-gluing honey.

Shortly after they met, he started calling her honeybee. He didn't know why, but it fit her perfectly. Three syllable nicknames didn't exactly roll off the tongue, but Bay deserved something special. Something more. Or maybe he was compensating for their unusual combination of monosyllabic names. *Bay* and *Vole* had risen their fair share of eyebrows over the years. They chose to spare William, but joked about naming him Jake or Jack or Todd.

"Did I lose you?" Bay asked. "You're being weird tonight."

"You're the loveliest woman I've ever laid eyes on. You're like Sleeping Beauty. You never change."

"Well now." She blushed. Took a sip of her wine. "I love you too, husband."

"I have to tell you something."

The mood between them became electric the instant he said it, and his hands slid across the table toward her. She reached out to grasp on to him.

"What?" she asked. "What do you have to tell me?"

"I spoke with Marc today. He had news about Etobicoke."

Hands tightened, eyes widened.

"And, I didn't get the position—" Vole shook his head to stave off her murmur. "I didn't get the position, but—and I know I said it had to be that location or bust, *but*..."

"I'm all right with not getting it.

"See, I've been doing a lot of thinking," he continued without breath or pause, "and I don't think taking on a bigger branch makes sense for us at this stage of our lives. This past while has sucked. Why would I take on more responsibility, now, as all the chaos is winding down? Is a little more money worth all the added stress?"

Vole was staring at his outstretched hands, willing them not to betray him.

"Would you please look at me?" Bay asked, squeezing his fingers.

He said nothing, didn't move.

"Vole?"

Slowly, he raised his head.

"Vole Gibbons," Bay said with a broadening smile. "You've made me the happiest girl in the world!"

"I have?"

"If you're happy with how things are, I'm happy with how things are." She looked satisfied and content. "Answer me one question. Who got it? Who got the Etobicoke branch?"

The question made Vole pause.

"You know," he began, slow, heat rising in his face. "I don't know. I didn't ask. I can't believe it didn't occur to me to ask."

She laughed again.

"Now's when I tell you I've been thinking about getting a dog," she said. "It'll be easier for me to get one now, before William's gone away to school. Trust me. You don't want me moping about a childless house without a dog."

"A dog?" He hadn't known she wanted one.

"I want a schnauzer."

"A schnauzer!"

"A miniature one. I want to name him Jock."

Vole was elated. The moment of danger had passed, and Bay was happy.

He hadn't deliberately withheld news about the London offer. It seemed much simpler to leave that part out once he'd gotten started, and now that he'd left it out, if he were to tell her now, she might think he was trying to keep it from her.

Vole wasn't trying to keep the truth from her. He tried to be honest with Bay. He knew how important it was to her they make big life decisions as equals, together. Sometimes timing was poor—Bay understood that.

"I don't understand you, honeybee," he said with a rueful shake of his head, vowing to tell her, when the time was right.

"Love's not meant to be understood. It just *is*. I trust you, and I love you. I don't need anything else. Know your numbers, know your heart. The rest will take care of itself. Those are your words."

"Of course."

Sunday, June 21, 2015
Stonehenge, United Kingdom
7:03 p.m. local; 2:03 p.m. eastern time
4,281 sleeps since

Bay's dream was simple. She wanted to slow dance with her beloved, and the dance floor was to be none other than the emerald stage of Stonehenge. One of the most inexplicable and wondrous creations on the planet. It was exactly the sort of place his honeybee would lay claim to, Vole thought to himself, as he considered how to set the scene.

A yellow plastic fence was installed around the towering stone slabs for reasons Vole couldn't infer. He took it down, not wanting to obscure Bay's view, and he vowed to put it back in place afterward. The official parking lot, two hundred meters from the site on the other side of the highway, had few tour buses in it. A crowd of people stood around, looking down at their cameras in the parking lot, but they appeared to be going back inside their bus.

"What's the worst that could happen?" Vole considered out loud. "People see a couple of kooks dancing on the grass?"

Still, Vole dreaded having to explain his sudden appearance to strangers, and he didn't want anyone to yell at him for taking down the yellow fence.

To calm his hyper mind, Vole thought about the hills they passed by on their way through Wales. Sheep with white bodies and black faces grazed in almost every pasture. He'd never seen any like them back home. The sheep in Ontario were all white, white bodies and white faces. These were different and reminded him of garden grubs. Bay said grubs reminded her of maggots, both important parts of any natural ecosystem, and would scold William for removing them from the soil.

It worked. Thoughts of her brought calm to him.
Vole glanced down at his watch.
It was time.

Bay didn't wake from her slumber, which she'd fallen into while on the moors, shortly after listening to William's voicemail for the fourth time. Her rest gave Vole the chance to lie with her in his arms, her head atop his chest. He could feel her steady breathing, her chest expand and fall; he matched the pump of his lungs to the pump of hers. Vole missed being surrounded by perpetual movement, but more than anything, he missed lying quietly together, while their two chests rose and fell as one.

He heard her breathing change before he felt her stir, exactly how it happened back at home.

"Vole?"

"Yes, honeybee?"

Bay pushed herself up off his chest and rubbed her eyes. Touched soft grass beneath the blanket they sat on with her fingers. Blinked hard a few times.

"Where are we?"

"You don't know?"

She was looking around at the stones, and he was certain she would recognize them. Bay took in a quick breath and Vole knew she'd put it together.

"Ooo . . ." she cooed, and then blurted, "They're so *big*! And there are so many of them! I had no idea there were so many. Did you know?"

"No, honeybee, I didn't. How are you feeling?"

Amazement changed to soft satisfaction as she recalled what they recently shared.

"Sensational," she responded, and she licked her lips. "Especially now we're *here*. Do you have any water?"

He handed her a bottle. She drank greedily from it before popping the medicine he handed her into her mouth. She gulped back more.

"I have such a headache," she complained. Vole looked at her with concern, but she waved it away. "Need the meds to kick in."

That didn't make him feel better.

"Here," she said as she poured a glass of the scotch he laid out. "Have this for me."

"For you?"

She shook her head.

She wouldn't be having any more.

Jock looked up from the bottom of the blanket they sat on as Bay moved around.

"Is he eating again?" she exclaimed. Vole blushed. "Please tell me you gave him water too. What did I ever do to deserve you?" Before he could answer, "I suppose I must be lucky."

"You know what I think about luck," he teased. "No such thing."

"Then what did I do to deserve all this?"

Vole ignored her protest as his left ankle made him wince, and together—he lifted as she pushed—they stood.

"You taught me how to dance, for one," he said in reply to her question and placed one arm around her waist. "You taught me how to kiss." He bent to press his lips against her soft pillowy ones. "You taught me how to love," he whispered, and pulled her close, pressed his hips against hers.

They swayed to the music playing in each of their heads, and soon they were humming a song they both loved dearly.

When the sun dipped low and the moon's silhouette glowed pale above them, Bay arched her back and looked up, trusting he would keep her from falling.

"Have you ever seen such a sky?"

He had, and he hadn't.

Vole wasn't prepared for the full weight of Bay's body as she slumped in his arms.

"Bay!" he cried out, pulling her back up, horrified by the loll of her head. He laid her down on the soft grass and shook her as much as he dared. "*Honeybee?*"

Jock trotted over to lick Bay's face. Vole panicked and time stopped.

THIRTY-ONE

Sunday, June 21, 2015
Stonehenge, United Kingdom
7:28 p.m. local; 2:28 p.m. eastern time
4,281 sleeps since

VOLE COULDN'T LEAVE her slumped over like that. When he touched her neck, it felt like her skin was on fire. She was burning up. He didn't know what being stuck in a fevered state, unconscious, might do to her.

"What do I do?" he pleaded.

More unsure than ever, he carried Bay to where he left the boat and his bicycle—a strange dark shape on an otherwise empty hill. He laid Bay down on the soft grass and retrieved what remained of the ice.

"Will this help you? What do you need? Please tell me what you need."

Vole emptied his lungs, cleared his mind, collected himself, and asked time to restart.

"Bay," he begged. "Can you hear me?"

No response from her, but he could tell she was still breathing. Each breath was quick and shallow. Her eye pockets were waxen but the rest of her face was pink and hot.

"What's happening?" he murmured, and he laid the wrapped ice against her neck. "What should I do? Please wake up." Second after second stretched. It was a lifetime alone spent crossing the desert, across another desert—each an eternity, no end in sight.

When Bay's eyes opened, Vole found he could think again.

She tried to raise herself up on her elbows, but Vole stayed her. "No, don't," he said, sounding more brusque than intended. "Don't get up." His voice caught and silence emerged between them.

When she offered no comment, he asked, "How are you feeling?"

"Fine. But . . ."

Vole tensed.

"But what?"

"I-I can't see."

After minutes of anxious waiting, Bay's eyesight returned. The doctor told them there would be episodes of blindness, but it still came as a shock.

The headache was gone, she said, though they both recognized the work of powerful drugs, and when he looked critically, he saw her bones were sharp. She looked thin; ready to float away on the breeze. *She's turning into a feather.*

Vole touched her neck with his hand. Where she felt hot moments before, she felt cool, now. Too cool.

I've done this to us, Vole thought to himself. Would a miracle have happened if they stayed in Dorset? Would some magical drug have been discovered, and would she have lived long enough to benefit from it? Maybe her condition would have somehow cured itself. Vanished without a trace. More impossible things had happened. *I've done this to her. We're in the middle of nowhere, in the middle of some foreign country, and she needs a doctor. I'm an idiot. A stupid fucking fool.*

Back on the waters off the coast of West Africa, Vole imagined the responsibility of the world was his to bear. The truth was much less noble, it turned out. He was only a man, who loved a woman, and he didn't want to say goodbye.

"We can keep going," she assured him.

"You should be in a hospital," it hurt Vole greatly to admit.

"No!"

"Bay . . ."

"Not yet. I can keep going. Show me the list—What's next? Italy?"

"Bay."

"Tell me, dammit!"

Deny her this too?

"The Wall," he responded.

"Berlin." Her lips drew tight together. "I've been waiting a long time to visit."

Bay was right. They couldn't stop yet. They still had seconds together left to spend.

"To Berlin we go," he said. "Onward."

A smile lit her face, making his broken-hearted capitulation worth his distress. He stopped himself from considering all that could possibly go wrong.

"I want to get into *Molly* myself this time," she said. "Can I do that?"

"Of course."

Vole helped her to stand, but her legs, now the frailest of stems, folded beneath her weight, as scanty as it was. By now the buses with tourists were leaving. No one was near enough to notice them as he lifted her in his arms and limped to the side of the boat. The setback to her health was a dagger to his chest.

Once he placed her comfortably in her seat, Vole lifted a subdued and wide-eyed Jock and laid him in her lap.

"Oh," she gasped once settled. "It's *wonderful* up here. This seat is more comfortable than my chair back home. Sitting passenger makes me itch to get behind the wheel again! I've sat here the whole time?"

Vole nodded. Jock stretched his neck out to lick the tip of his nose.

"For how long, exactly?"

How long it took didn't matter to him and he didn't want it to matter to her. That wasn't the point. They'd lived their whole lives by his clock—it was time to live by her clock. When he didn't answer, she asked again. Vole shook his head and gave her the same answer he gave every other time she asked.

"For just the right amount of time."

Years spent pedaling them around the world hadn't made him any younger. In some ways, he'd become ancient; Vole knew every long moment he'd labored showed on his face, his body, and increasingly quirky behavior.

"Will you let me look at you when you do it this time?" she asked.

A lump grew in Vole's throat. The last time her eyes were left open and trained on his back, he forgot who he was. Fear swallowed him up from the inside, whole. It took facing a consummate hunter, a jolt of feral intent, to knock him back out; fight or flight, and he chose both. It was impossible to count on another such shock.

Vole sank into Bay's open eyes. By the time he whispered, "Stop," he already willed the world into stillness a long time prior, but he found it impossible to look away.

Sunday, June 21, 2015
Berlin, Germany
8:28 p.m. local; 2:28 p.m. eastern time
4,312 sleeps since

When Vole started time again, the low sun had yet to set. It hung above the horizon and blazed through clouds; it cast a burnished glow over everything it touched. The Wall looked and sounded nothing like he imagined. It stood next to a road streaming with cars. Vole had difficulty not being blown over by the area's turbulence, and at first, he had trouble seeing straight through all the noise.

Day's dying sun flickered as birds flew by and drew his attention. He found himself able to focus on red-painted concrete slabs; winged shadows whispered new life into images of turmoil and oppression, of liberation. Some stones were marked with bold slashes, graffiti scars, and other stones with different scars. Deep pits and grooves, these.

Only a few minutes had passed when Bay began to shiver uncontrollably in Vole's arms. Her subtle motion added to the dense noise that threatened to overwhelm him.

Bay's eyes were closed.

"I wish I could tell Mum what it's like," she murmured. "She'd never believe I got here too."

"Who are you talking to, honeybee?"

She hid her face against his chest and pleaded like a child. "I don't like it here. Please take me away."

She was the weakest and most scattered she'd been yet.

Vole stopped time and took to Rome.

Sunday, June 21, 2015
North of Milan, Italy
8:49p.m. local; 2:49 p.m. eastern time
4,399 sleeps since

He rode with a grim face. For once, Vole found himself able to maintain a steady and rapid pace. His legs pumped and his wheels turned like windmills. Everything blurred. Cattle became cars, people became pastures. It didn't matter what he passed, all he saw were the same three things: lines on a map, street signs he didn't know, and the one place he needed to take Bay next.

One, two, three; three, two, one.

Ever onward.

Dr. Sheppard said two days at most. They were approaching twenty hours. Vole knew, deep in his heart: Bay's endurance was reaching its limit.

As Vole neared Rome, he diverged from his steady path. He turned onto a dirt driveway, unkept and curving. (A little ways back—the last time he stopped to use his binoculars—he noticed a barn peeking out from behind an overgrowth of trees. Overgrown barns tended to be abandoned barns, and an abandoned barn was particularly useful to Vole.) Twin hedges, once pruned but now unruly and wild smelling, lined either side of the drive. Low-lying green plants sprouted on the ground where worn tire tracks used to be.

At the end of the driveway, about one kilometer in from the road, tucked next to a grove of tall leafy trees, he found the barn. It was held shut with a metal chain and padlock, and it smelled like a forest.

Vole hefted bolt cutters, borrowed from a small hardware shop in Wales, and cut through the padlock. The doors seemed to whisper as he pulled them open.

A wall of air, warm and stale, met him inside. It was a dry smell, old rot, and he imagined it to be like the inside of a sarcophagus; he covered his face as he inspected lumps of cloth and roughened fiber that lay on the ground.

"Mummy wrappings," he muttered, eyeing up the skeleton of a rat, a peak of dust and bones in the corner. The barn was otherwise empty. "It's no five-star hotel," he told Jock. "But at least they've got the pest problem under control."

Vole blocked any space wide enough for a miniature schnauzer to fit through. He told the dog they'd be back soon.

"Whatever you do, Jocko, don't bark. Ignore what I told you about biting strangers. Forget I ever said that. Lie low, and if anyone comes inside, pretend they can't see you.

"Here. I got a small something for you."

Vole dropped a dried cow knuckle next to a full bowl of water—*thunk*—and cupped the dog's face between his hands. He looked deep into his animal brown eyes and bid the stalwart creature a solemn farewell.

With his pack on his back, Vole carried Bay outside the barn. He laid her down to wrap the chain back through the barn's door handles. This time he locked it with his own lock and zipped the key inside the fanny pack he was rarely without.

With Bay in his arms once more, he started down the driveway. When he reached the two-lane road, he turned and followed it all the way to a different highway, one he intended to follow east until he reached the hospital, fifteen kilometers away, according to his map.

The sun burned low on his right. When he reached the highway and turned, it burned low at his back. Had he cast a shadow, it would have matched his every lopsided stride. He imagined it like a beacon, dark and stretched out on the pavement before him. Without a shadow, Vole himself became a shade, passing invisible through a sea of sunlit statues.

"Bay," he whispered, hugging her closer to him.

Vole barely noticed the exotic cars with catlike features, and he ignored the vibrant farms he passed. Villas, the likes of which he'd taken note of in the past, faded away like everything else. Bodies in the landscape were more ephemeral than light. He didn't rest until he came to a shut gate. It blocked his entry to the hospital parking lot, and when he saw there was a different way forward, he stopped resting and carried Bay through to the other side.

"Will you help us?" he pleaded, breaking his long silence as he limped along.

The heavy thump of his right foot, followed by the light thud of his swollen left, *thump thud, thump thud, thump thud,* up the hospital's front steps.

"Hello!"

Two people, both dressed in business wear, passing a beige folder between them, didn't blink. They kept looking at each other. Kept ignoring him.

"Can you help? Will you?" he begged to know. "Do you speak English?"

He carried Bay past them and through the front rotating doors of the hospital. Inside, to his left, stretched a narrow gray hallway leading to *pronto soccorso*—the emergency room. In front of him was another set of glass doors. He tried to open them but found them stuck stubbornly shut. On the other side of the doors was an atrium, white and open and round. A steel staircase dominated its center. The staircase connected the main and second floors, and on the second floor a hallway with floor-to-ceiling windows traced the curve of the atrium. Vole counted two dozen people behind the glass, and he knew he had to get there.

It was nearly nine o'clock in the evening. All the daytime doctors would have gone home already, Vole presumed. Only emergency staff, night nurses, and restless patients would be spending the evening. Important doors would be locked, critical entrances barred. What were the chances an oncologist was in the hospital at such an hour? How would Vole know who he was looking at? What if they spoke no English?

Vole located an empty stretcher in the emergency intake wing. He laid Bay down on it and disappeared into the first stairwell he could find. Years of poking his nose in places he wasn't invited served him well. It wasn't long before he found an empty bed in a private room on the ninth floor in *oncologia pediatrica*—the ward where children with cancer were cared for. *Passionate doctors,* Vole thought to himself as he retrieved Bay. *That's where the most kind and passionate doctors will be.*

He laid her down in the private room before continuing his search.

When Vole found Dr. Lorenz, Medical Oncologist, MD (name and credentials were written in Italian and English on a panel outside her office door), she was sitting in her private office on the ninth floor, drinking tea. Vole wondered what sort of work merited a private office in such a well-equipped hospital, and he wondered what kept her there late at night.

"Then again," he said as he considered her studious profile from the center of the room, "I probably don't want to know anything about it."

It was clear to him the doctor wasn't your average medical practitioner. The sophistication she brought to the room was palpable. Vole could taste it on the air—clean skin, natural soaps, arcane knowledge. A German medical journal lay open in her lap. An English medical thesaurus, among other impressive-looking volumes, graced her shelves. He liked the aloe plant on her desk. It was one of the few plants he cared to remember, and only because he'd found its succulent flesh soothing over the years.

"Do you understand what I'm saying?" he grated at her, a whisper forced between the cracks. Despite the teacup in her hand and open journal in her lap, the doctor's eyes were closed. "Can you see me? Do you know I'm here?"

Then he straightened, stretched his neck from side to side, cleared his throat.

"Dr. Lorenz: I'm sorry for what I'm about to do and for everything about to happen. It's—Well, I don't have a choice, you see.

"Now, before you burn yourself . . ."

Vole removed the small porcelain cup from her hand. Set it down on the table in front of her. An electronic tablet, bright with a recently retrieved article, caught his attention. The text was written in yet another different language.

"You must be a genius," he muttered. "Genius people appreciate the insane ones. Right, Doctor?" Then, "I'll be right back. Don't you go anywhere."

On a whim, Vole left and returned with an empty wheelchair and seated the doctor down in it. He'd learned, from experience, no two people were equally pliable in a time-frozen state. A body's range of motion, flexibility in limbs and trunk, was variable, person to person. Perhaps it had something to do with a person's intent in that moment, blood's chemical ingredients leftover from whatever activity their brain and body were up to at the time. Vole could only guess. Holding Bay in his arms was one thing; carrying a strange woman was something else altogether, and he was shocked to find the seemingly at ease doctor to be stiff and unbending.

"Not a work-life balance type, are you?" he observed, doing his best to tuck her rigid elbow by her side. Before cocking his arms to ready position, he placed the thesaurus on her lap, just in case, and muttered, "Never thought I'd be doing this again." The wheelchair propelled effortlessly forward.

Down the hall, in Bay's room, he positioned the wheelchair so that Dr. Lorenz faced the bed. Vole stood in front of her and studied her face for a final time.

"What are you thinking?" he asked, breathing heavily. She did nothing.

He pulled Bay's schedule and medicine from his pack and set them out on the narrow table tucked next to her bed. The loud, rattling pills added to the turmoil inside his head.

"Good luck, Jocko," he said. "We'll be back soon."

Having run out of preparations to make—infinite circumstances waited for him and Bay on the other side of the moment—Vole whispered, "Go," and restarted time.

THIRTY-TWO

Sunday, June 21, 2015
A hospital just outside of Rome, Italy
8:50 p.m. local; 2:50 p.m. eastern time
4,416 sleeps since

VOLE DROPPED TO his knees as a siren blared throughout the hospital. Throbbing noise filled his every crevice, expanding and expanding. Every bone in his body vibrated beneath the pressure. Nausea gripped him. He clutched his head between his hands and willed the wailing to stop.

Loud, Loud! LOUD! Why is everything so LOUD?

He'd forgotten about Dr. Lorenz. He didn't know a woman had lunged toward him and was trying to get his attention. When he looked up it was through watery eyes. *Why is she looking at me like that?* Vole watched her face, fascinated by how quickly horror could grow to consume an entire expression. *Who is she looking for? Who is she?*

Then, "Bay!" he shrieked, adding to the commotion. Vole staggered to his feet. He ignored the woman pulling at his arm and lurched toward the bed. Bay's eyes were barely open. Her cheeks were flushed. Was she moaning?

"Are you in pain?" he shouted.

The alarm stopped blaring.

An open door triggered it—Vole hadn't known what would happen when he stepped through the secure thru-way—but it was closed again, and the alarm reset.

Vole's knees gave way and he fell back down to the floor.

"Hello?" A female voice he didn't recognize. "Sir, can you hear me?" Flawless English with an Italian accent. "Nod if you understand."

...*Who?*

Vole raised his head and met eyes, dark brown, beneath furrowed and stern eyebrows. They were in a face, fierce, twisted in confusion.

"My wife needs help," he gasped. "*Please.*"

A moment passed.

Dr. Lorenz made a sound deep in her throat before her frown cleared and she stepped into the hallway. Vole didn't understand the string of words she uttered in command, but before he could blink, there was a team of nurses buzzing over Bay.

"Come with me," Dr. Lorenz's low voice came to his ear from behind. She took firm hold of his elbow and lifted him with warm fingers. "You must explain yourself and what has happened here. We have words to share."

Vole, who hadn't slept or eaten anything in some unknown measure of time, slipped from her grasp and collapsed to the floor for a third time.

Vole regained consciousness to discover he was sitting in a wheelchair, the last place he expected to find himself. A needle was inserted into his arm. A narrow tube ran from the needle to a rolling metal rack, which held a small plastic bag filled with clear liquid. Sitting across from him was a woman. She was wearing a white overcoat with big pockets sewn in.

Dr. Lorenz.

They were back in her office. She was watching him and he found he couldn't look away.

"Mr. Gibbons," she said in a clear voice, giving nothing away. "The man who is like a ghost."

"How—" he began, but she waved his question aside.

"You identified Bay Gibbons as your wife. Her medication and photo identification was laid out. It was simple deduction on my part."

"Right." The wheelchair he sat in creaked. "Of course."

Then he saw his journal, stark and soiled in her sterile hand. It was supposed to be in his backpack. Which, as far as he could see, was nowhere nearby.

"Yes, I looked through your book," Dr. Lorenz replied in answer to his visible alarm. "Like I said. You're the man who is like a ghost. You take things that don't belong to you from people who don't know you're there, and you can't get caught because you don't exist."

Oblivious to his deep shame—or not one to care for it, he could only guess—she reached for the tablet on the table.

"How's Bay?" Vole demanded. "Is she doing better?"

"She's resting. I'll tell you more in a moment. First, you must see this."

She handed the tablet over to Vole. His calloused fingers scraped across its glass surface. The device was cold. Strange. Familiar, oddly.

"We're all riding bicycles," he muttered under his breath. "Fall off, get back on again. Or is that what you do with a horse? Hm. Perhaps a horse. I'll have to ask Will."

"Are you speaking to me?"

"What? Oh, no. I'm sorry. My manners are . . ." He stopped short, unsure of what to think of a stranger who listened attentively.

Vole turned back to the bright screen he held in his hand. What was he looking at?

Twitter.

Twitter?!

He kept his lips pressed tight together to keep his thoughts inside. The more he read, the looser his lips, his thoughts, everything around him, became, until all his understanding fell apart in a messy tangle of confusion.

"I don't understand," he mumbled, "what is all this," though he recognized it as something he feared.

"You see, Mr. Gibbons, your travels haven't gone entirely unnoticed."

The first tweet he read—the one at the bottom of a long list—was from a young man in Toronto. He claimed his hot dog vanished from his hand in the same moment a vision came to him. *Bearded white man apparated, stole my sausage, fed it to my dog. WTF! #GhostThief #Wizard or #Jesus?*

"B-but that was ages ago!" Vole burst, recalling a cat-sized dog, puffy with white fur, sitting nicely on the ground next to his trunk-ankled owner. He'd been hungry at the time. "I didn't know any better. I didn't give it to the *dog*. Good grief. What a waste of a good sausage that would have been. I ate it. On the roof of a tall building. As I recall, it was tasty."

"I see."

All over the world, over the past twenty hours, in the moments immediately following when Vole restarted time, people took to the internet. They tweeted about a man who visited them in daytime visions, or who came to them in their dreams. Sometimes the man was middle-aged and healthy. Sometimes his cheeks were hollow, his face gaunt, or covered in a ragged beard. Some people claimed he was crippled and wore no clothes; wore too many clothes, wore stolen clothes. Every account was different, all had one single thing in common: the man appeared in one second and was gone the next. As Vole scrolled through the comments, his journey came to life in new ways, and he was confronted by a world he no longer felt a part of.

Fueled by the impossible, conspiracies abounded. Government mind control, genetic targeting, vigilantes. The claims that made Vole most uncomfortable said the Ghost Thief wasn't a thief at all, but a test of faith, a sure sign of cosmic trouble to come.

"Good grief . . ." Vole whispered as he looked at a photograph someone posted. It was the note he'd written on the checkout card in the little library in Uruguay. *Thank you for the book. I'm looking forward to reading it as I cross the Atlantic. I hope to return it to you one day. In the meantime, please take these in exchange.* No desert was without its end—the internet brought everyone within reach. How could he have forgotten that?

The feed updated to show someone else had made a tweet. Someone from Sheffield said, *#GhostThief left me a dozen bags of plastic bottles to recycle*; and another, from a restaurant outside Hamburg, *#GhostThief dropped a deuce in our toilet*

"I did *not!*" he exclaimed, though he feared all of it might be true.

He handed the tablet back to Dr. Lorenz.

"May I go see her? We can't spend long here. She's sick. We don't have much time left."

"I understand, Mr. Gibbons. You must understand these are strange circumstance we find ourselves in." Her receptive regard turned piercing, and her tone left no room for negotiation. "If I'm to help you, I need you to explain what's going on."

Vole leaned back.

"Do you have anything I could eat?" he asked.

"You didn't come all this way for hospital food, Mr. Gibbons. Now talk. I want to hear every single thing. Every, single, thing."

"Of course."

They had already spent more than two hours in the hospital. Seven thousand nine hundred and forty-eight seconds, to be precise. Vole counted each and every single one while Bay rested. It wasn't difficult to do. Which was odd, because when time was stopped, it was entirely the opposite; the seconds became impossible to keep track of.

Dr. Lorenz stepped into the room and shut the door behind her. The sound woke Bay.

"Honeybee," Vole breathed out in a sigh of relief. "You're awake."

"H'llo," came her fuzzy reply. "Where are we?"

"The hospital. Dr. Lorenz has agreed to help us."

Bay swiveled her head on the pillow to look at the doctor.

"Where are we?" she asked, visibly perplexed.

"Italy. Twenty minutes outside of Rome," Dr. Lorenz replied.

"I-I thought we were going to Germany."

"We were there," Vole said. "You weren't doing well."

Bay nodded, but said nothing more.

"We have to discuss your health," Dr. Lorenz said to Bay, "but first you should know I spoke with Dr. Sheppard. He told me the police came to the hospital asking questions about your sudden disappearance." She made a disapproving sound with her tongue. A noise Vole had already come to recognize from their short time together.

"Your son is worried about you," she said, and turned to Vole. "You didn't think to leave a note at the hospital before you left?"

"Ah, no."

"Will," Bay said, the fuzziness in her voice gone. "He doesn't know anything."

Moisture fled Vole's mouth; his tongue became dry like chalk.

No, he doesn't. That's my fault too.

"How do you feel?" Dr. Lorenz asked, turning back to Bay.

The question distracted her, and the doctor continued. Where does it hurt? Describe to me what it feels like. Are you nauseous? Is there blood in your spittle? Your urine? Stool? When's the last time you had a bowel movement? So on and so forth. The doctor looked over Bay's chart, crumpled and dirtied but legible; and compared it to a fresh printout her team of nurses provided.

"Your levels are wrong." Dr. Lorenz spoke definitively—her words the period at the end of a punchy sentence. "We'll do what we can to fix that. Did Dr. Sheppard tell you what happens when your organs fail?"

Vole blinked.

"Yes," Bay answered.

"So you know what will happen to you, and how being with doctors inside a hospital like this one can help?"

"Yes."

"Good." She handed the printout to Bay. "Here's a revised schedule. You aren't dead yet. I don't see any reason why you should behave as though you are. If I never see you both again, I'll be happy." Addressing Vole, "Tell me. How do you sleep? When did you first notice your cough?"

"Oh. Fine. I sleep fine. And, um, it's nothing new," he fibbed.

Dr. Lorenz shook her head. Shrugged.

"It's your business, though I believe it isn't good."

She turned to leave, pausing to pull something from her pocket. The doctor placed an object, hard and shiny, down on the table next to Bay's medication.

"Call your son," she commanded, and left them alone.

Bay and Vole looked at each other, at the cell phone she'd left for them, and back at each other. Their faces both wore the same stupefied expression.

"How did you do that?" Bay asked.

"Do what?"

"Get her to help us."

"I don't know. I don't think I did anything."

When he asked Dr. Lorenz why she was helping them she told him he hadn't given her a choice. "You steal into my office like a bandit, transport me to the bedside of your wife who is dying of cancer, what did you think would happen? The disease is the enemy! I fight every battle to its end. All I can do is what I do best and pray maybe one day you'll be back to teach me your trick and help me to win the war." But the doctor's impassioned words died unborn on his lips.

"This isn't what you had in mind when you wrote that you wanted to come to Italy, was it?" he asked instead.

"No. Not exactly." Pause. "Vole . . ."

"Will."

"Yes. Will." She bit her lip before continuing. "Listen to me when I say this: You don't need to be the hero. Dying for a noble cause is still dying, and you've got a son, who—God willing—will one day have his own children. Being here for them makes all the difference." Vole protested, Bay ignored him. "You're *alive*, for Christ's sake. Do you know how fortunate you are? You have the chance to talk to your son. A chance your father never got, and you suffered for it."

Vole scoffed.

"My father saved lives," he insisted. As impactful as the statement was, his protest was a weak one.

"Yes, and he died while doing it, alone, for a war your mother never wanted him to fight in, without his family anywhere nearby."

"It wasn't—he wasn't there for *war*."

Vole didn't know why he found it impossible to talk about his father, a decorated soldier who died on a peacekeeping mission overseas when he was seven, and he didn't know why it felt like Bay needed something from him he couldn't give.

What do you want from me?

"All ever I wanted was freedom," Bay said, speaking definitively, like the doctor. "Freedom to dream, freedom to love. Freedom to choose my own grand adventure. Staying in love is an adventure. Making a baby is an adventure. Changing together is an adventure. We *have* that. How can I be disappointed?"

"You should have been an explorer, honeybee. You were made for it."

"You're not listening to me!" she insisted. "I was an explorer. I still am. Our life is an adventure, together."

"But . . ."

"It's not hard, Vole!" she cried, her patience having run its course. "Be the father to William your father never was to you—while you still have the time! *Talk to your son.*"

"But, Bay, I'm not—I don't—I-I can't—"

"*What are you so damned scared of?*"

The question burst out of her, and Vole knew. Neither he nor Bay had time left for excuses.

He sat down at the foot of the bed. Placed his hand on her leg. She looked at it but didn't move to touch him.

"I have to tell you something," he said.

"So tell me," came her anguished plea. "Talk to me. I don't know what you're feeling if you never tell me."

What if she didn't like what he had to say?

"Do you remember when we went for dinner," he choked, "and I told you about the Etobicoke offer?"

She nodded.

"I never told you they gave me a choice. I could stay in Dorset and continue running the old branch, which they intended to scale back, which is what ended up happening, or I could accept a twenty-five percent raise and they'd pay to relocate us to London, where I'd manage a growing branch."

"They offered you more money?"

"Yes."

"A lot more?"

"Yes . . ."

"To go to London?"

"Yes! If we had, we could have done all this sooner! You could have experienced the world when you had the health to enjoy it, like you wanted. You could have lived the life you wanted for yourself, but you didn't, you couldn't have, you never got the chance to, because, b-because . . ."

"Because you lied," she finished for him, voice level, flat, cold. "And because, when it came right down to it, there was never a valid enough reason to spend our savings on those sorts of things."

"I-I guess I—" he began, but the cough he'd been holding back couldn't be contained any longer. Bay watched him, dispassionate, as it choked him, until his miserable fit subsided.

"Hear what I'm telling you, Vole Gibbons," she said once he'd regained composure. She took his hand in hers. Gripped his fingers.

Strange, he thought, *to see her lips loose and brow clear.*

Where was her frown, her tight lips and scowl?

Her body was warm, her lovely face gentle; compassion poured from her, washed over him.

That coldness. Where had her coldness gone?

Had he imagined it in the first place?

"You need to accept that this is happening," she implored. "You can't prepare for everything. You can't control death, and you shouldn't live the rest of your life with regrets."

"But," he wheezed, his throat still tight and painful. "It's not fair. I don't want to lose you."

"Death is the only part of living that is fair."

"How can you give up so easily?"

"I'm not giving up. What we're doing isn't easy."

Vole didn't want Bay to die.

"I never knew if I was doing the right thing," he whispered. "I still don't."

"No one ever does," she said. "I'm not going to pretend to be happy you lied. I deserved your honesty. I deserved better. I shouldn't have to tell you it was never about the money for me. The way I see it, we spent our time together doing our best, making the best of things. I have no regrets. I don't plan on making new ones.

"I forgive you. Now would you please stop being such a sap, listen to the doctor, *and call your son.*"

"What is going on?" William demanded when he realized who he was speaking to. "You've both disappeared—you didn't tell anyone where you were going—and now everyone is talking about this old kleptomaniac weirdo who writes thank you notes. Of all the fucking things! He has the same god-awful chicken scratch as you, Dad! Have you seen the pictures?"

"U-um, uh," Vole stammered.

"Where are you? Where's Mom?"

"You don't, um, need to worry. Your mother and I are happy. We've decided to go on a trip. We, uh, love you. Say hi to Gina for us."

Silence.

"For fuck's sake, Dad. What are you, some kind of robot? I'm not ten years old anymore! I spoke with Dr. Sheppard. I know about Mom's condition getting worse. There's no way you two decided to go on a last-minute vacation. She's in no state to travel right now. *Where are you?*"

"We're in a hospital."

"Where? What city? I'll be there as soon as I can."

"You probably shouldn't do that."

"Put Mom on the phone."

"William—"

"*Put Mom on the fucking phone!*"

Vole handed the phone to Bay, who regarded him with sad, glistening eyes. He looked away as their warm conversation left him feeling cold and remote. A lifetime had passed since he felt he belonged together with Bay and William on the inside.

"I'm feeling much better, sweetheart," Bay said into the phone. "Rome—Yes, we're in Rome right now. Yes, at a hospital, with a specialist. I don't know when we'll be back. It's very, hmm, difficult, for me to describe how we got—Don't worry about the dog. Jocko's with us.

"I'm sorry this is causing you and Gina stress. It wasn't our intention . . ."

When Bay hung up, she collapsed into sobs. Vole held her skeleton frame in his arms until she stopped heaving. *She's no more than a clatter of bones,* he thought to himself in bitterness.

"Well," she said after some time, sounding as though she were speaking from the bottom of an aquarium. "That was terrible. At least I got to speak with him one last time and tell him we're fine. I don't think he'll do anything rash." She rubbed her face and grimaced as she blew her tender nose on the white sheet across her lap. "He's distressed."

Vole gulped.

"I-I couldn't—I'm sorry, honeybee. I froze. I didn't know what to say."

She bit her lip.

"Do you think I'll ever get to see him again?"

This is all my fault too.

"Does it change anything if you don't?"

Bay stared down the length of her legs to where her toes poked up beneath the blanket.

"No," she whispered. "I suppose it doesn't."

THIRTY-THREE

Sunday, June 21, 2015
A hospital just outside of Rome, Italy
11:02 p.m. local; 5:02 p.m. eastern time
4,400 sleeps since

BAY INSISTED ON washing her face and brushing her teeth in the hospital restroom, though it was no bigger than a closet. She felt more herself with a fresh face, she said to Vole, eyeing him in the mirror's reflection. Dark bruises beneath her owl eyes told a different story. *It will all be better when we get back out there,* Vole thought. *I've gotten much better at avoiding traffic accidents and squeezing between cars. Though, I'll have to avoid concentrations of people. Because if—*

"Where to next?" Bay asked.

"You don't like being surprised?"

"I do, but I want something specific to look forward to too."

She was sitting on the hospital bed's edge. He leaned down, pressed his mouth against her forehead, weathered lips against soft tissue. Vole rushed past his ritual preparations this time, and it surprised him to feel her lean into his parchment-paper caress.

Vole had become accustomed to the impossible, and yet, after all they'd been through, Bay surprised him.

"To Egypt we go, honeybee."

"Queen Hatshepsut's temple!" she exclaimed, clapping her hands in delight. "The oldest place on my list. My childhood dream."

"Not Paris?"

"Can you think of any child who would want to go to Paris over Egypt, where the pyramids and mummies are?"

"Hmm."

"That's very far, Vole," Bay said, becoming unsure. "It'll be a desert. You can't survive in a *desert*."

"It's not as bad as it seems," Vole replied. He tried to shield her from seeing him glance at his watch.

"I'll close my eyes this time," she offered, still dubious, but she closed her eyes anyway.

When it comes right down to it, she never did miss much.

As soon as everything came to a halt, Vole cradled her against him. Embraced her tight. Clutched her frail body and breathed in the scent of her hair. He grieved until his body, spent, could heave no more and stayed still in the same position for what could have been eternity.

"It's not over yet, honeybee," he whispered into emptiness he told himself was hope. "We still have more time."

Sunday, June 21, 2015
A hospital just outside of Rome, Italy
1:40 a.m. local, next day; 7:40 p.m. eastern time
4,416 sleeps since

I forgive you, she had said. All she asked of him was that he be the father to William he never had. Nothing more. Following his grand confession, there'd been no sticky aftermath to pick his way through. No teary-eyed insistence he dredge up every detail since. Bay hadn't placed any blame or demanded he justify his lies. She'd simply forgiven him.

"You know why," Vole muttered as he pushed her along in silence. His left leg was too sore to carry her the whole way back. "Stop avoiding it. Forgiveness is simple for people who are dying because they don't have a spare second for regrets. Forgiveness doesn't undo the past. All it does is make people all right with it, and I can't be all right with what I've done. That's not fair to yo—*oof.*" His outcry ended in a cough, and Vole winced as his ankle tweaked in pain. He caught his foot on a prominent stone, stubborn and hidden.

"Focus," he told himself. "You've got to focus."

It was dark out. For the first time, Vole was traveling at night. The sun set three hours before, moments after they arrived at the hospital.

Clouds, a patchy layer, blanketed the moon, making the sky around it glow silver. The nighttime air was cool, chemical free, and in it Vole recognized dusk's lingering sweetness. The occasional car changed that, made the air taste industrial and like oil, but Vole appreciated their headlights.

It was a long but uneventful walk back to the barn where he'd left Jock. Without a flashlight, on the stretches of road where no cars waited, moonlight guided him forward. He could see, but only when all his attention was focused on the immediate path ahead of him. Progress was slow until Vole rounded the bend and saw a warm light glowing from inside the abandoned barn.

"Jock!" he cried out in alarm, charging over the remaining distance as quickly as he could without jostling Bay.

The chain he'd hooked through the door handles was gone and the doors were swung wide. Inside the barn were two men, each with a flashlight in hand, slackened mouths agape. They were staring at *Molly*. Vole traced their outstretched arms and flashlight beams with his eyes.

"Oh, Jocko," he said when he realized what must have attracted the farmer's attention to the barn.

Jock was sitting on Bay's seat with his eyes closed, head tilted up, muzzle open in what Vole knew from many firsthand experiences to be a haunting howl. "I'm sorry we left you alone, little wolf."

A quick sweep of the area settled Vole's nerves. "We got lucky this time, Jocko." He grimaced because the dog looked miserable.

By the light of the two men's flashlights, Vole lifted Bay back into *Molly*. He fell asleep in his own seat, next to her. When he woke, he took the flashlights from the men's hands, and he affixed them to the bottom of his bicycle's handle bars. He recorded his sleep, stretched a bit, ate, drank water, and was on his way.

Sunday, June 21, 2015
Lecce, Province of Lecce
1:40 a.m. local, next day; 7:40 p.m. eastern time
4,417 sleeps since

The flashlights didn't project the way he hoped they would. They did little to illuminate Vole's path, but the lights did help him keep track of Bay when he left on short foot excursions for supplies. Overall, progress was slow and the dark was maddening. Vole had been mad once before. He recognized the signs, and proceeded to pick his way forward through perpetual shadow with great care.

Vole said farewell to Italy from the tip of its heeled boot and pedaled them south across the Mediterranean. They disembarked at the upside down mouth of the Nile, outside the shining city of Cairo. He led them south along winding roads and followed the ancient river to where Queen Hatshepsut, the legendary pharaoh, built her legendary temple complex.

Bay gasped in delight when she looked upon it. Tall ancient columns glowed white. They were the bones of giants, emerging from a long-forgotten grave. When she exclaimed the heavens above were the most sensational she'd seen yet, Vole nodded in agreement. Words evaded him. They were lost to a night that never knew dawn; language fell short of his need to express how brightly stars twinkled when time was stopped. Their diamond light kept him from falling into depression.

"Why Hatshepsut?" he asked instead.

"I like her beard," Bay answered. "It seemed like such a smart thing for her to wear."

Whatever magic Dr. Lorenz and her team of bustling nurses worked in Rome faded quickly after that. Bay kept nodding off. He took to carrying her in his arms. For the brief moments she was awake, she would blink, over and over, and stare into the night. Every time, her eyes would fill with tears but she'd blink them away and keep on staring.

It wasn't until they were on the road again, headed to the next place on Bay's list, when he realized he never got to tell her where they were going next.

THIRTY-FOUR

September 2005

"I HEAR THE Senators look promising this year," Vole said.

William took a steamy swallow from his cup before setting it back down on the table in front of them. He jostled his hand and scalding hot coffee spilled over the lip. William swore before soaking up the puddle with his sleeve. His cursing drew the appraisal of an adolescent girl with blue streaks in her hair, who watched him from her barstool perch by the coffee shop window. William didn't notice.

"Could be," he shrugged, eyeing his pink and tender skin. "I don't follow hockey."

"Me neither."

"That was grandpa's thing."

They fell quiet. William stopped nursing his hand and began to text someone using his silver flip phone, and Vole itched to throw the device into the trash bin.

"Hey," Vole said as he forced a chuckle instead. "I won something for the first time in one hundred cups. A free doughnut. You check yours yet?"

William smiled without looking up from his screen.

"You're winning all the big bucks," the young man replied, distracted.

"They're getting chincy with their freebies, eh?"

"Mmm-hmm."

They were sitting together in silence when Bay returned from the restroom. William slipped his phone into his pocket.

"There's always a line," she said. "All set?"

"All set," William replied.

Bay and Vole clasped hands and followed their son out of the busy corner coffee shop a few blocks from the University of Ottawa. They walked past their parked Sebring—bought to replace the Mercury—and chitchatted for another two blocks. When they turned left onto a small street off Somerset, and William told them they were close, Bay squeezed Vole's hand.

"It's not the most well-kept neighborhood, is it?" she observed.

They strolled past a three-story house with bins overflowing with garbage out front. The home had been converted into a student house, not unlike the one William recently moved into.

"The only thing worse than student tenants are student landlords," William explained. It sounded like the catchphrase off a student council election poster. "But it's Ottawa. The government won't let student ghettos get half as ugly as elsewhere. The stories I've heard about what goes on in cities like London and Toronto would make your skin crawl. Think rat eat dog, cockroach eat rat."

"So, you only have to deal with bedbug eat human?" Vole joked.

William ignored him.

"This is it," their son said as he took them up a set of steps, broken stone crumbling, into a front entrance covered in peeling laminate. "Home sweet home."

He was going into his second year at school, and three of them—William, another young man, and his girlfriend—were pooling their resources to rent two floors of the house.

"It takes a brave girl to live with two boys," Vole stated.

"Gina's not a girl, Dad," William objected. "You can't say things like that anymore. She's going into her fourth year, and she's smart. She could be your prime minister one day."

Vole chuckled at his son's response, until he saw how serious William was about it, and he muttered an apology.

"Gina sounds like a confident and brilliant young woman," Bay interjected. "Is she here?"

"Nah. She's in class. Next time. So. What do you two old timers feel like having for dinner? You brought your chewing teeth, right?"

"*Har-har*, you're funny," Bay said. "Lesson One of Moving Out on Your Own: Learn How to Host."

William laughed.

"I'm a good host! We have only one house rule: Open the Fridge at Your Own Risk. The demons that spawn . . ." He made a grotesque face and shivered dramatically. "Mom, you like Italian. There's an Italian place around the corner. They serve a mean linguine."

As William locked up behind them, Vole whispered to Bay, "Remind me, when did you become the funny one?"

William had lots to share about his classes and about the lab he'd begun to volunteer in. "We literally count cells in petri dishes," he joked when Bay told him working in a lab sounded glamorous. "It's nothing like Hollywood makes it seem," he assured her. Vole smiled often at their son's enthusiasm but didn't do much more throughout the entire meal.

On their drive back from Ottawa to Dorset the next morning, Vole interrupted Bay's reading to ask what she thought.

"He used to laugh at my jokes," Vole complained. "Didn't he?"

"He's focused on school right now."

"I don't think that's it, honeybee."

"I think he's becoming a serious young man who cares about big ideas, like climate change and social justice. He's developing values. It's only a matter of time before he starts challenging our political views. You remember what it was like at his age."

"Hmm."

"You could just ask."

"You think?"

"I think you can handle having an adult conversation with your adult son."

"I suppose . . ."

"You should talk to him."

"Of course."

Bay's eyes bored into the side of his face.

"Don't say *of course* and then go and do the opposite like you always do," she insisted. "Or else I'll stop sharing my advice, no matter how nicely you ask."

"I don't do that," he protested. Vole glanced over at her when she didn't reply. She returned to reading the book in her lap. "I don't know what I'd say if I were to talk to him."

"Maybe you should try writing him a letter?"

"Sounds difficult."

"It's only as difficult as you make it."

After that, Vole stopped talking, and Bay continued reading.

Sunday, June 21, 2015
South of Wadi El Gemal National Park, Egypt
2:40 a.m. local, next day; 7:40 p.m. eastern time
4,645 sleeps since

Vole never spoke with William, and he never wrote his son a letter either.
What else would I change?
The force of his question drove him through the long night, across the Red Sea, south through Saudi Arabia, all the way to the isle of Bahrain. He could have taken a northern route, led them across Israel and Jordan and deeper south after that. But, like Bay, Vole was getting tired. He'd witnessed unspeakable pain—the type of mindless torture only people can inflict on one another—and didn't think he could find his way out of those distant corners of the world he knew little about.
Vole knew shadows trapped people everywhere, and he was grateful Bay's eyes were closed.
When Vole came to the Tree of Life, an alien form rising from the sand, he walked up to it as though he'd come upon a friend's door. He brushed its branches with his fingers and pressed his cheek against its trunk. Tears left dark marks on its surface, and black cracks emerged beneath the moisture, revealing ridges on its bark, like lizard skin. The tree reminded him of the Atacama. It reminded him of dinosaurs and planets. It reminded him of everything old and spent and easily forgotten.
"I found you," he told the tree as he held it close. "She led me here. She led me to you."
He didn't know why he said those words, but he felt as though the tree was a kindred spirit and may have been waiting for him. Time stood still in deserts, whether it was moving forward everywhere else in the world or not. The tree knew

that. It must've known that, and other things, because there was no other reason it should still thrive, no water or vegetation nearby to nurture it. Nothing else flourished. The tree was the only thing.

"What should I do?" he asked. "You must know things."

Vole pleaded for answers. He agonized about whether he should start time again, so far from a hospital. He wondered if the time had come to call a halt to his mission, to let Bay live forever in this alternate state, for him to fade away none the wiser. The longer he kept time stopped, the longer he could put off saying goodbye.

"What would you do?" he whispered. The tree, in all its wisdom, said nothing; the sequined sky kept its counsel.

"I can't keep pretending, honeybee, can I?"

No, Vole, her voice came into his head, *you can't.*

Sunday, June 21, 2015
Tree of Life, Bahrain
3:34 a.m. local, Monday; 8:34 p.m. eastern time
4,821 sleeps since

Deep as night grew here, the sun always seemed ready to rise. The barest hint of blush dusted the horizon. Beneath the incandescent canopy, Vole looked down at Bay, whose head lay in his lap. Light was dim and that made seeing difficult. After gazing into her open eyes for many minutes, Vole realized she wasn't looking back. He lifted his arm—careful not to disturb her position or wake Jock, who slept pressed next to her—and caressed her face. She pressed her cheek into his palm.

"What are you thinking about?" he asked.

"William. The other two."

They spoke rarely of the two they lost, long ago. Life had a way of stacking the past to keep memories dormant, quiet and undisturbed. Perhaps the passage of time was intended to blur and blend, turn memory into dream, so the present could remain in focus and pressing. Vole didn't know. He could only guess, and guess again, and then doubt the way of it

"What about you?" she asked. "What are you thinking about?"

Nothing, he wanted to say. *Everything. You. Nothing but you.* He didn't answer.

The only sounds between them were of her labored breathing and the occasional warbling trill, reminding them the sun was climbing and their time left together was dwindling.

"Can I see . . . Will you read me the list, again?" she rasped. Every word cost her.

Vole pulled his first journal from the pile of things he'd brought to be with them beneath the tree. He held the paper close to his face and read Bay's List of Wonders out loud to her, mentally checking off the places they visited as he spoke, agonizing over those they missed.

"On to the Ganges then," she said, "where I can dip my big toe in the river and swoosh it around."

"What's wrong, honeybee?"

She took another breath, sharp and rattling.

"I'm dying."

Her words, stark and resounding, carried to him from across the dunes. He shivered, chilled by a cool breeze blowing across his skin.

She continued.

"I miss our home. I want to be surrounded by reminders of our life together, things I love, like Will." A weak laugh escaped her. "I want to be near Will."

"But," he began, "we're almost there . . ."

Vole knew he shouldn't insist. He wanted to be near William too, but to give up on their quest would be to admit the disease won. Admitting the disease won meant giving into the black hole he'd barely been holding back since Dr. Sheppard delivered the news. Admitting meant turning around and going back all that way, and spending year after year, alone, without Bay.

"It's lonely out there," he whispered.

"I'll be with you."

"No," he choked. "You won't."

Bay's sightless eyes forced him to look at her.

"Hear me when I say this," she said with as much force as she could muster. "As long as we are both in this together, you will never be alone."

"You don't understand what it's like. I can't—"

Her skeletal form became rigid with effort and for a moment she was as strong as the tree they sat beneath.

"Vole Gibbons, you stubborn sap! Do you think I fell in love with you because I thought you were perfect?"

"Oh. No. Definitely not."

"Trust me when I say I love you. I love *you*, all of you, even those muddy and annoying doubts you insist on keeping to yourself."

"But—"

"If you're worried about what I'm going to think, instead of finding out by sharing how you feel, you'll get it wrong one hundred percent of the time. You'll go completely bonkers if you keep it all inside.

"I know your flaws. I love you because of them. I love *you*. Your family loves *you*. We're with you because of it."

Her body softened and she stopped talking. Vole knew she was spent.

In that sinking pause, Vole came to understand something. Something, he realized, Bay had been telling him since the day she chose to share her life with him.

"You love... *me*?" he asked.

"All of you," she confirmed.

Vole grew wings and leaped into the sky; his spirit soared. He couldn't explain why. He didn't need to explain why. Bay already knew why. As long as he had her love, he'd never be without her.

"Not all questions are scary, eh?" Her chuckle, wry and dry like a fall breeze, ended in a fit that brought a red-tinted film to her lips, and he sank back down to whisk it away.

"Two people," he breathed, his mouth against her ear. "One decision. A unified front for the big stuff."

"You got it," she breathed back.

"Honeybee, I'm sorr—"

"Apologize once more, and I swear to you, we're getting a divorce."

He smiled.

"I love you too. All of you, too. Let's go home."

THIRTY-FIVE

Sunday, June 21, 2015
Dorset, Ontario, Canada
9:06 p.m. eastern time
8,996 sleeps since

THE SOUND OF my voice doesn't fade away when I stop telling our tale. It stops completely and I forget its notes and tones. That's what it's like, living in the space between moments in time. Bay's asleep again and doesn't notice.

    A breeze blows across our bodies. I listen to its whisper with greedy ears. I drink in the sounds of wood creaking around us. I wonder what I've forgotten and think about what I've left out. I'm done fulfilling Bay's last request, but in that, too, I've failed. I couldn't possibly tell it all. What about the shark with fury-black eyes, its sawtooth jaws spread wide as it looked out at us from behind a barreling wave? How to explain the majesty of soaring stingrays in Acapulco? Does she know stingrays soar? I don't think I ever told her, but that's how they look when they're caught, hanging there—like they're soaring through a liquid sky.

Then there were those times when my bicycle broke down and my well of reserves dried up altogether.

Like the places on Bay's list that were too far for our ambitious legs to reach, the parts of my story where nighttime reigned and hope diminished into shadow, my shadow—those parts of my story I left out. Somehow, when my mood turned against me, my legs turned for me, and I embraced my darkness, fated or not.

Her chest rises and falls rapidly.

I can hear her light snores in short bursts and then not at all for many seconds, and I grow scared that she's left me. I know it will happen anytime now because her lips tell me so. Once they were rose red, flowering for me under the rays of the western sun. Now, they are ocean blue as her heart abandons them. Faithless organs. Her body doesn't know there is no part more deserving than Bay's lips. Only I know that, and, despite all my power and ambition, I have no say in what will come to pass, so she is wilting.

"Why do you say you failed?" her weak voice rises, barely making it to my ears.

My beauty's awake! She's so quiet now. Or I am so old I must strain to make out her words?

"Why do you say you've failed?" she whispers once more.

I do this often, I've learned. Talk out loud without knowing I'm doing it. Before, I would never say a word, and now, I don't know how to stop.

"You didn't get to see all you wished for."

Her unseeing eyes remain closed. The sun's evening glow makes her look young again.

A shadow rises from a chair in the bedroom doorway, and I'm reminded of the most important thing I forgot in my devotion to Bay.

William, our son, steps into the lowering light. I don't see his movement; I sense it. My eyes, like Bay's, have worsened. Crossing deserts and staring into the sun's flaming core has rendered parts of my vision milky and thick. I turn my head to watch him in my tired peripheries.

Copper strands flash, like he was forged from the burning orb itself, as he steps toward us. I'd put the chair there, positioned in the doorway to help him immediately see. I placed him gently down onto it. It only just happened. How could I have forgotten?

He's carrying the letter and journal I left in his lap and the note I left tucked between his fingers. *Be calm. Fear not. We're well. Let us take our time. We have such little left. Quiet, now.*

On our way home, I collected him from the house he shares with Gina, overlooking Fort Henry on the St. Lawrence. I thought he must be a mannequin, a replica of our son. He was perfect when I found him, seated in his dining room, reading the newspaper off a shining screen. *Is this human our son?* I wondered. Could we produce such a wonderful specimen? I touched my nose against his and stared into his face for longer than I had ever done before. Not a dream, I decided. He has as many freckles on his face as there are stars in the sky.

Did you know that, honeybee?

"Dad," he chokes, almost a question, and closes the distance between us. He's impossibly quick; I struggle to sit up in bed. "Don't get up," he insists as he leans over me, eclipsing both Bay and I in the bed he once thought was as vast as a swimming pool. He kisses me on the forehead, whispers, "Thank you," and walks around to the other side.

"Who is it?" Bay's voice rises from her pillow. She sounds excited, disbelieving, weak. "Vole?"

"It's me," William answers, his voice cracking.

"Will . . ."

She reaches her arms out and her fingertips find his face. She traces his features as incredulously as she did on the day he was born.

William clasps her frail hands. Wraps his arms around us both, careful of Jock, who is busily licking any bit of William's skin he can reach. The dog must be getting dull in his old age, too, to not have smelled William sooner.

When did our little boy get to be big?

If the story I told had been anything else, we may have shared words. Bay may have asked how Gina was. I may have asked how work was going. He may have asked how we were doing, but for once, there were no questions.

"I love you both. You too, Jocko," William says, his voice muffled. His head is pressed against the pillows, sandwiched between ours. "I don't—I don't know what to think." He is pleading with us to give him answers; a child's plight. My heart squeezes, and I wish his was a pain I could have protected him from. "We need to get you two to a hospital, right now."

"*Shhh*," Bay shushes him. She struggles to lift her arm to rub his back. "They can't do anything for us now."

"Mom!" he insists. "You can't give up. Not now! I-I haven't told you—Gina's pregnant. You're going to be grandparents. You can't give up. Not after what you've been through. I'm going to call an ambulance. There's got to be something they can do." Our son moves to leave, but leans back down to kiss us each once more. We have become old and precious, and I'm glad for it. "I love you," he says, and walks out of the room.

His voice grazes my ears from beyond the door, where he's pacing the hallway. He's trying to explain to the emergency medical services operator what he believes needs to happen next.

"I would never have known," Bay whispers. "Our baby's having a baby of his own. He's all grown up."

The room darkens as the sun dips farther below the horizon. It must have waited for me to finish telling our tale, or maybe I left too much out, I don't know. The air around us grows heavy. I worry it's become too heavy for Bay's lungs to lift.

"I don't want to be alone," I whimper. I'm not embarrassed by how my hands tremble, but I am disappointed by how frightened I am to lose her. Still. Nothing, not even the plump promise of new cheeks, can make me let her go.

"We won't be," I think I hear her say.

"How can you be sure?"

I tell myself, as I've always done, the choice I make to hold on is for her. But, as her flame dwindles, I feel a new world order take shape.

The ending of my life's adventure must be my own.

Bay's eyes open. She looks up at me because she knows I'll be watching her, before her lids shut. In that brief glance I see that she understands, and she forgives, and she accepts; like how I have come to understand, and forgive, and now must accept; and my throat closes around the sweetest honey for the last time as I whisper her name.

Bay.

In these final moments, I do what she has always done, and lay claim. I'm happy knowing I've done things no man should be able to do. I've lived my life for reasons I'm proud to call my own, and that, at the end, I don't want to say goodbye. How could I? My hold on our life's love is all that's left of me. Knowing that, more than anything, as a man whittled to his core, brings me peace.

I'm much weaker now. The things I've come to know have done to me more than any bone-rattling cough or lame leg ever could.

I raise myself enough to bend my neck and place a final kiss on the top of Bay's head, and then place a hand on Jock's back. The dog won't leave Bay's side. I wonder whether he'll live long enough to go home with William and meet the new baby, or if he's become too much like us through all this.

Once more the evening breeze flows through the open windows of our bedroom, and I feel my temperature drop. What remains of my breathing lightens to the same shallow depths as Bay's, my honeybee beauty's, and I feel an enveloping quiet return to me. I open my arms and greet it, like it was my beloved, and I'm welcoming her home after a long and tiring journey. I think I hear William step back into the room, but I don't stir. Stillness has taken over my body, as it has Bay's. Our molecules merge as the moon rises. We embrace the peace night brings and we disappear with the sun as we finish our last grand adventure, together.

THIRTY-SIX

Dear William,

Countless times I've put my pen to paper to write you, and countless times I've laid my hand down and turned my face the other way. For guidance, I try to think of what my father would have said, and there I stop. I must remove myself and think of what a father like me would say to a son like you, and I believe he'd say these things.

Know your numbers and know your heart. Let the rest be. Consume the stories of others, but not at the cost of creating your own. Love unabashedly. You will be vulnerable. Embrace it. Admitting your weaknesses is the first step to growing beyond them. Draw strength from knowing that your doubts are no uglier than anyone else's. And, for the love of your wise mother, listen to Gina. For every strong woman in this world there is a man not far behind, struggling to keep up. Learn from her, share with her, and proceed side by side, together.

I love you. Your family loves you.

Your actions, however, are a different story. To be clear, I still dislike that you took the car. But holding such things, big or small, against ourselves, generates as much trouble as trivializing the trauma. I couldn't see it before. Now that I'm in the end, I can see straight through such walls. I'm sorry, my boy. I'm sorry.

Also, don't be rude and groan when your old man leaves you sage advice. I'm wise now, you know. Of all the negligible wisdom this chicken scratcher seeks to impart, I suggest you retain this one thing: There is no right way forward. There is only today's illusory promise of tomorrow. How you proceed through time is perception, mostly, and managing that is entirely up to you.

I almost forgot. There's one more thing I have to tell you. I left my name and address, and your phone number, just in case, in a note for a child who I encountered off the coast of Mauritania in West Africa. Please keep an eye out for a call. The child might need a friend like you one day.

Goodbye and good luck, William.

Dad

POST SCRIPT

BAY DIDN'T MAKE it to all the places on her list. In fact, of the original eighty-four destinations, she visited few. Her dream to witness the remaining passed with her, unfulfilled.

Vole considered sharing her list with William. Perhaps a kinder father would have, but Vole knew that drilling questions would make their son lose sleep. Questions like: What places were so private that Bay worshipped them her entire life in silence? Did she get to visit all the most important places, like the gravesites of her great-grandparents, and if not, which places did she miss? Could he, her only child, pay respect to the dead in her stead? What did each place on her list mean to her? What should each place mean to him?

Vole could've helped their son with answers, though from experience, he knew from every new answer countless new questions are born. That wasn't why he chose not to divulge Bay's secrets. He chose not to because such an artifact, an inventory of unrequited dreams, in any hands but the dreamer's, would weigh heavy. Bay's list would be as much a burden of questions as it would be a gift of answers, in Vole's opinion.

Besides, it was their secret. A memory made for two. He'd spent an entire lifetime earning her trust, and then spent another learning how not to betray it. Vole never told anyone what else was on Bay's list, and she didn't make it to all the places she dreamed of one day visiting.

She did, however, make it to all the places that mattered. Because the ones she visited, detailed in this story, she visited with Vole—and those dreams became her memories, proof of their little life spent with great care—proof of their little life spent with great care.

All the other details were too secret and not important enough to share.

The End.

GRAND PATRONS

Adeline Litt
Alana Rodrigo
ANA Book Club
Anne Toner Fung
Brenda M.
Dianne Sarkadi
Elizabeth Gallagher
Elyse Haid
Heather Campbell
James Toner
Jason Zan
Jeffrey Gadway
Joe Fung
Joel Widmeyer
Joseph Fung
Katy Innes
Lai Fong
Michael Litt
Michael McCauley
Nick Toner
Nicole Morin

Paul Teshima
Peter Panacci
Robert Doherty
Ryan Good
Shaddi Fahel
Sharon Gilmour
Sheila Fung
Shelley Cybulski
Sunnika Long
Sylvia Borza
Tina Nguyen

INKSHARES

INKSHARES is a reader-driven publisher and producer based in Oakland, California. Our books are selected not by a group of editors, but by readers worldwide.

While we've published books by established writers like *Big Fish* author Daniel Wallace and *Star Wars: Rogue One* scribe Gary Whitta, our aim remains surfacing and developing the new author voices of tomorrow.

Previously unknown Inkshares authors have received starred reviews and been featured in the *New York Times*. Their books are on the front tables of Barnes & Noble and hundreds of independents nationwide, and many have been licensed by publishers in other major markets. They are also being adapted by Oscar-winning screenwriters at the biggest studios and networks.

Interested in making your own story a reality? Visit Inkshares.com to start your own project or find other great books.

CPSIA information can be obtained
at www.ICGtesting.com
Printed in the USA
FSHW01n0912181018